THE BLACK ROOM MANUSCRIPTS

VOLUME ONE

The Black Room Manuscripts
Volume One

First Published in 2015

Executive Editor: Daniel Marc Chant
Compiled by: Daniel Marc Chant, Duncan P Bradshaw and J R Park

Copy Editor: Cheyenne DeBorde
Associate Editors: Duncan P Bradshaw, J R Park and Duncan Ralston

Cover design & layout: Vincent Hunt (@jesterdiablo)
www.jesterdiablo.blogspot.com

ISBN Paperback 9780993279348
ISBN eBook 9780993279355

CONTENTS

HORROR TODAY
FOREWORD BY JIM McLEOD
(GINGER NUTS OF HORROR)

What is the state of the Horror genre today? It is a question that never seems to go away. I think the reason that it is a perpetual question is the fact that the answer is always in flux. Like many things, the horror genre is a tidal beast, subject to moods, fashion, and critical response. If you asked me this question a year or so ago, I would have said that it is not in a good state. At that time, it was at risk of drowning in a sea of poor zombie novels, even poorer sparkly vampire novels, and a never-ending horde of just badly written books -- written by people who have no respect for the craft of writing. And there was something more insidious -- something that could really cause the genre to break. A total lack of sense of community. It felt that everyone was just shouting over everyone else. Ensconced in their own little bunkers. desperately trying to grab their own little piece of fame from the genre's rotting corpse. No one was listening to anyone else; no one outside of the genre websites and magazines seemed interested in the promoting the good within the genre. There was a time it felt like I was doing a vigil in a wilderness of mirrors.

It was a period when I was seriously considering packing it
all in; a taking a break from a genre that had been a constant
companion from the beginning of my reading life. Then
something happened. It was a subtle change at the start; one
or two authors started producing stuff that really was ground-
breaking and original. More importantly, people started
talking about horror again. Don't get me wrong, there are still
those who go about the whole "being a horror writer" thing
the wrong way. These are the ones that are more in love with
the idea of being a writer than the actual writing itself. These
writers will never make it; writing has always been and will
always be about the writing and nothing more. But enough
about them; let's focus on the positives.

Probably now more than ever, the fate and health of the
horror genre doesn't lie with the big hitters. It used to be that
you had the big four -- King, Koontz, Barker, and Herbert.
Then below them, you had the second runners McCammon,
Masterton, and Struab. Then came the mid-listers -- Keene,
Lanagan, Pinborough, and Ketchum. Then everyone one
else. These days, apart from King and Koontz, it really feels
as though everyone is pretty much in the same boat. There
will never be another big four contender; there just isn't the
market for it. Which, to be honest is a good thing. Since this
shift of power, the genre has become more alive.

Gone are the restrictions of big publisher remits, where every
new release felt like it was just a rehash of something else.
This allowed the small press to flourish, and gave them the
freedom to produce books that may well not have seen the
light of day. And more importantly, it allowed the talented
authors an avenue to some degree of recognition. We now
have wonderful presses such as Spectral Press, Horrific Tales,

Crowded Quarantine Publications, Dark Fuse, Small Beer Press, Thunder Storm Press, and Deadite Press, to name just a few. These presses have allowed the genre to breath and expanded in ways that, a few years ago, would not have been possible -- to the point that it is slowly making its way back into the bookshops.

It has given authors like Nathan Ballingrud, Gary McMahon, Adam Nevill, Helen Marshall, and Sarah Pinborough the opportunity to really push the boundaries of what the genre can do. Their stories show that horror can be not just scary and frightening, but also have a heart and soul. I challenge anyone to read any of their stories and not be moved. From the lyrical writing of Balingrud, to the gut crunching emotional rawness of McMahon's writing, horror is in a good place.

And that's just what some of the bigger names are producing. When you have talent like Laura Mauro, Mark West, Rich Hawkins, Thana Niveua, Cate Garnder, Simon Bestwick producing first class horror, and new and emerging writers such as Paul M. Feeney, Kit Power, and Kayleigh Marie Edwards just starting out on their literary journey, it really does look as though the genre is heading into a golden age. No matter what your preferred type of horror is, there is great writing going on -- writing that new authors can and should aspire to.

Let's not go back to the dark times where it felt that only bad books seemed to sell. We can stop this from happening again; it is really rather simple. Keep talking about the great books. If you are on Facebook, share the writers you genuinely love; mention them in discussions; share any interviews they do in websites. Don't, however -- and I mean this with all sincerity -- just promote an author because they are a friend. Promote the writing, not the author. The one thing that will bring the genre down again is if we only seem to promote the poor writing. I've seen it happen. Hell, I have been at the front end of a backlash from an author's fan base just because I didn't like their book. The genre lives and dies by the quality of the writing; this is how it has always been and how it should always be.

The Black Room Manuscripts, sums up perfectly the current state of the genre. With its fantastic mix of authors, this is an anthology that shows the breadth and depth of what is available out there. Pay attention to some of the authors here, for they are destined for great things.

PROLOGUE

My temper will be the undoing of me! Why did I kill the old man before making him reveal where his gold was hidden?

Because he took me for an ignorant peasant, who believed the tales of his sorcery. He thought to scare me off with a spell, as if I was of feeble mind, and that's when anger got the better of me and I drew my knife across his throat. It was a mistake.

I have searched high and low for the gold and found nothing. And now I am in the last room in the house -- and still there is nothing!

The room is bare. It can hold no secrets. I must begin my search all over again.

What was that? It sounded like a key being turned.

The door is locked! How can that be? The old man lived alone, and none but I would dare enter uninvited.

There must be another way out. Why are there no windows in this room?

The air tastes stale. It grows cold. Shadows creep

across the floor. The walls whisper. But no! It is the wind --
that is all. And as for the shadows -- they are still. Very still.

Wait! Are those footsteps? Yes. The sound is
unmistakeable. And again -- the whispering. Now I can
make out words. They are the ones the old man uttered as I
took his life.

Pasher tagoth imra... Pasher tagoth imra...

The words are alive. They invoke terror and feed
upon my fear.

And now I know the truth of it. The old man was
a necromancer. With his dying breath, he called forth the
Nameless Ones to exact his vengeance upon me.

They creep ever closer. There is no hope for me now.

The door handle turns and...

THE STRANGER
DANNY KING

I can't remember much of the evening. I'd only gone there to meet a girl, but ended up sitting at the bar like a mug all night, before accepting that she'd stood me up.

I downed the dregs of my last pint and was about to leave, when a voice beside me said, "Here, friend, let me buy you another."

Before I knew it, a fresh pint was put in front of me and some odd-looking guy sat down beside me. I thought he was trying to pick me up at first, but something in his eyes told me otherwise.

He started to talk and tell me stuff; stuff about his life, stuff about his week and himself. It was like he was trying to unburden himself. By the time he mentioned his dream, he'd downed his drink and had ordered two more. He looked hurried and anxious; as if his last bus home was almost at the end of the street.

The stranger in his dream had approached him in this very bar. He'd never even been in there before, but he knew the place intimately before he'd set foot in the place -- every shadow, every cobweb.

The stranger had glanced towards the darkest corners of the room with his eyes and asked him: "Do you hear them?"

"Whispering? Planning?"

"Do you see them?"

"In the corners of your eyes?"

"Moving? Nearing?"

The stranger in his dream talked in riddles for some time, each question punching his heart like a cold fist, and although he had no answers, he felt that they were just beyond his imagination.

He uttered not a word, yet the stranger learned all he sought through the beat of his heart and the static shrill in the air. The stranger shuffled closer, and silent terror turned my new friend's limbs to stone, freezing him on the spot.

"Are you ready?" whispered the stranger.

"Are you ready?"

He awoke to sheets soaked through with fear, and to a night as black as death itself. He hadn't slept for more than a week by the time I saw him, and his nerves were as tattered as the clothes he now wore. When he finished his story, he reached for a cigarette.

"I'll be back in a moment," he told me, shuffling outside to smoke.

That was the last I saw of him -- the last anyone saw of him.

The barman asked me if I knew who I'd just been speaking with. I told him I didn't, and asked who he was. The barman told me he didn't know, but he'd seen him a few nights earlier, looking smart -- like anyone else -- and sitting at the bar, drinking and talking with some wretch of a man he now resembled.

That was last week.

Or was it last night?

Was it real?

Or was it a dream?

I don't know. I can't tell anymore.

Can you?

Do you know the difference?

Does anyone?

But look at me, talking when your glass is nearly empty. Are you ready for another, my friend?

Are you ready?

TIME FOR TEA
DUNCAN P. BRADSHAW

"Shall I be mother?" asked Shaun through a forced grin. The others around the table nodded. He picked up the tall China teapot and looked across the thick oak table to Mandy. Her tightly curled hair cascaded off her shoulders; she was looking down nervously at her invitation to the tea room opening.

Shaun coughed gently, rousing Mandy from her study. She looked up like a startled panda, cast wary glances at her fellow patrons, and then slid her cup and saucer across the expanse of the table, past the sugar bowl and small jugs of ice-cold milk. It squeaked slightly as it cruised across the join of two planks. "Oops," she said timidly, instantly withdrawing back to the invitation in her thin, bony hands.

Shaun's hand trembled gently; black-brown liquid poured from the spout and into Mandy's delicate bone China cup. It slopped around within, some splashing onto the table.

"Careful, mate", said an annoyed Tony, "You nearly got some on me there." Shaun looked across at Tony, who sat to his right; his short blonde hair, blue eyes, and brusque manner gave him all the airs and graces of an SS officer.

Around the tea room there was a gentle undercurrent of murmuring. In total, three tables of four people were seated; engaged in hushed conversation, sipping tea or reading through the menu. Shaun slowly slid the cup and saucer back to Mandy, being careful not to spill anything. Tony held his cup and saucer out to Shaun, who took it off him and laid it on the table.

"Bit of an odd place to have this gaff -- in a basement." Tony looked around, checking out the other customers; each seemingly lost in their own worlds. Shaun passed the filled cup and saucer back to Tony and asked, "Have you not read your invitation yet? Might be some useful information in there."

Tony shook his head, "Nope, not yet, mate; will do in a bit. All very odd though, huh? Cheers for the tea, mate." A thick arm covered in near-transparent blonde hair reached out for the milk; between his sausage-like fingers, the jug seemed comically small.

Shaun poured himself some tea and turned to Carl,

"Pass me your cup," he asked politely. Carl looked at Shaun and put a hand over his cup, "No thanks, I'm good. Can't stand tea; makes me gaseous, you know? More of a latte man, comprende?" He replied snidely.

Shaun and Mandy gulped as one; wide eyes looked at Carl, who regarded each of them in turn with disdain. "What?" He asked aloofly, Mandy started biting her lip; the grip on her invitation tightened, the card started to creak under the pressure. She started muttering under her breath. Shaun rested the teapot on the table and looked at Carl,

"Mate, seriously, have you read your invitation? I really think you should have some tea, please." He started to frantically look around for some person unseen. The gentle hubbub of the basement continued. Someone at one of the other tables shot them a glance, before a kick under the table got their attention back to the ongoing conversation.

"I said, I'm fine. Thank you." Carl enunciated. He placed his gloved hands on the table, resting on a closed envelope bearing his name.

Shaun shook his head and looked angrily at Carl, "Why did you accept an invitation to a tea room opening if you don't like tea?"

Carl lowered his red-tinted sunglasses so they rested on the end of his nose. His slick-back hair reflected the light from the ceiling. "I go to all of these pop-up places; it's what I do. Just yesterday I was at a smashing little Tibetan restaurant in a caravan setup in Victoria Park. I turn up, am seen, and then leave."

Tony laughed, "Ha-ha, we've got ourselves a genuine, bona fide hipster -- what a dick." He stirred his cup with a small silver spoon, the clinking tolling like a miniature bell. He tapped the spoon on the cup's rim and placed it back on the saucer. "Right, let's see what this is." He said to himself and picked up the envelope with his name on it. A chunky finger plunged into the join and tore it open; as he pulled out the card from within, his face froze, the colour drained away in an instant, "No fucking way…" was all he could muster. Carl pushed his glasses back up the bridge of his nose, "Now, I better go; got some acquaintances to meet before dinner tonight at Il Maestoso Salmone in town. Have to go and get a pick-me-up first though." He placed his hands on the table and began to push himself away. As he did so, the air conditioning vent above his head swung open with an ominous creak.

A rusting telescopic metal pipe descended from the yawning hole directly above Carl's head, "My, my, Health and Safety will have a field day with this place." He said with utter contempt, looking up into the murk of the pipe.

All eyes were now transfixed on their table. From above came the sound of a stubborn, creaking valve being turned, followed by a gush of liquid. The pipe was around a foot from the top of Carl's head, who still sat in his metal chair, shaded eyes looking into the abyss.

There came a hissing sound as a viscous green liquid poured from the tube and straight over Carl's head. Shaun and Mandy, who sat on either side of him, pushed themselves away instinctively.

Carl emitted a ball-shrinking screech and started to swat at his face with his gloved hands. As he did so, globules of skin and flesh came off in his frenzied swiping. His slicked hair began to slide off the top of his head, taking his creased forehead with it and exposing the skull underneath. By now, his screams had subsided to nothing more than a wet gurgle -- the acid eating through his throat.

The tea room patrons shrieked in horror, petrified in their seats. As his ears dissolved into flesh-coloured slurry, Carl's sunglasses slipped off what was left of his face and onto his lap. From his eye sockets ran a reddish pink goo; tendrils of optic nerve slopped out before crackling and melting.

Carl now consisted of a skeleton, wrapped in a slowly disintegrating leather jacket. Bubbling crimson liquid popped and burst the length of his body as he was slowly eaten away. With no muscles to support it, his skull plopped forwards; the bottom jaw hung from one side before falling onto his lap, clinking against his sunglasses.

Underneath the screams of the patrons, there was a gentle fizzing sound like cola bubbles tinkling in a bottle. The pipe clumsily retracted back into the ceiling cavity; the plastic air conditioning cover still swung gently. The smell of burnt flesh and tissue hung heavily in the air, Mandy coughed and wretched, trying to clear the taste from her throat.

Tony looked back to the card contained within the envelope and the simple note within. "Follow the commands and enjoy afternoon tea, or they die," was printed next to a grainy picture of his mother gardening outside her house. Someone had drawn a crude knife sticking from her back. He looked over at Shaun, "You got the same thing, I'm guessing?" He asked solemnly, showing the card.

Shaun nodded, "My brother, he's just started Uni. Got a picture of him passed out in the toilets after a night out. How did they-" he was interrupted by the sound of piped music. An easy-listening version of Way Out West's Melt played through tinny speakers positioned within the walls. A burst of static crushed through the music. Silence descended upon the room. "Oh dear, looks like one of the patrons didn't want to play along. How silly. I don't see any of you enjoying your tea," said a creepy, high-pitched male voice.

From one of the other tables, a burly man shouted out, "This is bullshit! You can't keep us here. I'm gonna phone the filth and they'll be here to arrest your sick ass." Shaun, Mandy, and Tony looked across at the man who pulled a phone from his pocket and started to unlock it.

The voice warned, "Now, now, this is a respectable family establishment. We won't have potty mouths here, and we most certainly will not have mobile telephones being used. You all need to enjoy the ambience -- the lovely, lovely ambience."

The man raised his middle finger, "Fuck you, pal, I'm calling them now... Has anyone got a signal in this craphole?" Silence fell over the remaining customers; the air grew thick with tension and wariness.

It was broken by a cackling from the speakers, "Oh my, you seem to have discovered that our little boutique is a haven from the modern world; quite unable to pick up mobile telephone signals-"

A slight lull was broken by the sinister voice again, "Now, you have to pay for your insolence, young man. All I asked was for you to enjoy your afternoon tea. Maybe even sample our crumpets later; they're simply divine."

The man grew in surliness, "Fuck you, pal. Why don't you get your sick ass out here and I'll shove your crumpets up your arse. See how you get on with that, you fucking squeaky fuck." People shot glances at each other, perhaps sensing that this was just some kind of prank -- an elaborate one, admittedly, but that was possible, right?

"Thought so," yelled the man and he slumped back in his chair. The lights flickered momentarily. Mandy whimpered. The lights then gutted completely, leaving them all in darkness.

A loud clunk sounded, switching the desenter from incandescent rage to screaming -- yelling unintelligable curses. Through the gloom, four crackling, barbed tongues of lightning struck him at once, causing his arms to be flung stiffly out to his side, with his head arched back violently. A distorted pain-filled similie that was his voice was stuck on one half of a word "Fu...fu...fu...fu...fu..." like a broken record player.

The only light source in the dingy basement was eminating from the man as the electricity coursed through him. Bones wrapped in now translucent skin cast him like a ghastly Jack-O-Lantern. He thrashed around in his chair, as if some miscreant had vile control over him. A pall of acrid smoke started to rise from his head. Without warning, his hair caught on fire, disappearing in a fleeting woosh of flame. Eyes bulged from their housing, wide with pain; glowing from within, they projected a tributary of scarlet veins over his upper cheeks and forehead.

Through his pain-wracked features, the basement
dwellers could tell that the current had increased. The shaking
became more vigourous, bones in his hands cracked as they
contracted, skin crackled with coruscating waves of grotesque
light. His eyes burst in an explosion of fetid fluid and
fleshy pulp, the goo flying over his fellow table dwellers. A
smouldering tuft of back hair caused a ripple of blue flame to
wash over his body, as if he had been dipped in kerosene.
As quickly as it started, the electricity stopped. The room fell
dark again in the gloom, Shaun could hear people breathing
heavily, crying, gagging with fear. The ceiling lights flickered
back to life, showing a scorched corpse resting on the table.
The face had been petrified like a giant block of charcoal;
only kernels of yellow teeth offered any variance in colour.

The speakers sparked into life again, "My my,
electricity really can be quite dangerous; especially in these
old buildings. You go careful down there, my pretties; we
don't want any more accidents, do we?"

Shaun shook his head and looked over to Mandy,
who was now catatonic with fear. The speaker crackled again,
"Your waiter, Dirk, will be with you presently. He has your
Specials menus. Please show him a degree of courtesy; good
staff can be so troublesome to find." A muffled clunk signalled
the end of the speech.

On cue, the door at the top of the stairs, leading from
the basement, clicked as it was released from the frame.
It whined open before slamming shut again. After a slight
pause, they could all hear a thud-thud-thud from heavy boots
stomping down the wooden stairs.

The stairs were contained behind a thin partition
wall. The stomping grew louder; each step ratcheted up the
anxiety in the room. The clomping stopped and the waiter

was revealed; a hulk of a man, dressed in a grubby white shirt covered in all manners of unidentifiable stains. A pair of equally filthy, tight grey trousers clung to his tree-trunk legs, which ended in heavy army surplus boots -- the ends scuffed and slightly grey.

Over his clothes, he had a blood stained apron tied tightly around him. Shaun looked at the man's face. From where he was sat, it looked like it was hung wrong, as if someone had tied weights to the skin under his chin.

Dirk clutched a wad of paper. His jaw hung slack, a steady stream of saliva ran from the corner of his mouth. He looked around the room dispassionately, as if he was looking at a daytime television show. Tony kicked Shaun under the table, gave him a slight nod, and then another towards the teapot sitting in the middle of the table. Shaun realised his intention and shook his head slightly. Tony squinted with frustration and looked down into his lap.

The giant of a man lumbered over to the first table, still resplendent with their full complement of four people. He forced a piece of paper into the hand of every terrified occupant before moving on to the table with the still-smoking corpse.

He again passed out a piece of paper to each person. Seemingly unaware of the smouldering body, he squashed the paper into a blackened hand, which cracked and separated at the wrist, before moving towards Shaun's table. As he got closer, Shaun could see that the man's face swayed slightly with every step. He focused on the odd movement, and then realisation kicked in.

The waiters face was not his own -- it was a cross-stitch pattern of human flesh. Differing tones were cobbled together with thick black cotton; some patches had outcrops of hair, others still daubed with make-up. He recoiled at the sight of it, forgetting entirely about Tony's intentions.

A piece of paper was given to Mandy and Shaun. The goliath, again, seemed unaware that Carl was nothing more than a pile of bones and a puddle of melted flesh and tissue. The paper fizzled as he dropped it into what was left of Carl's lap. It dissolved quickly in between Carl's pelvic bone. Dirk's gormless gaze turned to Tony, who seemed enthralled and repulsed in equal measure by the sight of the ragtag assembly of the waiter's face. He wavered briefly, before grabbing hold of the teapot and clocking Dirk around the head with it.

The fine China teapot smashed instantly, showering them all with lukewarm tea and pieces of pottery. The waiter, though, remained unmoved; one hand still held the Specials menu out to Tony. The other hand reached round his back. Tony stood and looked up into the dull eyes of the waiter. The impact had done nothing except embed some small pieces of China in the man's facemask. Tony gulped, his Adam's apple bulged out. As he did so, the man slashed horizontally with a speed his ungainly height did not match. A jet of blood sprayed over Shaun's face, who gulped in surprise.

Tony's eyes widened. He clamped both hands desperately to his throat, trying to stem the bleeding. His fingers were red and sticky as he tried to hold his neck together; they went through the slit and into his windpipe. He could feel his own fingers tickling his tonsils, the sensation a stark opposite to the one of excruciating pain he was experiencing.

Mandy still sat there, shaking. A geyser of blood was being pumped over her, matting her hair. Tony collapsed like a taser victim; on his way down, his forehead smacked into the thick table. As his head bounced, it tore the last vestiges of skin and tendon which still held his head to his neck. A sickening slurp and crack later, his headless body finally met the floor. His head rolled around in a puddle made up of a mixture of his bodily fluids, eyes still open with shock. The man placed the paper where Tony had sat, slid the dripping butcher's knife back into his belt, and lumbered back to the stairs and out of sight. Shaun wiped the sleeve of his jumper over his face, trying to remove Tony's blood.

The upstairs door slammed again, and the speaker clicked into life, "Oh dear, another customer unhappy with our service. I'll have to mark Dirk down as "average" on the satisfaction survey. Nevermind, friends, you have your Specials to look forward to now. Enjoy."

Shaun looked across to Mandy. Her face and hair was drenched in blood; it dripped lazily from her hair and onto the table. He could hear her muttering to herself, though he couldn't make out what she was saying.

"Hey. Hey, Mandy," he said softly, moving his hands across the table towards her. She flinched involuntarily as they reached her personal bubble. She looked up at him, as if woken suddenly from a dream.

She looked back at him; the whites of her eyes a stark contrast to the drying blood over her face. "He... he... he... he's..." she tried to say, unable to form words into a coherent sentence.

Shaun nodded and looked at her, "It'll be okay, Mandy; we'll get out of this." Over her shoulder, he could see one of the other guests stand up from her table, dab a napkin gently across her lips, and walk towards them.

The lady stood behind Mandy. She was short and squat, her midriff bulging from where her jeans were fastened tightly around her waist. "I'm sorry," she said softly, holding the napkin in each hand. She reached over Mandy's head and pulled it against her throat. Mandy started to wheeze; the lady pulled tighter.

At first Shaun was too shocked by what he saw -- his brain unable to comprehend this latest act of violence, even beneath her blood-soaked face, Shaun could make out a blue tinge; veins pulsed and rose to the surface. "What the hell are you doing?" he demanded angrily. The woman repeated her apology and pulled tighter.

Shaun stood up and moved around the table. The woman paid him no heed and continued to drain the air out of Mandy. "STOP!" he shouted. The woman looked at him sympathetically and again offered her apologies. Before he knew it, he had lashed out; his fist had connected with the woman's nose. Blood was smeared on the top of her lip, her hold on Mandy relinquished.

He looked at the woman, and her nose was now flat against her face. She raised the napkin to her own face, dabbed it, and saw the blood. She looked at it impassively. Mandy turned to face the woman, rubbing her throat, trying to get some feeling back. The woman looked down at her and closed her hands around Mandy's throat, desperately trying to throttle her.

"Get off her!" Shaun bellowed again. He smacked the palm of his hand into the woman's face again, meeting the base of her nose. Her eyes rolled back into her skull as a thin river of blood trickled from one of her eye sockets. Her grip fell slack and she dropped to the floor, dead.

Shaun knelt down by Mandy, gently shaking her,

"Hey, Mandy, it's okay, I dunno what the hell she was doing, but you're okay now." The peace was short-lived -- a scream broke the air from the other table.

They both looked over; on the table of the electrocuted man, there were two men locked in a struggle. A glint of metal could be seen in a hand, though it was

impossible to see who held it. The men seemed to embrace --
one then suddenly jerked upwards. The other fell back, hands
clutching a savage wound in his chest.

"I'm sorry, I'm really sorry," his assailant was telling
his victim.

He knelt down by the stabbed man, who appeared to
be whispering, trying to give his valediction. "What's that,
buddy, I can't hear you," said the knife-wielder, who bent
closer. As he did so, the man slammed a clenched fist into
the other's skull, before collapsing back onto the floor in an
expanding pool of his own blood.

The man stood up. Bloodied knife in one hand, the
other clasped over his ear, he staggered uneasily, steadying
himself on the table. "Oh god," Shaun said, his voice laden
with disgust. As the man withdrew his hand from the side of
his head, Shaun could see a long-necked screwdriver had been
driven through the ear and deep into the man's skull.

The knife clattered to the floor, quickly followed by
the man, landing on his victim and attacker. Shaun reeled
from the sight of the blood and gore; a whip-like crack broke
his introspection. He looked across to the other table and saw
a woman trying to staunch a chest wound. He traced a path to
the sole survivor from the burned man's table, holding a small
smoking pistol. His forehead was sheened with sweat.
The man walked forward purposefully. As he neared the
person he had just shot, a woman in her early fifites lashed
out at him with an old-style wooden police truncheon. The
man's head rocked to one side, a purple contusion already
forming by the man's temple. He staggered like a drunkard on
a Saturday night. The pistol fell from his hand and he slumped
to the floor. He started to convulse; a thick white paste laden
with flecks of blood vomited forth, and he fell still.

Shaun looked at the other table. The woman who had

been shot was leaning back in her chair, arms hung limply by her side. He ran his hands through his hair; his jagged nails scratched his skin, "No, no, no, NO," he wailed in anguish. He looked over to Mandy. She was still rubbing her bruised neck with one hand; the other idly held the piece of paper the slasher had dropped off moments before.

That was when the madness started. He rubbed his head, trying to make things clear, trying to get some sense of what the hell was going on. His thinking was interrupted again by a banshee wail. He looked across to the table where the only other survivors were seated. The woman in her early fifties was crawling over the table; she had ditched the truncheon and now held a meat cleaver. The steel caught the ceiling light and seemed imbued with an inner glow.

The man was studying the piece of paper he had been given when he heard the cry. He tried to dodge to one side, but the cleaver bit deep into his shoulder. He screamed in pain. The older woman had fire in her eyes, her grey fringe rubbing across her eyebrows. She fought to heave the blade from his collarbone.

As she pulled, he screamed louder, like a semi-stunned animal at an abatoir. The weight of the woman toppled them both over onto the floor. The blade dug deeper into his chest, fully embedded within; he screamed again. The grey-haired woman now straddled him, still trying to yank out the cleaver buried in the man's body. The man's one free hand scrabbled desperately around for something -- anything -- to try and get this mad woman off him -- to try and buy himself some time. His hand fell on the small pistol. Gritting his teeth through the pain, he pulled the pistol up, holding the gun to the woman's temple. He squeezed the trigger. The force of the point-blank shot caused the woman to fall to one side. As she did so, she maintained her grip on the cleaver's handle; the pressure on it caused the man's collarbone and neck to be opened up like a bear trap.

The man screamed in agony as his arm was practically severed from the rest of his body. His heart continued to pump blood in his arteries, chugging his life force onto the concrete floor. He let out a pained growl and fell silent.

Shaun looked around the basement. Bodies laid in various states of dismemberment and agony. He looked over to Mandy, who read the piece of paper and folded it in half. He crouched on the floor, panting; his mind still awash with images of complete and utter horror. He reconciled something internally and brought himself to his feet. A wave of determination surged through him anew; this place and madness would not claim them -- he was going to make sure of it.

"Mandy. Hey, Mandy, it's okay. I don't know what the hell they were doing, but we are not like that, okay? We've got each other. We're going to be okay." Shaun picked up a napkin, starting to try and rub some of the congealing blood from her face.

Mandy put one hand on the folded piece of paper in front of her, and slid it across to Shaun. He looked at her quizzically and dropped the blood-smeared napkin onto the table. He picked the note up cautiously, "What's this, Mandy? What does it say?"

He unfolded the paper and saw on one side was a picture of himself. It was a few days ago, when he was shopping for some furniture. "Huh, that's odd." he remarked. He looked at the words on the other side;

YOU MUST KILL THIS MAN.

THE LAST ONE LEFT ALIVE WILL LIVE.

THERE IS A CHISEL TAPED TO THE UNDER-

SIDE OF THE TABLE.

GET IT.

KILL.

Mandys hand wrapped around the hilt of the woodworking tool, Shaun looked down at her in surprise,

"What? But you won't..." Before he could finish, Mandy thrust the dull, thick blade into his stomach and twisted it sharply. Shaun put out a weak hand, trying to fend her away, but his strength had deserted him. He patted her feebly. Mandy looked into his eyes, struggling to hold back the tears that welled inside.

"I'm s... s... s... sorry, Shaun," was all she could muster. He fell to the floor, still clutching the chisel interred firmly in his intestinal tract. The bottom half of his body felt warm and tingly. His head rolled to the side and he looked into the death stare of the cleavered man. He coughed up a thick wad of spit and blood, and fell slack.

Mandy stood up from the table, looking around at the carnage which had unfolded so quickly. The speaker popped and played a chorus of Queen's We Are The Champions, before the eerie voice came back on.

"Well done, my dear. Well done indeed. We hope you enjoyed your time here with us today. Please don't forget to leave feedback for our staff, and remember your complimentary shortbread as you leave."

The speaker crackled off. The door at the top of the stairs clicked open. Mandy, awash with adrenaline, ran up the stairs to freedom.

HIDE AND SHRIEK
VINCENT HUNT

"How long have we been in here now?"

It must have been at least thirty minutes that Gretchen and Andy had been in their hiding place. Gretchen was pretty sure that the game of Hide and Seek hadn't started that long ago, but as soon as Andy started fidgeting and whinging about getting "achey legs" -- after about five minutes -- it made the rest of their wait seem like an eternity. Her mood was certainly a million miles away from how she felt when the fun started.

Danny Blanks' birthday party had kicked off in fine style. Having his birthday fall on October 31st made him one of the luckiest kids in town. After all, what kid wouldn't want to have their birthday on one of the nights of the year when parents let their kids eat all the candy they wanted? When you added that to the stories that the old Blanks' house (which had been in the family for generations) was haunted, it made for a party of the year -- one everyone in the class was desperate to be part of.

Gretchen had prepared her costume with her mother

all week. It was her take on the classic "Wicked Witch of the West" look, with stripy tights; curled up boots with shiny plastic buckles; a pointy hat; and, of course, a mean-looking broomstick. The only thing that was missing was her skin not being green, but her mum wouldn't let her do that. "I am not having you running around this house making everything green with your mucky hands, little lady," were her exact words, and seeing as she helped put the rest of the costume together, Gretchen felt that she would let her mother have this one. She still thought she looked awesome though.

It wasn't until her mother insisted that she also took her younger brother Andy with her that she started to get upset. Andy, with his whiney voice, seemingly bottomless pit of a stomach and constantly runny nose. There was a year between them, but to Gretchen, it felt like a whole lifetime; a lifetime of having to put up with her younger brother, watching him stumble about and idiotically storm through life like a hyperactive bull in a China shop. Why couldn't she go to the party by herself? She wasn't a toddler anymore, and was certainly more grown-up than her brother. Surely she could be left to enjoy something herself for once -- that wasn't much to ask, was it? It was so unfair. She looked over her shoulder to give him an evil stare, but if she was expecting any kind of reaction, she would be disappointed. Instead Andy just stood there, tucked into the back of the closet, with his robot costume made from old cardboard boxes and mum's tin foil, looking back at her uncomfortably. He began shuffling his feet.

"I really need to wee."

Gretchen scowled. "Shut up, will you? They'll hear you if you keep moaning all the time!" Gretchen said with a hushed tone that barely concealed her annoyance. She turned back to keeping watch over the crack in the door, noticing

him curl his lip in disgust and give her a nasty look as she
did so. No doubt he thought she didn't notice it, but Andy
never was that subtle and, quite frankly, was oblivious of
his actions from day to day anyhow. Another minute passed
and Gretchen's eyes darted from left to right, scanning for
whatever movement she could see from the crack in the door.
Still nothing. She started to think that maybe this hiding place
was almost too good for this game. She should have known; it
certainly seemed too good to be true when she found it.

The Blanks' house was an old place, set on several floors
that seemingly got narrower and creepier the further up they
went. As the game kicked off, Gretchen noticed that most
of the other kids picked some of the most obvious spots to
hide immediately. With Andy clinging to her like a bad fart
in a lift, she never stood a chance at getting some of the
prime places for hiding on the first couple of floors. At first
that annoyed Gretchen; it was just another example of how
Andy was slowing her down, holding her back. Then as they
hurriedly travelled up the stairs, she felt a strange sense of
excitement. By the time they reached the penultimate floor in
the house, the other players had picked their little hideaways;
the only remaining people left 'out in the open' were her,
Andy the annoyance, and little Jonno Carpets -- one of the
fatter kids in the school. Jonno was puffing and panting by the
time they reached the last flight of stairs, but it was when he
looked up to the floor above that she noticed he had lost his
colour.

"You're not going up there, are you?" Jonno said in
between deep breaths.

"You know anywhere else we can hide?" Gretchen
replied.

Jonno bit his lip, which was one of the only parts of

his face clearly visible under his crude mummy costume. He
told everyone when he arrived that he had come as an ancient
Egyptian pharaoh, but Gretchen thought he looked like
someone had thrown a grenade into a toilet-roll factory.

Andy nudged him, "You're scared, aren't you!"

Jonno shrugged off Andy's playful nudges
aggressively. "Piss off! I'm not scared!"

"Danny's mum and dad told us not to go too far
into the house." Jonno looked nervous. "They looked pretty
serious when they said it, and I don't want to get told off."

Andy threw back his head and chuckled, his head
thudding into the sides of the cardboard box that rested on
his head. "Big Jonno's scared of Danny's mum and dad.
Brilliant!"

Before Jonno and her brother could argue any more,
Gretchen cut in. "We're running out of time and there's
nowhere else, so are you coming or not?"

There was a brief pause, Gretchen and Andy staring at
the round mummy in front of them. Just when she thought she
was going to have to ask him again, he let out a big sigh.

"Sod it. I'm going back downstairs and getting
some cake."

Jonno turned on his heel and trundled down the stairs,
mumbling something about "not wanting to play this stupid
game anyway," and before long, he was gone. Andy turned
back to his sister, and found that she was already making her
way up the stairs to the top floor. To him, the floor seemed
vaster and a lot darker than he thought it was a moment ago,
but Andy being Andy, he strolled up after his sister anyway.

When they reached the top, Gretchen noticed how
little there actually was on that floor. The floorboards had a
threadbare carpet, well-worn and aged, with odd stains dotted
around. The wallpaper was old, with a basic floral pattern

that repeated over and over, making it look like some kind
of faded kaleidoscope of greys. There were only three doors,
each of them wooden and decrepit-looking. When Gretchen
tried the first door, she found that it was locked. They tried
the second door, which opened with an agitated creaking
noise, only to find a small box room with a small window
-- no furniture or contents of any kind and, more importantly,
nowhere for them to hide. Andy was about to speak, but
Gretchen cut him off. She heard from below the sound of
Danny Blanks' voice, calling aloud; the hissing lisp his
retainer still made him audible, even from this distance.

"Ready or not, here I come!"

Gretchen turned and grabbed her brother by the wrist
and led him over to the last door on the hallway. It was their
last chance to hide, and if this one wasn't good enough, then
they would have to head back downstairs to be caught early;
and then face the humiliation of being the worst players of the
day (she didn't count Jonno, as he seemed like he wasn't even
playing anyway). She turned the handle, and with a quick
moment of relief, found that it was also unlocked, followed
by an even greater moment of excitement when she saw what
was behind the door. It was a vast closet, which was filled on
either side with odd and old-looking bric-a-brac on shelves.
In the centre stood a large, ornate coat rack, which clearly
hadn't been outside in daylight for years. More importantly,
and to Gretchen's great delight, there were three or four vast
fur coats hanging from it. She certainly didn't know what
kind of furry creature gave up their skin for them, and neither
did Gretchen care. All she saw was a perfect place in which to
hide. There was even enough space for both her and her idiot
brother.

In the background, Gretchen heard the excited cries of
the game commencing downstairs, and with a tug, she pulled

her brother into the closet. She pushed him deep into the fur camouflage den before pulling the creaky door shut with a triumphant click and a smile on her face.

That was almost forty-five minutes ago, and the thrill of the hideaway hunt and the exaltation at its perfection were nothing but distant memories. Now Gretchen stood in a stuffy old closet, hidden amongst a bunch of ancient and foul-smelling fur coats, having to put up with her increasingly irritating brother in a spot where they probably wouldn't be found anytime soon. For the briefest of moments, the thought of giving up and strolling back downstairs to be caught by Danny flickered through her mind. She forced it into the back of her mind, her inner monologue firmly standing its ground with a stubborn, "No!" Her brother, however, did not have the same resolve.

"I gotta go to the toilet!"

Andy surged forward, no longer concerned with the game or his hideaway and pushed past his sister. Gretchen, momentarily caught unaware, stumbled and almost fell onto her backside. Her fall was only stopped by a frantic grab onto the fur coats she was being engulfed by. Gretchen stifled out a cry of "Wait," but by the time she finished the word, Andy had already thrown open the door and rushed outside. In his haste to escape to the bathroom, he had neglected to shut the door after him, and murky daylight poured into the closet, illuminating the gloomy atmosphere briefly, and making all the dust in the air seem to sparkle like molecular weightless gemstones. Gretchen scrambled back up and, with a huff, reached out and grabbed the door handle. She pulled it back, and realised too late that she used too much force. The door swung back on her and slammed shut. Once again she stumbled back, grimacing and hoping that no one -- especially

Danny Blanks -- had heard the noise. Just in case, Gretchen retreated into the darkness of the coats and kept as still as she possibly could. Unless people could see through solid doors, she would have been totally safe -- but she didn't want to take any chances.

She listened carefully, waiting for the moment when she would hear someone exclaim that they heard a noise coming from her hiding place. A minute passed. Then another. Another four joined the others, and she realised that she couldn't hear anything. No one was storming up the stairs. No one was going to discover her hiding place, which she had been in so long. Gretchen thought that surely she must be the winner of the game by now. Why wasn't anyone looking for her? She reached forward slowly and reached for the door handle, turning it as quietly as possible. The old iron doorknob made an excruciating creaking noise until the signalling click of the mechanism told her it was open. She pushed the door open, careful not to give herself away, just in case Danny was in the vicinity, searching for her.

Nothing. The dank, old-looking hallway was empty. She pushed the door open some more, her steely resolve to stay hidden beginning to crumble. Just when she was about the leave the confines of her safe hiding place, something caught her eye. At first she thought she was seeing things, or maybe a bit of dust from those grotty coats had gotten in her eye, so she looked again and focused on it. It was the door at the far end of the hallway; the one she and Andy had tried opening when they first got up onto the top floor. The one that was locked. The door handle was... turning.

Gretchen retreated, pulling the closet door with her but leaving it open enough for her to see through. Face pressed close to the old wooden door, she kept her eyes focused on the doorway directly in front of her. She was breathing heavily, and realised that it was the only noise she could hear. It was completely silent everywhere else. It was almost as if someone had sucked all of the noise in the world out, and it scared her.

The handle continued to turn, achingly slow. To her surprise, it wasn't followed by the sound of someone trying in vain to push a locked door open, but instead the click and creaking wail of the old decrepit wooden door swinging slowly open. Gretchen's breathing increased in its intensity as she stared into the open doorway, trying to see as much as she could from the crack in the closet door.

It was dark inside -- impossibly dark. It was almost like someone had coloured the whole interior of the doorframe in with thick, black paint. Suddenly, Gretchen was hit by a wave of stench that almost made her gag. It was a sickly, damp smell with hints of rotten egg. If Andy was still in the closet with her, she probably would have blamed him for farting. Then again, if Andy was still in the closet with her, he probably would have. Gretchen turned away, blinking furiously, almost as if she was forcing the smell out by doing so. It seemed to work, as no sooner as the eggy smell had hit her, it seemed to fade away. Not completely, but enough to stop her gagging or throwing up some of the birthday party nibbles she helped herself to earlier in the evening. She turned back to the crack in the door, and that's when she saw it.

There was something in the doorway. Something lurking in the shadows. She couldn't make it out properly, but shining out in that impossible darkness were two hideous eyes peering out. They had that same eerie shine that a cat's eyes have when they are caught in a cars headlights. They seemed to be bobbing up and down ever so slightly, which made them even creepier. Gretchen gasped, and then quickly moved her hand over her mouth to stifle the sound. Whatever was in those shadows, she certainly did not want it knowing where she was. That was a sensible idea, but when whatever the eyes belonged to stepped out of the darkness, it took everything in her power not to scream in horror.

It walked unsteadily -- no doubt due to its size and shape. It was like its bones were too big for its body. It would have been immensely tall, with the top of its head no doubt touching the ceiling of the hallway, if it had not been hunched over. Due to this, its back was oddly misshapen, with a large hump visible on its back. The rest of its body was equally as grotesque, with overly saggy skin hanging from a thick skeleton-like material hanging off a table. The skin itself was a sickly, almost translucent thing, covered in boils, blemishes, and almost glossy in nature, as if it was wet. Its palette was a sickly pale green colour. More horrifying was how thin the skin seemed to be. As the creature moved, you could see the muscles, sinews, and bones beneath it stretch and move with it. It was hard to tell, but it seemed as if you could also make out the shapes of internal organs within as well. Its face was not immediately visible, as it sat behind a curtain of long, greasy, and slick black hair hanging in front of its face. That said, Gretchen could still make out the eyes. The cold, pale, menacing glare burned out from within the shadows, the pupils darting in every direction.

It didn't take a genius to know that, whatever it was, it was searching for something. Gretchen knew it, and she was terrified.

Her whole body tensed up, frozen to the spot in fear. She began to tremble. It walked incredibly slowly, as if every step was a real challenge, before stopping at the bannister at the top of the staircase. Gretchen could hear the sounds of the excited partygoers running and playing around the house below. The creature placed both hands on the bannister rail and leaned its head over the edge, its hair hanging down slick and wet. It too was breathing heavily, and Gretchen could see its chest inflate and deflate with each wretched, stale breath. It seemed to be observing something. Its head swiped from left to right in an almost feline manner.

Suddenly it leaned its head back and took in a deep breath through its long and crooked nose, now visible as its greasy hair fell back. As it did so, it made a high-pitched croaking sound that seemed to last forever. Gretchen was frozen on the spot within the shadows of the closet. She realised then that she was holding her breath. She watched whatever this 'thing' was, taking a good long nose-full of something that was pleasing to a disturbing amount, and it terrified her. In horror, she felt a sudden warmth running down her legs and realised that she had wet herself. At any time, she would have been hideously embarrassed by such a thing -- she was, of course, "grown up," as she kept telling her mum. Right now, though, all she could do was hope that the thing outside the door didn't discover she was there. She briefly glanced down at her leg, observing the growing darkness spreading down her stripy witch's tights. It was in that moment that the hideous, croaking noise had stopped. Gretchen turned back to the crack in the door as slowly as she possibly could, so she didn't make any noise. With a trembling bottom lip, she looked back out onto the hallway where the creature stood. It was still in the same spot, but something was different. This time, its head was turned towards the closet and it was looking directly at her.

And to her horror, she saw a large grin appear across its gaunt and hideous face.

She was oddly mesmerised, perhaps through sheer terror alone, by what was unfolding in front of her eyes. The creature slowly raised its right arm, and even from the distance that it stood, she could still hear the stretching of old skin, and the crack and snap of old bones moving. It extended its index finger so that it was pointing right at her, the grin still etched across its face. Gretchen's breathing intensified, and her heart pounded so hard that it felt like it would burst right out of her chest. Then, even more agonisingly slow, it raised the same boney and overly long fingers to its lips, and hissed out a long breathy and solitary sound.

"Shhhhhhhhhhhhhhhh."

That was the moment that Gretchen decided to scream. Until then, she hoped that staying silent would keep her safe. That clearly wasn't going to be the case. If she screamed for help, someone would come. One of the parents would hear her, and they would come running up the stairs to see what the fuss was all about. They would come up the stairs and save her before the creature could get her. So, with all of the breath in her tiny lungs, she prepared to let out the loudest scream she had ever done before.

What actually came out was a tiny, squeaking sound. It was as if she had lost her voice in an instant. She tried again, and this time there was even less sound. She reached for her throat, trying to feel if anything had happened to it. It was fine. Panicking heavily and tears streaming down her face, she tried to scream again, but all she could hear was the sound of air escaping her lungs. With her voice literally non-existent, she could only watch in horror as the creature turned the rest of its gangly, ungodly body and began to move towards the closet door. She had to do something, and quickly. With each thud of the creature's boney feet, it was getting closer and closer. When the creature lifted its arm slowly towards the door handle, she seized her chance. She pushed with all her might and the door swung outwards violently. Keeping her head down to avoid looking up at whatever horror lurked above her, Gretchen darted out from the closet as fast as she could, heading straight for the stairs at the end of the corridor.

She caught the creature by surprise, and it stumbled backwards on unsteady legs as she rushed past. She was almost at the top of the stairs when she tripped, stumbled and fell flat on her face, skidding along the wooden floor. Her two ever-growing adult front teeth bit deeply into her front lip. There was a brief moment of shock and the taste of metal in her mouth, before the hideous stinging sensation began. Tears were streaming from her face and she would have been screaming at the top of her lungs in pain, but all that could be heard was a breathy wheeze. She tried to crawl to the top of the stairs, but her foot was caught on something. Gretchen rolled onto her back to see what she had tripped on, and to her horror, realised that it wasn't on a loose floorboard.

The shiny silver buckle of her pointy, authentic witch's shoe that adorned her left foot was caught on something alright. Wrapped around it, like some kind of snake made out of pure bone, was an abnormally long finger. With tears filling her eyes, her gaze travelled from the shape of the finger, with its hideous ancient and cracked nail, along the rest of the huge hand it belonged to. It was twisted up in an almost claw-like manner, with only the index finger that held her fast being extended fully. The creature she had been so confident in outrunning had somehow lunged out and caught her before she could escape. How had it managed that? It would have had to be lightning fast, and it certainly didn't look capable of being that. The creature was on its hands and knees, hunched over even more than before, and with the tiniest gesture of its finger, began to drag Gretchen towards it. She tried to reach for the top step, desperate to crawl away, but it was too far and she slid smoothly along the wooden floorboards, pulled along as if she weighed nothing. The creature loomed completely over her, and Gretchen forced her eyes shut to avoid staring at what was above her. She felt its hair fall over her, thick and greasy like oily black liquorice. Its breath was hot, damp, and foul smelling, and crawled its way up her nostrils, threatening to make her gag. She clamped her hand over her mouth, and as she did so, she opened her eyes.

A huge, gaunt-looking face stared down at her, a pair of eyes like two burning hot coals deeply set into its skull. Its nose was oddly shaped, almost flat, as if someone has squashed it into its face. Like an animal, it sniffed and snuffled its way over Gretchen as she whimpered helplessly. Then, with lightning-quick reflexes, it grabbed Gretchen by her arms and sat her up like a rag doll.

Then Gretchen watched in horror as a huge, evil-looking grin grew across its face, revealing a mouth than contained way too many teeth. Suddenly its head twitched slightly, and Gretchen distinctly heard a sick popping noise. Its mouth opened, revealing a mouth that contained rows and rows of sharp, needle-like teeth. Its jaw stretched, as if the creature was letting out a huge yawn. Like a snake, the jaw continued to stretch and open, distorting the already hideous face to even more nightmarish proportions. It hissed as its sickly cracked lips pulled back, revealing huge discoloured gums, and its eyes widened in pure, unadulterated excitement. As the creature lowered its head towards her, drooling and hungry, Gretchen tried once more in vain to scream.

After the mysterious disappearance of Gretchen Hollow on that day, children never came to Danny Blanks' birthday parties anymore. Eventually, none of the parents would let their children anywhere near the Blanks' house, and would avoid the family whenever they could. Ostracised by the community, they moved away two years later. They left suddenly in the night, taking everything with them, leaving the old house an empty husk, ready for the next tenant. No one ever heard from the family again. The only evidence that they even existed was the cryptic note they left on their front door.

It simply said,

We did what we could to keep it fed, and but now it is your problem. May god have mercy on your souls.

ROOM AT THE INN
ADAM MILLARD

The carriage crunched its way along the gravel; the semi-darkness served to remind its passenger that he had not eaten a proper meal all day. His stomach rumbled at the thought of ham legs and buttery potatoes. He hoped the Kirkstone Inn would still serve him food; perhaps if he asked nicely, informed them of his unfortunate forgetfulness, they would construct something for him, for even a rudimentary repast would do.

As the carriage steadily meandered along what appeared to be a never-ending path, Dr. Beaman glanced towards the Inn. In other circumstances, he would have asked the driver to turn the carriage around and continue until they arrived at somewhere more becoming, but he was tired and hungry, and he didn't like the thought of searching for alternative accommodation after dark. Besides, it wasn't utterly abhorrent; he'd sojourned in much worse, albeit not of his own volition, and certainly not through forward planning.

The Kirkstone Inn was a pastel-shade of yellow. It might -- or might not -- have once been the purest white;

Dr. Beaman could only imagine the torrential weather an
entire winter would bring to Cumberland. Enough to remove
even the thickest coat of paint, or at least taint it until it only
bore a passing resemblance to its intended colour. There were
pillars on either side of the large, oak door; large columns that
were also decrepit, blistered, exfoliated by Lord-knows how
many terrible seasons. He wondered how many years it had
been since the proprietors last stumbled outside with a ladder
and a paintbrush -- for it certainly hadn't been during this
decade. Hanging in the windows were age-stained curtains
-- none of which had been positioned neatly on their rails. The
upstairs curtains were drawn; a sign of already-retired guests.
Dr. Beaman could only assume they had been unfortunate
enough to have run out of alternate options, thus resigning
themselves to The Kirkstone Inn for the night.

"Looks like a nice place." The voice startled the
good doctor, and only after a few moments did he realise it
belonged to the carriage-driver.

"One can only hope it's a little fancier on the inside,"
Beaman replied, a faux smile curling at the corner of his lips.
"Are you absolutely certain that there are no other Inns in the
vicinity?"

"I'm not from 'round these parts," the driver huffed.
"So I couldn't be certain. I can guarantee that it'll be cheap,
though." Beaman could tell the driver was smirking simply by
the tone of his words.

Impertinent, inbred moron, Beaman thought.
Delivering him to such a ghastly dwelling wasn't enough,
the driver was now outwardly mocking him.

The carriage slowed to a stop; two horses whinnied
simultaneously, apparently pleased with their performances.
Dr. Beaman disembarked, plucking his brown-leather case
from the seat. The first drops of rain gently pattered his coat.

It was Christmas, and yet there was no sign of snow. The ground beneath was solid, stable, when it should have been slippery with frost. Beaman was not feeling the joy he had come to know in previous years, for Christmas had always held a special place in his heart. Perhaps the lack of whiteness was the cause for his absence of merriment. Maybe he would feel happier upon returning to the city. The thought filled him with hope.

"You hear such things about places like this," the driver said in a hurried attempt at conversation. "Places that have seen so many things, so many people. I don't envy you on your night, Doctor." He didn't make eye-contact whatsoever; simply continued to stare towards the Inn, shaking his head in an apparent display of objection.

Beaman handed the driver a shilling. "Whatever do you mean?" His salt-and-pepper beard moved with his words, and he couldn't help noticing a hint of fear in his question.

"Well..." the driver grinned, revealing several discoloured teeth and not a lot else. He wore thick, silvery eyebrows that twitched nervously as he spoke. "Places like this see a lot of people come and go, don't they? I was just thinking about how many of them might go... in there." He extended a rheumy hand and jabbed a spiderlike finger towards the Inn's entrance.

Beaman didn't look to where the digit pointed; he could not look away from the churlish little man with whom he had spent the better part of an afternoon with in complete silence. He couldn't, for the life of him, understand the driver's intentions. "Are you mad, man?" he asked, somewhat brusquely, though he didn't think it was uncalled for. "There are no such things, I tell you. I'm a man of science, not of faith. If people have died in there, which I'm certain they have, they were brought out in sacks and never heard from again." His temper had betrayed him, though he felt better for it.

The driver, on the other hand, simply grinned. "You might tell yourself that," he said, "but it will be different when you're up in one of those rooms, alone. You mark my words—"

"Now, listen here," Beaman interjected. "I will not have fear driven into me by an uncouth specimen such as yourself. The things of which you speak are of no consequence, and it would do you well to remember that for your next paying passenger." He sighed, composed himself ever-so-slightly. "I must thank you for the pleasant journey, for it is rude not to, and bid you a good evening."

The man smiled, once again showing teeth that had been either neglected for years or completely forgotten about. "And a good evening to you, Doctor." He tightened his grip on the reins and steered the horses away from the Inn. Only when the carriage was out of earshot did Dr. Beaman breathe a sigh of relief.

"The man's a fool," he said, brushing rain from his shoulders.

He made his way to the door, the gravel crunching beneath his shoes. The first thing he encountered was a sign comprised of a set of rules. Hanging there at eye-level so that guests had no choice but to meet it, he began to skim through them. Most of them were customary: show consideration for other guests at all times; returning to the Inn beyond the hour of ten would result in admonishment at the hand of the owners; dinner is served promptly at seven, therefore tardiness is no excuse for missing meals. These were all self-explanatory, and Beaman skipped over them as quickly as possible. He was getting wetter by the second, and the downpour was worsening. He knocked the door three times and continued to read, and it was at this point he came across the most irregular policy of them all.

"Room seven is out of bounds. Guests attempting to gain access to room seven will be ejected without refund."

He was about to mutter something about the absurdity of such a preposterous law when the sounds of bolts unlocking and keys turning interrupted him. He took a slight step back into the rain, and watched as the door swung inwards, revealing the tiniest, elderly lady he had ever seen.

"Bit late," she grumbled, her neck craning so that she could make eye-contact with the man standing out in the rain. She was wearing a beige hand-knitted cardigan over a brown knee-length dress. Her stocking-ed feet were so tightly-packed into her slippers that her ankles blossomed outward, spilling over the edges like loaves of bread. Beaman was usually a good judge of character, and he surmised -- with some confidence -- that the landlady was not a person to upset. As tiny as she was, Dr. Beaman knew he would be treading carefully for the duration of his stay.

"I heard there might be vacancies." He shifted nervously from one foot to the other; the squelching of rainwater in his shoes was audible over the shower. His discomfort played on his expression, contorting his face so much so that the landlady would have no choice but to take pity.

She offered him a cursory glance, as if his appearance would somehow sway her decision. After a few moments -- moments that felt like eons to Dr. Beaman, who was beginning to resemble something that had crawled up from the sewers -- she nodded and stepped aside, allowing him just enough room to squeeze past her. He caught a whiff of her on the way in; lavender, perhaps, or rosewater, not the musty odour he had expected.

Once inside, Beaman placed his case down and shook his sleeves. Rain peppered the highly-varnished floorboards, and when he glanced up, the old lady was staring at him reproachfully.

"I'm sorry, do you have something I can mop this up with?" It seemed like the right thing to do, though it was simply a courteous gesture, and not one that he expected her to accept.

She closed the door, and immediately everything was decibels quieter. "Don't bother," she grimaced, stepping over the tiny puddles. "It'll be dry by morning."

Beaman removed his coat and looked around for somewhere to hang it. The Kirkstone Inn had been advertised as possessing most modern amenities, though this apparently didn't extend to a coat-rack. There was, however, a sparsely decorated Christmas tree in the corner; even from where he stood, the dust on the decorations was visible.

"You'll be taking your coat up to your room with you," the woman said as she reached up to where a row of keys hung precariously on the east wall. "Payment can be made before you leave, since you don't look like the type of beggar who's going to run off without paying." She handed him the key; a large, bronze thing that was also coated with dust. "I take it you read the rules?"

Beaman was in the process of wiping the thin film of dust away from his palms. "I did, but there was one that I found rather odd. It was the one about—"

"Stay away from room seven," she interrupted. "Pretend it doesn't exist, you hear?"

Beaman was confused, but the woman sought confirmation. "Room seven," he said, "doesn't exist."

She nodded; her neck seemed to only be connected to the rest of her by a small thread as her head wobbled about atop it. "There you go. Don't you feel better already?"

Beaman, in all honesty, didn't feel better about anything. "Much better," he lied.

"You're in room one," she said, gesturing to the stairs.

"Top of the stairs, turn right, it's the door with number one on it."

"Thank you," he said, ignoring her patronising wit. He thought about questioning her with regards to food, then decided against it. She was already shambling along the hallway, her tiny, bowed legs threatening to give beneath her. Something rumbled deep within him; and he knew it was going to be a most uncomfortable night. He would push all thoughts of meat and vegetables to the back of his mind, and hope his stomach reacted accordingly.

As he ascended the stairs, past paintings of long-deceased monarchs and sumptuous landscapes -- though made less sumptuous by the thin coating of grime -- he was taunted by three things. The first of which was the carriage-driver and his ridiculous words upon their arrival. Then there was the fact he had been put in room one. Surely he wasn't the only guest at the Inn, though the more he pondered it, the more he realised that Christmas was probably a quiet time for any temporary accommodation. The only reason he was here -- and such a waste of time it was, too -- was because one of his old patients had succumbed to consumption. Finally, there was that strangest of rules about room seven. Why, oh why, would such a nonsensical law be enforced? What could possibly be wrong with the place? As a man of science -- not of faith -- he found it most bizarre, and by the time he reached the top of the stairs, it was niggling at him like a rotting tooth.

Room one was where the old lady said it was. Hanging on the door, somewhat out of place, was a garland. The proprietor, miserable old so-and-so, was apparently clutching at remnants of Christmas, despite having nobody to share it with. Beaman slipped the dusty, bronze key into the lock and turned. There was a click, and then a rattle -- no doubt the dust falling from the keyhole on the inside, or a mouse running for its hole. Pushing his way into what was going to be his room for the night, he felt a sense of forebode wash over him. There was, of course, no reason to feel so ill of the place, the room, the inn in general, but it was there; depressing, compressing -- every feeling that had no place at such a joyous time of year.

Leaving his coat and case on the floor near the door, he walked across to the table which occupied the majority of the north wall. There were three candles and a box of matches, and he proceeded to light them so that he might gaze upon his bed for the night.

It was as expected. One pillow, and a thin, brown sheet which looked itchy -- and would prove to be. The large window on the east wall overlooked the pathway leading up to the inn and the forest at the edge of the road. It was now completely dark; the cessation of the rain did little to quash his unwarranted nervousness.

"Pull yourself together, you fool." The sound of his own voice startled him, subsequently rendering his words obsolete. Perhaps the carriage-driver had been right. Maybe there were forces at work that could not be explained by science alone. The fact that Beaman was even entertaining such thoughts made him realise just how tired he must be.

He began to ready for bed, hoping that when sleep came, it would be enough to carry him through to morning; to a breakfast of warm bread and tea and disinteresting conversation with guests that may or may not be present.

When he woke -- to a feeling he could only describe as

horrific -- he knew he had been sleeping for less than an hour. Hairs were standing up on his arms, his legs, his head; it was as if the entire room had become statically charged. Pins and needles in his limbs prevented him from moving right away, and so he lay, whimpering, until the paralysis subsided. The candles -- of which only two remained lit -- flickered on the table against the wall. There wasn't a draft, was there? Dr. Beaman didn't think so.

Finally, he managed to swing his legs 'round and off the bed. His head was thick with sleep that had yet to come -- sleep that would not be forthcoming while he remained at The Kirkstone Inn. His mouth was dry, and he slapped his lips together in a vain attempt to generate even the smallest amount of moisture.

Standing, he paced across the room to where his case sat on the floor. Down onto his haunches, he began to riffle through its contents. "Where are you?" He was certain he had packed a small bottle of something or other amongst his various medicines and equipment, but as he ferreted around, he soon arrived at the conclusion that he might have -- must have -- forgotten to bring it. He cursed beneath his breath and straightened; his back audibly cracked, a sign of increasing age and desiccating bones.

Pushing the notion of inevitable death and impending twilight to the back of his mind, he found himself struggling. His mind was telling him to return to bed, that tomorrow was Christmas Eve and he would return to city and meet with his friends for drinks and celebrations; his heart was driving him, unwillingly, towards the door of his room. The hairs on his body continued to tingle, to dance on his flesh; a miniature party to which he was not invited, but was instead the venue.

Before he knew it, his hand was wrapped around the doorknob, which also seemed to be affected somehow by the inexplicable atmosphere. It thrummed in his palm, tickling, and he almost laughed aloud at the sensation.

He pulled the door inwards and stepped through and out onto the hallway, almost knocking the hanging garland from his door with a clumsy shoulder. It swung back, brushing noisily against the wood, and he reached up, fearing it would unhook itself and clatter to the floor. Quite how much noise he believed a small garland could make was beyond him, but he didn't want to test it. The old lady didn't appear to be very forgiving, and would not be best pleased with a rude awakening, despite the countless excuses Beaman could formulate to placate her.

Where was he going? His inner monologue was telling him, in no uncertain terms, to return to bed, to ignore the mysterious air in the room and sleep, for tomorrow would come soon enough, and bed was a much safer place to be than where he was currently heading.

The atmosphere in the hallway was as preternaturally intense as the room he had just left. Beamon's tongue tingled, such was its reach -- its power? -- and he scratched at it with his teeth, being careful not to bite down too hard. Surgery, he could do -- he was trained for it -- but he had never self-treated, and now was not the time to begin practising.

He reached a door with a number two upon it; a garland, identical to the one on his own door, hung here too. He continued, his flesh buzzing, his insides seemingly bubbling inside him, either through sheer excitement or implausible fear -- or an amalgamation of the two. The voice in his head had fallen silent, possibly realising that no amount of deprecation would change the mind of its possessor. The truth of the matter was: the good doctor didn't feel in control, and was therefore not the best person to try to convince.

He didn't want to go where his legs were taking him

any more than his conscience; it was, for want of a better word, inescapable. He was being pulled inexorably forward, past doors three and four now -- which both had garlands... of course they did -- and as he reached the fifth door, he could no longer control the pace at which his body carried him.

"Blaaaaggghh," was all he could manage. The scientific part of his mind -- not of faith, remember? -- told him to stop talking nonsense and return to his bed, but no matter how hard he tried -- how much thought he put into turning around and heading back to his two flickering candles and forest-view -- he could not. It was as if he was sleepwalking, a somnambulist with his destination pre-determined, yet he was fully conscious, and moving faster than ever down the hallway.

His whole body oscillated; bone, muscle, tendon, skin, every inch of him was crawling with invisible parasites. He willed himself around, pleading with incomprehensible sounds, but it was of no use.

Room seven, he thought. I'm going to room seven whether I like it or not...

He reached another door, though this one was different. There was a garland, but no number. The tinny sound of Christmas carols pouring out of a phonograph emanated from the room beyond. "Meuurghhh!" he said, meaning to ask for help. It was a terrible noise, one that seemed to be in another person's voice. The numberless room must belong to the proprietor; it was perfectly positioned on the landing, directly opposite the stairs. The old lady was in there, listening to carols in an attempt to lull herself to sleep. He willed his arm to move, to raise and bang upon the numberless door. Her grievances with him would be nothing compared to the relief he would feel at the sight of her. The arm, however much he tried, remained firmly at his side, stuck. "Maurgggh!"

And then he was moving away from the door, continuing down the hallway. If she had heard his incoherent utterances, she made no attempt to investigate.

Room six... his legs were weakening from trying to fight it. The tendons were sore, no doubt in need of treatment, but that was the least of his worries as his recalcitrant feet carried him onwards.

The Christmas carols were still there, albeit muted, and the joviality of God Rest Ye Merry Gentlemen was something of a conflict to how he felt inside. Lonely, morose, violated...

He didn't have time to dwell upon the melancholy within him, though, as the door to room seven was now in front of him. The number was loose, hanging down so that it appeared as an L. On this door, there was no Christmas adornment. Beaman wondered why, and then he knew why. Because this door belonged to room seven, and room seven was different to the others...

The carol emanating from the landlady's room changed, and Beaman suddenly found himself listening to the opening sequence of The First Noël, straining to hear it over the incessant drone in his head. And from in front, from beyond the door to room seven, he could hear whispers; children's' conspiratorial whispers that both terrified and intrigued him. More than one voice, too, as they bickered back and forth. There was another sound; a crackling, as if the room was possessing an welcoming fire.

The hallway was ominously cold. The doctor hadn't noticed it before, but now that he had heard the roaring fire from within room seven, a chill ran the course of his spine, causing him to shudder uncontrollably. A thick plume of white vapour escaped his lips.

He wanted nothing more than to be in that room, to prattle nonsense with the whispering children, to sit in front of the fire and warm himself as the rest of the inn suffered the cold, midnight misery.

He reached down with trembling fingers and enveloped the doorknob. By the time the pain registered, it was too late. He hissed, pulled his hand back to discover it was already blistering.

> *They looked up and saw a star*
> *Shining in the East, beyond them far*

He could smell the flesh of his palm as it smouldered. The pain was numbed, momentarily, but he knew it wouldn't last, not if he didn't treat it quickly. If I could just get back to my room...

> *And to the earth, it gave great light*
> *Until so it continued, both day and night*

The whispers quickened, and the sound of a child's laughter penetrated the door upon which the doctor had singed his hand. He couldn't reach down and try again, for his mind had learnt its lesson. He didn't have to, though, as the doorknob slowly turned, the guest(s) in room seven wanted to see who had come to visit them so late.

> *Noel, Noel, Noel, Noel*

The door opened slowly, cautiously, as if the person on the inside was just as terrified as Dr. Beaman.

> *Born is the King of Israel!*

Holding his sizzling hand between armpit and chest, Beaman watched as the door opened to reveal the room's inhabitants. Creaking melodramatically, the door halted, and Beaman stared in at something that wasn't real.

It couldn't be.

There were no children here, at least not any more. A small blue flame -- solitary and flickering, much the same way as his own candles flickered back in room one -- sat in the centre of the room. There was nothing beneath it; no saucer to prevent the flame from spreading; no sand to control it. It was completely free to cause whatever damage it so desired.

Though it wasn't real. Flames are orange, yellow; this was blue and white and growing. The thrumming that he had felt back in his room, all along the landing, in his head now as the carol continued in the landlady's room, was emerging from the flame, calling him deeper into the room, into room seven where he had no right going because the rules said so.

If only I'd listened...

He watched, unable to move, as the strange, flickering light grew brighter and larger, a dancing orb that pulled him inexorably in. He stood fast, leaning back so that the flame -- whatever it was -- didn't have its merry way with him. When it was big enough, he saw faces within, pushing outward. Heads and limbs jutted out of the light, beckoning him to come closer. The conspiratorial whispers returned along with the child's laughter. The flame continued to expand, exponentially bigger now than when the door had opened of its own accord a moment ago. The children in the flame continued to press; bright, glowing fingers slipped out of the mass momentarily, only to be drawn back in.

"What have you done?" A voice screeched from the landing behind. Beaman didn't need to turn to realise it was the proprietor, clearly dissatisfied with his actions.

"Not me!" he said, finally able to speak once again. "I didn't want to come here. I wanted to sleep!"

The woman moved up alongside him, her jaw wide open as if it had been dislocated. "I told you! Pretend it doesn't exist! My, my, my, this is just terrible!"

Dr. Beaman found his limbs were working again, and stepped back, away from the door, away from the expanding azure flame which threatened to swallow the Kirkstone Inn entirely. "If the sign wasn't there," he said, "then people wouldn't be so inquisitive." Not that he had had any control over it. One way or the other -- call it fate, or destiny -- the door to room seven was opening. If it hadn't been tonight, it would have been another. Why couldn't it have been another? Beaman thought.

The woman screeched, her eyes almost luminous as the contents of the room reflected upon them. "The children!" She was gasping, for both air and words. "The fire!"

The tenderness at Beamon's calves prevented him from moving quickly, but he did move. He backed away towards the head of the stairs, never once taking his eyes from the strange conflagration expanding in room seven. "What is it?" He could feel it pulling him in, as if they were two magnets, attracted regardless.

The lady -- Dr. Beaman hadn't the foggiest what her name was -- turned to face him, and what he saw almost sent him toppling backwards down the stairs. Her eyes continued to glow, blue, white, blue, gray, a display of iridescence that caused his heart to leap up into his throat. It was then that Beaman realised he was in the presence of something otherworldly, for she oozed the ethereal; the doctor could smell the death.

"Almost ten years!" she gasped, her words a chorus of voices. "I kept the room shut for ten years! You foooooool!"

As the last words trailed on for an eternity, hands crept over her from the doorway, from the glowing orb silhouetting her. Tiny, merciful hands that gently encompassed her, pulling her back into the light. Beaman wanted to help her, to pull her away from whatever coveted her so passionately, but he couldn't move. His legs were frozen once again; useless tendrils dangling from his trunk.

The heat was intolerable, and Beaman turned his head to escape its fiery assault. Sweat seeped from his pores, dripped from the tip of his nose. In his periphery, he could see the woman blackening, curling up at the edges in much the same manner as newspaper does when you take a flame to it. Her screams were not of pain, though, but disappointment, resentment. Beaman wondered whether she was actually feeling anything as the fire engulfed her.

With his head turned away from the chaos, his ear was perfectly positioned to pick up on the choral performance of O Little Town of Bethlehem drifting from the numberless door. Oh, the insanity of it all! The music played, joyous and festive; the lady screeched, guttural and resigned; the children whispered and giggled as they licked at the lady's kindling flesh; and Beaman regulated his breathing -- if indeed he was breathing at all -- for the simple purpose of keeping his heart beating. It was then that he slipped on the landing; a folded corner of carpet his ultimate demise. And so began his descent of the stairs; over and over, his body folding in on itself like a marionette with severed strings. Upon reaching the bottom, he crashed into the dust- and grime-covered Christmas tree, sending decorations and adornments across the perfectly-polished floorboards. He didn't know it then, but his neck was broken; he was dying, draped in glittery festivity and listening to the only sound in the entire Inn.

The phonographic carols emanating from the landlady's private quarters.

He closed his eyes and listened; never once questioning the insanity of what he had just witnessed. On one's deathbed, there are much more favourable things to reminisce about.

Article from the Carlisle Journal, Christmas Eve, 1887:

A fire broke out at the deserted Kirkstone Inn yesterday, causing minimal damage to one of the rooms and partial damage to the first-floor hallway. It is believed to have been set by hoaxer's intent on adding to the legend that the abandoned Inn is haunted. The perpetrators also hung Christmas decorations to further embellish the hoax. It is the second fire to strike the Inn in a decade; the first being 1878's unfortunate blaze, which killed the proprietor, Ms Elizabeth Becket, her daughter, Mrs Anna Porter, and her granddaughters, Polly and Lisbeth Porter, aged 8 and 9 respectively. Luckily, no guests had been frequenting the Inn at the time of either fire. The Inn is due to be pulled down next year.

CLANDESTINE DELIGHTS
J.R. PARK

Clouds of dust flew into the air, kicked up by the screeching tyres of a 1965 black Ford GT40 as it hurtled along the sun-baked city roads. The driver gripped the steering wheel tightly as his muscles responded to the excitement and impatience that possessed his spirit. He clenched his teeth as he overtook a truck on a blind bend. Clearing the HGV, he swerved back onto his side of the road, narrowly avoiding an oncoming van amidst the blast of an angry horn.

Hours ago his phone had rung, and although he had not answered the call, it told him everything he needed to know. The wait was over. It was time.

The Maid of The Wave was a beautiful hotel. An oasis of luxury, privilege, and pleasure, positioned overlooking the water in the city's industriously active harbour. It towered above the neighbouring warehouses and boatyards with its ten storeys of modern elegance. The rounded corners of the stone work, criss-cross of angled glasswork, and sleek marble finish made it a striking sight -- a piece of functional art that had clearly allowed the architect to realise their wildest ambitions, but with the restrained filter of carefully applied taste and class.

Its beautiful exterior was matched with an equally exquisite interior. Plush, crimson carpets lined grand hallways whilst marble pillars reached up to high ceilings, decorated with breath-taking murals depicting the great ships that once sailed from this historic site. It would have been no surprise to anyone walking through the foyer of the hefty price tag each room commanded. But this was not a place people stumbled across by accident. With its remote location and refusal to advertise, this was a place frequented solely by direct invitation. The only passersby consisted of fishermen, lorry drivers, and crews from great cargo ships. The Maid of The Wave held no welcome for these types and, therefore, it was largely ignored by the local workers that merely viewed it as a bastion of upper class snobbery -- a world in which they felt they had no place and no desire to enter.

So the hotel remained in perfect seclusion amidst a bustle of daytime activity; a calm, monolithic presence in the centre of a commercially industrious storm. As the evenings drew in and the workers retired to their family life, the harbour fell into the same peaceful state as the hotel -- its seclusion becoming momentarily absolute.

It was a cool summer breeze that caressed Ben Varrey's tanned neck as he stepped from his 1965 black Ford GT40, panting from the breathless effects of adrenalin. He straightened his suit jacket, gliding his fingertips across the pristine fabric with a smile. The touch of such quality had never ceased to provide him with pleasure, no matter how often he wore these clothes. The suit's tailor had long since lost his eyesight, and with it his business. Ben knew there might never be suits made again with such precise, handcrafted finesse, and this exclusivity made his own self-satisfied pleasure of ownership even sweeter.

The door to his car clicked shut and he breathed in the salty air, tinged with the aroma of fresh fish and diesel. He thought back to fun-filled family holidays on the coast at Stanswick Sands, but this did nothing to placate his nervous excitement. Ben licked his dry lips and walked up a set of large, granite steps, making his way into the grand entrance of the hotel.

The evening sun shone its final seductive moments through the lobby window, bathing Ben in a cosy glow. He felt the golden rays gently warm him through his clothes and remembered how the sun used to shine like this when he was child; how it used to magnify through the window of Mr Coats's sweetshop and, when the sun was at the right strength, it would slowly melt the sweets on the shelf. Ben was unsure of the exact moment he first discovered this, but he'd found that if he was to wait for a carefully estimated time in the evening, the rays would have exerted enough influence to have melted the cola bottle gum sweets in their packets. Timing and patience were crucial. If he bought them too soon, they would only be soft and sticky, whilst still retaining their original shape; too late and the packet's contents would be reduced to a syrupy liquid. But get it just right and the sweets would melt together in the packet to produce a ball of delicious, chewy gelatine, whilst the sugar was forced to separate, running to the edges and forming a thick crust. Its taste was an intense burst, so sweet that at times it seemed sour, so pleasurable that his jaw clenched in disgust. This childhood ecstasy was a secret Ben had kept to himself --a joy too exquisite to be shared. It was, perhaps, this experience that shaped the path he trod now; a lifelong pursuit of clandestine delights.

The squeal of false laughter pulled him back from his reverie. Irritated, he flipped a circular token impatiently in his pocket as he waited for the people queued in front of him to finish their business.

The couple were of a type Ben was familiar with, moving in these affluent, social circles. The man looked to be in his seventies, whilst his glamorous partner was at least thirty years younger. Wealth and power initially lured these trophy wives. It seemed this one had remained with her man; the aphrodisiac of big spending and luxurious living must have been enough to secure her vacuous soul.

He caught the look of wonder and amazement in their eyes as the couple gazed around the hotel, waiting for the receptionist to book them in. He'd held a similar look when he first made his way here all those years ago. And like he did then, no doubt the couple would fill their bellies with the five-star cuisine before enjoying more base pleasures at the casino and bar.

Ben had lost a large amount of money here in the past, gleefully handed over at the roulette tables, but it had barely dented his wealth. The rush of putting so much money on the line was a thrill he still indulged in, but this evening, his heart pounded for a different reason. There were other pleasures to be sought in this hotel. In a haven that pampered to the rich and powerful, the entertainment had to go beyond the threat of poverty.

A bead of sweat rolled down his temple.

"Mr Varrey, how lovely to have you back," the receptionist flashed a pair of beautiful green eyes over the rim of her glasses.

"It's lovely to be back, Jenny," Ben replied, mesmerised by the living emeralds that scanned his features, momentarily allowing him to escape from his unease.

"I didn't realise you were staying tonight," her brow furrowed in agitation at this seeming disorganisation. "I'm sure we can find a room. Would you like me to speak with Mr Trewhella?"

"N-no," Ben stuttered, his nerves returning as he thought about what lay in store. "I'm not staying tonight."

"Are you okay, Mr Varrey?" Jenny asked with genuine concern.

Ben smiled weakly without replying and pulled his hand from his pocket, handing the receptionist a small, clay disc. The object was a black poker chip. Its edges were marked with white and gold patterns whilst its face was decorated with a picture of an old fashioned galleon, up turned on its end and half sunk beneath cartoon waves. On the flip side was an unknown marking scratched into the surface. The chip left his sweaty palm and fell into hers. He grew pale and began to tremble, a pathetic smile hung like guilty shame from his face, giving off the air of a young boy that had been caught masturbating.

Jenny nodded with a look of understanding. She smiled reassuringly at the man stood in front of her and placed the chip carefully into a drawer. Without any further words between them, Ben passed her a bank card. She ran it through the payment machine and handed it back to him along with a key card. The key card was jet black with no markings, logo, or room number.

"Thank you," she replied softly, before turning to a colleague that approached the desk.

"Miss Hanivers," her boss began, "we have the Eldos'

arriving late, so could you…"

The world around Ben began to melt from focus. He was given no guidance, no further instruction. It had all been explained before and was now up to him. The chip of the sinking galleon was the key to start tonight's journey, but it had been the final piece of the puzzle, handed to him by Lorelei, slipped into his palm as she'd brought him to orgasm during his stay here last week.

She had been his guide, giving him the clues and codes, piece by piece. But it was not her decision when to reveal each instruction; she was merely a conduit. Ben waited, understanding that it could not be rushed. Maybe he was being tested. But like the melting cola bottles in the sun, patience was key.

"You've got the sinking galleon," he remembered Lorelei's silky, breathy voice whisper in his ear, "but you must wait now. Wait for a call that is not answered."

That call came this morning. A missed call from an unrecognised UK number was left at 5:30am British Summer Time. He knew not to question. If he called back, it would break the contract and his chance would be lost forever. So the decision to cancel all business meetings, to make his way to the dingy harbour and most exclusive of hotels, was a decision largely based on hope and desire -- a feeling reacting to the most discreet of signals.

He prayed he'd gotten it right.

Ben walked away from the reception desk, through the lobby and down a long, regal hallway. It was a path he knew well and the first of the secrets he was shown. This was where he'd met Lorelei. He walked past the casino entrance and to the end of the hallway, he took a left and just before the kitchens was a set of large double doors. A bouncer stood menacingly by the entrance, his shoulders almost as wide as the doorway he protected.

Entrance through that doorway was a coveted privilege, even amongst the exclusive guests of the hotel. No one talked about it. No one dared breathe a word about the Wunderkammer.

A secret in a secret.

"Good evening, Mr Varrey," the bouncer politely nodded with a smile, opening the door for him.

"Thanks, Terry," Ben returned the greeting, forcing his words through a throat that was dry with anticipation.

The door creaked closed behind him as his nose met with the familiar, perfumed scent of the Wunderkammer.

"Ben, my darling," a woman approached him with a hug, pulling him close to her body. She kissed him on both cheeks, then leaned back to look him in the eyes. "You're a little early."

Madam Mami Wata was perhaps forty-five, but looked ten years younger. Her long, red hair flowed down to her green, sequinned dress that split at her thigh, revealing a toned, slender leg that ended in a five-inch stiletto. Her makeup had been applied with a heavy hand, but her eyes sparkled with a sexual cunning. Ben remembered those eyes when she first spoke to him at the casino two years ago, tempting him with her whores. She held his gaze then as she did now, but at the time, he knew her peripheral focus was squarely on the huge pile of chips he had on the roulette table. This was nothing new to Ben. He'd made his first millions ten years ago when he became the market leader in internet dating. His website CupidsBar had been set up with a few hundred pounds, but sold for six million. Since that first experience, he had found himself to be quite the businessman, involving himself in whatever took his fancy, from wine production to car parts to computer components. He was now the owner of Memory Inc. -- the most forward thinking of technological brands -- and one of the richest people on the planet.

Mami had crudely described her girls as the best fucks in the world, and when Ben met Lorelei, he found the Madam had not been wrong. But this pleasure only went so far; only satisfied him so much. Ben could own almost anything he wanted, so what he really desired was the rarest, the most exclusive; those experiences that only a select few could say to have witnessed. These things had to be sought for, to be searched out, and to be hunted down.

His suit had been made from a tailor living in London. His shop was tucked away on a side street off the beaten track; a cramped and deteriorating building that was sandwiched between a second hand book shop and a laundrette. Only a discreet few knew of his trade and they never discussed it with their peers, only absorbed the admiring looks their exquisite garments attracted.

Whether it be clothes, food, wine, sex -- whatever the pleasure -- it needed to be exclusive. It needed to be as special as the cola gum balls he coveted as a child. A prostitute for hire could not appease this appetite, no matter how well practised she was in the delights of sexual gratification and eroticism.

"Lorelei's not here; you know that, don't you?" Mami asked, looking questioningly into his eyes.

Ben didn't reply. As he grew closer to his goal, his jaw tensed through adrenalin, making speech a discomfort. He tried to smile and held out the blank key card.

"Then you know what to do," the Madam whispered. Mami stepped aside, allowing him access down the corridor of the Wunderkammer. Each side was lined with doors and, as he walked through the passageway, he felt the eyes of the girls follow his every step. Excited whispers tickled his ears, but by the time they reached him, their meaning had faded into an unintelligible buzz.

He had not come for Lorelei.

He had almost given up on the sex here completely, but at one tiresomely debauched party, his interest was piqued by the rambling tale of a drunken, high court judge. He spoke about an unproven fable of the hotel that was only whispered of in hushed tones, and then laughed off for its ridiculous nature.

Although the judge seemed adamant about it at four in the morning -- after the seventh bottle of Bordeaux had passed his lips -- when questioned through the fog of a hangover the next day, he denied ever having spoken of it. Intrigued by the secret, Ben paid vast sums of money to various insiders, but all he ever received in return were the same rumours he'd already heard. Scraps of hearsay were all his influence could obtain.

This at once infuriated and excited him. This secret was so closely guarded, so exclusive; he had to have it. Its search became his obsession and he'd uncovered enough to know the search started at the Wunderkammer.

"Where are you going?" Mami called out after him.

Startled, Ben momentarily paused, but remembered the words of Lorelei as he had shared breakfast with her last month.

"There is a table at the end of the hall," Lorelei's full lips pouted as she whispered her instructions like a child reading a story. "You have to slide that table to the side and use the key card. It may sound weird, but no one will stop you."

With her words in his mind, he carried on, his eyes fixed on the round table and ornate lamp that stood in its centre.

A large fist grabbed Ben's shirt, knocking him from his feet and forcing his head to smash against the solid wall. The strong arm of the bouncer held Ben upright, pinning him whilst his feet scrambled to find their balance. His assailant snorted aggressively through his nostrils, baring his clenched teeth.

"Terry?" Ben attempted to say through breathless panic.

"She asked where you're going," Terry spat his angry words into Ben's face.

Ben got to his feet but was unable to shake the iron grip clenched around his collar. His mind chased after lost memories, looking for boltholes of information that might save him.

No one will stop you.

That's what Lorelei had said. He had it memorised. Had she told him a lie? Was this all for her amusement? A way for a high class hooker to get her kicks?

Terry leaned closer, his thick beard prickled Ben's clean shaven chin. The sound of a private lift arriving chimed in his ears, dislodging a memory.

Ben's mind cast back to last September. His back pushed against the mirror wall of a lift car. Lorelei was crouched in front of him, delicately balanced on her stiletto heels. Her shapely legs, seductively dressed in a pair of luxury satin, sheer stockings, held her steady as she unzipped his trousers

and slid his swollen erection deep into her mouth.
Her lips skilfully glided up and down his manhood until the
sensations sent small electric jolts of pleasure through his
body. She took his penis from her mouth and began rubbing
it between her breasts, gyrating it against the groove of her
cleavage held firm by a green and black corset. She panted
with excitement, anticipating the rich bachelor to come at any
moment.

The lift was approaching the next floor. A small bell
sounded, alerting them that the doors were about to open. Ben
willed himself to ejaculate, to be caught at this very moment,
to feel shame and revel in the disgust of his accidental
audience.

As he heard the mechanism of the lift doors beginning
to activate, Lorelei looked up into his eyes and cooed an
instruction between her gasps.

"When you're on the path to your goal, you will
be asked where you're going," she felt his cock spasm as it
reached its moment of climax. "When you are asked, you
must tell them…"

"I will tread where Blackbeard fears," Ben recited.
Terry released his grip on Ben's shirt. His expression softened
and an apologetic smile glinted across his lips.

"I have to be sure. You understand," Terry said,
stepping aside and letting Ben continue. "He's early," the
bouncer called out to Mami.

"It does not matter," she replied dismissively before
turning her back.

Lorelei stepped from the newly-arrived lift and
looked at Ben as he pushed the table away from the wall. Her
thick, black hair framed a face softened with sadness.

Taking the key card from his pocket, Ben waved it

in front of the oak panel walls, unsure of what he was doing.
A high pitched beep sounded for a second, just on the edge
of hearing. A panel slowly peeled back. revealing a corridor
dimly lit by lanterns fixed to the walls. The light flickered.
making ghostly shadows haunt the tapestries decorating the
passageway.

Ben looked back at Lorelei and saw the melancholy
in her eyes.

"Are you sure this is what you want?" she asked with
a tenderness to her voice he had never heard before.

"I have to see. I have to know," Ben replied, before
letting out a deep breath and intrepidly stepping into the
corridor.

"Stay with me," Lorelei called out so gently her
words never made it to Ben's ears.

The secret door closed behind him, leaving only the orange
glow of the lantern's dancing light to illuminate the passage.
Ben walked deliberately slow, allowing himself to take in this
new environment. His eyes strained to make out the patterns
and symbols woven into the tapestries on the walls. He
stopped and traced his finger over one of them, recognising
it as the same pattern scratched into the back of the sinking
galleon poker chip. They reminded him of runes.
Did they hold a purpose? He wondered as he made his way
to the end of the corridor. If not, it made for good theatre.
Ben smiled at this thought in a vain attempt to trivialise the
situation. But it did nothing to ease the tension.

The passage ended with a large metal door; its solid
steel front shone in the lantern light. There was nothing
hidden about this entrance. Ben recalled the next instruction.
He thought back to the beginning of all this, over a year
and a half ago. After spending months quizzing Lorelei and

only receiving a bewildered look as an answer, this was the first instruction he'd been given; the first clue that he wasn't chasing a myth, but that it was real.

The instruction came unusually outside of the hotel. Ben had been in a restaurant on the other side of the city, waiting for the arrival of two potential business partners. He hoped the best seafood in the country and hundred-pound bottles of wine would provide the required lubrication to secure the cheapest manufacture deal he could get. It was while he waited, preparing himself, that Lorelei appeared. With confidence and purpose, she walked up to his table, turning heads with her thigh-high boots and leather skirt. Ben did not see her to begin with, but lifted his head when he felt the uncomfortable wave of astonishment from the other diners in the restaurant.

He was shocked at her presence, but smiled to see the beautiful face that had charmed cash from his wallet on so many occasions. He watched her sensual lips -- those that had expertly brought him to orgasm -- recite an instruction.

"In order to receive what you desire, you must..."

"...knock on the door," Ben raised his fist and banged three times on the steel.

The sound echoed off the stone walls.

A small peep hole opened, revealing a pair of inquisitive eyes. They bored into Ben's face with an unwelcoming intensity.

The next part Ben knew well. He had recited it to himself over the last eighteen months, and held the memory so clear. As he recalled it once more, he could smell the salty freshness of the seafood restaurant mixing with Lorelei's perfume. He remembered a glint of emotion in her eyes; something he had not picked up on until now. Had that been sadness?

Her words were clear, the verse committed to memory.

"I have heard them singing each to each," the voice behind the door barked.

"I do not think they will sing to me," Ben replied.

The peep hole slammed shut, followed by a long silence. Ben questioned his memory. Was that right? Had he got the line memorised as perfectly as he had been instructed? A clunk from a large bolt confirmed his answer and the heavy door slowly creaked open.

His eyes took a while to adjust as Ben made his way into a room lit with harsh, fluorescent tube lighting. The room was nothing more than a small square with a few seats lined up against the bare stone walls. Ben sat on one of the seats and felt the damp of the wall as his back made contact, the moisture seeping through his suit jacket. He looked around to see another door opposite the one he had come through; in front of it stood a muscular man with a fierce expression. He was dressed in combat trousers, an armoured jacket, and riot helmet. He gripped his Heckler and Koch tightly, holding it across his chest. Another man sat by a small desk, a computer monitor rested on its surface. The screen flickered with a grainy, black and white picture of such low quality that Ben was unable to make out any identifiable image.

He looked to both men for instruction, but neither of them said a word. It seemed this far in, the airs and graces of privilege had been forgotten; his money and power meant little here. He was at their will and command.

Ben had gone as far as he could with the information he had been given; all he could do now was wait.

"I can really smell the salt," he offered as a conversation starter with the two men. "This room must be right by the water."

The man by the monitor looked at him, then back to his monitor. Neither replied, allowing his words to drown in the silence.

Ben thought back to the journey he had taken to get here. He had to admit this wasn't what he'd expected. A wave of excitement rippled through his body, causing his scrotum to tighten and goose pimples to rise on his neck. The journey had brought him joy. First there was the initial discovery of the rumour; how he'd lie awake at night thinking about the possibility. Then the careful preparation of finding the right girl to put pressure on, all the while charming her Madam; understanding the delicate balance of money, influence, and desire that was required to get what he wanted.

He had gotten the combination spot on, and now he was here.

His thoughts went back further, recalling how he'd waited outside Mr Coats's sweet shop after school for the sun to complete its work on the packets of cola bottles. Waiting for that feeling, that intuitive whisper of thought that told him the time was right. He'd sat on the edge of the pavement and thrown stones into the quiet road to pass the time; and thinking back to this, he remembered the pleasure he felt. The knowledge of what was to come, and the build-up of anticipation was almost as joyous as the taste of the sugar-encrusted gumball itself. Maybe it wasn't a matter of timing to get the perfect cola bottle gumball; maybe that feeling of knowing when the time was right wasn't an esoteric ability. Maybe it was just a matter of wanting to wait, to feel the excitement of what was to come. To revel in the intoxication of anticipation, building it up to such a high as to enhance the experience of what was to follow. To further elevate his secret sweet treasure to pleasures beyond that which mere taste could allow.

"Open the door," the man behind desk spoke to the armed guard, disturbing Ben's idle thoughts.

The guard pulled back a heavy bolt and began opening the large, metal door. He'd only got part of the way when a figure half fell, half scrambled through the opening. The man collapsed on the floor, turning to look back through the doorway, his face wild with terror. The guard pushed the door closed again, grunting with the exertion. As the entrance sealed shut, the terrified man tried to get to his feet.

Water ran off his soaking clothes whilst large tears in his garments revealed cuts that had seeped red patches through his shirt. His body shook and he gasped to catch his breath, unable to speak no matter how hard he tried. In an attempt to communicate, he began waving a hand around, stumbling on his feet as he did so. His other hand gripped his stomach as a trickle of scarlet liquid dripped from underneath his pressed palm.

The armed guard took him by the shoulders and guided him to a chair.

Ben looked at the man in shock. Anticipation and excitement turned to fear as the adrenalin pumped faster round his body.

"This one's early," the armed guard pointed to Ben.

"No matter," said the man behind the desk, "No point him waiting any longer."

"Everything clear?" The guard asked, placing his gun by his side and unbolting the door.

His colleague put his face inches from the monitor and squinted at the blurry, black and white image. "We're good to go."

The guard took Ben by the arm and hoisted him from his seat.

Ben looked back at the shivering, bloody mess that sat slumped in a chair. The man leant forward and vomited a small puddle of blood. He continued leaning further forward, losing his balance and falling flat on his face. His arm fell away from his portly belly, releasing a jagged gash he had been trying to hold together. Blood flowed from the horrific wound and his intestines unravelled in the growing crimson pool.

"Please," the man begged as he tried to clamber to his knees, slipping on his own innards.

Ben looked at the guard and felt a tear run down his cheek. He held his mouth in an attempt to prevent the vomit that climbed his throat from escaping. The guard pushed him through the doorway. He tried to stiffen his legs to stop it, but was easily overpowered. What had he done?

Partly thrown, partly pushed, Ben stumbled into the darkness. The huge iron door echoed as it slammed shut behind him, leaving him alone, confused, and scared.

With his eyes of no use in the pitch black, his other senses heightened, making the salty smell of seawater so strong Ben could taste it on his lips. He made his way carefully down the darkened corridor, checking the footing of each step before committing his weight to it. The walls dripped with condensation, leaving a slimy residue on his fingers as he ran them along the exposed brickwork. His hand found a railing, and following it, he came to a descending staircase.

As Ben made his descent, he began to feel a damp, warm tingling around his ankles. The sensation moved up his legs and, as the wet fabric of his trousers began clinging to his skin, he realised he was walking, deeper and deeper, into water.

He had found it. At last he knew he was here. This was what he had been looking for -- the treasure he'd sought in the private brothel, hidden within the exclusive hotel.

A secret in a secret in a secret.

The staircase ended and opened up into a large room where daylight crept in through small horizontal openings near the ceiling, each no wider than a letter box. The room was filled with water that lapped around Ben's chest whilst the air was thick with steam. The vapour clouded Ben's vision as the dim evening light shone a red glow, struggling to penetrate the mist. Through it he could just make out the wooden shell of the room and chains that dangled from a pulley system near the roof -- remnants of a time when this was still part of the working harbour. Everything else was lost to the cover of the steam.

As he waded through the water, a sound began to drift across the mist, interacting with the thick vapour, as if in a dance. Its melody caressed his ears with such beautiful tones it seemed to lay aural kisses of adoration gently on his neck. He closed his eyes, intoxicated with the sound, and felt his soul move within the confines of his body.

Ben turned to find the source of this divine sound as he fought a giddiness that rolled his stomach. Hidden in the blood red glow from the setting sun, he made out the silhouette of a female figure perched on a crate above the waterline. Through the mist he watched as she ran her fingers through her waist-length hair. He traced the pleasing curve of her body and found himself salivating at the outline of her breasts. Ben's dick grew hard in the water, straining at the crotch of his trousers. He bit his lip in an attempt to regain some control, but dared not move, entranced by the vision he saw before him and enraptured by the song that floated from her lips.

The stories had not been lies. She was real.
Forgetting all he had been told, he waded towards her, unable
to withstand any longer the enticing allure of her song and the
dream-like image her silhouette cast.

But no sooner had he made two steps towards her
than she stopped singing. Her monochrome image looked in
his direction then gracefully dived forward, sliding into the
water with the gentlest of splashes.

Ben continued to wade through the gloom, desperate
to find her, to hear her song and gaze upon her beauty. He had
to see her close up; he had to touch her, to feel her.

"Don't be frightened," Ben cooed.

Something swam past his leg, sending electric sparks
of delight through his body. Looking down, he made out the
flash of a fish tail; the U-shaped fan of its caudal fin spread
over a metre. He tried to follow the ripples in the water, but
they were soon swallowed up by the covering mist.

All fell silent and Ben licked his lips with excitement.

She was indeed a beautiful creature; one whose
mythical reputation seemed to be proving all too real.

He'd heard rumours of how she'd been accidentally
caught up in the fishing nets of a trawler, and when dragged
aboard, the crew had fought for her ownership. The returning
boat had only three men left alive. Seven mutilated corpses
had littered the deck, slaughtered as greed and madness took
hold.

How she then got into the hands of the hotel was
another mystery altogether; a tale that was surely just as grisly
and soaked in even more bloodshed.

He felt the wake of the water as she circled him.
A pair of hands gripped his thighs from below the surface.

Ben dared not move as he sensed the wondrous touch of this mermaid. Her hands moved slowly up his thighs towards his torso. This is what he had paid for; this was still a brothel after all. He let out a groan as her fingers brushed past the bulge of his erection and continued their upward journey. A head of blonde hair rose from the water, and as she brought her face level with Ben's, she rubbed her body against his chest, stimulating his nipples with the brush of her breasts. Her eyes were a beautiful green that sparkled in the ever-vanishing light as she held his gaze. She smiled as she pulled him closer to her, holding him in a position where their bodies met completely.

Ben's bravery grew as he cautiously placed his hands on her, one at a time. As each fingertip met her soft, warm skin, his breathing momentarily stopped and his mind filled with the most exquisite of raptures. The mermaid placed her hands on his chest. He looked down to see each finger ending in a large powerful talon. Ben watched, motionless as those talons ran over his sodden shirt, gently slicing it with ease.

Stories told of the unimaginable carnal pleasures this creature provided, but there was no mistaking that she was a wild animal. Ben thought back to the man he'd seen burst from this room. How he'd cried out with his innards spilling from his injuries. The mermaid was a predator and as feral as any of nature's killers; he may as well be locked in a cage with a hungry tiger. As this realisation dawned on him, a feeling of absolute terror mixed with his unfettered euphoria producing an emotional cocktail beyond comprehension.

This was the experience he'd been promised!

Ben gently moved his hands up her naked torso, following the smooth lines of her curves. "Carefully does it," he thought. He'd have to show the same patience as he did to get here.

Instinctively, he lowered a hand and rested it on her rear. He gasped as he felt the human-like skin fade into the slimy grooves of fish scales. His affectionate action was returned as she hung her arms around his neck and began to hum a tune that brought him close to orgasm. Ben delicately pulled at the mermaid's flesh; the intoxicating melody caressing his lust. He brought his face to hers and moved his lips towards her seductive pout. As he felt her lean in, he closed his eyes, ready to kiss the fantastical creature. With his lips puckered, he held still, awaiting the sensual contact.

But none came.

He opened his eyes to find himself alone in the water, his brow dripping in the dark. Night had claimed the sky and had taken the last slivers of light from the room. The water was perfectly still.

Confusion enveloped his thoughts.

Had this all been some kind of hallucination?

What was in the steam? Had they been pumping some kind of drug into the room? Had the months of preparation only existed in order to ensure he reacted in the right way to the narcotic vapour and atmospheric surroundings?

Ben lifted his fists and smashed them into the water, furious of this deception.

How could he have been so stupid?

A splash of water and a sharp, throbbing pain across his cheek cut short his rage. Instinctively, he cupped his face then, pulling his hand away, he saw his fingers drip with blood.

His blood!

Another splash signalled a second wave of pain, this time striking against his chest. He looked down to find his shirt torn open, exposing a gash that ran from nipple to nipple. He clutched at the wound and gritted his teeth, desperate not to cry out. His legs burned with agony as he felt the mermaid swipe her sharp claws against the back of his thighs. Unable to control his reaction, Ben called out a feverish wail that was abruptly silenced as he was dragged under the surface, the mermaid pulling his legs from beneath him.

His lungs screamed for air as he struggled to free himself from the mermaid's grasp. Through the murky water, he saw the creature's face flash in front of his. A frightening aggression had possessed her beautiful features; the killer had awakened.

Ben punched out, hitting her side, but this did nothing to abate the striking of claws slicing into his defenceless flesh.

What had he done to provoke this reaction?

Whatever her reason, he was not prepared to die.

With one last burst of energy from his oxygen-starved body, he brought his legs to his chest and kicked out, catching the mermaid squarely in the side of the head and knocking her back. Ben shot to the surface and gasped for air. Looking up, he saw the chains hanging from the ceiling directly above his head. He jumped, grabbing hold of the damp metal links. Heaving himself up, he lifted his legs clear of the water, and not a moment too soon. Splashes below him signified the frustrations as the mermaid lost her prey.

But his escape was only momentary. He was still trapped in the room with her, still locked in her domain. Ben pushed these thoughts from his mind as he hung on the chain and tried to climb the wet, slippery metal. Tensing his muscles, he fought back the pain, pulling himself higher whilst his wounds bled profusely. The blood looked black in the darkness as it fell into the water, increasing the deadly creature's appetite as it circled below.

Looking through the steam, he could make out another chain hanging a few metres away. If he could get himself to that one, it was possible to climb up it and reach the vents that lined the wall near the ceiling. Through the vents, he could make out the silver glow of the moon, the outside world, and a chance to escape.

Holding himself straight, Ben swung his legs backwards and forwards, slowing building up a gentle motion. As the momentum increased, he began to arc back and forth, going further and further with each pass. His hands burnt as he gripped hard on the chain, but his progress gave him encouragement, spurring him on.

One, two, three, four. Ben counted the timing of each swing, preparing to make the switch. After two more swings to set himself up, he reached out and caught the other chain. The first one began to swing back, pulling him from his goal. He let go quickly, fumbled on the links of the second and fell, twisting in the air. Instinct took hold and his legs clamped together, catching the chain between his thighs. His stomach convulsed as his fall abruptly stopped and he found himself hanging upside down, his head only metres from the water. Desperately, he scrambled to right himself, climbing his hands up the chain and pulling himself further from the water. The mermaid leapt into the air like a dolphin. Ben reacted quickly, pulling himself out of reach, and heard her hiss as she failed to lay a talon on her prey.

Fighting through the agony that tore through his body, Ben hauled himself further and further up until at last he was level with one of the small openings. Reaching out, he grasped at it and felt relieved to feel the night air on his fingertips.

Peering through the letterbox-sized hole, he watched an elderly gentleman walk to his car.

"Help!" Ben called out.

The man turned to Ben's direction.

"Help!" he shouted again.

Squinting his eyes, he recognised the man to be the high court judge. There was no mistaking his crooked hunch and steep nose.

"Help!"

Had he heard him? Had he seem him? It was impossible to tell. The car park was so far away and separated by a chain link fence.

The judge appeared to make some kind of hand signal before turning his back and climbing into his metallic blue BMW seven series.

Was that a thumbs-up? Had that even been at Ben?

Below him, the softest of lullabies cooed its way upwards and persuasively pulled at his thoughts. His hands began to slip as his resolve gave way. The heavenly sounds ignited a lust in Ben that dissolved his feelings of despair and entrapment into nothing more than an abstract memory. His grip relaxed as he looked down at the mermaid swimming in hypnotic circles beneath him, her alluring verse growing louder as he slid down the metal links, landing back in the water.

The melody stopped and, turning around, he saw a rush of white water heading towards him. Fear coloured his infatuation and he tried to block the advancing monster, but she was too quick, striking out with her claws and slicing across his belly. He held his stomach as he watched the water around him turn black.

He waded across to the crate she'd been sat on when he first saw her, and tried to pull himself up. As he strained to lift his own weight, he felt the tear on his stomach rip further. He reached down to feel the gristly tubing of his intestines spill from his injury.

Ben slumped back into the water, turning to face the marine predator -- the illustrious creature he had spent his whole life searching for. Was this the ultimate in clandestine delights?

The mermaid drew close to him and placed her claws softly on his chest. Ben had lost all strength to fight and instead regarded the creature, her face once more a portrait of softness and pleasing symmetry.

The mermaid pulled Ben close and he felt her tail tenderly wrap around his legs. She gently tightened her embrace, forcing all water between them to depart. Ben looked into her eyes and marvelled at the wild green orbs that even now seduced him.

She had been his ultimate prize. A life spent looking for the finest the world could offer had culminated in an experience that mined his entire emotional, sensory, and spiritual responses. It had left him questioning everything he thought he knew.

What a fitting way to end.

The mermaid placed her palms on his cheeks and pulled his lips to hers.

He closed his eyes as he felt her lean in, and swore he could feel the sun on the back of his neck. Its golden rays were warm and powerful. The sweets in Mr Coats's sweetshop would slowly be melting.

As their lips met in a passionate kiss, he savoured the taste of cola bottle gumballs.

WAITING FOR THE RIGHT STOP
MADELEINE SWANN

Lilly jumped when the phone rang in her pocket. She answered it, glancing about the unfamiliar, darkening city streets to see if she had reached her destination. It was Terry, of course. She briefly panicked about remembering her way back, and if she would need to. "I'm here," he said. Her guilt was immediate on hearing his voice.

"I won't be too long," said Lilly. "The map said it was close by. Regent Road -- that's where I need to get off." She squinted as she turned the corner, blurrily spying a dilapidated bus stop surrounded by hordes of people. In the queue, no one glanced at the dark blue jacket swamping her body or her curly black hair scraped into a ponytail. Her dark skin was free of make-up and every tired line exposed. From what she could see, the others weren't too pretty either; the older ones sported creaking knees and wheezing chests, and a few slender youths displayed a half closed eye or some kind of skin complaint. Some smiled politely before looking away.

"I can't wait to see you," said Terry in a voice that made her sad, "I miss you. It's weird not having you here."

Though his words were grimy with age, Lilly was
sure he meant them. She promised she'd be there and hung
up, windpipe tightening. The B&B she'd found last night was
cold and dreary, and left her fuzzy from lack of sleep. She
really didn't want to have to go back.

The double decker bus pulled up so quietly it reminded her
of a dream. Odd for a bus, thought Lilly, most of the time
they sound like unhealthy old men. Her phone rang a second
time. "Mum," announced the screen. Her mother's calls had
dwindled to once a week then once or twice a month, and
were now rare -- there was so much to say, it was easier to say
nothing. Lilly pressed the hang-up button. She would answer
the next one for definite.

Lilly inhaled the attic scent as she climbed the steep steps,
once more a child in her old house, reading in hiding places
under insulated rafters. She grabbed hold of the rail when
the bus lurched forwards. "Blimey," she grumbled crossly,
wobbling past blank faces staring out of windows, settling
down in the centre of the back seat. An old lady in a filthy
floral coat and hair net sat hunched at the far end. She turned
her wizened face to Lilly and grinned. Lilly smiled back.
"Don't talk to me, don't talk to me," she begged silently. Her
request was, of course, ignored, and the old lady shuffled
closer. Her washed-out appearance reminded Lilly of the moth
that had turned to grey dust under the sink.

The old lady -- Ruby -- twittered about the closing
of the local supermarket, and Lilly realised she couldn't
remember buying a ticket. She checked her purse, worried
she might be accused of trying to get a free ride. There it
was; she must have purchased it on autopilot. "Do you have a
husband?" asked Ruby.

"No," Lilly hoped brief answers would diffuse further chat. Ruby nodded slightly, expectantly, "A boyfriend."

"Oh," she seemed surprised, "That must be nice."

Lilly fought the memory of screaming at Terry like a drunken harridan while he turned away from her in disgust. She bunched her fists tightly, focusing on the pain to avoid thinking about what happened next. We're going to talk tonight, she thought in a loud, distracting voice, we'll talk and sort it all out.

"Are you alright?" Ruby's voice deepened with concern.

"Yes," said Lilly. "Fine."

"I still talk to my Harry all the time," said Ruby. "Who else would listen? He was the only one who ever did."

Lilly felt sudden sympathy and turned to her companion, eyes wandering over the old lady's face. Lilly had thought there was something strange about the hair net and now realised what it was; it was a cobweb, crawling over the grey head and stretching with delicate tendrils over her ears and cheeks. Lilly stood suddenly, muttering something about needing to see where she was going. She stumbled over other passenger's knees and feet, keeping her head down but occasionally catching other's weary eyes, aware her own must look wild.

She climbed to the top deck, eventually finding a seat at the front beside a middle aged man with stick insect limbs.

"I've not seen you around here," he said with a surprisingly firm voice.

"No," she said, unsure of what else to say. He nodded and leaned his head back against his seat.

Lilly felt she should speak, but nothing came to mind. Instead, she stared out of the large window ahead. The

roads were grey and unfamiliar. She tried to remember what
the map had said, which roads she needed to keep a look out
for, but reality never resembled the neat lines of a drawing.
She glanced at her companion; his outline seemed fuzzy, as
though he had been rubbed out. Their silence pressed on her
like shrinking walls. "Do you... live around here?"

He looked up and tilted his head to think. Large
flakes of something fell from his hair onto his lap, and Lilly
struggled not to retch. "Yes, I have a bedsit nearby." He
paused. "I go to the café in the mornings and read my paper.
I like to listen to the conversations around me." A maudlin
film coated his eye and Lilly regretted speaking. She thought
of the last time she had been amongst friends, how much
easier it had been to let them evaporate. She felt displaced in
any company since meeting Terry. She tried to push aside his
revolted face once more...

"...He was a lovely dog," the man rambled, "Went
with me everywhere." Lilly sat through his descriptions of
Pip. Other people's memories are impenetrable, visible only
to the speaker. All she could do was nod and wait for it to be
over. The memory of shrieking drunkenly at Terry stumbled
forward and this time she couldn't stop it.

"My friends say you're an arsehole." It was night and he was
walking away. The sight of his turned back enraged her and
she pushed his shoulder hard, too hard, "and I think you're an
arsehole too."

"It's not so lonely when you go for a walk, though," said the
man beside her. Lilly nodded and shifted in her seat. When
was her stop? Why did everything look different? Behind her
someone coughed and she realised how quiet it was. Nobody
else was saying a word. There has to be someone else who

knows someone on here, she thought, but when she glanced behind, everyone meekly stared ahead or out of windows. Some eyes connected with hers, faces expressionless. Why did they seem so odd? Her eyes strained at fuzzy road signs.

"Still," the man sighed like a dying dog. Lilly waited for his next sentence but it never came. Daring to hope her ordeal was almost over, she prayed for Regent Road to appear, placing her hand on her chest. Wait, what was that? It wasn't her own gasping she could hear, but the man next to her. She turned to him, desperately trying to remember any first aid tips.

"Get them to cough," said a know-it-all schoolmate in her head, "get them to lie on their front," shrieked a former colleague. Lilly grabbed the man's shoulder, staring uselessly when it crumbled in her hand. "That shouldn't happen," said her brain, "that really shouldn't happen."

"Oh my God," said her mouth. The grey lumps in her hand shrank to grains of dust and fell to the ground. The man beside her didn't even look up. Lilly backed away from him, perching on the end of her seat. She felt the eyes of the other passengers on her before she saw them, and when she turned everything was in sharp focus. The closed eye of the nearby blonde wasn't some genetic problem after all. In her socket was a spider's nest, eggs ready and waiting to burst into a seething mass. The grey figures were alive with spiders, earwigs, woodlice, and thin, brown, clothes moths. Cobwebs swamped their shoulders and faces, sticking them to the seats, each other, and the windows she now saw were black with filth. She recognised one or two youths from 'Missing' posters on cracked walls. The attic smell was no longer comforting, but sickly with mildew and mould.

Something tickled her lower lip and she pulled absently at it, whimpering when she saw strands of cobweb in her fingers. Wiping her mouth over and over, she stood, inching towards the stairs and descending clumsily, keeping her eyes on the passengers who watched her every move with what ocular power they had left.

Alighting unsteadily on the lower deck, she grabbed at the yellow poles and pulled herself towards the driver. "Excuse me," she said, her throat closing, "I need to get off here. I'm sorry, but I need to get off now." His back remained resolutely facing her, only pale ear lobes and stringy brown hair beneath his driver's cap visible. She wondered what his face was like. "Excuse me," she raised her voice squeakily, glancing behind, "I need to get off." Nothing; the driver stared ahead. Shaking now, Lilly realised she would have to press the button and wait for the next stop. She made her way back to the threadbare seats, keeping her eyes firmly on the ground. She knew they were staring, but she forced herself not to look.

The broken handle of a passenger's pink, plastic umbrella crawled with insects. With a sweating hand, Lilly pressed the stop button firmly. She brushed away an earwig trundling onto her knee with barely concealed hysteria. Just wait calmly, she thought, just wait calmly and keep your mind on nice things.

The full violence of her argument that night with Terry stared back at her; the cold delight in his eyes, his hand crushing her neck, her feet dangling mid-air, the stone of the wall against her back, her smashed glasses on the street below. Sensing danger, the alcohol had abandoned her brain, exposing her to the whole debacle. The worst part had been the dying fish noises she made.

Lilly now placed a hand to her chest and struggled for breath, aware that each noise drew further attention. Her fingertips skimmed the strings of a web connecting her shoulders to the seat and she tore at it furiously, "No," she said aloud, "I won't let you." Lilly grabbed her neighbour's umbrella, ignoring the grit and writhing creatures beneath her fingers. The woman made a vague attempt to grab it back, but the effort proved too much and she fell against her seat, exhausted.

Lilly stormed to the front, gripping the handle so hard that blood tingled in her fingers and bugs were crushed. "Let me off now," she ordered, jabbing the back of the driver's head. It lodged wetly into the back of his cranium. Retching, Lilly yanked it back and a stream of watery, red brain matter spattered down the aisle and onto her jacket. Nobody seemed the least bit concerned. She turned to the glass on the door and smacked the umbrella against it with all her strength, expecting it to shatter or even just crack -- but nothing. Lilly hit again and again, losing control and flailing her arms, weeping and howling. She dug her fingers into the crease of the doors, trying to separate them, pulling hard until all the air left her body...

The vehicle creaked to a halt and the driver turned to her, a disgruntled frown on what was left of his face. Tears balled inside Lilly but she swallowed them down. Nodding slightly, she trudged back to her seat, handed the umbrella back to its owner, and waited for the right stop.

EQUINOX
CRAIG ANDERSON-JONES

```
**************************************************
./System_boot
./DATETIME = 3252/7/9-1532
./…
./Artificial_intelligence/E771e = Active/.
./Craft_designation = DS-Explorer Type 2/.
./Craft_ID = Epiphany/.
./Crew_manifest_call = 4.0/.
./Captain = Yokohuri, Sian/.
./Specialist = Falwasser, Kurt J/.
./Engineer_first_class = Shepherd, Alvin T/.
./Engineer_second_class = Tan, Amy Y E/.
./Location_scan
./…
./Equinox region CONFIRM/.
./MC-671/.
./Initiate +captain_evocation_alpha+ /.
**************************************************
```

The chattering text sent strips of light strobing in the darkness. Computer screens in turn blinked awake from their slumber, sparking into life with beeps and lights, triggering a hive of activity amongst the electrical components on board. In a dark room, lights flickered on as four polished chrome tubes began to lower from a central cylinder. Interred inside each tube, lay prone a member of the deep space exploration team.

The frosted glass covering of one tube slid gracefully open; a drowsy female head rose from the yawning fissure.

"Ellie, are you operational?" her voice asked; soft, but stern, despite the sudden awakening.

"Hello, Captain Yokohuri. I trust your sleep was a pleasurable one," replied a monotone, feminine voice.

"Yes, marvellous, thank you, Ellie. How are my crew? Give me a status report," said the Captain, rubbing the sleep from her eyes.

"Vital signs are good. You are all lacking some vitamins and minerals, which is to be expected from your stasis," replied the disembodied voice, matter-of-factly.

"Okay, how long until they are awake?" Yokohuri demanded, seeking confirmation for an answer she already knew.

The AI responded immediately, "Three hours, standard time, as you requested, Captain."

Sian Yokohuri stood up on uncertain and shaky legs. Stepping out of the stasis tube, she stretched her tall, athletic form and ran a hand through her short, black, bobbed hair. Cracking her neck to one side, her face hardened.

"Are we here?" she demanded, her authority restored like Lazarus.

"Yes, Captain," replied Ellie in a heartbeat.
Sian nodded and looked over the other three stasis tubes, still holding her crew in a frozen embrace.

"I'm going to the bridge," she said as she pulled her pristine uniform from a tall metal locker.

Sian pressed the cold, aluminium button and the frosted glass doors slid apart. As she made her way down a maze of walkways to the bridge, she could feel her heart beating faster. A pang of claustrophobia washed over her. She could feel sweat chaffing her armpits as anticipation surged through her body.

This could be it; another Earth, a new home, and I would get the credit... finally.

Overpopulation, greed, and a severe lack of moral fibre had inevitably descended to anarchy, social disintegration, and riots across the world. True to form, this led to recrimination, which bloomed into war. International neighbours fought and bled over long-held quarrels, escalating to the deployment of nuclear warheads and pinnacling with the use of particle weapons. The environment waved a white flag and surrendered; the Ozone layer developed gaping holes as vast as continents and started to deplete quicker than ever. The world entered a second dark age. Hope was extinguished. After five hundred years, things finally stabilised. People and nations began to communicate again. The horrors of history forged a new desire to make the world better. Money was consigned to history; working together became the goal of humanity. In this new age, technology flourished. Ships were being sent further and further into the void; new ways of interstellar travel were discovered, harnessed, and mastered.

This ship -- her ship -- was the first to venture beyond our galaxy and into another.

The Epiphany and her four-man crew had been sent into the abyss to explore planets that had been identified as potential replacements for Earth. Despite humanity's enlightenment, the punishment meted to its home had been terminal.

"Are you okay, Captain Yokohuri?" asked Ellie, interrupting Sian's moment of introspection.

"I'm fine," she growled back.

"Your heart rate is elevated, as is your skin temperature. It would suggest that you're experiencing anxiety," responded Ellie, oblivious to the Captain's irritation.

"I guess I am," Sian replied softly, more to herself than anyone else. As she entered the bridge, the shutters that covered the fore windows started to open. Console lights flickered on and she saw the familiar, cold, white, hygienic bridge.

Facing the huge front windows was a large, white leather chair, fitted with a motion display above it. Upon her entrance to the command hub, the display started to track her, following her every move so that she could issue commands to the ship at any time. The shutters finished their ascent and ground to a halt with a loud clunk.

Sian looked through the window and revelled momentarily in the vast emptiness of space. It felt comforting, though the myriad of stars surrounding her were unfamiliar compared to the ones she used to navigate back home. In the distance -- growing larger every second, like an explosion under water -- was the planet known only as MC-671.

"Ellie, have you done any preliminary scans?" Yokohuri demanded, her mind back on the task at hand.

"Affirmative, Captain," Ellie responded in its usual, disconnected way.

Sian sighed, "What're we dealing with here; is it good news?"

"Affirmative, Captain; initial scans indicate there is a breathable atmosphere, though the levels of oxygen are much lower than Earth. Prolonged exposure and exertion will affect human physiology. I am also registering water and organic material," Ellie reported back.

"Organic material?" Sian asked with a raised eyebrow. "What do you mean exactly by organic material?"

"It's difficult to objectify, Captain. Scans are only preliminary, and only provide very high-level results. For more accurate findings, we will need to move into orbit and conduct further tests," Ellie answered immediately.

Yokohuri nodded and rested both of her hands on the edge of a console, "Move us into orbit and begin to wake the crew."

There was a brief pause before Ellie replied, "Are you sure, Captain? This request does not comply with normal operational protocol. Regulation three-dot-one clear-" Sian interrupted curtly, "Yes Ellie, now! They need to be briefed and given this new information. We need to begin our work. Send all the results of your scans to my quarters," she turned and exited the bridge.

"Affirmative, Captain Yokohuri."

"Christ almighty. I can't stand these long stasis trips. Nothing but nightmares and scary fucking shit all the time," growled Kurt Falwasser, Specialist on board the Epiphany. He frantically scratched his short ginger hair, "Fucking fleas." He was nicknamed *The Ginger Psycho*, following one notorious shore leave when he was detained for picking a drug-induced, hallucinogenic fight with a tree. Despite his short stature, he won by a Technical Knockout.

"Falwasser, you don't get nightmares, man; that's what hyper sleep is all about. Just pure, unadulterated sleep. Hmmm, mmm, baby," came a voice from behind another tube.

Kurt tilted his head in the direction of the voice he'd

known since he was a kid, "Shit, after all this time, I gotta wake up to your ugly face. Put me back, man, put me back."

Shep clutched his hands to his chest, "Man, your words. Sometimes, man, they really fucking hurt." The two men laughed and clasped hands, "Good to see you, K-Dog; who else we got on this little pleasure cruise? Please tell me there's some ladies. Shep's gotta get some."

"Sorry to break up your little bromance, jerks, but you're in my way," Kurt turned to face a woman's chest.

A cough brought him back to reality. He looked up into Amy Tan's frowned, unimpressed face. She looked at him with a mix of impatience and barely-checked annoyance.

Kurt stepped to one side, "Why, I'm sorry, Miss Amazonia; me and my pal here were just about to look our best for you, oh gracious one."

Amy towered over the two men, "Really? I wouldn't bother; you're both so ugly that if you were the last two men left in all of creation, and I had to select a mating partner to repopulate the human race... I'd choose celibacy," as she turned from them, her ponytail swung from one side of her head to the other.

Shep looked in the mirror; his balding head and short, podgy body peered back, "Hey, man, that's uncalled for. We had that moment on Talus Five, if I recall."

Amy spun on her heels and looked down at Shep, "From what I can remember, your ugly bastard face met my fist at high speed."

Shep chuckled, "Still, bitch, couldn't keep your hands off me, huh?" He offered a fist bump with Kurt, who obliged and started laughing.

Amy moved in closer, her glare set to maim.

"First, asshole, you're not a tower rat, so don't speak like one. Second, you call me that again and I will introduce

your face to the…" Amy's admonishment was interrupted
by the hissing of the stasis room door opening and the
appearance of Captain Yokohuri; her face like thunder.

She scowled at the three of them, "Okay, kids, we
have a situation. Be on the bridge in five minutes, is that
clear?" Her exit was as abrupt as her entrance.

"Why, hello, Captain. How was your sleep, Captain?
Are you feeling okay, Captain? What the fuck has burrowed
up her ass and died?" Kurt muttered to the space where
Yokohuri existed for the briefest of moments.

Amy let out a small chuckle.

"Dude, that's basically third base," Shep whispered to
Kurt as they slipped each other a low-five.

Kurt smiled and walked towards the exit.

"Right then, twats. You heard the good lady, off we
toodle-pip," he said in a pretentious English accent.

"What's the crack then, Captain?" Kurt asked gruffly.
Sian ignored the tone and replied, "This planet has a
breathable atmosphere, potentially able to support life."

"Seriously?" replied Kurt, the surprise etched across
his face. "I didn't think that we would actually ever find
another planet that… you mean… we could have somewhere
to relocate mankind?" His voice trembled with excitement.

A solemn silence fell over the group, broken by
Ellie's digital voice, "Captain, the ship is in orbit. Shall I
conduct further scans?"

"Yes, Ellie, please do," said Sian, the group lapsed
back into silence, transfixed on the green planet that loomed
large through the window.

"Scans confirm initial findings, Captain," whirred
Ellie. "Additionally, I conducted a routine scan of the ship and
detected a minor electrical fault with the port thrusters. It will

require imminent repair, or we may struggle to maintain our orbit."

Sian looked across to Falwasser and barked, "Kurt, that's your baby, get your gear and get out there. The quicker it's fixed, the quicker we can get down there."

"On it," replied Kurt. He mock saluted and started to exit the room. As he reached the doorway, he turned back to his crewmates; his face birthed a small smile. "It's exciting, huh? We might have just found a new home for all of mankind."

Yokohuri interjected, "Let's not get carried away Kurt. At the moment, all we know is that there is a breathable atmosphere... end of story. Now get to the airlock and get suited up."

Kurt grappled with his space suit. He locked the bulky gauntlets into the wrist slots. In keeping with superstition, he picked up the pen knife from his overalls; it had been given to him as a child. Slowly, he turned it in his hands, unfolded the blade from its stiff home in the hilt and smiled.

"Still got it, dad," Kurt looked up briefly, folded the knife and slid it into a compartment on his belt. "Let's get this done," he muttered to himself.

Kurt punched the release button and stepped outside of the ship. He couldn't help but notice that the all-pervading silence seemed louder than ever; the blackness of the void, somehow even more claustrophobic, whilst he himself, seemed... less calm.

The sound of his breathing echoed in his ears, whilst the metronome beep of the life-support systems reassured him that everything was normal. Inside though, he didn't feel normal. Something just felt off, yet he could not determine the cause of this sensation. He did, however, like his new lightweight suit. Much better than my previous piece of shit.

He made his way towards the thruster when his thoughts were interrupted by the Captain's voice over his headset, "Kurt, can you hear me? It looks as though there is a small meteor shower en route. Nothing major; just be careful out there, will you?"

Yokohuri checked the comm's channel, "Can you hear me Kurt?" she asked.

The intercom fizzed back.

"Can d-" the voice cut short by static.

"Kurt!" demanded Sian. "Kurt, come in…"

The speaker crackled back.

"It's… a… little… hai…" the voice flitted in and out of existence.

Sian shared an anxious look with Shep. After a few minutes of asking for updates, greeted only by static, she asked, "Ellie, where is Kurt?"

"Captain, Kurt Falwasser's current trajectory is set to a collision course with MC-671," Ellie responded with no hint of worry.

"Shit, will he make it?" she asked. Sian felt as if she herself were falling.

"There is a twenty-three-point-six percent chance of survival, Captain," responded Ellie.

"Get hold of him, now. Keep me updated, I'll be in my quarters," Sian snapped back, before she turned and stormed out of the bridge.

The planet grew large in his eyesight. Kurt managed to stabilise himself, but the influence of the planet's gravity pulled him faster and faster towards the ground. His shoulder still ached from the piece of rock that knocked him from the ship's hull.

"FUCK IT!" he screamed. He smacked himself on the side of his helmet, which forced him to regain focus. He started to tap at the computer housed in the sleeve of his suit. "Ellie, come in. This is Kurt."

Silence.

"Ellie, where the fuck are you, man?"

Silence.

He looked up and stared at the rapidly approaching sphere. Through the ether, a familiar voice sounded through his earpiece, "Kurt Falwasser, this is Ellie. Can you hear me?" Kurt tapped the side of his helmet, before he replied, "Thank fuck, Ellie; what's my status?"

"Kurt Falwasser, you have a twenty-three-point-six -- and falling -- percent chance of survival," Ellie answered, before descending back into silence.

"Not that fucking status! Fuck sake, if you're going to tell me that, fucking lie!" Kurt yelled; the inside of his visor flecked in spittle.

"Kurt Falwasser, my reports indicate that you have a dislocated shoulder and a possible fracture of the humerus. However, your suit reports that there is no lack of integrity, no oxygen leaks, and no loss of pressure. Aside from your increasing velocity and current course setting, you could say that you have been lucky," Ellie replied.

Kurt rolled his eyes, "Thank you for your words of encouragement, Ellie. Can you guys come and get me -- like, now!"

Silence.

"Kurt Falwasser, this is not possible. Given the disrepair to the port thruster, any attempt to break this orbit would result in a rapid, unplanned descent to the planet's surface," Ellie reported in her detached manner.

"Okay," grunted Kurt. "We'll have to do this old

school." He exhaled deeply; pain flared down his arm, "Ellie, please tell me the flight chute is not an optional extra?"

"Affirmative," Ellie answered. "If I have determined your theory correctly, you will need to deploy the chute at the precise moment you break into the atmosphere. This should decrease your velocity sufficiently. I estimate your chances of survival could then increase to sixty-seven-point-one percent."

Kurt laughed, "Ha, excellent. Let's do this shit."

His suit's temperature display started to flash. Not today, Pedro, he thought and pressed the parachute deployment button. The force jolted him violently and he lapsed into unconscious.

"Captain, I have Kurt Falwasser. He is planning on releasing his flight chute as soon as he enters the atmosphere. It has increased his chances of survival by for-" Ellie began to report, but the A.I. was broken off sharply by Yokohuri.

"Will he survive, Ellie?" she demanded.

Ellie paused before it answered, "Kurt Falwasser's chances of survival have been increased. It is now reliant on external factors to ensure his well-being."
Sian sighed deeply, "How is he doing, Ellie?"

"Captain, I have just lost signal with Specialist Falwasser. This would indicate that the contact signal has been damaged due to either re-entry or sudden, terminal impact," responded Ellie.

Sian lowered her head into her hands, "Tell everyone to meet me on the bridge, now."

"Okay, guys, this is the situation..." Sian proceeded to explain what had happened.

The crew's faces changed from disbelief and shock

to acceptance, and finally to the expression she wanted to see: focused and determined.

"…So, that's the long and short of it. Kurt is down there; we don't know if he's alive or if he's… Either way, we need to find out. Suggestions?" Sian asked. She casted glances at each of the crew.

"I can go and fix the thruster. We can get this heap of shit down there and find out," said Amy. She pulled her hair back tighter into its ponytail.

"Are you sure?" asked Shep. "Kurt was resident expert on those damn things."

"It's okay, I have a little experience. We trained together. I can do this, I promise," responded Amy, her outlook exuding positivity.

"Okay…" said Yokohuri "…get your gear and make a move. Shep, you work with Ellie and try to re-establish contact with Kurt."

Shep hesitated, "Captain? Can he survive down there?"

Sian fixed him an icy stare, "I don't know, Shepherd. All I know is that the atmosphere is breathable, if only for a small amount of time. Which is why I need you all on this now."

Shep nodded and hurried out of the room. Amy followed in quick pursuit.

A dull ache surged through Kurt's shoulder and into his head. The pain forced him to come round; his eyes struggled to focus. The helmet visor had been smashed and was now lined by a row of cracked glass, like a shark's jaw.

Fucking hell, that must have been one hell of an impact.

He pulled the clips down around the neck joint and

removed his helmet.

He didn't know how long he had been unconscious, but he noticed the freshness of the air. He took a huge gulp and it felt like a drug. It coursed through his veins, filling them with a sense of vibrancy and life.

He rose groggily and looked around. He was in a forest; tall trees loomed over him. Their gnarled bark merged into a face which appeared to study his every move. Light struggled to find its way down to him through the dense canopy. His breathing increased. He felt as if the forest was closing in on him; the tendril-like branches groping for him, the interloper in their midst. He tried to calm himself, but his breathing increased further still. He sat down and closed his eyes.

"Focus," he whispered to himself. "Just calm down." He closed his eyes so tight he could make out the veins pulsating in his eyelids. He waited a few minutes until he could feel his body finally heeding his call to calm down.

He opened his eyes and stood up, breathing in a deep lungful of air.

There we go; nothing to worry about.

As if it had been waiting for this moment, a loud piercing scream -- sounding as though a child had been slowly pulled apart -- ripped through his heart. He fell over, panicking; his head spun. Instinct kicked in, and he got up and ran. He didn't know where he was going, but he hoped it was away from whatever made that sound.

After ten minutes, which felt like an hour, he stopped to catch his breath. The cloying atmosphere constricted him and he could feel the effects filling his lungs like cannonballs. Kurt buckled over and fell to his knees. He panted and dry-wretched, running the back of his hand across his brow.

"Kurt..." a whisper scratched at the back of his head.

It sounded close.

His sweat dribbled down his face, stinging his eyes.

"Kurt... Can you hear me?" The voice, at once sinister, also sounded familiar. "Kurt, come in. If you're there, pick up the fucking mic."

Kurt stuck a finger in his ear and realised his earpiece wasn't in. He fumbled around his chest, found the dangling wire, and put it in his ear.

"I'm here... I think. Come in, anyone," he tried to shout, but it emerged as a hoarse whisper.

"Thank fuck, buddy..." screamed Shep. "...Where have you been, man? We've been trying to get hold of you for ages."

Kurt wiped the sheet of sweat from his face, "I don't know. How long have I been out?"

There was a pause before Shep answered, "About ten hours, man. What is going on down there -- where have you been?"

"I honestly don't know. Last thing I remember before waking up in this goddamn forest was the warmth of the atmosphere..." Kurt said slowly, trying to recollect his thoughts. "...Then, I punched through and pulled my chute... that's it."

"Well, my friend, you are fucking lucky to be alive," said Shep, his voice laden with relief. "Just stay where you are, we are working on fixing this thruster and getting down to you, man."

"I was hit by something. Guess my harness didn't lock on properly," Kurt mumbled. He cracked his fingers just to feel something.

"Well, don't worry about that. Just sit tight, man. Once we get this fixed, we'll figure out a way of getting to you. You're going to be okay" said Shep. "Hang on, man, I need to let the Captain know I have you. I'll be back. Don't go anywhere."

"Okay, Shep, I ain't going anywhere," Kurt replied, he let out a small laugh and sat down. "Hang on, Shep, how long have you been able to hear me?"

"Dunno. I guess since you woke up?" replied Shep distractedly. "I managed to create a connection about an hour ago... Why?"

"Did you hear anything?" Kurt asked.

"No, what do you mean? Are you alright? You sound to me like something's happened," Shep's tone changed to one of worry.

Kurt massaged his damaged shoulder; the pain was subtle but still there. "A scream... It was fucking awful... and loud -- like nothing I've ever heard."

The line crackled, before coming back clear.

"I didn't hear anything, man. Listen, just sit tight; we will be there soon," Shep signed off.

The line fizzled out into crackling static.

"Huh. Well at least they-" before Kurt finished his sentence, he was interrupted by a scream.

It sounded as though it was all around him; as if it was following him, maintaining the same distance. Like it was stalking him. He got up and ran. The screaming restarted, providing the soundtrack to his fleeing.

"Amy, come in," Captain Yokohuri spoke into the intercom. "How long 'til you get this fixed?"

"Not long, Captain," she responded, her voice straining with effort. "I am nearly finished; just give me ten minutes."

"Thank you, Amy," responded Sian. "Keep me posted. Shepherd, talk to me, what do you have? Shepherd?"

Shep burst into the bridge, breathing heavily, barely able to squeeze the words out, "Captain, I got him. Ellie, patch Kurt's connection to the bridge."

Shep and Yokohuri listened as the feed fizzed into life. The sound of fabric rubbing, heavy breathing and the cracking of broken branches blasted through the speakers.

Kurt's voice shrieked through the background noise, "What the fuck do you want? Leave me alone!"

"Kurt? What is going on down there?" Sian asked, grabbing hold of the console.

Kurt's voice cut through the background noise once more, his panting and sobbing becoming a background layer.

"There's something down here, Captain!" he stammered out.

Sian's hold on the console started making her palms squeak against the metal, "What is it, Kurt?"

"I don't know; it just keeps following me. It won't show itself. It seems to hide in the darkness. It's everywhere," Kurt replied manically.

"Kurt, listen to me, yo-" Yokohuri started to say.

The background noise instantly ceased.

"Oh my god…" whispered Kurt. "… It's…no…"

His words faded to nothingness.

Silence blanketed the bridge but was quickly interrupted with a bloodcurdling scream that sliced through the comm's system.

The radioed whined for a moment, then went dead.

Kurt came to an abrupt stop. The darkness enveloped him. Claustrophobia seeped into every pore. His eyes were fixed directly ahead, unblinking. A human-like figure stood in the distance; its naked body dripped with blood that poured from the lacerations and gouges that chequered its skin. In one hand, it held the head of a child; in the other its torso, held by the foot.

The creature's hair was long and lank, through which two long horns protruded. It stood staring back at Kurt with a mesmerised, barbaric look. A smile cracked and crawled across its face whilst thick black blood seeped from its eyes and mouth. It cast the child's mutilated and battered torso to the floor as it raised the infant's head to its mouth and bit into the neck. It tore a piece off and chewed it slowly. Blood continued to drool from its lips, and sharp fangs flashed as it savoured the torn flesh from the juvenile corpse.

Kurt watched, catatonic with fear. His head began to swim as tears streamed from his eyes. His face was nothing more than a mass of congealed dirt, tears and sweat. As he watched this beast devour its food, he fell to his knees. The animal discarded the child's skull and let out a scream. It was the same one that had tormented Kurt since he made landfall. The beast slowly put a taloned finger to its own face and dragged the claw across, rending flesh and exposing muscles and bone.

Kurt's heart kicked like a bass drum, faster than he thought was possible. He tried to scream but a choking gurgle was all he could muster. As he watched the beast defile its visage, he felt a searing pain travel across his face. His scream was finally released from its flesh prison, matching the one the creature had made; both bestial and barbaric.

He patted his face with his hand and felt a deep pulpy chasm run from the tip of his left ear, across his cheek, below his eye, and finishing on the opposite side just below his right ear. His hands shook as blood gushed from the wound. He looked at the beast and his eyes grew wide with pain. The creature laughed and ran another single claw upwards, from its groin to its chest. With every inch, the thing smiled and chuckled, its laughter like huge bells tolling.

Kurt gulped and looked down. Through the tear of his suit, he could see another savagely carved channel through his body. Overcome with agony, he wretched and vomited as the pain took hold.

The torment subsided. Kurt looked up and saw the animal slowly walking forward. It cocked its head as if it were revelling in the suffering it had caused.

"Why are you doing this?" Kurt gurgled through wads of blood and bile.

The beast smiled and growled, "For your sins and weakness."

Kurt's face contorted in confusion. "I... I... I don't understand... I don't know you. Get away from me!" screamed Kurt, his body wracked in bouts of agony.

"Don't you, Kurt?" grunted the animal.

It crouched down; its face inches from Kurt's head.

Kurt swatted the air as his body felt heavy. He could smell the wretched stench of death emanating from the animal. Its jaws cracked open and let out a horrifying scream.

Kurt passed out.

"Kurt Falwasser is point-eight kilometres to the west of your location, Captain. His vitals are low and life signs are dropping. He does not have long until he expires. In addition, I would recommend keeping your helmets on, due to the dangerously low oxygen levels," Ellie's voice rang through their headsets.

"Okay, guys, you heard her; let's get moving," said Yokohuri, pushing through the dense forest.

Though none of them could put their finger on why, ever since they set foot in the forest, a deathly silence had befallen, interrupted only by updates from Ellie.

"Captain, I can see him," shouted Amy.

She picked up her pace and the others followed in a desperate sprint. As they got closer, they all saw the horrendous wounds on his face and torso.

"Shepherd, keep your eyes peeled. Scan the perimeter," ordered Captain Yokohuri.

Shep nodded, pulled his gun from its holster and scanned the horizon. He walked over to Kurt's prone figure, human compulsion forcing him to eye the gruesome sight.

"What the fuck did that, Captain... It's... it's..."

"Shepherd, I gave you an order; do your job," Sian demanded as she got closer.

The Captain had to keep her revulsion in check as the grisly scene made her gorge rise.

Amy crouched down by Kurt's body, "Captain, this is odd. I don't think it was anyone else. I... I think he did it himself. Look."

Shepherd and Yokohuri looked down at Amy and traced a path to what she was pointing at. In Kurt's hand rested his gore-splattered knife.

Sian shook her head, "We don't know what happened yet. He could have been holding it in self-defence. Let's get him back, patch him up, and then he can tell us himself."

The crew stood around a stainless steel gurney. Kurt's butchered body rose and fell gently as it lay on top. Rivulets of blood ran from his wounds and into a soakaway chamber.

"Ellie, diagnosis," demanded Yokohuri.

"Captain, from my examination, I can confirm that the wounds were self-inflicted. Both from the weapon used and the angle of attack. Kurt Falwasser suffered extreme injury to a number of his primary internal organs; his h-"

Ellie was interrupted by Yokohuri, "Did you scan the forest for life?"

"Of course, Captain. I detected no sign of sentient life within a five hundred kilometre radius from the landing zone. If I may, Captain, I have a suggestion as to what happened," Ellie reported.

Sian looked over Kurt's wounds, "Go on."

"Given that when you woke, you all had vitamin deficiencies which were not replenished, combined with the trauma he suffered attempting to repair the port thruster, and his descent onto MC-671, in addition to suffering from Hypoxia... I believe that this combination of events created a psychiatric breakdown resulting in a paranoid delusion," Ellie said, her voice detached and cold.

"Fucking Hypo... what?" Blurted Shep, his hands balled into fists.

"Hypoxia, First Engineer Shepherd. A lack of oxygen to the brain can result in-" Ellie started to reply.

"Enough. We've got a job to do here. I need to report back and advise that this planet needs terra-forming to be habitable. Ellie, will Kurt survive?" Sian interjected.

"Affirmative, Captain. His injuries, whilst severe, are treatable. I am more concerned with the psychological damage inflicted. I will conduct further scans on MC-671 to complete your report, Captain," Ellie finished.

"Good. Let me know when we can leave, Ellie," responded Sian. "Come on. Let's see what else we can find out about this place. Suit up, all of you."

The team made their way back out of the infirmary and headed towards the airlock.

Shep stopped in his tracks and cocked his head to one side, "What the hell was that?"

"What is it, Shepherd?" asked Yokohuri.

"Did you hear that?" Shep asked, still scanning the corridor for something unseen.

Sian sighed and looked back at him, "Hear what?"

Shep stared straight into the Captain's eyes, "It sounded like a scream."

HE SAID, IT SAID
LEO STABLEFORD

Despite all his careful preparation, the acolyte almost fudged the final words in the enunciation. Tucked at the back of his mind, indestructible, was a single nagging doubt. Would the creeping things that dwelt beyond the Outer Dimensions follow at his bidding? And if they did, would they find themselves in thrall to incantations culled from a volume the summoner won in an eBay auction?

Too late now if they would not; the transaction was complete. Nothing left for it but to utter the last few syllables with all the seriousness that the acolyte could muster.

He had to admit to doubting his own meagre competence. Even so, the gathering thickness of the smoke that issued from the ceremonial censers began to drop the whiff of brimstone. This loosened the knot in his throat and caused the bottom to drop from his stomach. His hands twitched. The grimoire almost found itself dumped to the floor.

The acolyte discerned motion beyond the roiling veil of smoke. Something shifted forward into three-dimensional space, cloaked in wisps of grey-black smog. The seller had, it appeared, been the real deal. The acolyte was both mollified and gleeful.

"Mortaaal," the demon intoned, its voice sculpted from leaden screams of torment. "You sssummoned me forth from the wasteland of deliciousss torment. For what reeeeassson?"

The acolyte shuffled the notes he had taken down from the book. He had thought about bookmarks, sticky ones. In the end his mind revolted at the idea of sticking little red plastic tabs into the imposing tome. Cheery primary colours did not jibe with the catchy title: "Libris Ex Enunciato Pandaemonium Mortis."

To think that, at the time, he had worried about the authenticity of a product that's auction listing had read:

GENUINE ancient grimoire wrapped in AUTHENTIC HUMAN SKIN! Communication with the dark hosts of the Outer Hells 100% GUARANTEED or your money back. Product almost as new, a couple of signs of age besides the natural wear and tear. Several tiny spots of blood staining Page 47. Written in Latin and Sumerian on alternate pages. A 40 page A4 typescript of an English translation included at NO EXTRA CHARGE! No reserve.

When the product had finally arrived, the acolyte's doubts retreated just a little. The binding did indeed seem crafted from a fine, soft, and fleshy leather, decorated with actual bones. The cynic in him said the provenance of these refinements were undetectable; unless he wanted to run the risk of awkward questions from the police.

When he opened it for the first time, the cynical voice had retreated further. Something in the hand-inked pages of pleasing rough vellum gave the volume gravitas. As one read it, the book also appeared to be reading its owner right back. Being an educated man, some aphorism about staring into the abyss had popped into the acolyte's head. The product did its best to appeal to an undeniably sexy nihilism in the acolyte's soul. The acolyte had never found any part of himself sexy prior to receipt of the book. No doubt, at the least, the product itself was massaging the ego.

Still, doubts lingered. After all, he had paid someone called Drk_Wrshpr23 for the book using PayPal. If it was not for the seller's 96% positive feedback score, the acolyte would have passed. Drk_Wrshippr23's profile boasted the shipment of over 800 occult items in the last two years. Also, of course, the volume had only cost the acolyte $40. So, however you looked at it, this was an experiment with a low cost for failure.

The evening of receipt, the acolyte had prepared a ceremonial circle and set about his ritual. He'd obtained the design from Otherside443's Tumblr. At the time, the design's intricacy had made up for its posting on a public social network.

Now that the precise concentric circles and arcane symbols were in service, he had to pause. Was the best course of action to base his choice of containment circle only on the resemblance to one in that episode of Buffy he liked? He opened his mouth to speak. His voice caught in his throat, mired in insecurities. Should he be using the English translation, printed in grubby Courier New on bog standard 80 GSM copier paper? His mind wandered to the neglected "Teach Yourself Ancient Sumerian" course he had ordered. The tape now sat gathering dust on top of the closet.

It was way too late for regret now. Either the English

would work or the demon would eat his giblets. He'd made his ceremonial circle; now he had to deal with it.

"O Demonic Host!" he said, wishing he sounded more like Alan Rickman and less like the adenoidal douche he believed himself to be. "I offer thee supplication in the names of Baphomet and Baal, in the names of Azazel and Ashtoreth. I deny the pretender on his gilded throne who would turn our eyes from greater gods. In return for my eternal soul, I ask of thee that my every worldly desire find fulfilment in the mighty hosts of the Infernal Flame."

"Sssnivelling Mortaaal," the demon replied. "The forcsssesss of the Outer Hellsss hear your requessstsss. If you have proven your devotion to usss by the offering of sacrificssse, then the deal must be forged."

The acolyte's grin faded a little. He hoped the set designers on Buffy had some experience with dabbling in the occult, or he was about to be in serious trouble.

This latest deal had led Gu'lor-atha to a place where he was feeling better about existence. For about three centuries now, it had been nothing but bum lead after bum lead. It was hard enough to meet soul acquisition targets for Xeno-ha-atep-ra Inc. at the best of times. Harder still when all the cards you got handed from the market research department were as stale as week-old prana.

Now he just tried to keep his sense organs out of the view of management and turn in some decent paperwork. One day he might put in for a transfer. He realised he had become too comfortable, but he could not face change; it was a vicious circle.

"Gu'lor! Rockin' it old school, baby!" one of the new kids said as Gu'lor attempted to sup at the prana cooler that morning. "Man, you pulled off some sweet stuff back in the day. How's it going?"

"Oh, you know," Gu'lor sighed, "working on my targets."

"Things are tough in acquisitions, I hear," the kid replied with a sigh. Gu'lor explored the kid for signs of mockery. The upstart was wise enough to dance right up to the line but not over it.

How old was this one anyway? He had only five hundred eyes; most of them still glowed. He can't have been more than twenty-five aeons. Depressing.

"It's not all bad. The naked monkeys developed some new technology since I got in this morning," Gu'lor said. "I got assigned to courtesy massacres whenever they play back a recording of this one incantation. Some academic of theirs read it out of a summoning tome set down a couple of aeons back. They never even have a summoning circle chalked out when they play it. It's tasty, and pretty fun."

"Yeah, but courtesy massacres?" the kid said, sloshing some prana around in a feeding tube. "That's some marketing ichor, no mistake. You shouldn't have to bother with that stuff; you have SLAs to meet."

The upstart withdrew his tube from the prana dispenser.

"Hope things pick up for you, really," it said, voice filled with hideous pity.

"No, I'm in a solid negotiation right now," Gu'lor objected. It was too late; the kid was already phasing into the trading zone. No one was listening to the old demon from sales anymore.

Gu'lor wasn't fooling anyone. This deal could very well be his last chance; he couldn't afford to blow it. The acolyte had brought his soul to the table and Gu'lor had to be ready to close it. Fired up with a muted, hopeful enthusiasm,

Gu'lor phased back into the negotiation. He took a good,
long look at the acolyte and arranged the Xeno-ha-atep-ra
disclaimer in his head before he spoke. Naturally, clients
expected legalese from the Outer Hells to be something less
technical. Gu'lor was proud of his authentic baroque copy; he
felt it came from a time with more class.

"O Demonic Host!" The acolyte said. That address
was already becoming stale. Gu'lor decided to nip it in the
bud.

"You will know me asss Gu'lor-atha Magna!" Gu'lor
boomed in his best 'command presence' voice. He felt a warm
glow of accomplishment as the acolyte's pasty face turned
a light blue. Even the nerdish figure's acne seemed to be
cowering at the command.

Of course he wasn't really referred to as *the Great
Gu'lor-atha* by anyone; a good thing too, because that
sounded like the stage name of some Middle Eastern-themed
conjurer. In actual fact, his friends all called him plain old
Gu'lor. Not that this naked ape was ever going to come within
screaming distance of being someone Gu'lor would consider a
friend.

The acolyte looked like he might throw up. That
would be a trial if he did. The smell of ape vomit always
made Gu'lor hungry. He hadn't consumed fresh prana since
the last company party he'd got into. Sure, there was the
binding circle protocol policy to worry about; but the fact
remained -- when an entity from the Outer Hells got a sniff of
something tasty, instinct could overrule common sense.

The moment passed. The acolyte pulled himself
together and spoke:

"Gola Arthur Magnet!" he mangled Gu'lor's name.

Gu'lor felt a twitch from a many-toothed feeding
tube in non-space and suppressed it. He didn't want to lose

his job over something so stupid. "Please accept the humble supplications and devotions that I have followed for thee. If I am wanting, I deserve no more than to burn forever in torment for disappointing my true lord and master!"

Gu'lor didn't believe this obsequious toadying. He was willing to bet this precocious little flesh-bag didn't believe it either. Things had really changed in this dimension since they'd had an *Age of Enlightenment*. One inter-dimensional moment later, a monkey worked out a couple of tricks; the kind of basic maths Gu'lor had learned in kindergarten. These meat parcels were absurdly proud of their childish grasp of space-time basics. All of a sudden, acolytes had disappeared up their own posteriors.

Acolytes used to be appropriately awed by the manifestation of a being from a higher plane. They used to become filled with unholy dread and decadent rapture. They used to do things properly. In their modern era, they dabbled with computerised renderings of true reality in the name of entertainment. Designed games where consumption by beings from the Outer Darkness was no more than an inconvenience. Some insist even childish primates could tell the difference between reality and video games. All Gu'lor knew was that he couldn't deny acolytes seemed to lose all respect for the Outer Beings.

"Your binding circle isss poorly rendered!" said Gu'lor, allowing a good measure of truculent threat to enter his voice. It was obvious -- this meat sack had just sketched the design down in a slap-dash manner and hoped it would do.

"However," he added and couldn't help letting a little regret leak through. "It isss within accssseptable limitsss for the firssst invocation."

The acolyte looked relieved. Even so, Gu'lor could sense a little righteous indignation -- and even boredom -- in the flesh sack's demeanour; it wasn't much, but creatures in three-dimensions were terrible at hiding their thoughts. Gu'lor bristled. Something in the monkey's mind irritated him.

He directed a jet of sensory spores skidding over the chalice of blood that rested on the altar. The gory soup inside was cold. Not only that, but it wasn't from one of the three most preferred sacrificial animals; not even in the top five, in fact. This joker was cruising for a million years of extended torment before being rendered down into prana.

"Your sssacrificial offering," he said, not even attempting to hide the irritation. "It'sss pigsss blood! And not even fresssh!"

"Now, wait just a minute!" the acolyte spluttered, but then bit his tongue. "Gola Arthur Magnet!" He resumed his ceremonial drone. Gu'lor supposed the acolyte considered his pitch and tone 'appropriate'. Gu'lor would characterise the nasal wheedle as 'annoying'. "I presented to you the freshest offering I could find. In this modern age, access to livestock is not as widespread as it once was. The butcher I received the offering from assured me that, even now, it is less than twenty-four hours old."

"Greater should I had received the butcher than the pig!" Gu'lor thundered, forgetting the Xeno brand guaranteed sibilance. This wiry little prick's attitude had grated on him from the very first moment of manifestation. He'd done the barest of bare minimums in the way of preparation, and now he was arguing over the quality of sacrifice. Gu'lor's feeding tube was beginning to itch. He decided to get this first meeting finished.

"You have technically fulfilled the requirementsss. The Outer Hellsss will consssider your requessstsss," Gu'lor grumbled. "Tell me, what are your wishessss?"

The acolyte grinned, perhaps the most irritatingly

smug moment in the business relationship yet. Then the
grin faltered.

"Oh," he said. "Hang on! Er, O, Gola Arthur Magnet!
The all mighty and all powerful!"

The acolyte fumbled in his pocket and pulled out a
crumpled sheet of note paper. Gu'lor's main mass, still safely
ensconced in its dwelling matrix, sighed heavily. This was
going from bad to worse.

Still, at least it wasn't a courtesy massacre.

"Did you just say *So let's recap?* " the acolyte asked.

It wasn't the first time he had noticed the demon's
bizarrely modern speech patterns. So far, the second
summoning wasn't anywhere near as exhilarating or as
terrifying as the first -- not by a long way. The acolyte didn't
want to seem ungrateful. After all, the demon was a genuine
obscene lurker from the outer darkness. Though the novelty
had run thin with alarming rapidity. The acolyte didn't want to
barter away his soul using language common to management
review meetings. The acolyte already had to clear his throat
loudly at the concept that they were going to get his demands
down on the table. Eyebrows had been raised at the notion
that he should "really tighten up the wording" on demonic
boon number four.

The acolyte didn't want to be unkind, but Gu'lor's
demonic vibe had definitely eroded over the course of the
meeting. The acolyte had stopped feeling grade-A quality
dread. Things had declined a long way since the beginning of
the ceremony. Gu'lor emanated an atmosphere of hangdog; he
seemed harassed and maybe just a little stressed out.

"Sssilencssse Mortaaal!" Gu'lor rumbled. At first, the
timbre of the creature's voice had chilled the acolyte's bone
marrow. He never thought he could miss an unpleasant prickle

of nerve pain. Over the course of this evolving relationship, some things had become clear to the acolyte. He was sure that sometimes the demon found its own declamations tedious. On occasion, it even sounded like it was reading from a script. The acolyte was starting to feel that Gu'lor could really do with a little more positive attitude... Or negative aura... Or both, whatever.

Gu'lor cleared its mouth parts, disrupting the acolyte's confusion.

"It is non-negotiable! Your pitiful requessstsss mussst be clarified for the Hossstsss of Material Manifessstation." Gu'lor admonished the acolyte. "So it issss written, so it hassss been, so it shall ever be," he added. His tone was probably supposed to be menacing. To the acolyte's ears, it just sounded a bit overplayed and hammy.

"O Gull Or Arthur Magnet," the acolyte intoned. "Here are the desires of my material body, which must be sated in exchange for my eternal soul..."

The only desire the acolyte wanted satisfied as he said it was finishing this meeting. He never expected hell to have gone this corporate.

"No, you infernal idiot, I don't want to hold!" Gu'lor shouted but to no avail. The worst thing about being put on hold in the Outer Hells was that it filled your essential being with its nature. You weren't just on hold in some vague semantic sense; you were actually the embodiment of 'on hold.'

A mood of frustrated anticipation filled Gu'lor, one he could not resist. He thought of upbeat guitar rock with the strained tones of a chorus of lower-level homunculi singing the company song:

Xeeeeeenooooo-Haaaaaa!
Aaaaaatep-Raaaaa!
We find every dimensional direction,
For delivering the finest soul collection!
Wheels grind! Cogs Turn!
We don't rest 'til souls burn! (Souls burn)"
And so on and so forth.

Gu'lor had started closing respiratory sphincters to cause pressure build up. After the pressure got to a certain intensity, some of his smaller eyeballs exploded. This brought discomfort, but at least it distracted him from the singing.

There was a click as he found himself put through. Something manifested adjacent to Gu'lor's dwelling matrix. The entity appeared to have a thing for chitin-covered tentacles. He surmised whatever it was must be female, because chitin was traditionally a bit of a feminine feature.

"Office of Nurg'hrnath Zadfragget!" it said with a voice like pinholes blowing fetid screeching notes from the openings in a rotting corpse. Definitely female; probably Zadfragget's secretary.

"Is Zadfragget Magna available?" Gu'lor asked with mounting depression. This was the run-around if he'd ever experienced it.

"Zadfragget Magna is in a meeting right now; is there anything I can do to help, or a message I can pass on?"

"It's just..." Gu'lor felt his own whining desperation like a foul disease, gnawing at his self-confidence. "Look, I have this lead and he's all ready to sign. I just need the requisition order for a small amount of three-dimensional lucre and biological matter. I wouldn't normally bother Zadfragget Magna with this, but... You see, the Fulfilment Operative said that I would have to get this new form..."

Gu'lor waved one of his own tentacles (which sported more masculine-toothed suckers) in the direction of the form. It manifested as a small purple creature, globular with sixteen eyes. It sported seven feet growing from the crown of its head, forcing it to walk everywhere upside down.

"Matter Requisition Order #876/G," the secretary supplied. Maybe it was intended to sound helpful, but in fact, it just seemed pedantic.

"Yes, er, that," Gu'lor said. "So it needs Zadfragget Magna's signature..." he let the sentence trail until it was plain that, in fact, it had come to a stop.

"I'm afraid Zadfragget Magna is not available to sign anything. I'll pass your message on," the secretary said. It was evident she did not care.

"Any idea when I might hear back?"

"Not until after the next aeon closing nourishment cycle," the secretary said. She managed one part apologetic to ninety-nine parts condescending.

Gu'lor was outraged. "But," he said, "that's not for seven hundred thousand of the Earth creature's years!"

"I'm sorry, sir."

"Couldn't you just PP it now?"

"I'm afraid I'm not authorised."

"But I have targets to meet!"

Gu'lor felt the secretary's 5000 ocular ports looking at him. They were all saying "So what?"

"Fine," Gu'lor said. "I'll see if I can find some other way."

"Thank you for your c-" said the secretary, but was cut off in her indecent haste to dematerialise.

Gu'lor let his central torso hang in abject depression. He felt that the world was moving too fast. Five centuries ago, Xeno-ha-atep-ra had been a company motivated on soul collection numbers. Now in the blink of an eye, it was all about chains of supply and potential relationships.

In Gu'lor's mind, a soul was a soul. You chipped away one soul at a time, contributed to the prana vats, did your fair share. It seemed things had taken a turn in the lower dimensions. The implications for the Outer Beings were unpalatable, to say the least.

Gu'lor got the distinct impression that if an acolyte wasn't going to lead to the establishment of a cult, then that acolyte was of no use. Never mind service, never mind reputation. It was all about volume.

Not that anyone had openly told him that his lead was a dud -- not directly anyway. He had been issued several new internal forms during the registration process; all of them seemed focused away from the individual acquisition.

The Zadfragget Magna situation replicated whenever he needed to get in touch with a colleague on a higher plane of being. Every communication was treated as an imposition. He could be told to wait for an answer, sometimes for up to three or four millennia. In a business that ran on ridiculously short three-dimensional solar calendars, this wasn't acceptable. The higher ups didn't seem to care about client concerns, nor the first-line staff who dealt with them.

Maybe it was time that Gu'lor thought about finding another career path in the Outer Hells. Soul Acquisition was a young being's game. He'd finish up this one and then that was it. He'd find something else to keep tentacle and central thorax together.

"What do you mean you can't get me the harem? Or the ziggurat?" the acolyte whined.

Things had definitely turned sour. In literal terms, every piece of fresh produce in the room always rotted and withered when Gu'lor appeared; the acolyte assumed that was intentional. On a metaphorical plane, sourness was less welcome; the deal was looking shaky.

"Look, kid," Gu'lor said with a distinctly non-terrifying, light, East Coast accent. "I've run a couple of dozen queries up the chain about your contract and I get back precisely buttkiss. We're going to have to face it; we both got the backyard shaft on this one."

He'd dropped any pretence of being a nightmare hewn from shadow, voiced by the tormented wails of a million damned, about an hour ago. The acolyte hated having to do business with a small, bright orange frog crowned with the head of a cow. Gu'lor had explained that the smoky-nightmare-tormented-wailing-thing was way too difficult. Everyone agreed it was a bit inappropriate under the circumstances. Sure, there was purple ichor weeping from the thing's eyes, and wisps of blue smoke curled from its ears when he spoke -- A for effort. Overall, the whole thing had left the realm of H.P. Lovecraft and was pitching far closer to the neighbourhood of Friz Freling.

"Well, what can you get me off my list?" the acolyte asked. He could feel the edifice of his megalomaniacal schemes crumbling into a vast ocean of disappointment.

Somehow the frog with the cow's head managed to shrug.

That just did it. A fortnight ago, he'd been on the brink of global renown and unending material luxury. He'd been about to take the title of player number-one. Now he was stranded in a desert of apathy, complaining to an orange cartoon that had little in the way of tangible power. A cartoon, moreover, that didn't seem to care about the acolyte's sense of personal betrayal. Worse, the unimpressive demon had lost all pretence of quality customer service.

"This is your fault!" he thundered, wagging his finger in Gu'lor's direction. "If you hadn't misled me about your appearance and nature..."

"Hey, kid!" Gu'lor shouted back, and a little of the old, cold steel crept back into the frog-cow's voice. "That's enough of that. I already explained this is the easiest manifestation into this plane I can muster. I'm sorry that you find it less than ego-massaging, but since I'm unable to deliver the full service, I took a risk on a personal touch. Can't you at least appreciate that I'm trying to level with you?"

That -- it had to be said -- was perhaps the least comfort the acolyte had ever experienced in his miserable life. He felt himself pout and vented a brief, ungracious snort.

"Isn't there anything I can say or do that will make the situation a bit more bearable for you?" Gu'lor asked.

The acolyte stared at the edge of the ceremonial circle.

"I doubt it," he grumbled.

"So I guess that Xeno-ha-atep-ra cannot rely on you providing positive customer feedback?"

That definitely deserved no more than a derisive snort. The acolyte provided one.

"Then... I guess there's really no harm in a brief lapse of judgement with regard to protocol," Gu'lor said, more to himself than to the acolyte.

A gust of uncomfortably warm breath disturbed the hair on the acolyte's neck. The acolyte turned slowly, noting that the orange frog-cow had gone. He'd have mentally processed what replaced it, but whatever it was took place in far too many dimensions. Trying to see it caused the acolyte's mind to turn into warm porridge. In a moment, his entire body was sucked into one of Gu'lor's feeding tubes.

Gu'lor realised afterwards that he had been eating far too much processed prana lately. The over-consumption of raw human flesh was linked to a variety of unpleasant feeding tube conditions. While it tasted so sweet, Gu'lor found it hard to care.

The minute he had stored the acolyte's remains in a vestigial digestion chamber, he knew he had made a mistake. The major clue was when the script on the communication tablet at the edge of his domestic vat changed to a flash of deep orange flame. The high scrape of the stone re-carving itself ended in a flourish of rushing wind and hideous animal screaming. The fanfare announcement that the prana-rays swam free from their singularity cages and set about the hunt. Gu'lor oriented a moon-sized gelatinous eye towards the stone tablet. He read the message with mounting depression:

Employee,

It has come to our attention that you have been defying company protocol. You have broken a containment circle nd devoured a soul promised to the greater prana vats of Xeno-ha-atep-ra.

In lieu of disciplinary action, the organisation intends to terminate your contract with immediate effect. We also reserve the right to immediately discipline you for extruding a feeding tube into a lower dimension. This is in full accordance with Outer Hell Ordinance #45194/12. Your essence will be dissolved for processing in the vats.

Hail Xeno-ha-atep-ra, 5000 ageless aeons and still a leading Soul Acquisition Service Provider.

As the prana-rays took possession of his dwelling matrix, Gu'lor just sat and waited. This netherworld was no place for an old-school guy like him. At least in the prana vats, he didn't have to think about targets anymore or, indeed, about anything else for the rest of eternity. And there was no dimension that could offer him any more bliss than that.

PLAGIARISM
MARTIN JONES

Hey there, I'm Dave Reynolds. Pleasure to meet you.

So, where should I begin?

Well, the better you get to know me, the more you'll realise I'm a pretty average bloke, much the same as everyone else here.

Not much has changed really; even as a kid I never stood out, and certainly wasn't particularly good at anything at school. I was what you might call a 'C+ pupil.' I remember Mum used to come home from parent evenings wearing a nondescript look on her face whilst congratulating me on studying hard and keeping out of trouble. Dad had passed away from cancer when I was four, so it was only me and mum.

Of course, when you were a kid in those days, being nothing special was a blessing -- particularly when you were an only kid without a dad. I lived in constant fear of being classed as 'a mummy's boy', and who wanted to stand out from the crowd at that age? No, it wasn't like it is now; we didn't celebrate 'geek chic' or 'individuality.' It was much safer to be part of the pack in my day.

It wasn't until the last year of senior school when I realised I didn't have to be that person.

A group of us were knocking about outside the shops on a Friday night, as kids do, and a sixth-former called Tosh -- or Lee McKintosh as he was known to his parents -- approached us. He had a determined look in his eye, and as he got closer, my mate, Kev, shouted out, "Alright, Tosh, whatcha up to?"

"Alright, Kev. It's my turn to buy the booze for the boys," replied Tosh.

"Bloody hell, Tosh, you'll never get served in here. Old man Banks always checks everyone's age," said Kev. "You'd be better off going to Threshers."

"Bollocks to that, it's half an hour from here and we've got some serious drinking to do." Tosh dropped his roll-up and ground it under the toe of his trainer. I noticed they were a brand new pair of Puma G Vilas. Jammy bastard; all mum could afford were Hi Tecs. "I like your trainers, Tosh." I said. He ignored me.

"Besides," Tosh said to Kev, "I've got the secret weapon. Banksy will be throwing cans at me as fast as I can ask for them." With that, he pulled a £10 note and a card from his jacket pocket.

"What's that?" Kev asked.

Tosh smiled slyly, "My brother's driving licence, mate. I'm now Daniel McKintosh, aged nineteen." He started chuckling. "Do you lads want me to grab you anything while I'm in there?"

We quickly scrambled around in our pockets, producing coins in both hands.

"How much have we got?" asked Kev as we put all of our change into his cupped hands.

"I reckon there's about a fiver there," said Mike, another mate of ours. "Should be enough for two four-packs and twenty B&H."

"Give it here, lads. I'll sort you out." Tosh said, winking at us. Kev handed him our shrapnel and Tosh walked around the corner to Banks' shop.

"He'll never get served." Kev said. "Banksy turns people away for fun, the miserable old bastard."

"He'll be okay," said Mike. "Give him a chance. Besides, he's got ID."

"We'll see," I said.

Five minutes later, Tosh reappeared with a huge grin on his face. He was swinging three full carrier bags as he walked over to us.

"Trust your Uncle Tosh, lads! Or rather, trust your Uncle Dan. I told you the driving licence would work, didn't I? Banks never questioned me." He handed over a bag to Kev. "Four cans of Strongbow, four cans of Tennent's Super, and twenty Bensons. Enjoy yourselves lads, I'm off to get pissed." And with that, he strolled off.

We quickly split the four-packs and stowed the cans away in our pockets, in case there were any coppers about, and headed off to the park. I got home three hours later after puking four times, stumbled out of my clothes, and flopped onto my bed. As I laid there waiting for the room to stop spinning, I was thinking about what a brilliant night we had and how easy it had been to fool Banksy with just a slip of paper. Tosh's face was a picture when he came out with the booze that night, and it was a massive buzz for all of us. Tosh was a hero.

I think that night was the beginning.

From that point on, I couldn't stop thinking about it. Could you really get something that you wanted simply by pretending to be someone else? Obviously in Tosh's case, he had his older brother's driving licence, which was all above board, but Tosh must have walked into that shop a thousand times during school. Why didn't Banksy recognise or question him that night? The answer was clear to me; Tosh was someone else.

Now remember, this is long before the internet, so I went to library and looked for books about people with secret identities; books about spies -- anything I could find really. I devoured these stories, real and fictional, and I wanted to be like these people. Anyone other than myself.

Term finished and we had just started the Easter holidays. Two weeks off with sod-all else to do other than eat Easter eggs and hang around with your mates. It was Wednesday night and me, Kev and Mike were walking to the shops when Mike said, "Anyone fancy getting pissed? I've nicked my brother's driving licence for the night."

Kev stopped and stared at him. "You did what? If he finds out, he's going to kill you!"

"Nah," said Mike. "He won't even know it's gone because he's too busy shagging his missus. C'mon, let's get some cans."

"Who's going in?" Asked Kev. "I'm not. I only look about seven years old!"

"I'll go." I said.

Mike handed me the slip of paper with his brother's details on it and his contribution to our drink fund. "Good luck, mate; don't let us down." I took Kev's money as well and headed off to Banks' shop. I have to admit, I was shitting myself; but I was determined to see if it would actually work. I stopped at the shop door and took a deep breath, reaching into my pocket to check the licence was there, and noticed that my hand was shaking. I closed my eyes and took another breath. Now or never...

I entered the shop and headed towards the counter. Banksy had his back to me, adjusting the sweet jars.

The booze was over the counter to the right. You have to remember, we're talking local shops in those days -- all very Open All Hours. Not like today, where you have CCTV cameras and security guards. In those days, you kept all the expensive stuff behind the counter to stop kids from nicking it.

I coughed to get Banksy's attention. "Hello, son, what can I do for you?" he said as he turned around.

I froze. Oh bollocks. I just stared at him for what seemed a full minute, but was probably seconds. "Can I have four cans of Tennent's Super, four cans of Strongbow, and twenty Benson & Hedges please?"

Banksy looked at me. "Are you eighteen, son?"

"I am," I replied. At this point, my stomach felt like a washing machine on fast-spin and my asshole felt like it was about to release the spag bol mum had cooked for tea.

"Can you prove it?" asked Banksy.

I reached into my pocket, making a conscious effort not to shake like a shitting dog. "There you go," I said as I placed the driving licence on the counter.

He picked the licence up and studied it for a couple of seconds before looking up at me. I stood there, staring back at Banksy, who was staring at me. Looking back, it must've looked like the world's shittest Mexican standoff. Eventually, Banksy put the licence on the counter and walked over to the booze. "Four cans of Fosters and four of Tennent's Super," he said.

"It's Strongbow, not Fosters," I corrected.

Banksy turned around and fixed me with a stare.

"Yes, you're right," he said.

I nearly shat myself. I won't lie to you.

He bagged the cans, and grabbed the cigarettes and threw them into the bag. I'm pretty sure I was holding my breath and let it out in an explosive "humph" as he handed the bag to me.

"There you go son, that'll be £7.53." I managed to pass £8 in coins to him and waited for the change. Banksy handed the change to me, and I grabbed the bag and headed towards the door.

"Have a good night," he said as I walked out of the shop into the warm evening.

I walked around the corner, and Kev and Mike let out a cheer as they saw the carrier bag in my hand. "Piece of piss," I said as I approached them. I handed Mike the driving licence back.

We bumped into a group of girls from school as we were heading to the park. Karen, Emma, Sophie, and Ann from our class were there. "Any of you ladies fancy a drink and a smoke?" asked Mike.

"Don't mind if we do," said Emma on behalf of the group. We all headed off in the direction of the park as usual. Once we were firmly ensconced in the safety of the bushes, we distributed the cans and fags around the gang, and drinking and smoking commenced. I was sat next to Sophie, and we began to chat about school, teachers we liked and hated, lessons that were crap, etc. The usual stuff.

The thing is, Sophie never really acknowledged me at school and this was the first time we had ever had a proper chat. No doubt the free lager and fags helped loosen her lips, but as she talked more, I found myself noticing her blue eyes and the smattering of freckles across the bridge of her nose, and thinking to myself what a very pretty girl she was. It also helped that I was half-pissed and was a horny teenager, and

I was thinking about how her arse wobbled during the cross country runs (I was never fast enough to pass her for some reason…).

"Do you fancy going for a walk?" asked Sophie after we had shared a couple of cans and smoked a fag each. "Yeah, okay." I replied. We both stood up and started to head off towards the lake. Kev wolf whistled, and I turned and gave him a V sign.

Sophie and me chatted some more, although I couldn't for the life of me tell you what we were talking about. I was too busy sneaking sideways glances at her bum. We settled on one of the benches and, before another word, she kissed me full on the lips, sliding her tongue into my mouth. I flinched and Sophie pulled away from me.

"What's wrong?" she asked.

"Nothing," I replied. "I just wasn't expecting that."

"Shall we carry on then?" she smiled.

"Yeah," I said, grinning back at her.

We kissed again and Sophie took my hand and placed it on her boob. I was shaking harder than when I was in Banksy's and I could feel her smile as we kissed. I squeezed gently and felt her nipple stiffen against the palm of my hand. I can't tell you how long we sat on the bench kissing and groping each other, but it started to get dark and Sophie said, "Bollocks, I need to get home. Will you walk me back?"

"Yeah, of course," I said.

We walked back to hers and I stopped short before reaching her front garden. You don't let dad catch you with his little princess if you want to make it home with both balls attached.

"I should be about on Friday night if you're coming out," said Sophie.

"I might be," I replied. "Not sure if I have to go and

visit my gran. If I'm out, we'll either be by the shops or at the park."

"Okay, I'll see you then," Sophie said. I walked home in a daze. I got away with buying booze in Banksy's, got off with a fit girl and she wanted to see me again!

I won't bore you with the rest of the holiday, but Sophie and me started going out. We made it to the end of the term, and broke up just after school finished and study break began. Sophie put it down to the stress of having to study and the upcoming exams. I'll be honest, I didn't care that much. I was fifteen years old and school had finished. What more could you ask for?

The next couple of years were spent at college and then gainful employment with an insurance company as an office junior. I kept my head down and worked hard, and week nights and weekends were spent in the pub with Kev and Mike. No need to borrow ID then, as we were all over eighteen, but I'd never forgotten the buzz of lying and getting away with it.

My next attempt at pretending to be somebody else didn't go so well. I met a bird in a club in town and told her I was the sales director of a company. A totally harmless white lie, but when she suggested we meet the following week, I knew that I'd have to put some work in to carry it off. Saturday morning, I went into town and spent some serious cash on new clothes. I reckon they cost me the best part of a weeks' wages. I knew that sales directors didn't drive an old Cortina, so I had to borrow some decent wheels. Of course, nobody I knew earned enough to run a posh car, so I ended up spending another week's wages hiring a BMW for 24 hours. Plenty of time to take this bird out and get it back to the rental company.

I picked the car up, drove to her local where we had a drink, and then headed into town for a meal. The night went well, and we stopped off on the way back to hers for some al fresco shagging. Thank Christ for BMW's wipe-clean leather upholstery. Once we were dressed, I started the car up and continued driving back to hers. We made it back to her house and said our goodbyes, agreeing to see each other again (although I had no intention of seeing her again). So far, so good. It all went wrong when I took a left instead of a right turn and got a bit lost. I say a bit; I was totally lost, to be honest.

As I was staring at road signs, trying to find a street name I recognised, a cyclist appeared from nowhere and, before I could hit the brakes, the poor bastard went over the bonnet. I stopped the car and jumped out. The lad was lying in the road, not moving. I ran over to him and tried to see if he was breathing without moving him. I was looking around to see if anyone had been alerted by the collision, but couldn't see anyone. I quickly grabbed his bike and dragged it over to a hedge, then ran back and grabbed the lad under each arm, dragging him over to where his bike was propped up.

I ran back to the car, got in, and drove off. I was sweating, shaking, and had to pull over to puke twice. I eventually found an area I knew; I drove at a steady thirty miles an hour. I pulled up outside of my house, composed myself, and walked in, heading straight to my room. I didn't sleep a wink that night, expecting the coppers to knock on the door at any point. I avoided calls from Kev and Mike over the weekend, and was too scared to put on the radio or TV. I eventually found out the lad had had concussion and a broken arm, and despite a policy enquiry, there were no witnesses to the accident. Once again, I'd gotten away with it, but that was too much of a close shave.

The internet became my greatest tool. Not only could you meet people through dating websites, but the profiles you could create meant you could be anyone you wanted to be; no questions asked. Well, questions were asked, but if you got your story straight, it was no bother. I couldn't tell you how many woman I met online, and not once was I myself.

Props never hurt either. I bought clothing and a kit from an army surplus store when I told a bird I'd met that I had been in the army and had just got out; and I ordered some medical equipment online when I pretended to be a doctor. It had never been easier to assume a false identity.

This carried on for a number of years. Every couple of months, I would select someone online I liked the look of, then spend a few weeks chatting to them. If they wanted to meet up, we would exchange numbers and talk on the phone, eventually meeting up. I don't think I ever met anyone more than once, and they had no way of contacting me again, as I deleted my profile and set up a new one. I would throw away my mobile phone SIM card and buy another. I reckon I used to get through six or seven new phone numbers a year. Trying to remember your number if someone in a pub or a club asked for it was a nightmare.

Mum got sick early last April or May. She started getting breathless when she was out and about, and mentioned that she had a dizzy spell when she was gardening. I assumed she was overdoing it or had picked up a bug. I told her to take it easy, and offered to do the running around for her.

I popped over to mum's on a hot sunny Saturday morning in July to cut the grass and was shocked when she opened the door. Her face was drawn and she looked grey.

"Bloody hell, mum, you look terrible." I said.

"Oh thanks," replied mum. "I made a special effort too." She winked at me.

"I think you should go and see a doctor, mum." I said.

"If I don't feel any better by the middle of next week, I'll make an appointment, love." said mum. "Although it'll probably be a fortnight before I get to see anyone. Anyway, sit yourself down and I'll put the kettle on."

"Don't be silly, mum, I'll do that. You need to rest." I said.

I made us both a cuppa and got mum some lunch. We chatted for an hour about the usual stuff, and then I went into the garden to cut the grass and tidy up. After forty-five minutes, I came back in and washed my hands in the kitchen.

"I'm off now," I said as I gave mum a kiss on the cheek. "I'll call you in the week to see how you are."

"Okay, love, you look after yourself and don't worry about me. I'll be fine." Mum closed the front door as I walked to the car.

Mum called me on Wednesday evening. She had managed to get an appointment to see her GP on Tuesday and they referred her immediately to hospital to see a specialist. They found a lump in her breast and it didn't look good; the specialist thought it was stage four breast cancer; more than likely spread to her lungs and was inoperable. They could only provide pain relief to make her as comfortable as possible, and due to the advanced state of the cancer, they had given her until the end of the year. Mum was completely calm as she explained all of this to me.

When the call was finished, I ran to the toilet and threw up.

Cancer.

Just like dad.

Why mum?

Why me?

I didn't have any other family, and with mum gone, I'd be alone. I just wanted to run away. Somewhere. Anywhere. I couldn't leave mum though.

The hospital arranged for end-of-life care for mum; palliative care involving a lot of pain relief medication that knocked mum sideways, so half the time, she didn't know who or where she was. At least she wasn't in pain though.

Over the next few months, I watched mum turn from a vibrant, fun-loving woman who was always quick to laugh and quicker to help others into a skeletal, frail, grey facsimile of a human being who couldn't move from her bed. It broke my heart. I began to drink in order to sleep, but sleep evaded me. I spent a lot of time thinking.

Mum died at the end of November. There weren't many people at the funeral, but it was a decent affair. I was so numb I couldn't cry. Once the coffin descended, everyone left the crematorium to look at the wreaths and tributes people had sent, and I listened to people offer their condolences. I thanked everyone and eventually I was the only one left. I walked to my car and drove home.

I sat on the sofa with a large whisky in one hand and a cigarette in the other. I had nothing left. I needed to escape. I didn't want to be me anymore.

I ground my cigarette into the ashtray and drained the glass in one gulp. I knew what I needed to do.

I picked up my laptop and switched it on. Once I logged onto the dating website, I set up a new fake profile; this time as a woman. I found some photos of a reasonably attractive brunette. A total random; nobody famous -- that wouldn't work.

Now that the hook was baited, it was just a case of seeing how many takes I got. Within twenty-four hours, thirty-seven blokes had sent 'Louise' a message. I selected four that I thought would be suitable and gave them my number. Within half an hour, all of them had messaged me, and one even sent me a naked photo. I deleted it as soon as I saw it. 'Louise' flirted outrageously with the men and offered to meet all of them, and it was agreed that they would pick her up from 'her' house the following week to go out for a drink and see how they got on. I wasn't sure any of them would fall for it.

Well, they all turned up on the dates and times agreed to pick 'Louise' up. It's amazing how a sniff of fanny can make a man throw caution to the wind. Silly bastards.

It took me seven hours to remove the skin from Dave Reynolds' body, and I'll be honest, he's not the best fit in the world -- but what can you do? I really need to invest in some decent tools for this job; after three attempts earlier this week, you'd have thought I would have learned my lesson by now.

That's problem with being somebody else. It makes such a fucking mess.

LANMÒ
THOMAS S. FLOWERS

Chapter 1
Lost

Greenwood, Mississippi. 1964.

John Turner burned his dad's 1953 Cadillac down the country
dirt road. Soft pebbles pinged against the side. Del Shannon
wailed over the speakers, "I wah-wah-wah-wah-wonder."
The windows were down; spring winds gusted in over John's
sweat soaked white button dress shirt that clung to his brown
skin. It wasn't even summer yet and the humidity was already
high. It's going to be a hot summer this year, John thought.
The last of his "Support the Mississippi Summer Project"
leaflets stuck out the back pocket on his black slacks; the sad
face of a small girl glared from the glossy surface, her eyes
told the story of so many in the south -- hungry for change.
On the passenger seat sat a stack of One Man, One Vote
bumper stickers and a clipboard with a list of names and
addresses. John glanced at them briefly, feeling a strong sense

of pride and hope and fear stir within him.

In the summer, volunteers from all over the nation would be flooding into the rural Delta of Mississippi. Despite the relative success from Montgomery's Bus Boycott, the Freedom Movement had been painfully slow here in the south, with phone threats, bombings, and beatings, and the like. John had even heard of a man over in Houston who was lynched in the bayou by men in hoods and sheets. They had carved the letters KKK into his stomach. He was found dangling from a tree, still alive somehow. Terrifying as it was, in the Delta -- it was worse.

John thumbed the steering wheel. He had been on this dirt road for too long. Violence made his stomach spin. What if someone sees me talking to folks about voting? He thought. What if... Eyeing the road, he reached over for the clipboard and balanced it on his lap. With his thumb, he flipped to the second page and glanced down at a crudely drawn map. He had one more stop he wanted to make before calling it a night. Some hermit woman some of the locals called a witchdoctor, a voodoo priestess. Whatever they had called her, John did not care. He needed votes. Looking back to the road, John watched for a moment as the sun fell into the horizon. Dark orange exploded into wisps of thin red and yellow clouds. He smiled and returned to the crude map. Shouldn't have been on this road for this long. Must have missed my turn. Better double back, he thought. If I miss the sign again, I'll just head back to Jackson and rendezvous with the others. I'm sure Moses will forgive one vote missed.

Sirens blared behind him.

John looked up into his rearview mirror. Hands unsteady. A white Chevrolet police cruiser was flashing its reds and blues. Where did they come from? John wondered. He slowed down and pulled his dad's Cadillac over. Across the bank, deep pinewoods shielded the setting sun. Everything seemed darker here. He left the engine and lights running, but took his hands off the wheel. The police cruiser pulled up behind him, leaving a wide birth. Bright spot lights flashed, burning through the Cadillac. John squinted, struggling to see anything.

"License and registration," demanded the officer, suddenly appearing beside him.

John blinked wildly against the glare from the spotlight. The officer was white and bald. Soft around the midsection. Too much of Mama's pulled pork, John joked, but not out loud -- oh no, not out loud. The officer had on a dark blue uniform with a Mississippi state patch on one shoulder and a Greenwood county patch on the other. His badge reflected some of the glow from the spotlight. John reached in his back pocket, whispering a small prayer of thanks that his dad insisted he have it. "You don't want to give 'em a reason," his dad had said.

John held up his license and registration, "Everything okay, sir?" he asked gently.

The officer collected the items and spent a few long silent moments reading it over. "Where you headed, boy?" he asked, indignant and surly, his southern twang dragging out boy, making it sound more like buoy. The officer continued to study John's license.

"I'm afraid I'm a bit lost, sir. Trying to make my way to the highway," John said, not wanting the officer to know why he was really out here in this part of town.

"You gonna make me ask again?" his cold blue eyes searched the Cadillac.

"Meridian," John lied.

"Why?"

"Got a job interview in the morning, sir," John lied

again.

"Where at?"

John hesitated, he hadn't expected the interrogation -- well, at least not this intrusive of one. "Weidmann's," he said without thinking. The restaurant had been the first thing that came to mind. John had only been there once and the experience wasn't exactly what you'd call hospitable.

"Oh yeah, Weidmann's," the officer said. "I've been there a time or two."

John held his breath. Shit.

"Weidmann allow niggers in his place?" The officer was looking directly at John.

"Dishes, sir."

"Awful long way to wash dishes, don't you think, boy?"

"Take work where I can find it, sir."

The officer glared at John for a while, silent. John noticed the officer eyeing one of the One Vote bumper stickers and the clipboard on the passenger side.

"Know why I pulled you over?" asked the officer.

To John's credit, he remained calm as rain. "No, sir," he said. But John knew. He had been canvassing the area long enough to know how the authorities were toward coloreds. And if the officer noticed the bumper stickers and guessed the real reason why John was out here in the middle of the Delta, then there was no telling what would happen.

"You got a taillight out."

He's lying.

John remembered checking the car this morning, before heading out. John always checked the car while canvassing in the Delta. But again, to his credit, he remained right as rain.

"I'm sorry about that, sir. I didn't know. It was

working before I left home," John said.

"You calling me a liar, boy?"

"No, sir."

"Step out the car."

"I'm sorry, sir. I didn't mean any offence."

"Get out -- NOW!"

The calm rain in John's mind turned tempest. Dark clouds flooded his eyes. John readied himself for the worst, undid his seat belt and climbed out. It will be okay, John. You've had training for this sort of thing. Just remember your training. The officer gestured for John to walk toward the back of the car. John rounded the trunk and noticed another officer standing near the woods, his back turned to them, taking a piss along the tree line. The blue eyed officer shoved him from behind.

"You gonna come clean, boy?"

"Come clean about what, sir?" John stumbled toward the center, now he was between the two men. The one taking a piss joined in. He was thin and tall in a crisp dark blue uniform. His face was awfully young, but John could tell there was meanness there, hidden underneath his boyish looks. His eyes were dark, hair an Irish flame, his smile wicked and cruel. John looked at the back of his dad's Cadillac. Both taillights were glowing red. The older officer pulled out his Billy club, gripped it tight in his hand. John nervously watched. Eyes darted between the two men.

"Niggers never learn," hackled the ginger officer.

"See, boy," said the other officer while taking a swing with the baton, shattering a taillight. Glass fell in the dirt, red light flickered and died. "You got a taillight out. Now, that's a driving violation, right?" he smiled.

John remained motionless in the middle. Silent. Watching the baton cautiously.

The officer stopped smiling. He pointed the baton at John. "You gonna tell me why you're out here?"

John put his hands in front of him, as if calming some wild boar. "Please, sir," he said, "I'm just trying to get back to the highway. Just let me go and I'll be gone."

"Oh -- it's too late for that, don't you think?" said the older officer. "See, I know who you are. You're one of those smartass college niggers coming to educate us poor stupid southerners, right? You come down here to tell them shit-mouthed coloreds they got to go out and vote," he hissed.

John said nothing. He had an overwhelming urge to take a piss.

"You think a vote will change things down here?" asked the ginger. "Coloreds voting? Hogwash."

"Got you scared, don't it?" John whispered.

The officers were silenced. The sun disappeared. Night had come. Slowly the song of crickets and locus came out in droves. John glanced to the forest, dark -- thick. Should I run? No -- no John, don't make it worse. Taking a deep breath, John held a hand against his chest. His heart thundered. Oh, Lord, please let me make it out of this alive. The older officer glanced over at the ginger, nodding -- some kind of code? They closed in, laughing, sneering. Eyes burning with fierce determination. Malice. Hate -- murder.

"You know, boy, we're smarter than you think. Brother Pullman warned us about niggers like you. He and our grand wizard Beck told us everything. See, civilization can only survive while the whites and the blacks are separate. We cannot coexist, sing kumbaya, and hold hands. 'The Highest allocated the races when He divided the sons of man, fixing the bounds of the nations,' as the good book says. And here you come…" said the older officer. He took a step and swung his baton. The thick wood struck John's abdomen.

Something cracked. John wheezed. Doubled over, he held his stomach.

"And here you come," he continued, stepping away, "threatening our way of life."

The ginger swung at John this time. The baton struck his knee. Blinding hot pain brought John to the ground, whimpering he clutched the throbbing bruise.

"But you're not just threatening my way of life or my children's way of life or their children's children, but your own. Do you understand me?" continued the older officer.

The ginger swung again, striking John's forearm. John rolled into a ball. The pain was white hot. He held his other arm against his gut. The officer swung again, stomping the ground with his boot. John could see the older man looking off into the distance. Keeping watch -- maybe? The officer above him continued to spew rage. Spit flew, slithering down John's blood-soaked face. He grimaced against the pain of each swing, each stomp, each kick. John fought to stay conscious. If he allowed the dark curtain to fall over him, who knows where or if he'd wake up. Please, Lord, let me make it out of this alive...The sound of rusty hinges came closer. Is that a car coming? John prayed. He hoped. The clunker came to a halt on screeching brakes and crunching gravel. The ginger officer began to giggle. John's heart froze. This was not his Calvary.

"I thought you were going to get that fixed?" laughed the ginger.

"Like I can afford new pads," said a man from the truck. "We're in a depression, haven't you heard?"

The older officer walked toward the vehicle, putting on a mock frown. "About time, Huckabee, I thought maybe you got lost or something," he said.

"Not hard getting lost out here -- hell, I didn't even

know this road existed." Huckabee hopped down to join his friends. Another man followed behind him, he was thinner, eyes fixed to the ground.

"Well -- well, what do you got here, Bill?" asked Huckabee, grinning at the older officer.

"One of them college coloreds from up north," said Bill.

"Oh, do we?" Huckabee hocked, clearing his throat, and launched a chunk of dark brown matter on the red clay ground. He gleamed, hitching his thumbs inside the pockets of his jean overalls; his wavy hair slicked back and wet.

"Well, I think we know what to do..." he said, somewhat contemplatively.

"Let's-- let's take it easy, now. Remember l- last time? We don't want things getting out of hand, do we?" asked the other man standing behind Huckabee. John looked him over from the ground. The man was young, as young if not younger than the ginger officer. But he was thinner than the rest; small frame, but tall. He wore stained painter's pants; uneven globs of white, blue, and red covered his thighs. His hair was short, crew-cut -- or at least as much as John could tell in the dark.

"Billy," spat Huckabee, pulling out a pack of Camels. "We're doing what needs to be done. You want this boy to go about stirring up coloreds? You want them marching in town or boycotting your daddy's Piggly Wiggly?" he sparked a match, the flame bright in the growing darkness. John watched him take in a deep, languorous breath, and puff out grey smoke.

"Don't be such a pansy," teased the ginger. "We got a higher purpose. Besides," he voice rose, "there ain't no room for cowards in the Knights of the Klan, for Christ's sake! You want to go back in town and tell Brother Beck, the most ornery grand wizard since Theodore Poole, that we decided to cut this nigger some slack?"

"Damn Poole was a mean son-a-bitch," said Huckabee dryly.

Billy shied away, stuffing his hands deep into his pockets. He stared at the ground. "Sorry, Sean, I was just... I don't know."

"You call me Officer Hannity, you fucking limp dick," spat the ginger. His shoulders hunched, eyes wild. The baton swung like a winged predator in his hand.

"Okay, you two, that's enough. Remember who the real enemy is, okay?" said Bill, throwing up his hands. "Beck gave us a mission and we're going to make good. We all swore an oath; let's not make liars of ourselves." He glanced at Billy.

"Well said, Officer O'Reilly," hummed Huckabee. The others nodded. Hannity beamed yellow. Billy was grey. John remained on the ground. His eyes darted between the men and back toward the woods across the bank. What they said terrified him. There was no use for nonviolent resistance here, not the way he was trained back at Chapel Hill. These men meant to kill him -- and there was no one here to stop them. Hell, even the law is involved! But where can I go? Anywhere but here... the woods look deep. I could hide. Maybe find the highway. Flag someone down -- but will they stop to help? Sounds like this is a private party; doubt these assholes want anyone else involved. Might back away if I could just get to someone -- anyone. John looked back over at the men as they talked about rope, shovels, axes, or whatever it was. That old fellow they called O'Reilly probably won't give chase, or at least not enough to worry me, even with a hurt knee. Nor that fat one they called Huckabee. He might run, but that lard ass couldn't catch the flu. The ginger,

Hannity, and that other one -- Billy, I think they called him...
they look like they could run. Might be fast too, by the look of
them -- I'll just have to be faster. John slowly, carefully, began
to shift. He positioned himself on his knees. Stretched out one
of his legs; anchored more weight on his hands.

"Go on and get the rope, Billy," ordered O'Reilly.
Hannity turned to Huckabee, "You bring the shovels?"

"Son -- did I bring the shovels? Let me tell you what.
I've been lynching niggers before you was born!" Huckabee's
belly danced as he laughed.

John had heard enough. It was now or never.

Chapter 2
Lynch Party

John Turner sprang from the ground in a cloud of red dirt. He
crossed the bank before the first shout echoed into the night.
John didn't dare look back. He pumped his legs, hurling
himself over broken tree branches and pounding dead leaves
with everything he had. Ignoring his burning lungs, he sought
some kind of intuition -- headlights, markers; something to
direct him away from his would-be assassins. There was
something up ahead -- yellow, but dim in the haze that hung
just above the forest floor. John sprinted toward whatever
this light was. His eyes blurred from exhaustion. Hot tears
streaked his face, blinding him to the large root that stuck up
from the ground ahead of him. John hit it full tilt. Searing
pain shot up his leg. He stumbled, and hit the ground hard.
White stars filled his eyes. Can't stop, he thought. Can't stop.
They're behind me -- somewhere. Gotta keep moving. John
braced himself against a nearby tree, tested his hurt ankle.
He bit his lip, but kept pressure on it, slowly moving forward
again.

"There you are!" shouted a menacing voice.

Panicked, John started to trot.

"We're going to kill you, you son of a bitch!" the man screamed.

A thunderous crackle broke the otherwise silent woods. A sharp whistle snapped the air behind him. In a flash, his leg erupted in red mist. John fell to the dirt once more, crying out against the sudden and terrible pain. He clutched with wet hands at his wound.

"Got you, you nigger!" hollered the man. "You fucking skuzz!"

"Please—" John fought to say.

The face of Hannity loomed above him. He aimed his service revolver at John. Giggling manically, he fired. The bullet impacted John's knee, showering him in dark red flesh and splintered bone.

John screamed.

"That's a gas!" hollered Hannity, dancing a jig as if he'd won some ill-gotten prize at the county fair.

John gritted his teeth, taking deep and rapid breaths. He wanted to collapse, his vision blurring.

"Jesus, Sean! You shot him?" cried Billy, coming up from behind. O'Reilly and Huckabee joined soon enough.

"Shut up, you square. Yeah, I shot him. What? You think I want to chase him all night? What if he got away, huh? The highway's not far from here." Hannity kept his gun on John, but his eyes fired at Billy.

John winched as he craned his neck toward the soft yellow glow in the distance.

"That's right, coon. You almost made it -- all the way to the promised land!" Hannity laughed.

"Enough fooling. Let's get this done, okay?" said O'Reilly. "Eventually someone will drive by and get curious.

I don't want nothing linking us, got it?" he eyed his boys.

"Here," said Huckabee, letting down the large brown sack he had strapped across his back. He threw the rope to Billy. "Put this around his neck. I spotted a good tree a few yards from here."

Billy's eyes went wide, but he remained silent. John cried, trying to move; but his legs were going numb.

"Please, mister. Please don't do this," he blubbered. "I promise I won't tell anyone. I swear it! What? What is it you want? You want me to tell the others to stay away? I will -- I'll do that? But, Jesus, you don't have to do this... You don't have to do this..."

Billy held on to the rope. His hands shook violently.

"Well, what are you waiting for, Billy? Put that rope on him," O'Reilly barked.

"Please don't," cried John again.

Billy did as he was told. With sweat pouring from his forehead, he batted away John's weak flaying arms. In a quick lasso motion, he tied the noose around John's neck. Billy locked eyes with John. He could see spit hanging from his lips. One leg -- the one with the gapping bullet hole in the thigh -- lay limp and twitching; the other seemed oddly misshaped, hardly held together by sinew and shards from John's black and bloodied slacks.

"I'm sorry," Billy whispered.

"You can do something -- if you wanted," whispered John, his voice hardly audible against his hazard, jagged breaths.

Billy said nothing. He looked at John and skirted off to join the others. Hannity took a portion of the rope and along with Billy, began to drag John through the woods, scraping what remained of his clothes against broken sticks, collecting dirt and dead leafs that clung to the forest floor.

John pulled at the rope, allowing a few precious moments of air to flow to his lungs. He wanted to kick. He wanted to run. But his legs would not budge. John couldn't feel anything below. Huckabee and O'Reilly followed behind the committal parade, as silent, watchful mourners.

"That's the one, up yonder!" Huckabee suddenly shouted, pointing forward.

The death march came to a halt. The men -- even John -- gazed in wide wonder at the tall weeping willow before them; an alien among the dense pine and bald cypress -- an ancient sentry germinating at center of the dark woods. The willow tree's thick, gnarled branches arched high into the air and drooped back low with lush green curtains of flowery leaves nearly skirting the red dirt below.

"Someone must have planted this one," O'Reilly said to no one in particular.

"Who?" asked Billy, bewildered.

"I don't know, you iggit. But it's not native, I can tell you that," barked O'Reilly.

"Sling your end of the rope over that branch there," said Huckabee. He pointed to a tall branch.

The boys obeyed. With the rope slung, Billy and Hannity began to pull down on the slack. Slowly and painfully, John was corralled to the trunk of the large willow 'til the noose finally tightened against his burning neck.

"Please—"croaked John.

Billy wanted to piss himself, but the fellers would have seen. He took hold of the rope, readying to hoist. His guts boiled. His eyes inflamed. He looked at John -- one last time. There was pleading in those dark browns of the Negro. *I didn't know we were going to do this... I didn't know!* Billy shut tight his eyes, and joined Hannity, heaving John's weight up into the air. Chunks of bark came raining down as the rope scrapped across the tall branch. Billy got some in his eye.

"Don't drop him, you piss ant," shouted Hannity, struggling with John's weight.

"I'm not, you kiss-up," snorted Billy. He readjusted his grip, ignoring the stabbing pain in his eye and heaved, and heaved, and heaved, 'til John dangled some five feet from the ground. They anchored the rope around the base of the willow. Finished, they stood back.

Billy refused to look up.

Hannity beamed.

Huckabee lit a smoke.

O'Reilly folded his arms across his chest.

John's neck burned hot as coals. Thoughts flashed in white lightning as his brain fought to stay alive. He tugged futilely against the noose. He could feel his eyes bulging. He had a terrible image of what his mother called his "baby browns" popping like squeezed grapes. In a last ditch effort, he swung. Using his hips to carry his dead legs, John's body began to sway back and forth. He could feel the dizziness turning into something darker -- something beyond, astral. His vision blurred. This is the end, he thought.

A loud thunderous crack woke John up. Suddenly he was free falling. The others were shouting -- something vulgar. And then he thudded hard against the clay ground. Sharp white pain shot through his shoulder. John rested his head in the dirt.

"Well -- shit," said Hannity.

"Let's just get out of here," Billy whined.
John yanked off the noose, gobbling deep breaths of hot humid Mississippi air.

Huckabee dropped to open his bag. "This is going to get messy, boys. I hope you came with an empty stomach."

O'Reilly knelt beside John. Keeping his service

revolver on him, he surveyed the damage already done. John's
face was swollen and busted from Hannity's baton strikes
and punches and kicks. An aggravated red whelp was etched
around his neck where the noose had been. But, for the most
part, bleeding from his leg wounds had stopped -- congealed
in a dark red paste.

"This isn't how I wanted to do this," O'Reilly
whispered to John. "I'd prefer you were dead before we -- it'd
be merciful." O'Reilly looked up into the night sky. "But we
ain't got all night."

John watched in silent horror. Fear had swallowed his
tongue. He glanced over at Huckabee, his eyes shot wide as
he watched the fat man in the jean overalls hand the ginger a
long wooden handled axe. The blade twinkled in the bright
star light from the heavens above.

This cannot be real, John thought. This -- this isn't
real. I'm having a nightmare. As soon as they swing that axe,
I'll wake up in my bed, sweating -- but alive. I'll wake up in
Jackson. Andrew will be snoring in his bed. Bob Moses will
be up reading a week's old New York newspaper, something
from Harlem maybe. There is no way this is happening.

Hannity brought his blade down first. The axe sunk
deep into John's shoulder, nearly severing his arm. He jerked
it out. Blood showered from the gash, spraying Hannity in
the face.

John was silent -- at first. His thoughts muddied into
reality. He looked at his ruined shoulder... his dangling arm.
And then he looked at Hannity; and finally let out a deafening,
awful screech. It was the sound a lamb makes at the slaughter
house -- a nightmare of bleating.

Huckabee brought his axe down on John's mangled
knee. The flesh severed clean from the bone. A long, noodled
tendon whipped out as Huckabee yanked on the blade.

Another arterial spray drenched John's already mucked white dress shirt.

Billy shied away, hiding his face in his dirty palms. Huckabee hoisted the heavy axe above his head -- readied for another blow. He stopped, looked John in the eye.

John had stopped screaming. Blood gurgled in the back of his throat; but his eyes were fixed on Huckabee.

"I'm going to get you -- all of you," John wheezed. Huckabee smiled. With a labored grunt, he brought the axe down with all his weight. The symmetrical blade lopped a large chuck of John's face and skull clean off. Red mist sprayed from John's mouth. Malleable flesh dribbled down his cheek. John's eyes rolled -- twitching. As Huckabee brought his axe away, Hannity came down with his. The blade sunk deep into the top of John's head. In a horrifying dance, his legs shook violently, and then were still.

Huckabee and Hannity continued to hack pieces of John Turner for another ten minutes. They saved removing his head for last. Satisfied their work was done, O'Reilly dug in Huckabee's bag for a camera. He took a picture of the carnage.

"What the hell is that for?" cried Billy, his skin pale white.

"All this wasn't about just one nigger. This is about those northern agitators. I'm going to develop this film in my basement. And then I'm going to mail it to them CORE sons of bitches. They'll think twice before they ever set foot in Mississippi again," said O'Reilly.

Billy quickly turned away, lurching. In a hot, stinging convulsion, he messed the ground with partially digested catfish, corn bread, and pecan pie.

"You done?" asked O'Reilly.

"Yeah," said Billy, turning back to the group.

O'Reilly handed him a shovel. Hannity took one as well. Then the boys dug 'til dawn first broke into the night. Quickly they buried the remains of John Turner in a shallow grave beside the old willow tree. Collecting the shovels and axes, the men made their way back to the unnamed red clay road. O'Reilly grabbed the gas can that had been tied in the back of Huckabee's truck. Without haste, he drenched John's father's Cadillac. Huckabee lit a match. The group watched the car ignite in dark angry flames, and then drove off.

O'Reilly and Hannity went north into downtown Greenwood. Huckabee and Billy took off south, toward Sidon Lake. The Cadillac burned for three hours before anyone drove by. It took an additional hour before the Greenwood fire department and the Leflore County Sheriff's department arrived on the scene. By the time the investigation started, there was nothing left but ash and soot and gnarled steel.

Chapter 3
The Woman in the Woods

A week had passed since John's mutilation. A week since his father's ruined Cadillac had been hauled away to the city dump. A week since his father had refused to make the trip south to Mississippi to find what had become of his boy. A week since the Leflore County Sheriff's office report regarding the disappearance of John Turner had been added to an already stupendous pile of unsolved crimes. The detective given the case had commented to a colleague that the boy was probably dead, buried somewhere out in the woods. A week had passed and John's body remained undiscovered.

A few days after the search had been officially abandoned, the CORE office in Tennessee received an unmarked envelope. Bettie Palmer, a volunteer student from

Seattle, was working the front office that day. After collapsing
to the floor, fellow CORE office personal came to her aid
and found the contents of the letter face up -- a disturbing
photograph of what was assumed to be John Turner hacked to
bloody bits in a grizzled black and white image. The Leflore
Sherriff's office received the envelope, added the photograph
with a few statements collected from Bob and Andrew
Garfunkel, and poor Bettie Palmer, and subsequently filed
the case back inside a moldy brown, water-stained box
marked 'unsolved.'

On the afternoon Andrew Garfunkel made a collect
call to John's parents in North Carolina.

Ronna Blanche was trudging knee-deep through a
thicket of red berried thorn bushes. The sharp organic blades
ripped and pulled against her long flowing olive dress. No
matter, she thought, girding the loose material and pushing
her way through the gnarled snare. Up ahead stood her old
friend, the Willow Tree -- a mighty sentinel rooted deep at
the very heart of the delta forest. I've missed you, Ronna
thought. Gracefully, she came to its trunk. With tender hands
-- lover's hands --she stroked the coarse bark. Ronna was
not certain when this particular tree had been planted, but it
was not ingenious to the overgrown pine and kudzu woods of
Mississippi -- of that much she was sure. She had stumbled
upon this tree when she was just a child -- no older than
fifteen -- running from a mob of drunken men. She hid in the
tree and watched the white fellows pass in a haze of cheap
bourbon. And as she hugged the branch that saved her from
-- something she dare not think -- she swore the tree spoke to
her. The Willow had called her, 'Little One.'

Ronna paused only briefly to greet her old friend
before turning to the fresh mound by her feet. The length of
the mound was long enough for a body, but looked shallow.

Claw marks were visible in the red dirt, as if some animal or creature had tried to find an easy meal buried beneath. Ronna wiped fresh beads of sweat with a purple bandana and tied it back around her frizzy powdered afro. The afternoon heat was beating down through the tall tree opening. Ronna tossed her bag from her shoulder and retrieved a shovel from within.

"Okay, Mr. Turner. Let's let you out," she said.

The red clay dirt had been packed tight by last week's heavy rain. The job took longer than she had anticipated. The sun was starting to set when she unearthed his head -- or what was left of it.

"Aw, there you are," Ronna sang sweetly, holding up the mutilated flesh of what had been John's face -- ignoring the awful yellow stink of decay. Abandoning the shovel, she quickly dug with her hands for the rest of John; shoveling up, with soiled fingers, maggot-infested mounds of dirt from the grave. She stored each rotting chunk in the canvass sack she had brought with her. His torso had been the hardest to retrieve. Rooted, Ronna heaved with both her legs, heels digging into the red ground. Finally, it came unglued. She surveyed the parts, but had to forego bringing both his legs and one of his arms, as they were all too far gone to salvage.

"We'll fix you; don't you worry, John. We'll fix you right up," Ronna said. With a grunt, she hoisted the bag over her shoulder and marched carefully back through the deep woods, across the lonesome highway, toward the bright and shimmering yellow light that belonged to her hut.

Chapter 4
Voodoo

Agonizing pain woke him. Flashes of coagulated memory seared from his mind. John fought to remember.

He could recall the old Greenwood police officer, O'Reilly -- wasn't it? John remembered his callousness; the officer's deep concern for justice. He watched the others set upon him with as much interest as taking out the trash.

More pain. More flashes of images John cared little to relive -- but he had to see, he needed to remember. And there he was, laying in the abysmal nightmare of his own demise. It was both strange and otherworldly; John felt stretched between what was and what is. He swam in the soupy memory and watched as the fat redneck in the overalls -- Huckabee? -- and the ginger they called Hannity went to eager work with axes. Axes? How am I... alive? Am I dead?

John pondered and watched as Huckabee swung the killing blow. John could feel the blade sink in, the severing of nerve endings coming apart like serrated slippery cords.

And suddenly he was conscious. He felt -- strange. Like floating fully clothed in a pool -- heavy; weighed down by something. John took deep breaths, filling his lungs with burning liquid. On his lips, he tasted something sweet. In his mind, the faces of his killers danced before him, laughing, calling him cruel, unimaginable names. Beyond the faces, another image took form. Shadows dancing to the beat of drums. A deep vibrating bass. Shouting, screaming, howling fell into rhythm of some ancient, powerful rite. John gritted his teeth, trying to focus his eyes. The shadows began to clear, little by little. There were people all around him, dancing in step with several large drums that sat in the corner. The dancers were decorated in something -- John wasn't sure; it looked native and wild. Chicken bone necklaces and feathers donned the dark skins of those that whirled and leapt and spun and jumped and jittered almost hypnotically.

The macabre masquerade intensified 'til finally he saw her -- a woman in the crowd; a priestess, perhaps,

draped in a long flowing crown of dark, elongated feathers,
of some creature John could not place, reaching all the way
down to her buttocks. She wore the same necklace as the
others, except her flesh was painted in white chalk -- a bright
and bold contrast to her midnight skin. She danced just as
hypnotically as the others. The dancers slowly backed away,
surrendering center stage. John watched, mesmerized by her
presence. It was -- intoxicating. The music blended in potent
cerebral electricity that crawled and burrowed into his heart.

    "Gen lavi..." the woman shouted.

    "Gen lavi..." she repeated.

    "GEN LAVI!"

    The music pounded louder and louder. The dancers
became more chaotic. Several from the crowd were having
seizures, as if possessed by some demonic spirit, moving and
jerking their bodies like ill-fated marionettes. A lamb was
brought to the center. Its neck slashed. Blood poured over
the people. The wicker flames surrounding the ceremony
-- is that what this was? -- burned brighter than the midday
sun. Whatever John was contained in, the thick syrupy liquid
began to boil. Bubbles enveloped him. He could feel the surge
of something powerful passing from the people to him. A
sensation -- wild, rapturous, spiritualization -- rushed over his
flesh as if the nerves beneath his skin were just waking up.
John could feel his legs; and then his abdomen, and arms. He
could feel his head -- pounding with the drum beats. And then
-- he could move. John pulled an arm into view, but he did not
recognize it. There was scarred, and black wires stitched in
the waxy flesh. The color seemed- - off, as if not his own, or
at least not as how he remembered it. John craned his neck.
Peering at his form. Gashes and similar scarring marked
his body. Black wire stitches coursed throughout like some
nightmarish map. The destination led to suffering and pain

unimaginable. Stupefaction was replaced with rage -- rage for what had come of him, his mutilated form. Rage for the life stolen from him, and even rage for this new life given. Rage for...

What will come of me now? John hissed. Shutting his eyes tight.

(Retribution.)

The thought came suddenly, from -- somewhere in his head. It was and wasn't his own; a foreign tongue licking his mind.

Retribution -- how -- what?

(They need to pay, John.)

Who? What is this? Am I losing it?

(No, John. The four men need to pay. They've hurt and done worse. And they'll keep doing worse 'til they get caught.)

How -- what am I supposed to do? Look at me!

(Open your eyes.)

John obeyed. Before him stood the strange woman. In his heart, John knew was a priestess. She was looking at him, standing at the forefront of the other dancers. Her hand pressed against the glass of whatever container he was floating in. The voice, it was hers; somehow it was her voice that found its way through the fade and into his mind. But how could this be? This is insane, right? He wanted to close his eyes again, to deny everything. This is all a dream, that's it. All a dream. Some nightmare from some story cooked up by Moses or Andrew. This isn't real. It can't be real. (Those men need to pay, John. For what they did to you. For what they'll keep doing...)

You're not real! This cannot be real! No -- no -- NOOOO!

(I'm sorry, John. I'm so sorry, son. But this is real.

This happened to you. They did this, and we put you back together.)

It's not possible…am -- am I dead? Is this hell?

(No, John. This is not hell.)

But I am dead, right?

(Not anymore.)

What does that mean? 'Not anymore?'

(Feel your skin. Look at yourself.)

John hesitated and then finally obeyed. His skin was ruff, malleable. The stitches were sharp and fresh. The liquid in the tank was sweet and intoxicating. He thought about pinching his skin, but perhaps that would be too absurd. No.

As much as John desired for all this to be some fabricated work of his imagination, the cold hand gripping his spine and the sharp pragmatic focus of his cerebral cortex told him otherwise. As horrible as it sounded, this was all real. Reality sunk in and John screamed. The violent quake muffled against the thick fluid that contained him.

(Hush, now. Everything will be made right again…)

How? What am I?

(You're you, but not you… You're something else.)

What?

(Lanmò.)

What?

(…death.)

Chapter 5
Honky-Tonk Decapitation

Hannity was alone at the bar. Some hole-in-the-wall place called Rooster's; an old Greenwood establishment that typically brought in a number of thirsty parishioners, each cooing on the nip for Mississippi Mud. But tonight the bar

was near empty. Hannity paid little notice. He simple sat
and drank, and fumbled with the bowl of peanuts. Off duty,
Hannity wore his favorite pair of Wrangler blue jeans and
the flannel button-up his mom bought him from a Sears &
Roebuck catalog. The King was vibrating across the bar from
the fat jukebox that sat in the corner next to a set of overused
pool tables. Some idiot on a date put in a nickel and selected
some sappy love song:

Are you lonesome, tonight?

Do you miss me, tonight?

Hannity hammered back his whiskey, poked the bar,
signaling another round. The bartender, some guy named Ted
-- but everyone called him Teddy -- lined 'em up. Teddy gave
Hannity a cocked eye, as if to say without words, "Know your
limits." It was something his daddy would have said. Hannity
sneered and downed the first glass. Grimacing, he slammed
it back on the table. Teddy shook his head, dismayed, and
walked to the other side of the bar. Another fellow was
waving his hands, ready to suck on the nipple tap of cheap
booze.

(Know your limits…)

That son-of-a-bitch was never one to practice what he
preached, Hannity thought. He eyed the next glass. Contempt
for his father brewed with the whiskey in his otherwise empty
stomach. Last winter, Hannity senior left some shithole bar
in northern Greenwood, drunk as a skunk, and took a sharp
turn off a steep cliff, as the saying goes. He'd been on a rather
rough binder and whoever had manned the bar that night
never bothered taking his keys. Though, to be fair, no one
could take his father's keys. Those that tried usually ended up
with a black eye or worse. Nope. Hannity senior drove home
after downing enough booze to kill a moose, pulled too hard
on the steering wheel and pitched his Chevrolet off Miranda

gorge (named after some woman who threw herself off back
in 1890 after being raped by some of the menfolk from town).
The truck didn't explode on impact. From all those action
flicks at the Cinemark, you'd think it would. No, instead
Hannity senior racked his brains against the front windshield.

When they pulled his body out, his neck was twisted
hideously backwards to the point where he was staring at his
own ass. Fitting, Hannity Jr. thought.

Know your limits.

Hannity slammed back his last glass, biting against
the wonderful burn inching down his jut. He stared into the
bar with a sudden sadness. Good things never last, he thought.
It was well over a week now since he and his friends served
up some of -- what his daddy would call -- Southern Justice
to that yank nigger. There had been some stink from the
local color, some questions regarding the burnt car belonging
to the kid's father, and John Turner himself, missing. But
all that came of it was a missing persons' report and some
photographs supposedly belonging to the victim that CORE
had mailed down, followed with a hysterical phone call. "Just
who's the law down there, sheriff?" they had asked. "Where
is the justice?" And that was that; just a bunch of stink. No
real nothing. Fear of Klan retaliation had kept everyone pretty
much quiet, or so Hannity assumed. But then again, good
things never last.

Hannity could sense the horizon. The world he knew
was slipping away. A new world was emerging where the
Turners and Moses of the world had little regard for tradition.
They scared them sure enough -- him and O'Reilly and
Huckabee and, God help 'im, even Billy -- but what they did
wouldn't last. Hannity knew that. Old man O'Reilly is a fool
if he believes hacking up one colored will stop the hands from
moving on the clock.

Times are 'a changing—

And good things never last—

Hannity wobbled from his bar stool, eyed the near empty joint. A couple sat at a table near the jukebox. Someone else had put in a nickel. Now Jimmy Dean was humming away in his deep cathartic voice. The bass rattled across the bar as Hannity made his way to the men's room.

He stood six foot six...

And weighed two forty-five.

Broad at the shoulder...

--Everybody knew, ya didn't give no lip.

To Big John...

Big bad John.

He kicked the door open; stumbled inside the empty restroom. The sour smell of urine was strong, causing his nose to twitch. Purging his whiskey into the commode, Hannity paid little notice of the door opening, and the heavy, slow, methodical footsteps coming up behind him. His thoughts were lost in the sundry of lust and booze. Hannity wagered how many more whiskey shots he should have before driving over to Mary Garner's place, getting him a piece of action. He was just delivering a final surge of steamy piss when a dark shadow came over him.

What the hell is this? he thought.

"Listen, you better beat it, pervert, before I boot stomp your ass into next Sunday," Hannity hissed over his shoulder, shaking out the last few drops.

The shadow remained, its breath as hot and raucous as death. Beneath the stink was something else -- something sweet. Some kind of fruit or alcohol -- rum maybe.

"Alright, faggot, you asked for—" Hannity spun around. His eyes bulged. In the gleam of his irises, a monstrous reflection burned bright against the white bathroom bulbs. No...this isn't possible.

"Hello, Officer," said John Turner -- or whatever he was now. His skin was dark and waxy under the unflattering lights. Black wires stitched into the skin and bruised in abysmal purple patches. His words echoed off the cold tile walls. The stink of mushed flesh caught in the undercurrent of rum.

"You're— you're-" stuttered Hannity.

"Dead?" offered the creature.

"We killed you. Chopped you up. There is no way— this is not real." The debate was ill conceived. The whiskey battered against his rational mind. Hannity and the others had killed this boy, a little over a week ago. But the irrational truth stood before him. John Turner was alive -- or whatever this was; its face sure looks like John Turner, but the rest? The creature before him was deformed, to say the least; a large chunk of its face mangled and crudely sown back together. Its arms were large, as well as its legs. The boy they buried was of average height and build. Hannity felt drawn to its face. It looks so much like him, though, he thought. Can it be?

The monster smiled. Its teeth yellow and viscous; lips wet with some kind of dark mucus. Its bulky arm shot out. Hannity was hardly aware it moved at all 'til it had a hold of his neck. He could feel his pulse thumping against the waxy warm skin of the creature's enormous hand. Inside its hot breath, Hannity swore he heard laughing. Its other hand came up and took hold of Hannity's ginger hair. Dean Williams continued humming along out in the bar.

Big bad...

Big bad John.

Hannity thought of Mary and the tail he would not be getting tonight. He thought of O'Reilly and the boys, not being able to warn them. And then he thought of his dad,

the old drunk fool who did not know his limit. And then
Hannity thought of nothing. The creature tore his head clean
off his shoulders, showering the urinal stall in a geyser of
malcontent.

Chapter 6
Late Night Evisceration

Ever since the Great Experiment, when they let that colored
fellow Jackie Robinson into professional baseball, segregation
in athletics has dissolved into a radical and fundamentally
new world (the same "New World" Sean Hannity feared), or
so Huckabee imagined. Sure, who cares if you let a few on
your team? They can jump real high and run real fast; natural
athletes that could well enough give your team a competitive
edge -- especially against those uppity yank colleges up
north. Schools have already started. But they've opened
Pandora's Box. Now these coloreds and their white traitorous
sympathizers are calling for integration everywhere, in every
aspect. Integration is bleeding through athleticism and into
our everyday world. What was it, no more than a year ago
when that darky ape walked up into Ole Miss? Registered
and walked right in. And what good came of that mess? Riots
and federal troops coming into our state and telling native
Mississippians how to think, how to act. There is no freedom
of speech or pursuit of happiness anymore. Niggers are
clawing at our backs with monkey paws. Nibbling away at
what's ours -- at our God-given constitutional rights. Brother
Glenn warned us and we failed to listen. He'd been talking
about this since that Montgomery bus boycott shenanigans in
'58. Folks nodded their heads. But no one was willing to take
action -- well, 'til now. Huckabee smiled at the memory as
he set up a tub of Turtle Wax next to his freshly washed and

dried Chevy Pickup. The driveway outside was still stained in streams of red clay. He had driven around for over a week now with the dirt clinging from that unnamed road -- that is, 'til O'Reilly gave him a good bark.

"Everyone else was too chicken shit to do anything," Huckabee confided in his truck. He smoothed out a few splotches on the hood with the shammy cloth. "But we did something. Taught those bastards a real lesson. The photo Bill took ought to keep 'em away for good."

Huckabee was getting ready to buff out the wax when he noticed a shadow pass by his garage. Lingering, a dark grey ghost through the faded window panel, and then slowly, it walked away.

Who the hell is that at this time of night? One of the boys? No, Bill told us to keep separate 'til he gives us the 'all clear.' So who the hell is this? Curious, Huckabee left the shammy on the hood of his truck and peered out the door. Nothing. It was pitch black outside; not even the moon was strong enough to pierce the abyss.

Huckabee opened the door. "Who's out here?" he called.

Nothing. Silence. Not even a cricket calling for a mate nor any lull of passing traffic. It was dead quiet along the side of his garage. Unsatisfied, Huckabee carefully walked the perimeter, peeking around the edge of the building, but found nothing to report; only two silver trash cans filled with motor oil cans, filters, empty tubs of Turtle Wax, and Coors.

"Must've been a tree branch or something," Huckabee whispered in the dark. Feeling a cold wind come upon him, he quickly fled back inside the garage. Leaning against the door as it closed, he shut his eyes for a moment to catch his sanity. Nothing there, you fat fool. He eyed the oval General Electric refrigerator over by his work bench and decided to get a cold one. The bright interior light blinded him for a moment. When his vision cleared, he stared in wide horror at the severed head of Sean Hannity propped up against his six-pack of Coors. Along the shelf blood pooled, dark red and coagulated. Hannity's eyes were open and rolled back. His skin looked waxy in the artificial light; his tongue dark and puffy, protruding from his thin lips.

"Jesus H. Christ!" Huckabee screamed, slamming close the refrigerator door, silencing the light, stumbling backwards. He wiped a cold clammy hand through his greasy, wavy hair.

Laughter bellowed throughout the one car garage. Huckabee spun around, but found only his newly washed Chevy pickup, and behind that, only shadows.

"Who's there?" cried out Huckabee, bewildered at the thought that someone, here with him in his garage, killed his friend. "Show yourself," he demanded, doing his best to subdue his fear.

More laughter, hideous and cruel, came from the dark spaces of the garage. Huckabee darted to find the source, from corner to corner, desperately seeking the intruder. He glanced at the door and started to inch toward it. Just get out. The stink of something sweet and thick washed over him.

"Who are you?" Huckabee cried to the dark, inching ever closer to freedom.

Something in the shadow moved. Huckabee bounded for the door. His hand reached the knob, but something large and hot took hold of his wrist. It spun him around and Huckabee came face to face with Hannity's killer. Its strength terrified him, but what he saw in its face was even more unimaginably horrible. Huckabee saw the boy he killed in the face of this monster before him. The familiar face on the body of this hideous thing forced Huckabee to flood his overalls.

"You..." he whispered.

John Turner -- or this creature that looked a hell of a lot like John Turner -- smiled. He smelled of rum. His skin was waxy. His ruined white dress shirt revealed black wire stitches underneath, covering most of his flesh. He pulsed with power, an energy Huckabee had never felt before -- altogether robust, dominant, commanding, and formidable. His odor was sweet yet somehow rotting, perhaps reeking of divine retribution. It held Huckabee firm.

"How are you... here?" Huckabee asked.

"Hush, now," the creature cooed. "This is for your own good."

Huckabee panicked. "What -- what are you going to do?"

The creature took hold of Huckabee's other arm and held him in a tight vise. Slowly, Huckabee could feel his limbs being tugged tighter and tighter.

"Oh— Jesus, please! No-- NO!" he screamed.

The creature yanked, severing Huckabee's arm as easily as pulling a wing from a boiled chicken. Blood gushed out in lapping waves of gore. It spilled on the oil-stained floor, pooling together in a strange crimson-brown nightmarish river toward the drain. Huckabee felt flushed and nauseous as a black curtain fell over him. He gritted his teeth, suddenly awake again, as the creature began pull on his remaining limb.

"Don't-- please... mercy..." Huckabee wheezed. His strength had left him, burned away by the lightning throb of pain coursing throughout his body from his mangled flesh.

"I wish this could be different," mocked the creature, "but it has to be this way." It smiled. Giving a final jerk, it removed Huckabee's remaining arm as easily as the first.

The bone cracked with a sound eerily similar to heavy logs collapsing under the heat of a brush fire.

Huckabee shrieked in a shrill waning howl. The black curtain was again falling back over him. He was hardly aware of the creature poising for another strike. Its arm moved down on him, its hand plunging deep into his gut. Huckabee felt the impact with terrifying disinterest. He looked down. He's inside me, Huckabee thought dimly. With another jerk, he watched in faded horror as the creature pulled out chunks of long, wet bits of flesh. What Huckabee would have called his inner-tubing -- it spilled on the garage cement floor. The creature plunged again and dug out more of the fat man's intestines. Huckabee could do nothing. He was paralyzed, feeling the cold shiver of death coming upon him. Inside the dark curtain, there were eyes watching him, waiting to devour his soul.

Chapter 7
Last Man Standing

O'Reilly pulled out of the Leflore Sheriff's Station on burning tires, nearly plowing into an elderly woman wearing her Sunday best on her way toward Greenwood First Baptist Church. He didn't bother checking his rearview to see if she was alright. He just kept going. Faster and faster down Main Street. O'Reilly needed to find Billy -- Jesus, let him be okay. Don't let him be dead too. A few minutes before, O'Reilly was at the station; called in on his day off. The Sheriff wouldn't tell him why.

When he arrived, they took him in the office; closed the door, shut the blinds, asked if he had heard or seen anyone suspicious lurking around -- watching him. "No. Why? What's going on?" O'Reilly had asked. And then they told him. His partner, Hannity, was found decapitated in the men's room at Rooster's. Some fellow on a hot date went to take a piss and found him there. Head was missing, but the bartender ID'd the body.

And then they told him about Huckabee; knew they were old friends. Played High School football together, for Christ's sake! They showed him the gruesome Weegee photos of Huckabee's garage. Even in the black and white, the carnage was incredibly heinous. Huckabee's head was also missing. One of the photos showed a name written in -- what O'Reilly assumed to be -- blood across the hood of Huckabee's truck. John Turner lives. And then they asked if he knew anything about the murders, about this missing boy from North Carolina. O'Reilly stuffed everything inside, locked it tight, and lied out his ass.

The Sheriff and the detectives seemed to have bought it. They figured it was probably a retaliatory crime against the two men. Hannity was a known hot head. And Huckabee -- well, let's just say his ancestry ran deep in bigotry. There had been some talk; the sharecroppers were taking action into their own hands. Talk of militantism. Talk of communism. They assumed the worst, but O'Reilly knew better. This wasn't some act of political unrest. This was plain and simple revenge. Somehow, someone found out about the Turner kid. And now that someone was taking them out, one by one.

Got to find Billy.

O'Reilly slammed his patrol car haphazardly into park in front of the Piggly Wiggly off Roane Avenue. He ran toward the large double doors, nearly falling on his face on the way in as the glass automatically opened when his foot hit the mat. O'Reilly remembered, with disgust, how Piggly Wiggly was the only store in town with those new contraptions. The lights inside glowed bright and cold. Locals gathered near the front registers glanced at him with mild disinterest as they waited in line. O'Reilly ignored the random

'Hello, deputy,' and ran towards the manager's office in the back. It was midafternoon. Billy should be just about getting off. Billy had always worked the AM shift, for as long as O'Reilly could remember. Billy worked the mornings because that was when they did their drops at the bank. There was some girl who worked at the Greenwood Planters Bank and Trust. Shelly -- wasn't it? I believe so. Rusty's daughter -- preacher's girl. Way out of Billy-Boy's league, but damn if he didn't try.

The Managers office door was closed, but O'Reilly could see light pouring through the bottom crevasse. It was a good sign. O'Reilly rapped on the door, rattled it against its hinges. He waited. Metal springs whined inside. The sound of slow lazy footsteps.

Not Billy.

The door flung open.

"Deputy O'Reilly, what can I do for you?" beamed Clyde Dalton, Billy's father. Sweat beaded along his meaty forehead. His face looked wet and greasy. He breathed laboriously through his short pudgy nose. His corpulent belly heaved with each inhalation. Clyde reminded O'Reilly so much of the cartoon pig depicted on the very store he owned and operated.

"Mr. Dalton—thought Billy would be working. Did he get off early?"

"Billy? No, he called in sick this morning. I had to rush out of bed and get here to open the doors before the blue-haired mafia tore it down! Crazy fools," Clyde laughed.

"He called in sick? This morning?" asked O'Reilly, troubled.

"Yes, sir. So what's this all about?"

God…is he?

"No-- just need to see him is all." O'Reilly locked it

up; face frozen with mock disinterest.

"Well— he should be home. Said he was coming down with something. Fever and the runs and all that mess. Sure sounded pitiful on the phone." Clyde looked away, lost deep in his own thought.

"Pitiful? How so?" asked O'Reilly.

"Dunno... just sad, I guess. Depressed maybe."

"Depressed?"

"Sounded like it. So, you gonna tell me what this is all about or what?"

"Like I said, it's nothing to worry about."

"Look, Goddamn it, he's my son, Bill. If he's in trouble, I want to know."

"No trouble."

Jesus...

Clyde said nothing more. Simply grunted, eyeing O'Reilly suspiciously. When the officer said goodbye, Clyde watched him disappear behind a rack of Post's Sugar Krinkles (the one with the demonic clown eyes) and then went back into his office, dialing Billy's house. The ringer rang several times. Finally, Clyde hung up. He thought about driving out there, checking in on his son, but then Fred Mathers busted in, screaming about one of the commodes flooding a river of shit in the men's room, and forgot all about it.

Chapter 8
Low in the Grave

The muted orange-red sunset seemed bleak by the stark contrast of the dark storm raging inside O'Reilly. He hummed some unknown tune, strumming his thumbs along the steering wheel. He'd killed the CB, allowing some peace and quiet to give him some time to think things though. But what was there left to think? Who could it be? How did they find out? Where are they now? Is Billy still alive? Or did they get him too? The dismal thoughts inked and clouded together. Nothing was in focus as O'Reilly yanked his patrol car on to Walton Avenue and skidded in front of the one-bed, one-bath matchbox Billy Dalton called home.

There was no car in the dirt driveway; Billy didn't own a car. He rode a bicycle to work every day. And for Klan meetings, Huckabee always gave him a ride in that 1940 pickup of his -- now smeared with black blood in the photograph O'Reilly was shown at the station. O'Reilly wandered up toward the house. Billy's home had never been pristine. The paint, even since its birth, had an off-color about it; faded, but not quite yellow. A garden of weeds barricaded the front porch. O'Reilly leaped over it, nearly slipping off the cement steps and busting his ass in the grass. Gaining his footing, O'Reilly went to pound on the door and found it ajar. Music was seeping through the crack. Some old-timey church song from the gospel station Billy was known for enjoying.

Low in the grave he lay…

Waiting the coming day…

Vainly they watch his bed…

"Billy—" O'Reilly called.

Vainly they seal the dead…

Death cannot keep its prey…

He tore the bars away…

"Billy? Come on, man!"

Up from the grave he arose…

…with a mighty triumph o'er his foes.

He arose!

He arose!

"Billy, answer me, damnit?"

Hallelujah! He arose!

O'Reilly stilled the cold panic rushing over him. He took hold of his service revolver and slowly pushed the door open. The living room was bare, except for an old, beaten sofa with stuffing showing through gashes and marks. Nothing out of the ordinary. His eyes darted to every stained corner; searching, readied. O'Reilly moved into the narrow hallway to Billy's bedroom. The door was closed.

"Billy?" O'Reilly knocked.

No answer.

"I'm coming in, Billy. You better be decent." O'Reilly joked but found little humor in what he said. His tone was grave and shallow. He led with the gun, pushing the door open with the barrel. Billy's dead eyes glared back at him from the other side.

"Jesus—" O'Reilly screamed. He jumped back into the hallway, rapping his head against the wall. He stared in horrified fascination at the last of his friends swinging from a cheap noose made of coarse manila rope.

His feet dangled lifelessly, grazing the soiled carpet with the toes of his shoe. Billy's face was swollen and blue, his lips pursed and purple, his tongue ballooned. His eyes looked like glass with a white film coating. His crouch was wet with what O'Reilly assumed was urine. He'd seen the same thing before, from time to time; being a deputy, you were bound to come across a dead body from time to time. Many had defecated. Jim Nilles, the County Coroner, told him once that it was the natural process when the body's muscles relax and then -- well, 'wham-bam-thank-you-ma'am,' he had said. O'Reilly held his own theory on the matter. As a firm believer in the good book, Bill O'Reilly fancied that when people, especially the rot of society, mess themselves, it's because they got a good glimpse of hell before being dragged off.

O'Reilly shivered.

Is that where Billy is now? he wondered. Jesus H. Christ!

He fled the house; jumped into his patrol car and pealed back out down Walton Avenue, and hung a right on Route 77. The evening sun had now fully disappeared among the lush green and darkening landscape. The faces of his friends flashed through his mind in sharp bolts. His belly boiled. His chest heaved in frantic bursts of breath.

"I'll kill 'em!" O'Reilly bellowed. Hot tears poured.

"I'll kill 'em all!" he cried again, punching the steering wheel.

But you gotta find them first, you iggit.

--what do you have in mind?

You're the last one, right?

--Yes.

They'll be coming for you next.

--Then I'll be ready.

You can bet the farm on that.

Just as O'Reilly was formulating a plan, a great and terrible shadow covered the road. He swerved to miss it, barreling the patrol car onto an unknown, unnamed red clay road. He hit a pot hole in the process, knocking his head against the roof.

"Shit-- shit, what the hell was that?" O'Reilly hissed, grinding his teeth.

Through the dark, O'Reilly sped down the country road. Mile by mile, the forest that occupied each side of the road became a strange and familiar sight. I've been here -- before, haven't I? he wondered. The recollection came on him suddenly, pursued by cheap denial. No! No! It can't be... it's just not possible. He's dead, Goddamnit. We put him in the grave. Ashes to ashes, dust to dust, and all that bullshit.

But Hannity and Huckabee and Billy-boy...

How?

Does it matter? They're dead. You're next.

An otherworldly mist drifted across the road. Thick as syrup, it clouded the yellow beams of his patrol car. O'Reilly padded his pockets, wishing to God he'd smoked. Leaning into the steering wheel, O'Reilly squinted against the growing macabre haze. A familiar shadow grew out from the dense dark fog several yards ahead.

"You son of a bitch! You want me? Well, you fucking got me," O'Reilly spat. He slammed his foot down on the accelerator. The patrol car hiccupped, galloping forward. The engine wailed. He squeezed tight on the steering wheel. Held his breath. Closer, and closer toward the gloom.

The dark shape did not move. O'Reilly hit it full tilt. The patrol car jerked violently as if running over some heavy, ruined carcass. A shadowed silhouette rolled upward. The front windshield flowered. He stared into the rearview, waiting for—whatever it was, to inevitably roll off the back.

But nothing came.

"Where the hell did it go?" he whispered, watching, waiting.

Metallic thunder roared above as the creature pounded the roof of the patrol car. Large and jagged indents protruded inside. One nicked O'Reilly's skull. Hysterical, he swerved the car back and forth on the road, desperately trying to unhinge the thing from his roof. Shit-- come on! Shit. Damn-- get the hell off my car! Come on -- come on!

The patrol car skidded too close to the bank. The tires slipped and skirted down the grassy embankment. The passenger side crashed into an adjacent oak. O'Reilly knocked his head against the passenger door. Hot white stars filled his eyes. His ears rang church bells. He could taste iron in his throat. Dismayed, he crawled out of the driver's side door and into the drifting, cold mirk. With dopey hands, O'Reilly reached for his revolver and aimed it at the roof. The dark monstrous form towered above him. O'Reilly fired.

The creature grunted with each round but did not move. He -- it -- whatever -- stood motionless. Waiting.

"What the hell are you?" O'Reilly screamed.

It laughed. The son of a bitch laughed.

Terrified, O'Reilly rolled over and heaved himself into a sprint -- charging through the other side of the woods heedlessly, without direction. He tripped over a gnarled root protruding from the ground. Rolling in the dirt, O'Reilly lost all sense of where he was. His knee throbbed. Heavy footsteps sounded -- somewhere beyond. He hoisted himself back up and limped toward a thicket of red berried thorn bushes. Craning his neck, he could see the shape in the dark coming closer. O'Reilly pushed through. Sharp jagged hooks took hold of his flesh, ripping, scraping.

Warmth trickled down his arms, his face, his hands, 'til finally he emerged into a clearing. A faint yellow glow pierced the haze of night. Not waiting to see -- or hear -- where the creature was, he lurched toward the light. Out of the fog came an enormous willow tree. The old deputy looked at it dumbly. This isn't -- the same -- no, can't be-- With each painful step, his pace quickened. Soon, he was at a full trot toward the massive sentinel in the woods, and in his haste, did not see the unearthed grave before him.

O'Reilly yelped as his feet came out from under him. He tumbled and fell for what seemed like ages. His back hit something hard -- wood perhaps, deep inside the large, cruel, sunken earthly mound. His head thumped the backboard. Blinded, he screamed for help. The soft yellow glow steadily brightened. Like a curtain, the night was pulled back. Suddenly, there were dozens of swinging lanterns held in hands of strangers dressed in white pants and dresses, looming above. The men were shirtless; strange drawings or symbols -- perhaps made in what looked like white chalk -- covered their bare dark skin. The women had faces of similar paint in the same queer design.

And there was another woman who stood out among the rest, dressed in a long flowing crown of dark, elongated feathers -- of some creature O'Reilly could not place -- reaching all the way past her hips. She wore the same bone necklace as the others, the same chalk-white design on the flesh of her exposed midnight skin. She stood at the center, just above his head. In her hand, she held a small lamb. Its feet bound with rough manila rope. Its small muffled bleat pierced the silence.

"What— what do you want?" stammered O'Reilly.

He waited for an answer, but none came. His eyes darted to each man and woman; darting into eyes of coal. Unmoving, unblinking. Jesus— what is this? What am I in? O'Reilly felt around. The hard wood and the loose dirt walls above him triggered an unsettling certainty. He was lying in a grave. Is this -- no -- NO!

"Let me out -- let me out!" he screamed.

Somewhere above, music -- tribal and vibrant -- began to play. The watchers that stood above him began to dance -- all but for the woman who held the bleating lamb. Their movements were fluid and intoxicating. Each stomp in the dirt resounded with the bang of a drum. Many were yelping frantically, shouting in a language Bill O'Reilly did not understand.

"Lanmò -- Lanmò," the dancers howled over and over.

O'Reilly began to thrash about, fighting to gain some footing in the makeshift coffin. But he had seemed to have lost all strength. Trying to catch his breath, he listened to the growing madness above, and the heavy and horrifyingly familiar sound of footsteps approaching the crowd. Petrified, he listened. Slowly, the dancers parted and made way for the mountainous thing that had hunted him through the woods. Despite its hideous face, O'Reilly recognized it as the boy he and his friends had murdered; the colored fellow from CORE -- John Turner. His skin was dark and sinister in the glow of the lamps. Black wire stitched along his joints and yellowed patches of flesh. His eyes bore down into the pit; down deep inside O'Reilly himself. Eyes filled with pain, malice and rage and judgment. His body was misshapen -- not as O'Reilly had remembered it. This thing that was perhaps John once was now larger. Monstrous, and appalling. They -- O'Reilly and Hannity and Huckabee and Billy -- had maimed him good. Whatever John's face was hemmed, it could not be from his body, but perhaps borrowed from someone else's.

O'Reilly lurched, spilling stomach acid on his sweat-matted shirt. "You—" he gasped. His throat stung with bile. "How are you alive? How is this possible?"

"You made it possible," said the woman, the priestess above him.

"Me?" whimpered O'Reilly.

"Your hate gave him life," she said.

"We didn't—" O'Reilly stammered.

"You think no one saw you pull the trigger? You thought there wouldn't be consequence? You believed you could murder a boy and not pay? To not suffer as he suffered; as we suffered?" asked the woman.

"We didn't mean—" begged O'Reilly.

"You did," said John.

O'Reilly noticed for the first time the cloth sack held in his hands; the fat bottom swollen in ghastly dark red stains.

The dancers around them continued with their macabre music and feverish dance as the creature -- as John -- reached into the bag and pulled out Hannity's bloated blue head.

"JESUS—" O'Reilly yelped.

The creature threw it in the grave with O'Reilly. Next, he pulled Huckabee's head from the bag and tossed it in the pine box coffin. Lastly, John held out Billy's head, still fresh but starting to yellow, and then he tossed it in with O'Reilly.

O'Reilly shut tight his eyes.

Just a dream— nightmare, nothing more. This can't be real -- can't be. Wake up, Bill -- wake up!

"LOOK AT ME!" the creature, John Turner, bellowed.

Terrified, O'Reilly obeyed.

John heaved his shoulder with each monstrous breath. His eyes burned into O'Reilly. He pitched the now empty sack to the ground, but he said nothing. Suddenly, the lamb cried out, gurgling, and then was silenced. Warm droplets fell on O'Reilly's face. He reached up with his hand and smeared its oily texture. Pulling back, he looked in horror at his crimson muddied hands. And then a flood fell over him -- dark red and thick. He choked on the deluge as it washed over his face. It tasted of iron and salt. The dance and deep moans above steadily increased in fever. The drums pounded malignantly. O'Reilly was intoxicated by the rhythmic chant; horrified by his doomed fate.

Dizzy, he again tried to plead for his life, but could not. His voice was gone. His body solidified. All but for his eyes -- he could not shut them. He watched in terror as the coffer lid was lowered into the grave -- his grave. Darkness came over him. The sounds above muffled through the pine box. The sound of rain began to pound unsteadily on the box. It came in slow spurts, proceeded with metallic crunching.

They're— they're— no, NO! You can't -- no, please God, no -- STOP! He knew this was no rain, but dirt from the unearthed mound above. They were burying him alive.

"Al mekomo yavo veshalom," said John, shoveling another pile of dirt into the near full grave.

"Al mekomah tavo veshalom," said the priestess, tossing a handful of red clay dirt into the pit.

Somewhere, far across town, a mighty hymnal rose above a gathered mourning congregation. A speaker, young but worn, declared to the parishioners:

"I'm not here to do the traditional things most of us do at such a gathering… what I want to talk about right now is the living dead that we have right among our midst; not only in the state of Mississippi but throughout the nation. Those are the people who don't care, those who do care but don't have the guts enough to stand up for it, and those people who are busy up in Washington and in other places, using my freedom and my life to play politics with."

WHEN THE PIN
HITS THE SHELL
KIT POWER

12

Time slows. When you're up against it. When it's you or
him. When it's just the hot wind rattling grit off the wall
of the tavern. Just a stray crow, calling out the dead. Just a
mud track. Just ten paces. Just the echoes of a bell counting
backwards from twelve. Just…

11

Dan is five. Playing in the dry earth outside his front porch.
Muddy face. Sackcloth, sharecropper overalls. Dirt poor. Not
a metaphor.

See him. Crude wooden horse in hand. He's running
it about a soil track he's scraped with his hands; the flaky
earth is gritted up under his fingernails. Black, filthy. He
runs the horse around, making clip-clop noises. Making the
horse jump invisible gates, yelling "Ye-haw!" when he does
it. Imagining jumping the gate of his homestead on a horse,

Mom hanging on behind. Riding out and across the endless prairie to become cowboy outlaws, and never taking no shit from no one.

Behind him, behind the crude wooden door to his home, he hears his father yelling. Angry. Cussing. Hears Mom yell back. Dad roars. Mom screams. The horse jumps. A chair falls. Flesh collides. His mother's scream cuts out. Another smack, meaty. His mother makes a high, gasping sob. She mumbles. Begs. Smack. Smack. Smack. Smack.

She stops begging.

The horse jumps.

Escape.

10

…the hard calibre in your hand. This is all there is.

The pressure of your trigger finger.

Time slows. Time crawls. Time seems almost to stop. Your finger pulls the trigger, pulls the hammer back, and it takes…

9

"I've got the money."

The girl looks at him. Squinty eyed. Piggy nose, wrinkled. Sizing him up. Unimpressed. Whore's rouge already smeared at eleven A.M. Dan is big for twelve, but his face is still young, boyish. She's unimpressed.

He holds up the half dollar. Her face shifts. Goes hard, then soft.

"Well, why didn't you say so? C'mon up, handsome." She takes his hand, leads him through the dark bar to the stairs. He's still half-blind, moving from the glaring sun to the dark inside, and stumbles on the first step.

"All right, young fellar, don't break yer neck before you break yer cherry!"

There's a roar of male laughter at this from the early booze-hounds. Dan scowls over at the bartender, hating. The 'tender lifts his hands -- I surrender.

"No offence meant, son. Enjoy Tallulah. She's a wild one."

Dan nods, scowl down to a smoulder. The girl tugs his arm once, gently. He follows her up. Wooden steps. Rough beams. Splintery floor. Through a thick door.

Small room, mostly filled with a double bed. Blinds drawn. Wall lanterns, belching out oily, dirty light and foul tasting smoke.

She walks to the bed. Drops her dress. It falls from her like rain. He takes in a sharp breath. She bends to move the sheets back. He stares at her ass. His mouth fills with saliva. His hands tremble.

She turns. Her face looks soft, but hard underneath. He doesn't see. He's staring at her breasts. Watching them rise and fall with her breathing. There's a faint sheen of perspiration. Her nipples are hard. His Johnson is throbbing, painful in his pants.

"Those four bits will get you a good time, cowboy." Her hands move to her nipples. Fingers squeeze. His whole body tightens, relaxes, tightens.

"But if you've got a buck, you can have me all day."

One hand strays down to the thatch of pubic hair. His eyes follow it, glued. She puts a finger either side, spreads herself.

It's a revelation. All at once, seems like, he understands what he has. How it works with what she has. How it fits. The knowledge is gunpowder. TNT.

Fire. He burns.

"What do you want, cowboy?"

His hand is shaking for real now. Reaches across his belt. Touches the knife there. He looks at her snatch, the first one he ever saw. Hand on the hilt. Remembering how it felt as the blade opened his father's throat. The blood. The surprised look on that bastard's face as he awoke, gushing red, dark. The way the look turned to anger. To fear. Then to nothing. He reaches past the blade, to the purse. Takes out another coin. Places it in his fist with the first. Throws them onto the bed.

"I want it all."

She smiles. It's not pretty.

8

…five years, seems like, to pull all the way back. The stretch is like salt taffy. It just gets longer, thinner. Never seems to break. The hammer goes back and back. The trigger goes back and back. Endless, feels like.

Finally,…

7

Dan looks up, and through the grim smear of his hangover sees the black smoke on the horizon. The still air holds the column in place. A thin dark tower stretching to heaven.

It takes him two hours to reach the source of the fire. The gritty, lukewarm water from his canteen helps with his throat, but does nothing for his pounding head. He crests a hill and takes the scene below.

Three wagons, on their sides. Wrecked and smouldering. Dan quick-counts fifteen bodies -- five men, three women, seven children. It's bloody. Severed limbs a speciality. Supposed to look like the savages did it, but Dan notes the dead horses. No red-skin would do that to healthy mounts.

So it's road agents.

Dan swings the rifle from his shoulder, drops from the saddle. Alert, nostrils flaring, hangover forgotten. A wolf with a scent he doesn't trust. Eyes scanning the surrounding high ground.

He contemplates going back over the hill, the way he came, but he's already halfway down. Too exposed. He heads for the ruins of the wagons instead, hoping for better cover there, pulling his horse along behind, eyes moving constantly. There're a couple of carrion birds circling, high and lazy, but otherwise it's quiet.

He hunkers down in the ashes of the nearest wagon. Notes the smashed open trunks, the looted packs. To his left, an old man, grey beard, lies in a pool of his own blood. The front of his dungarees are soaked dark red across his whole belly.

Wood cracks behind him, heat pop, and he spins on his heels, slips. His hand reaches for support, unthinking, and grabs a smouldering plank sticking out of the wreckage. The pain is immediate and intense. He yells a string of curses, snatching his hand back.

That's when he hears the cough behind him.

He flips back around, hurt hand forgotten, rifle coming up. Down the sight, he sees the old man, looking at him.

They stare at each other, in silence. The old man is breathing ragged, his face is white and slick with sweat. Dan's seen enough hurt people to be pretty sure that this guy has seen his last sunrise. Probably his last sunset too, come to that.

They look at each other some more, and then Dan

lowers the rifle slowly, feeling foolish.

"I... I'm not with them."

The old man nods, tries to talk, coughs instead, rattling deep, face creasing with agony as he does so. He waves Dan over instead. Dan shoulders the rifle and squat shuffles over.

Close up, Dan can smell the man is dying. The copper of blood, and the sharpness of his body letting go. The cough has died down but the old man looks to be burning up with pain. Dan thinks for a minute, then reaches for his pistol. Slowly, he places the barrel under the old man's chin. He's about to look away when the old man opens his eyes again, staring at Dan, blazing, and he shakes his head, once, firm.

Dan frowns.

"I can't help you, old man. You're bleeding out, and it's apt to be long and painful. I'm just trying to spare you..."

The old man waves his hand, dismissing. Dan trails off. Frowns some more.

Then the old man holds his hand out again, eyes never leaving Dan's.

"You... you wanna do it yourself?"

The old man pulls a face, which Dan reads as God save me from this fool, then holds his hand out again, fingers flat together, thumb out, palm towards Dan.

Dan nods, and takes the old man's hand, sitting down next to him as he does so. The old man grips his hand tight. A warrior's grasp. Dan grips back.

Slowly, so slowly, the sun rolls across the sky.

6

...you hear the trigger click. You feel it. It cuts across everything. The spring has released the hammer. The hammer doesn't move yet, but it will. It's inevitable, now. It's destined. It's physics, that's all.

Still, time is doing the taffy thing. You don't look down. You keep looking at the target. Aiming true. Just the same, you see…

5

Dan looks at the ugly bastard sitting across from him. Rotting teeth in a shit-eating grin. Week-old stubble. Shifty rat eyes. Grinning that idiot grin.

Dan looks down again at his hole card, sweating.

"I know you ain't got the straight."

Dan's eyes shift to the man's mouth, drawn by his words. That hateful, cocky grin. Christ, even his fucking voice grates. Whining. Weaselly. It makes Dan's knuckles itch.

"I. Know. You ain't. Got it." Pointing at himself, then Dan. Winking.

Dan looks over at the asshole's cards. Twos and six's, same as before.

The asshole cackles. Throws his head back. Dan sees himself sinking his blade into that scrawny neck. Sees the blood jet out. Hears that whiny voice gargle. It's so vivid it takes him a second to realise it didn't happen. That he's still sat down. Sweating. Stinking. Drunk.

The asshole starts humming Dixie. Off key. Dan tries to ignore him, looks back at the pile of chips. It's the hand of the evening. The one he's been waiting for, and now…

"No shame in folding, big man. No shame t'all."

Dan fucking glares at the asshole. The asshole shrugs big. Who, me?

"Take yer time, big man. Reckon we got all mornin'!"

He laughs at his own joke. The horse bray carries

spittle clear across the table. It covers the chips, stops just shy of Dan's cards.

The asshole scratches under his arms, oblivious. Dan can smell him from across the table. He smells like rancid cooze. Dan feels his stomach turn over. Sour, cheap whisky rises in his throat. He chokes it back.

"C'mon, dawn's rising and I need my beddy-bye! Shit or git off the pot, boy!"

Boy is what does it. Dan is seventeen now, with dark by-god whiskers on his fiz, a gun on his belt, next to the blade. He's taken lives with both, and no shit from anybody. No one calls him fucking boy.

"Call. Here's your fucken straight, asshole."

He flips over the Jack, drops it on top of his hand, grinning.

The asshole's smile falters. His eyes flick down. Dan feels his heart swell. It's savage. Primal. Got you, you bastard. The asshole reaches out a hand to his hole card.

"Guess you got me there after all, big guy."

He flips the card over, slowly.

Six.

Dan blinks. Hard. He feels sweat break out all over him. Feels his stomach lurch again, painfully.

"Well now, hold on here, what's this?"

Dan is still staring at the six. It's the corner of his eye that tells him the asshole is looking at him. His ears tell him he's grinning through his words. It all seems to Dan to be happening a long way away. He can barely hear it for the roaring in his ears.

"Holy sheeeet, looks like I got me a house! Wow! Talk about shit luck, big man! And here I thought you was bluffing me! Well, fuck your luck! Just fuck..."

The roaring drowns out everything. Dan looks up.

Things slow down. The asshole is still talking. Dan can see his jaw flapping, even as his face drops. So slow. Dan is up on his feet. The table flung to one side, chips bouncing everywhere. The asshole is still talking. Dan can't hear him. He reaches for his blade...

4

...that pin, a single jagged tooth. You see it, slicing the air as it falls. Springs pushing it forward. Relentless. Seems like you can hear it cutting the air. Seems like your target can hear it too. It's doom, sure and certain. Righteous. You have him dead centre of your sight, and...

3

Dan's about to take his first whisky of the day when it happens. The glass is halfway to his pursed lips. He's already tasting it. Already thinking about the next one. About getting drunk, getting some cheap pussy, getting the dust of the trail out of his throat and eyes and mind.

It's a good hard kick to his barstool. It does the job. Whisky down his shirt. Over his beard. Everywhere but his mouth. Shot glass collides with his tooth.

Dan takes a breath. In and out. The bar is suddenly quiet. Graveyard. Dan rises, pushing the stool back. Turns.

It's a portly gentleman. Handle bar moustache. Average, going on short. Smart suit, no badge. No badge is good. Dan can kill him and maybe not even have to leave town after. Can stay and get some pussy, anyway.

He's gonna want some.

The gent is eyeballin him. He's packing heat but hasn't drawn. He looks a little flushed. Like he's realised maybe he's bitten off more than he can chew. He ain't gonna back down though, thinks Dan. That much is clear.

Good.

"Mister, you made me spill my drink."

"Reckon I did."

His voice is high. Mushy. He's got a pretty good chew on. Dan feels himself coming alive. Lighting up like fireworks on the 4th. The way he does only when there's killin' to be done. Or the fucking that follows killing.

"You goin' to 'pologise?"

"Nope."

They stand. Eyeballin. Dan feels his head starting to throb. The world dropping away.

The stranger works his mouth. Spits. The dark jet coats Dan's boot.

"Alright, boys, take 'er outside. Don't want no killin' in here."

The barman's voice is calm. Bored, even. Dan sees his hands stray under the bar. Eyes darting between them. Casual, but wired.

Dan turns back to the stranger. Nods. The stranger nods back. They leave the bar, side by side. Walk out into the street.

2

…the pin bisects the air. Splitting off the living from the damned. It's a clean cut. It punctures the metal of the shell. Stabs it. There's fire. An explosion. Gunsmoke rises. There's a flash.

You feel a hard punch to your chest. Then you hear the bang.

The strength leaves your legs. You tumble into the dust.

1

Dan's breath is ragged. He can taste blood. His chest is whistling with each breath. Losing air to the hole in his lung. Drowning. At least it doesn't hurt much.

The stranger walks over to him. Dan hears him holster his iron. The face comes into view. The stranger kneels beside Dan. His eyes. Dan sees now what he'd missed in the bar.

The stranger offers his paw. Dan reaches, his own arm lead heavy. He makes it. The stranger's hand is warm.

A warrior's grip.

Dan holds tight.

HAND JOB ITALIANO
D.K. RYAN

Fatima Santan had moved from her native Italy for a better life in the United Kingdom, believing it to be a more stable choice for financial freedom. Stumpy in stature, with an awkward limp, and the carrier of an ugly hairy wart underneath her left nostril… it had done nothing to deter her from pursuing a lifelong dream to become the greatest hand model the world had ever seen.

She wasn't a fool, and knew that first impressions were, more than not, a driving factor in a company's hiring protocol -- whether that person could do the job or not. Many times back home, her chances had been dashed by bigger tits, or a bigger arse on slags Fatima wouldn't put in charge of making tea. But that was all in the past. England was going to be different. She could feel it.

Her morning had started in a greasy spoon, circling local agents from the classifieds of a day-old free paper. Fame was her ultimate intention, and starring in an advert with Lily Patel -- a recently famous swimwear model -- using the great Fatima's hands to pick up a glass of Johnny Walker was something to aim for.

Back home, after managing to secure a small role in a county-wide foot spa promotion (not her first choice), the experience was one that didn't end well; it was something she still suffered from, periodically, screaming at night until awake. But she had to start somewhere, and what caught her eye in the midst of tea-stained black and white words could be the first path on her road to stardom.

WANTED:

AN EXCITING OPPORTUNITY HAS OPENED UP FOR THE RIGHT PERSON TO AID US IN THE MAKING OF AN UPCOMING ADVERT FOR WORMING TABLETS.

THE SUCCESSFUL APPLICANT MUST BE AVAILABLE TO WORK THIS COMING WEEKEND, 22/4.

THE ONLY OTHER REQUIREMENT: PERFECTLY MANICURED HANDS.

THOSE INTERESTED ARE URGED TO CALL, DEREK ON THE FOLLOWING NUMBER...

Fatima swallowed her yolky bread, the hair from her wart brushing the back of her hand as she wiped her mouth.

A mobile phone was still on her to do list, but thankfully an old red box was situated on the next corner. She grabbed her bag, rummaging around for loose change, and made her way into the cold and a hopeful career in the hand business.

Derek Swanner was already in the hand business, and had

been for more years than he cared to remember.

It had started after a failed first date; the girl, Tracey, had linked her fingers through his, and that gesture alone was enough to make him reach a full erection and complete an ejaculation, all within the space of thirty-eight seconds. After that moment, he was hooked, and it became his life's work.

Today he was frustrated. The morning had started with such promise and his ad had brought in several potential prospects for his worming advert; but none had what he liked, and that was... FEELING. He studied the four sets in front of him; all clean -- nails perfect and free of visible biting.

On any other day, the sight would have him salivating, but unfortunately, the missing ingredient was cause for frustration. Set one had a skin tone that was too pale, like the owner had spent too much time out of direct sunlight. She could have actually lived in the dark for all he knew, but it was something that would have to remain a mystery.

Set two was from a Jamaican woman, and as smooth and silky as they were, his advert was strictly white hands only. He loved the hands, but with the relative sameness of dog colours today, the hands would surely become lost to a great Bernard's dark coat, deeming the whole thing pointless.

As he perused pairs three and four (wondering if, in this day and age, people just didn't see an opportunity for stardom if it smacked them in the fucking head), the bell rang on his outer warehouse door. He looked up at the camera, which revealed a short, podgy-looking specimen with an ugly wart plastering her face. She was disgusting, of that there was no doubt, but poking out from the ends of her duffel coat... Though the camera projected only black and white images, Derek couldn't contain his excitement for whoever this grotesque, deformed tree trunk turned out to be. She had what had to be -- a pair of the most beautiful hands he had ever seen.

He glanced once again at the thirty-two fingers and eight thumbs; their sight already causing a lump of sick in the back of his throat.

With one big scoop, he brushed them off the table into a waiting dustbin. The bodies were still scattered over the floor and their blood covered a wide area. Luckily the room had a big lock—more than enough to keep the likes of his new visitor from discovering his secret. A small mirror sat above an out-of-place sink, and after spitting in his hands, using his smelly saliva to flatten his hair, he stood tall, put on his business face and moving to open the door.

Fatima stood looking back out to the street, using her cupped hands to blow slightly warmer air onto her cold fingers. She'd been cursing herself all the way from the café for not being more prepared -- in not thinking that gloves would be a good idea, considering the weather. She'd never hid the fact that her mind was a sieve, which rarely held information or logical thought for much longer than it took to eat a bar of Dairy Milk. A slight giggle creased her face and her forgetfulness was erased from her mind. All she knew was that the person behind the door held a key to the rest of her life; and the sooner Derek opened up, the sooner she could show him, despite her looks, how talented she actually was.

With an injected dose of enthusiasm, Derek swung open the door and had to use all of his deceptive skills to force a smile he hoped looked genuine. Standing a foot away, she looked worse than the camera had first suggested. He wondered if she'd ever had sex, but dismissed the thought as utterly fucking absurd.

He had to admit that, there and then, he was losing

control, and no words had even passed between them. Her wart couldn't be avoided and it's where his eyes landed, like she had this kind of invisible magnetic force, pulling his optic nerves toward certain death. The hairy disfigurement gained his attention for the slightest of seconds as her hand came up as a gesture to be shaken.

Derek liked to think he was a man of the world; someone who was looked up to in the wider community, and a man with a face to thwart any game of poker. But on seeing the delectable, delicate, sexy, most beautiful long fingers, he nearly passed out.

Grabbing himself before he fell, Derek could do nothing but apologise profusely, blaming a recent illness for his unsteadiness. What he did know, as she guided him inside, shutting the door behind them, was that this was what he'd been looking for. The hands holding his elbow were going to make him a very rich man indeed.

Fatima had been surprised at the lack of speech from her potential employer and his near collapse, but she could see how he looked at the hands. His dislike for her wart was also something that wasn't missed. Initial fears aside, she knew that her features had that effect, but also knew that the right decision had been made.

Derek Swanner was going to be instrumental in her dreams, and the not-too-distant future was going to hold only good things for the Great Fatima Santan.

"You'll have to excuse me," Derek said, awkwardly, "I was sure I'd completely recovered."

"Think nothing of it," Fatima replied. "Are you alright to walk on your own now?"

He could feel the first stirrings down below, but stood anyway, eager to know more about this woman before taking her hands.

"I should be fine, thank you. It's been a long day, and if I'm totally honest, quite a wasteful one. Come— let's see if we can warm this place up; then you can tell me all about yourself."

In the back of her mind, she'd known how the place would look, expected nothing more than to start at the bottom, but actually being here was something completely different. The dirt and its unkempt appearance should have caused her more concern, but an embarrassing barrage of desperation had blocked out all but bright lights and Lily Patel.

She detected a strange smell. Metallic— like when, as a child, she'd licked the end of a battery. But never having ventured to such places, she dismissed it as normal.

They passed through a crudely erected partition and into a large, bare room, where a low table and two chairs sat opposite to each other.

"Please," Derek motioned, "take a seat and I'll get us some drinks. Tea? Coffee? Something stronger, perhaps?"

"A glass of tap water will be fine if you have it, thank you."

Derek was aghast, "Tap water? Are you sure? I do have a can of extra strong stout if you're so inclined? A drink and meal in one, and it'll put hairs on your chest."

Fuck! He thought. If there was one thing he was trying to avoid, it was mentioning anything about hair. She had enough external growth on the wart for fucking Rapunzel to break out of her tower.

Slow and steady, Derek, slow and steady.

Fatima was finding it difficult to take the man seriously. To be fair, her dealings with the English had been limited to old episodes of Allo Allo and Eastenders, so her knowledge of proper etiquette was slim. And she wasn't sure if she was the brunt of some private joke.

Dismissing his manners, she accepted a Stout, which produced a sultry smile from the strange man; one that increased as she took a full swig, waiting a moment before swallowing the heavy liquid.

"Now... Fatima— from your phone call, you said that you'd recently landed in the UK from Italy. Things must have been bad over there. Tell me, what do you hope to get out of today's visit?"

"Well, Derek, it has to be said that things were not as they should be back home. But I've always wanted to see this wonderful country, and with nothing holding me there, I thought it'd be a splendid chance to not only visit, but work here as well."

It was stupid of him to offer her the Stout. He was at odds as to how he was going to slip her some of his white powder which would enable him to chop off those beautiful hands.

He did have one thing in his favour, and that was Fatima's failed attempt to hide her pleading words. He didn't doubt there were other places for her to visit, and he knew of plenty where she'd fit in to some underground operation, run by individuals far more sinister than he could ever be. Yes, he did chop off hands and dismember bodies, but some of the things he'd seen made him look like butter wouldn't melt.

He'd wait until she asked for the ladies' room, then make his move. He was in debt to some nasty bastards and the last thing he wanted was to star in his own video, so this time he was going to pull out all the charming stops and make the stumpy Fatima feel like a star.

The conversation touched on previous work life, with Derek doing most of the talking and Fatima explaining why she chose hands for a career. She told of how her looks weren't the best, to which Derek scoffed, telling her to "stop it," and for the most part, they were having a pleasant time.

It was only when Derek had also started on the Stout, and kept asking if she needed the toilet, that she became suspicious of something amiss, prompting her to pay more attention and if need be, finish what she'd come there to achieve ahead of time.

A failed gastric bypass, shortly after her seventh birthday, had done little to stem Fatima's Goliath consumption of food. Over the years, her weight had steadily increased, and due to her unfortunate height of four-foot ten, it brought nothing but constant misery. Now her bygone operation was paying for itself in the form of protection. No matter how hard she tried, her body failed to recognise the effects of alcohol or any other foreign body, such as, say, a potent concoction of sleeping pills and heroin.

Derek had managed after much trying to lure her to the bathroom, enabling him to seduce her drink with his magic potion. Thinking this would soon leave the ugly woman speechless, and incoherent to her surroundings, he'd drank a further four cans, knowing full well his days as a heavy drinker were long gone.

Fatima seized her chance. Rushing to the back room, left unlocked and full of bodies, she retrieved an axe and returned to where Derek lay, slumped in his stupor.

The time for niceties was over, and she brought the axe down hard into his face, producing a slurping squelch as she pulled it back out.

Next, she laid his arm out straight and brought the axe down once again, lopping off his right hand.

So far so good. The warehouse was perfectly situated, and Fatima concluded that its position directly across from

a small post office was paramount during its purchase.
Derek was in the business of supply and demand—the post
office serving him perfectly for his everyday packaging and
distributing needs. This was something of a miracle, for
Fatima's next job came in two stages — the second slightly
more difficult, and the short walk to send off her gift boxes
was a trip that required her complete attention.

Half an hour later, she was making that walk, trying her best
to look normal, but unable to hide the pasty, near-collapsing
look which covered her face. A cupboard had held all she
needed in the way of small boxes and declaration forms, and
with a hurried hand, she filled out the correct forms, making
sure to mark Derek's label 'fragile' and 'prosthetic,' while
stating its value as under ten pounds.

For a moment, she considered forgetting the whole
thing; forfeiting her life-long dream; but she'd come this far,
and dismissed her reluctance.

With a final look, she bit her lip and brought down
the axe, severing her own right hand. Quickly wrapping the
bleeding stump, quickly dropping it into a similar box, she
packed it and made her way to the post office.

One thing she did know was that soon, medical
attention would have to come her way, but not before making
the call. She'd held tightly to the number since leaving Italy,
and with trembling fingers -- not even knowing if the number
would work -- took Derek's phone, starting to press numbers.

Her wait was short, and the refined voice of a woman
answered,

"Hello."

"—erm, hello... it's me. I've done as you asked."

"Why, Fatima, how wonderful it is to hear from
you. It was only this morning over breakfast that your name

came up."

Back in England, Fatima's excitement at hearing the voice brought on an involuntary bout of urine leakage, and she pissed herself, feeling warm, yellow liquid dripping down her legs.

The refined lady picked up a small handbook which sat beside the phone before speaking again.

"So, Fatima, darling, if I'm hearing right, you've proven yourself and I'm now able to cross 'Shifty Cockney, Hand Dealer' from my list?"

A smile of achievement overcame her. "You are indeed."

The refined woman held her pencil at the ready, hovering over the next line of words that read 'Fat ugly Italian woman with a hairy wart'.

"I think, Fatima, it's now time to tell me if you've completed the next part of our business?"

An overwhelming sea of emotion gushed over the fat Italian woman sitting in a London warehouse, surrounded by bodies, her hand in a box over the road.

"I'm pleased to say that it has indeed been completed, and I even marked the boxes 'special delivery,' so you should have them in the next couple of days."

The refined lady looked towards the ceiling, relieved; another piece was nearly hers to keep.

"Fatima, you have no idea how that makes me feel, and I can honestly say, it's been a pleasure working with you. But... as with all things happy, they at some point have to come to an end. You know what needs to be done, so if you wouldn't mind..."

She did know; she'd known from the moment she came to this country; but as a consolation, her mother would be taken care of. The woman had promised her that. Placing

the phone at arm's length, she shouted her goodbye, then
pressed end. She held the axe handle between her wet legs
and, with all of her remaining strength, brought it up with
frightening speed, forcing it into the recesses of her brain.

Before Fatima went to the place all fat Italian women
with hairy warts went to, she was glad that her dream was
going to be fulfilled, and her hand would finally be starring in
an advert with the beautiful, recently famous Lily Patel.

High in the Mongolian mountains, behind the tall, fortified
walls of a sprawling castle, Lily Patel replaced the receiver,
overjoyed at her ability to manipulate. It had started many
years before, when at the age of ten, her life had been one
of shapeless prescription glasses and a mouth full of metal.
Fortunately, things changed and through puberty, her looks
improved slightly. The metal, piece by slow piece, began to
empty from her mouth. Though subtle, the changes ignited an
anger at those who'd made her suffer, and one by one, she'd
made them pay.

Her body was far from perfect, but it suited her
antagonists, as week by week she waited for them to fall
drunk from the doors of varying nightclubs, where, hidden
in the shadows, she would lure in a sultry voice, becoming a
vision from their wildest dreams.

To this day, scattered over the breadth of the United
Kingdom, were eighteen young men, once full of spunk, now
fully eunuch.

Her life had come full circle and she really didn't
need to work that hard to please a wanting public. Her face
appeared on every magazine, and an hour in her presence
cost more than most made in a year. All this was thanks to her
race-car driver husband, Angelo, who loved her with all his
bodily might. From the start, he'd accepted who she was, and

her tale of childhood only made his love for her grow.

A month ago, Angelo appeared with a scruffy young man who had been hitchhiking down a dark and lonely road. Obviously he'd gone to work on the nameless man, breaking both arms and one leg before handing the present over to his beautiful and sexy wife.

At first, Lily didn't know what to say. She stood with a look of thanks, and as Angelo threw him down, he gushed with ecstasy, bring out her book from his back pocket. They had fun during the night, with the man crying and pleading to be let go. The greatest thing about the Mongolian mountains was that noise rarely travelled, and as morning started to appear, Lily was overjoyed at the pointless struggles from her 'scruffy looking hitchhiker.'

She could hear faint sounds from the panic room -- a large, closed off area at the bottom of a curving marble staircase, where her loving husband was, at this very moment, torturing a young goat header he'd picked up the previous afternoon. Despite the weather, she was a pretty little thing, looking less than her twenty-four years; but they had a tendency to age rather quickly after an extensive stay in his company. Angelo usually spent a week with the women, but he was sure to be up soon to hear the news -- she'd managed to cross two more from her list.

Excitedly, she walked towards a set of huge double doors, carved in the shape of hands. A beautiful calligraphy sign sat above the entryway, stating she was entering the Hand Room.

Pushing them open, she breezed into a domed airy space, its walls completely covered in small polished wooded plaques, each with a mounted, single hand. Underneath each was an equally decorative description.

Lily took in her surroundings, happy with her

growing collection. She read one of the plaques: 'German cafe owner' -- a recent addition from Angelo's latest trip to Europe after taking pole position in a very competitive race. Another: 'shop worker from The Natural History Museum.' Angelo really was a gem.

Her revere was interrupted by a beep from the panic room door.

Knowing he wouldn't keep her waiting, she rushed out to meet him as he reached the top stair, and told him of her list. Smiling, he held out another to be crossed off. The hand was dainty and beautiful -- certainly not that of a goat herder. But she took the offering anyway, pleased that her wall was filling along with a diminishing list.

It was only now, through her excitement, she noticed the lack of colour on her husband's face. Before she knew what had happened, she found that he'd collapsed at her feet.

After the goat herder, he'd reached into his pocket, pulling out another offering -- another prize for the wall of his beloved. Angelo had given her the ultimate gift of love.

The man who had loved her from the start decided that his career was nothing compared to his unrelenting love. With a forced smile, he handed her his own hand.

She started to cry.

Looking down and showing slight concern for his shallow breathing, she hurried back to her room where with great care and respect, she attached it to its own carved plaque.

Lily was a happy woman. She stood back once more, admiring her new addition. Her body and mind was complete, and as long as her average looks kept the public bringing up her name in connection with a Nobel Peace Prize (which she doubted, but could hope), she would continue to live a charmed existence.

An excerpt from old underground swimwear model magazine sat in a frame on Lily's wall:

AN EXCITING OPPORTUNITY HAS OPENED UP FOR THE RIGHT WOMAN TO BECOME OUR NEXT FUTURE FACE IN SWIMWEAR. IT SHOULD BE NOTED THAT THOSE WHO WISH TO APPLY SHOULD BE FREE OF PREVIOUS EXPERIENCE AND WILLING TO DO WHATEVER IT TAKES TO REACH THE TOP OF THIS HIGHLY COMPETITIVE INDUSTRY.

A CURVY BODY WOULD BE ADVANTAGEOUS BUT IS NOT ESSENTIAL, AS TRAINING AND EATING TECHNIQUES ARE PROVIDED.

ANYONE INTERESTED IS URGED TO CALL THE FOLLOWING NUMBER, AS PLACES ARE LIMITED.

IN CONCLUSION: EACH APPLICANT MUST BRING ALONG A SMALL NOTEBOOK AND PENCIL. HB IS RECOMMENDED, BUT OTHER LEAD GRADES WILL BE TAKEN INTO CONSIDERATION ON THE DAY.

THOSE WHO REMEMBER THIS FINAL DETAIL WILL BE LOOKED UPON MORE FAVOURABLY.

WE HOPE TO HEAR FROM YOU SOON.

LONG HAUL
DAVID JAMES

His entire world was burning. The blackness stretched out
before him, but the creeping fire filling his body was slowly
turning everything on the periphery red. It felt as if his veins
were being pumped full of acid, burning through every artery
and capillary.

He opened his eyes.

Even filtered by the frosted glass a few centimetres
from the end of his nose, the weak artificial light hurt his eyes.
His body suddenly spasmed once... twice... twin shocks of
electricity adding insult to the injury of the arterial acid pulse.

Though his arms weren't bound, they felt heavy.
Fighting through the burning and the dense fog in his mind,
the thought occurred that he might be submerged. There
was viscous liquid all around him, clinging to his bare skin,
weighing down his shocked limbs.

The initial surge of panic at waking, submerged and
electro-shocked, subsided as he recognised the oxygen still

filling his lungs, feeding his tired brain. The breathing tube, he now realised he'd been crushing between his teeth, felt thick and uncomfortable further down his throat.

The searing pain, now flaring at the tips of his fingers, in his toes, stabbing at the pit of his groin, was all surely sending him mad. He groaned gutturally against the tube in his gullet. The pain wasn't flaming out to a crescendo -- no, it was a consistent, constant agony now finally filling his entire body. The pain was everywhere, coursing through every vein, singing through every nerve; no longer growing, nor receding.

He weakly raised an arm, noticing through the murky pickling liquor surrounding him an inked pattern snaking up around his elbow. There were thick tubes and coloured wires going in and out of his flesh, but it was the tattoo which disturbed him. It felt like someone else's limb. He didn't recognise the pattern nor the arm he was battling to raise against the opaque screen in front of him.

He let his focus drift. He didn't know who he was.

A mad rush of panic surged again up his spine. His heart beat loudly inside his head. How could he not know his own name? He wanted to scream -- primal, obscenities -- but the only thing keeping him from drowning in his own brine was the plastic tube stuck down his throat.

Then something moved. A dark shape shifted a few metres beyond the frosted front of his jar. He weakly pushed a balled-up fist against the glass, hoping to attract its attention. He tried rapping the glass again and the shape moved, growing in his vision, shifting closer.

A gloved hand struck flat on the outside of the glass, just a few millimetres in front of his nose making him twitch violently back in his tank. The hand wiped away a smear of condensation in a single jerked movement. Through the murky liquid swimming in front of his eyes, he could make out a figure, wrapped in dark clothes, but no features where the face and eyes should be.

He could also see other tanks behind it, presumably like the one he was suspended in. The closest was missing the glass at the front and he could make out another figure slumped forward, almost spilling out of it.

The gloved hand frantically wiped away more of the moisture on his own jar; the figure's shadow-wrapped face pressed up against the glass again and again after each swipe. He began struggling inside his liquid cage, trying to bring more force to bear from the inside, thrashing arm and legs. But his limbs, enfeebled as if in a dream, barely resonated against the glass.

Then the dark-clothed figure withdrew, moving away, out of sight to his side.

He felt rather than heard the blows of metal against metal from behind his left ear. The figure was trying to break into his jar, he realised, panicked. Mere seconds ago all he'd wanted to do was escape from this prison; now he prayed it would just hold against its attacker.

Again and again the blows rang out, amplified through the thick soup around him. Something metallic was striking the tank -- it rang in his ears. Then stopped, as quickly as it started.

He shifted his body around in the liquid, straining against the tubes and wires piercing different points on his flesh, sparking fresh ripples of pain. He couldn't see the figure. Maybe it had left him alone, maybe he had time to try and get out on his own.

Suddenly those twin shocks returned, coursing through his body, sending it once more into spasm.

As the red receded from the peripherals of his vision with the shock, leaving only the familiar burning agony inside his body, he saw the figure return into view. It seemed to look over at him for a second.

Did it nod? he thought. Did I imagine a barely perceptible movement of the head?

It put both its gloved hands beneath each arm of the slumped figure opposite his jar and lifted it forward. Only now did he see the jagged opening of that other tank. The glass had been shattered and the occupant was now being dragged across the ragged glass teeth around the opening. He could already see pools of blood forming beneath the opened jar. He couldn't tell if the body was moving, or even whether it was a man or a woman. It may already be dead, as though, in his muddied thoughts; that might excuse the rough way the body was being treated by the figure. He shook his head, trying to wake his dulling brain into life. He seemed to be drifting, his thoughts growing more distracted. There's something out there and we're not going to be friends, he said to himself. I need to get it together. To get out. I can figure out the rest later.

But who the fuck am I?

Out of the corner of his eye, he noticed a red glow, throbbing in and out of sight. He shifted his head around to look over his shoulder in the cramped confines of his jar. There was a slowly breathing red light on the outer side of his shell. That was when he noticed the stale taste of the tube in his mouth.

There was no more oxygen.

He looked around to see the figure holding up a hand, as if to wave goodbye, claim responsibility, or maybe merely apologise. It dragged the body out of sight, just leaving a wet, bloodied trail on the floor behind. His head felt lighter. The acid fire in his circulation seemed to be receding now. Or at least I'm getting used to it, he thought. I always did have a high pain threshold. And then there it was. He felt the corners of his mouth lift slightly around the useless tube still held between his teeth.

Jacob. That's it, he thought with satisfaction. My name's Jacob.

Jacob's eyelids slowly flickered close. The next round of shocks sent the muscles into spasm once more, but the eyes would no longer open.

This is always the worst bit; why do I do it to myself? Was his first resigned thought on regaining consciousness.

Neural conditioning stepped in, compartmentalising the worst of the pain seeping into his long-dormant arteries. Not for the first time, Conrad wondered why they always sparked you back into the land of the living as the plasma-synth was still being pumped back into your body.

It was like some sort of spiteful punishment just for the privilege of visiting the farthest reaches of the heavens, for leaving everyone else behind. Terrestrial engineers were always such arseholes. Still, it made him smile thinking whoever had designed and built these creaking old stasis pods were long since dead. Probably their children too, he thought, their old bones now many light years away.

Riding that first seething wave of agony was always the worst bit of coming out of a long sleep. The icy stasis fluid took its own sweet time draining out of the circulatory system, slowly making room for the sterile, warm, plasma-synth to filter back into the body. It was like the worst pins and needles sadistically amplified and seemingly eternal, ever growing in intensity and all through your body.

He felt around blindly for the emergency release valve, somewhere around his right hip, and pulled the lever down. The viscous liquid slowly oozed out of the metal grating below his feet as the tank's ceiling vent creaked open and recycled air flooded in. Jen-Hui was probably going to be pissed at having to clear the filthy, ancient gunk out of the waste dump below deck, but they weren't going to be using these pods again anytime soon.

The oxygen shut-off indicator flickered into life, breathing red. He reached up and eased the breathing tube out of his throat as soon as the liquid level dropped below his chin, retching a little as he did. Every trip, every uncomfortable wake-up call, that tube scratched the back of his throat and made Conrad sneeze. Twice. Every time. This time, the first came with such intensity it blew off his nose-clip.

He tapped restless fingers against the frosted glass on the front of his pod, waiting for the rest of the thick liquid to drain out before the catch released, freeing the door. He wiped a little of the quickly congealing gunk from his sodden skin, looking forward to putting some warm clothes on. Well, any clothes.

Haven't been warm in a long while, he thought absently to himself, suppressing a shiver.

Conrad cursed violently as his body was suddenly racked by two spasmodic pulses of energy. He gritted his teeth and kicked the door angrily through the slowly receding pool of liquid still draining through the bottom of his pod.

Always forget the fucking shocks, he cursed his sleep-addled brain.

Reaching up behind his head, he grasped a corded cable connected to a socket at the base of his neck. With still numbed fingers, he unscrewed the connector and slowly withdrew the six-inch needle nestling into his spine.

The muscle-shocks were a total anachronism. Conrad was sure his bio-augmentations meant stasis atrophy didn't really apply to his level. The pre-wake muscle conditioning routines were completely irrelevant for pretty much all but the oldest of the engineering and pilot teams. But institute rules and regs meant they all needed the spinal sockets to get insurance. And so the meds always gleefully plugged them in dirt-side.

The fuckers.

With a hiss of compressed gas and a creak of long-dormant mechanics, the door catch on the front of his pod released, finally popping the door. Without the slight tint of frosted condensation on the outside of the pod, the weak, artificial light of the stasis bay still felt harsh on his long-unused retinas.

Conrad Drexler pushed open the hatch and took his first wobbly steps onto the slightly warmed metallic floor. His first in decades.

First Engineer, Jen-Hui Tsai, and Software Tech, Will Morgan, were already suited up by the time Conrad staggered out of the shower room and into the kitchen.

Jen-Hui was small, and her slight build coupled with her short, dark hair gave her a certain boyish quality too; something the unflattering company jumpsuit did nothing to assuage. She grunted at him as he made his way to the empty chair. She was nursing a branded company cup with some thick black liquid in it that was not entirely unlike coffee.

If anything, Will was even more slight than Jen-Hui -- currently a worthwhile trait in spaceflight -- though he was almost twice her height -- which wasn't. He never looked particularly in control of his gangly limbs -- an experience to behold in zero-G, Conrad reminded himself. His almost equine face and skittish nature really worked well with the newborn foal aesthetic he was capable of pulling off so well.

Both may have already been in their suits, but neither looked much like being capable of getting down to work anytime soon. Jen-Hui's dark eyes were heavily bloodshot and Will was resting, face-down, on the kitchen table, cradling his head in his arms.

Calling the cramped communal space the 'kitchen' had become Will's standing joke. The rations and protein packs they subsisted on for the last weeks of their long journeys didn't need reheating, but Jen-Hui had jury-rigged a warming plate from one of the charging points anyway. It at least gave them the illusion of cooking. And if they could find a way to break into the primary crew's module -- and their 'secret' stash -- in the next few weeks, it might also yield actual tea.

The kitchen was their entire living quarters, about the size of a small public toilet with a similar bleachy/fecal odour. It linked up to the stasis chambers and the sealed primary, secondary, and tertiary quarters via the shower room between them. In one corner was a set of four bunks, recessed into the wall, and in the opposite corner a small table extruded from the same dirty off-white polycrete material the rest of the living quarters were fabricated from.

Conrad mumbled a greeting to the others, scratching at the irritated puncture holes left by the tubes, electrodes, and monitoring feeds he'd spent the last half hour extricating from his protesting body. Maybe he'd been wrong. Maybe pulling the waste line from inside his urethra was the worst bit. He could swear the fuckers barbed that shit.

Will slid a mug of something black across the yellowing table where the two engineers were already sitting. Conrad swung a leg over the bench, also extruded from the floor, and sat down. He raised a weary eyebrow at the mug, contemplating whether things were desperate enough to try Will's coffee-analogue.

"Heard a peep out of the cattle?" he asked, still rubbing at his wounds.

"Will thinks there might have been a problem with a couple of the stasis modules," said Jen-Hui, dubiously squeezing a little extra matter from the protein pack in her hand.

"What sort of problem? If it's a couple stasis modules, we could be looking at, what, fifty individual pods affected?" He didn't need to hear this first thing.

"Not sure," she shrugged noncommittally. "The oxygen levels have been spiking and there are some caution flags being queried by the cattle grid. Will's going to break the seal and check the diagnostics down there once we're in any way functional."

Nope.

There it was.

This was the worst bit.

Busted down to Q Crew; first to wake and first to have to deal with whatever shitstorm had happened during the sleeping bulk of the trip. As the golden boy Primary Pilot, all he'd had to do was wake up just before the final big braking burn, get out of his tank, swing the ship into parking orbit, and find someone to cook him breakfast. He pretty much got to sleep for the whole trip.

"Come get me when you decide to pop the seal and check it out, Will," he said, rising from the table and shakily wandering over to the bunks. "I'll get on and start my checks soon too. Promise."

Fuck, I'd happily take Tertiary Pilot, he thought. Just to not have to deal with whatever the hell was brewing down among the cattle.

"How are we looking, Connie?" chirped Jen-Hui over the comm's.

"Fine... Hughie," Conrad sneered back. "All systems are in the green; the engines are barely ticking over; we're slowing as calculated; and we're aiming right at Dulos. Barely any point waking me up, really."

The hauler's navigation computer had the necessary smarts to adjust their trajectory by small amounts during the long trip through deep space. Managing the gravity braking manoeuvre around the system's star, though, needed some human intervention to avoid plunging the multi-trillion cred ship into the heart of Dulos' Class M star. Of course, their sleeping cargo was even more valuable to the company men down on the sixth planet.

"I was just saying the same thing to Will..." Jen-Hui's reedy voice responded.

He silently raised a middle-finger to the comm's console. It still took a little getting used to being first on the cramped bridge; he was used to the noise of a busy command module. Working the graveyard shift meant dusting down the aging controls alone and just getting on with coaxing the necessary systems back into life after their own long sleep. He hated the quiet.

"We've cracked the seal, but the access hatch has been a bit of a cunt to open; Will's going to go check on our passengers."

"Fine," he replied absently. "Tell him to not to worry too much about the diagnostics. Everything's still sitting between normal tolerances from what I can see. A few spikes aren't going to matter a hell of a lot."

"Sure, just need him to get down there and tuck them back in... I'll let you know the score though. Signing off." The comm's interface clicked off.

Conrad turned his attention back to the maintenance console and brought the monitor back into life with a light touch on the screen. Ignoring the seemingly endless component checklist he was tasked with wading through, he jabbed a stubby finger at the panel and projected an exterior view onto the main view-screen at the front of the bridge. It was the only window-analogue in the whole craft, and having it to himself was the only privilege of an empty command module.

To some, there would be nothing to see -- just empty space with their destination, Dulos, barely registering as a nanopixel in the projected image. But Conrad was still as enchanted by the inky blackness as he had been as a student back on Galileo. He'd spend hours just staring out of the station's cupola, dreaming of the days he'd get out there to touch the stars. He was still enchanted by the cosmos... the actual day-to-day grind of being a company pilot? Less so. Some heavy-going stocktaking wasn't exactly why he'd spent all those years studying astro-navigation.

He pulled his eyes from the barely-moving galactic vista they were hurtling through and went back to counting down the long maintenance manifest list.

Conrad's tongue felt furry and his throat dry as he peeled his face from the now-blank console interface. At some point, the tedium and stasis lag had gotten the better of him and he'd blinked. For a couple of hours.

There was plenty of time to fudge the checks later. Besides, his stomach must have thought his throat had been cut; it was probably his rumbling gut which had woke him. He eased himself out of the seat, massaging his sleep-stiffened limbs and stumbled sleepily back into the kitchen. He was surprised to find it empty. He grabbed a mealpack from the store without looking and activated the heatpatch. With the packaged protein matter gently warming itself in his hand he pressed a finger against the comm's panel set in the wall.

"Jen?" he called into it. "Jen, what the fuck are you two up to?"

Nothing.

"Will?"

Are they fucking with me? he thought. Again he jabbed the comm's panel.

"Jen-Hui!"

He stalked out of the kitchen to check the shower and deep-sleep chambers but his eye, and mind, was caught by the freshly-unsealed maintenance hatch leading into the depths of the freight-stasis levels. He stopped in the short connecting corridor, facing the waist-level hatch.

Seriously? Freight-stasis? he thought with a little shudder.

Conrad had only been down there once before, on a previous run out to Arcturus. The dark, freezing cold space felt claustrophobic despite its endless corridors stretching far out of sight, giving him the screaming shits. Rows of tanks; the cattle, suspended in their own brine, reaching off into the distance... he shuddered again.

Will, though, found the place fascinating. He hadn't been surprised the skinny wretch had been so quick to break the seal and go check on the diagnostics array down there. It was back on the Arcturus run where the ship's angry Chief Office had sent Conrad down to drag the fucker back up. He'd found him cross-legged on the floor, just staring at one of them with his hand down his pants.

To be fair, the tank-girl had a certain charm suspended in her stock company travel vest and pants combo, but there was too much of the necro' about it for him. He knew they were still kind of alive, but everybody looks like a corpse in stasis, he thought. And besides, she had been heavily pregnant.

He grimaced and turned away from the hatch. He checked in the only other two cramped living spaces Jen-Hui and Will could possibly be hiding, all the time knowing deep in his gut he was wasting his time. He knew where they were, just not why the fuck they were both down there.

It's going to be stupid cold down there, thought Conrad as he pulled down the edges of his woollen sock cap down over his ears. He'd already picked up the gloves and company jacket, and was once more facing the hatch.

Entering the access code, he flushed the outside hatch and it slowly swung open to reveal the miniature airlock behind it. Climbing inside, he cursed his two colleagues for

the thousandth time through clenched teeth. With the hatch
shut behind him, Conrad entered the code into the outbound
lock and the secondary hatch hissed and creaked open, stiffly
swinging inwards.

As the automated door swung towards him, it drew
an uneven curve onto the deck of the cramped airlock space.
In crimson. Conrad started, pressing his back against the
exposed metal of the airlock's bulkhead on seeing the mess on
the other side of the door. There was a pulpy mass of flesh and
congealing blood caught on the hatch's fittings. The chewed-
up meat was flecked with ivory and interspersed with clumps
of jet-black hair. It clung to the back of the door, slowly,
thickly dripping down onto the floor.

His throat tightened and he had to fight his limbs,
mentally screaming at them to move. He edged around the
burgeoning red stain on the floor of the airlock and crawled
out, terrified of what he was going to see in the murky half-
light of the freight-stasis level.

But there was nothing but an abandoned crowbar
lying on the deck. Ahead of him, he could make out the
shapes of the closest tanks, but the weak light given off by
the auto-phosphorescent panels in the low ceiling made it
impossible to see more than ten rows into the distance. The
inconsistent light from the slowly swirling luminous matter
in the ceiling strips only lit his frosted breath and made the
shadows shift barely-perceptibly in his peripheral vision.

He picked up the crowbar. Having the weighty lump
of metal in his hand was vaguely reassuring. It seemed as
good a protection as he could have hoped for at that moment.

The bag 'n' tag bay was a few rows down to his
left. When the med crew was roused from their slumber in a
couple of weeks, they'd be down here cataloguing the cattle
that didn't make the long trip. For now though, it was just
him, a bunch of suspended stiffs, and fuck-knows what else.
His knuckles whitened as his grip tightened on the crowbar.

Fighting the gnawing sickness in the pit of his
stomach, he turned to follow the bulkhead around to the left.
Before he could take a single step, something heavy cracked
across the back of his head, sending him staggering to the
floor. The half-light seemed to flare for a second behind his
eyes, and then it all went black.

Your first few trips off-world as a pilot are generally
always in zero-G. The simulated gravity of the longer range
vessels, like the company haulers, was needed for the long
trips, but for the odd taxi ride between orbital platforms,
it was simply unnecessary. Despite his familiarity with
the sensations, it took Conrad's throbbing, buzzing head
the longest time to parse his body's orientation when
consciousness finally flowed back into it. He was upside down
and hanging by his feet.

That didn't help the pounding in his skull, or his
swimming vision, as the blood was falling down towards his
battered brain even in the half-G false gravity the company
craft generated throughout its interior.

He raised a hand, which had been dangling an inch
or so above the floor beneath him, and touched the back of
his head. It was wet and the merest touch blazed with pain.
The bile rose in his throat and he thought he might vomit.

His vision swam again, and when it slowly pulled back into focus, he saw the crumpled form of Jen-Hui slumped against the white wall of the med bay. Though he could only tell it was her because of the name-tagged jumpsuit she was still wearing. Despite the gore-splattered tag, Conrad could still make out the name. Identifying her any other way would need dental records. Half her head was compressed into a concave nightmare, and what remained of her face was simply a pulpy mess of featureless flesh and bone fragments.

This time he did vomit.

Groaning weakly, he tried to take in his surroundings. The med-bay was essentially just a small, sealed room, coated in the same sterile polycrete material as the living quarters, with a pair of examination tables in the middle and stained drainage points in the floor. This was where the unlucky cargo would end up if they didn't make it through the lottery of the colony transfer. The med crew was revived only a couple weeks before landfall and their only job was to audit the cattle which hadn't made the journey. They were only ever cursory autopsies; the sheer volume was the problem. They'd quickly be filed into the database, then finally into the lockers on the far wall for processing and evacuation.

But someone had been living here. There was clothing on the tables, looking like makeshift bedding, and some of the equipment had been altered. There was exposed wiring and jury-rigged electronics spilling over the counters and onto the med-bay floor. Despite his aching head, he tried to swing his hanging body around to get more of a view of his surroundings.

And found Will.

Like him, Will was hanging by his feet from the ceiling. A loop of material had been slung over a cabling duct in the roof and tied around their ankles. Will's hands were also tied behind his back, and it looked like he'd received the same welcome as Conrad. He saw blood drying around a wound at the back of his head, dying his blonde hair a matted black-red.

His blood suddenly froze as he heard footsteps. He reached out against the wall to his left to steady his movement. Then, letting his arms dangle to the floor again, he closed his eyes just as he heard the door creak open behind him. Soft footsteps shuffled across the med-bay floor. They stopped nearby. There was a wet thud, a pained grunt, and a faint metallic scrape.

"Fuck. No," the rasping, ragged voice was altered by pain, but still unmistakably Will's. "Don't do..."

The half-finished sentence was cut short by a wet schnick, the sound of metal grinding against bone, then punctuated by an ear-splitting, pig-like squeal. Conrad's eyes flicked open to see blood pooling beneath his head. He could feel Will's body thrashing against its binds through the shared beam they were both suspended from. The scream crumpled into a wet gurgle, but the thrashing was subsiding as Conrad was bodily spun around.

"Did you want to watch?" asked the hooded figure now grasping onto him.

Conrad could hear the smile through those callous words, but the face was shrouded in shadow and a filthy rag pulled up over his nose and mouth. The waning light of the med-bay barely reflected in the sunken pale eyes looking down at him. The figure was clothed head-to-toe in old, ragged, ill-fitting clothes. They were darkly stained, crusted with... Conrad didn't want to know what.

He could see Will's eyes were wild, like a dumb, stricken animal. His mouth has moving, though all that was coming out were pink-tainted bubbles. The initial gush of arterial blood which fountained from the ragged, second mouth opened at his throat had died down to a slowly pulsing trickle.

"Who...?" Conrad started to say.

"You've got to let the blood out first," came the figure's muffled voice, "...or the meat spoils. Sorry, I interrupted you. Rude... Who am I? Just one of the herd." The figure flung out an arm, gesturing in the vague direction of the stasis tanks.

"I was just telling your friend before you popped up," he said, bending down to look into the dying eyes of the gangly software technician. "I woke up a few years back and have just been twiddling my thumbs ever since..."

Conrad's mind was ablaze. He was used to the old stasis tanks fucking up and drowning the odd cattle-class colonist, but this was un-fucking-precedented. A good percentage of them died en route. The company never released the actual numbers; the LocalNet media would have a witch-hunt if they ever found out. But no one had ever gotten out of the tanks mid-journey.

The pain in his head was intense and his vision was still all kinds of fucked, but he had to do something. There must be some way to get away.

Whether he had any conscious awareness of it in his shutting-down, oxygen-starved brain or not, Will came to his aid. With the ragged figure still squatting before him, Will's body went into its final, muscle-constricting spasm. A

violent contortion twisted his body and his head smashed into
the hooded figure's face. It staggered backwards, trying to
stand, but stumbling as it straightened its knees. The stained,
saw-toothed surgical blade the figure had still been holding
clattered onto the floor as he fought for balance.

It was his only chance. Conrad pushed against the
wall, propelling himself towards the blade, just snatching it up
off the ground with the tips of his fingers. With a strength he
had no idea he possessed, he swung his body up and grabbed
at his legs. He hauled himself up, constricting his lungs,
making it even harder to breathe. But he still managed to
bring the blade to bear on the rags looping his legs to the duct
he was tied to.

He crashed to the floor, knocking out what little wind
was left in his lungs. As he lay there gasping, he saw the
figure propping himself up against the off-white polycrete
wall. It tore the rag from its face, revealing a scraggly beard
and a snarling, bloodied mouth. As the hooded figure pushed
itself from the wall, Conrad dragged himself off the floor and
threw himself towards his attacker.

Conrad's momentum was greater, his bulk heavier,
and propelled the rag-clothed figure back into the wall,
winding it in turn. Despite the impact, the figure still held
Conrad's knife-hand in a vice-like grip. Pulling his right hand
back in a closed fist though, he punched into the hood. Again
and again, he smashed his fist into the figure's face, finally,
satisfyingly, feeling bone break beneath his onslaught. The
grip loosened and Conrad pulled his blade hand free, plunging
it into the rag-covered midriff of his opponent.

An anguished cry gurgled out of the hooded figure's
ruined face as it slumped to the floor, clutching its stomach.
Snarling, Conrad staggered to the lockers, hauling one open

and pulling out the morgue-style stretcher. He returned to the prostrate figure slumped against the wall. It protested weakly as he hauled it up, dragging it onto the fixed gurney. Pulling back the hooded cowl to reveal a surprisingly young, pockmarked visage, Conrad spat blood-flecked phlegm at his face.

"You're fucking done!" he snarled. "I'm going to mechanically reclaim your arse and spit the rest out into space."

He bounced the head off the gurney again and again.

"Fuck you!" He screamed, blindly raging. "Fuck you!"

Then Conrad felt an arm across his throat from behind and something ice-cold plunge into his back, scraping against his ribs. He gasped in shock, feeling the strength leaching from him. He looked down at the groaning form in front of him and then down at the scarred arm around his neck. He staggered, almost taking his assailant with him. But he was held up, the ragged blade forcibly pulled from his side. His head was roughly jerked backwards and he felt the first bite as the forgotten blade began tearing out his throat. He opened his mouth to scream, but only blood came out, spilling down his chin.

He watched wide-eyed as an arc of his own black blood sprayed against the low ceiling and sagged to his knees.

With the blackness creeping in from the edges of his vision, he saw a young girl's face staring down blankly above him. The figure on the stretcher pulled itself around to face Conrad's broken form. Blood dripped from the brutal, ragged smile playing across its bearded face.

"You didn't think I'd spent all these years alone, did you?" It hissed through smashed teeth.

CUTTINGS
DUNCAN RALSTON

Katie was in the kitchen when a low rumbling rattled the window. As she moved the curtain aside to peer out, a large off-white object filled her view, and in the next moment, the blast of a horn startled her away from the glass. Someone had pulled into the driveway.

Hanging half out the kitchen door, Katie took a cautious look at the back of an ugly old van spewing black exhaust into the carport. The tinted rear window was cracked, the bumper on a sharp cant, and every inch of it was covered in a layer of scum -- even the small silver letters spelling out RAM.

"What the heck is this?" she wondered aloud.

The driver door opened as she said it. She recognized her husband's designer jeans before he stepped down on the concrete slab, and she saw that he had clearly gone mad, because only a madman would have such a bright, goofy smile stepping out of such a filthy, run-down vehicle.

Gavin Leslie had only just recently lost his job, and now he'd lost his mind.

"Honey, before you say it, I got a great deal."

"Unless you traded for magic beans, a great deal is still too much."

"Honey," he said again, in the tone he used when he knew he was in the wrong, "you're gonna love this van. And she was only twelve-hundred dollars."

"Twelve-hun—" Katie let go of the door jamb and stepped out onto the cement porch. She had to, for fear of keeling over in shock. "Jesus, you really have lost your mind."

Gavin threw open the back doors, the biggest surprise saved for last. In the back stood a bathroom cabinet papered with faux wood, alongside a soiled mattress. Katie gaped at them. Gavin took her surprise for a favorable reaction, and the smile returned to his scruffy face. "You love her, right? I knew you'd love her."

"I know times are tough, Gavin, but surely you don't expect us to live in that van." Trying for patience, her tone sounded more like measured anger. Had he really just called it her?

"I'll take out the mattress," he assured her. "And the cabinet. I guess the previous owner must have camped in it." He squinted into the back, a forlorn quality to his look Katie didn't quite like. Then his eyes lit up. "I forgot the best part. It's got a tape deck! You remember cassettes."

"Honey, we're the same age. Of course I remember them."

"I found a whole bunch of old cassettes in the cabinet. It's got Mr. Big. You remember Mr. Big."

Katie rolled her eyes, and Gavin drew himself away from the van to stand below her at the steps. He took her hand. "I bought her for us," he said. "For the business."

"What business, Gavin?"

"The flower shop," he said, excitement creeping back into his voice. "Cuttings," he added with a hopeful look, reminding her of the name he'd picked as a joke only the two of them and his dead stepmother would get.

Katie peered over her husband's newly balding head at the beaten-up van with its tape deck, and '90s hair-band cassettes, and the moldering bedroom in the back. She knew what her sister would call it: she'd call it a rape van. Katie had a similar sentiment. Likely a previous owner had camped out of it, as Gavin suggested. Or lived in it, she thought uneasily. But they could take out the mattress. They could take out the cabinet. The flower shop had been a pleasant dream when they'd first started dating, before bills and real life got in the way. Before Gavin's stepmother, Deanie, who'd always filled the Leslie home with the colors and mingled fragrances of a hundred different blossoms, had passed away in a hospital room resembling a greenhouse.

"The flower shop," Katie said, warming to the idea. "I hate the name Cuttings, though. If we're going to go through with this, we really ought to call it Deanie's."

A smile crept onto Gavin's lips. He took her hand and kissed it gently.

Six weeks later, Deanie's Flowers was a living, breathing thing eating up a good portion of their life. But it felt good to be doing something other than banging out her latest book, and even better to see Gavin working again. The layoff had been hard on him. Secretly, Katie thought he'd felt emasculated living off the meager royalties of his wife's crime novels.

With a view of the back gardens, the glassed-in conservatory made an excellent workshop. They'd removed all the furniture, filled the space with tables, and covered them with asters and baby's breath and poinsettias and tulips. In the center of the room, they'd erected a long counter with a stone finish where the two of them could work side-by-side.

Gavin was an expert with flowers, but arranging wasn't his strong point. Here, Katie discovered an untapped talent. So while he cut the flowers and groomed them, kept them fresh and vibrant, she performed magic with vases and pots and floral foam. While Katie placed orders and created the budgets, Gavin's experience in marketing gradually brought in new customers. He also drove the delivery van, which, with its new paint job and Deanie's Flowers decal, began to look somewhat respectable, despite its shabby past.

Together, Katie and Gavin Leslie made a perfect team, and as Deanie's Flowers began to bloom, so did Gavin's libido. His hunger for her had waned after the layoff, but now it revved like the engine of his ugly old van. The day they cleared out the workshop, high from the news of their loan approval, they'd fucked on the cool ceramic tiles in the middle of the glassed-in room, oblivious to potential stares from over the back fence. Gavin devoured her with an enthusiasm he rarely showed, even during their courtship. Secretly, Katie had thought he felt inadequate, despite her reassurances. But that night and every day since, he pushed her to orgasm multiple times, until her own cries grew so loud she embarrassed herself, and the two of them lay their sweaty heads together, laughing and panting.

The Leslies were happy, healthy, and growing more successful by the day.

Gavin snapped awake. He'd been sleeping in an awkward position and his legs felt numb, belonging to someone else. His chest was constricted. His first instinct was to struggle, bound to a familiar chair, though his hands were unrestricted.

Where am I?

He blinked into the dark. As his vision adjusted, he saw the black slab before him, a glimmer of glass. He thought of the conservatory, of his chair at the work table, but here the glass was too close. Moreover, he didn't smell flowers and damp earth but a familiar musty vinyl.

Yellow light flooded the backyard, triggered by some creature of the night, and he recognized his surroundings: the van, the driver's seat. The pressure on his chest was the seatbelt. Somehow he had wandered out here in his underwear — Sleepwalking? he thought — and buckled himself in behind the steering wheel.

The yard light dimmed, throwing him once again into darkness.

"How did I get out here?"

As he spoke, he became aware of a presence at his side, the urge to turn both powerful and repellent. He unbuckled first, drawing his hand slowly across his lap, conspicuous of the erection tenting his boxers, the snap of the buckle like a dead twig to a prowler. When he was free, able to bolt if he needed to, Gavin stole a look at the pallid thing in the passenger seat.

The girl shivered in her flimsy bra and panties, bruised and beaten, rivers of mascara and saliva pooled in her sharp jugular notch. Someone — couldn't have been me — had tied thick nylon rope under her conical breasts and around her ankles, the flesh red and angry beneath, as if she'd been struggling.

"Who—?" Gavin tried to ask, but the tape player came on abruptly with the dash lights, blaring the three-part harmony of Mr. Big's "To Be With You." At the sudden din, the girl snapped her head toward him. Her eyes, dark brown and moist, bore the look of a beaten puppy.

She's afraid. Afraid of me.

Gripped by fear of his own, Gavin snapped on the dome light.

The phantom girl vanished under its harsh white glow. The music stopped and the dash lights dimmed like the picture in an old TV set.

Shaken, Gavin staggered out, bare feet on cool concrete, wondering what the hell he'd just seen. A dream? Never had a lucid one before. Never sleepwalked before, either...

Crickets chirped in the night. Otherwise, Dayton Street was silent. As loud as the music had been, it hadn't woken the neighbors. Gavin let out a small sigh. He crept into the house through the kitchen, aware of every creak.

Katie rustled in her sleep when he returned to bed, but she didn't wake. Gavin was glad for it, despite the persistence of his hard-on. He wouldn't have been able to explain where he'd been if she was awake. He couldn't explain to himself what had happened, let alone his wife of seven years. The image of the abused girl — whatever that had been — had disturbed him terribly.

Despite his worries, Gavin eventually drifted back to sleep. When he awoke in the morning, he found it easy enough to convince himself what had happened in the night was just a very bad dream.

The woman banged on the glass while Katie was at the grocery store. Gavin looked up from spritzing aphids off the primroses to see her dark figure standing at the door.

"Welcome to Deanie's Flowers," he said, letting her in. "You must be Madison."

"Yes," she said. Dressed in black from her cloche hat to her shoes, she sniffled as she slipped by. "Thank you."

Madison Davis had called in an order for her husband's funeral two days prior. Katie took the call, and later told him, "If you died, I wouldn't have the strength to make that call." Gavin directed Madison toward long-stemmed flowers, bunched tightly among white carnations into several slim glass vases and wicker baskets.

"They're lovely," she said, wiping her nose with a tissue.

"You can thank my wife for that," he said.

"I will."

"You know, callas aren't true lilies," he said, just to make conversation. "They're from the genus zantedeschia. They're mildly toxic."

"Why do they call them lilies?"

Gavin shrugged. "A rose by any other name..."

"Well, my husband always loved them," the grieving widow said, almost apologetically, shifting so their elbows met for a brief moment. Gavin stole a sideways glance at her round face. Her green eyes shimmered with tears; plump lips pouty; her thick, lined neck with the visible blue slash of her jugular. Her heavy breasts rose and fell under a cinched black trench coat ending at a knee-length wool skirt and thick leggings. Beneath a light woody perfume, Gavin smelled the mingled aroma of sweat and baby powder, involuntarily stiffening in his work jeans. He stepped away from her, blushing.

She turned her dewy eyes to him, so sad and broken — and suddenly Gavin wanted to swat everything off the work table and throw her down on the space he'd made, slamming the breath out of her in a terrified gasp, her fat tits popping the top buttons of her jacket. He wanted to jerk up her skirt and tear down her panties, thrust his face between her smooth white cheeks and savor the fragrant bouquet of her cunt.

Madison seemed to see something wrong. She took a step away.

Gavin flustered. Not now, he told himself. Please, not now. "I'm sorry for your loss," he said, hoping to cover whatever his face had revealed.

She thanked him again with a wary look at his dirty hands.

"Let's ring these up, shall we?" he crossed the workshop. Madison hesitated only a moment before following. The cash register stood beside the doorway to the hall, the master bedroom mere feet away. Gavin knew he could snatch her by the throat and the belt of her jacket and push her inside easily. He could throw her down on his marital bed and dry fuck the bitch while her tears dampened the comforter and she cried out for her dead husband—

STOP IT!

His hand shook. His head swam with her sweat and perfume and his balls felt unusually heavy. He caught her eye. Again, she looked down at his hand. "Sorry," he said, and forced a cough. "I think I'm coming down with something."

"It's been going around," she murmured.

"If you'd like, I could send you the bill?" Madison nodded a little too emphatically, her red-rimmed eyes on the door now, longing for escape. "That would be nice."

"I'll just bring them to your car then."

Gavin juggled two tribute arrangements through the door. Madison carried the third herself, eager to get away. Under the carport, the air was in motion, her scent not as potent, and the sudden, terrible urge to violate her disappeared. She wasn't his type to begin with, and worse -- her tears reminded him of the phantom girl from the van. He threw a look toward the van now, its fresh white paint job shimmering in the cool autumn air. I'll go for a drive, he thought. Play some tunes. Calm the nerves.

He stood the tributes up on the floor in the back of her Audi. Madison held the third out to him with an uneasy look. She wants me to do it, he thought. So she won't have to turn her back on me.

Gavin took the vase, eager to get her going and get behind the wheel himself. In his haste, his still-quivering fingers brushed hers. The widow snatched her hand away with such a look of fright she might have caught a glimpse of his twisted fantasies. He placed it with the others. "I'll get the last of them," he said anxiously, and hurried back to the workshop.

Madison Davis was already in the driver's seat when Gavin returned. She'd started the car while he crouched for the last of the bouquets -- a flower basket and the casket spray. He found the widow staring through the windshield at the back of the van, a troubled look in her eyes. Gavin loaded the last arrangements. She didn't acknowledge his presence until he said, "All done."

Only then did she shoot a brief, thin smile over her shoulder, flinching when he shut the door.

"Drive safe," he told her. The back tires squealed as she pulled out of the driveway.

The tape player blasted INXS when Gavin started the engine.

The first time he drove to Almond Street, Gavin met the van's previous owner.

He'd taken a circuitous route through town, clearing away the stress of the day, listening to the tunes he loved in high school. When he emerged from under the dirty, graffitied overpass, he found himself in a seedy neighborhood of potholes and brick-faced warehouses.

The street sign out front of a run-down convenience store said ALMOND in white letters on green. Gavin made the realization as if in a dream. He knew the area by reputation only: it was said a man could get almost any kind of woman he wanted here, even underage ones. He hadn't meant to drive here, had only been going by the feel of the road; subtle vibrations in the steering wheel causing him to twist the wheel this way and that. He wouldn't have driven to Almond Street if he'd been aware of his destination — if he'd entered it into the GPS on the dash. It had been entirely unconscious, almost as if the van had driven him.

Women in impossibly short skirts and heels of equally improbable length trolled the grimy sidewalk. Gavin pulled up to the curb, meaning to make a U-turn and go back home, but a pair of hands with black lacquered nails grasped the window sill before he could pull away, and a young woman peered in, chopped black bangs framing a pale, eager face and junkie's eyes.

"Hey, hot stuff," the girl said, before squinting at him uncertainly. "You're not Tony."

Another woman sauntered over, dark nipples like saucers protruding from a white tube top, cut-off blue jeans so short the frayed edges hugged her crotch and a waistband swallowed by her stomach. "How 'bout a threesome?" this woman suggested.

"Fuck off, Indica," the first girl said over her shoulder, ushering her competition away with a flick of her wrist. Indica stayed put, while the junkie hooker looked over the interior of the van. "Ton' let you borrow his baby?" She gave him a dubious look, absently flicking the piercing under her lower lip against her teeth.

Gavin's entire being screamed for him to leave. He

jerked the wheel and stepped on the gas, peeling the girl's fingernails off the passenger window with a clack as the van squealed away from the curb. He drove home with his thoughts thudding in his ears as loud as his heartbeat. What was I doing there? What the fuck is happening to me? I love Kate. I don't want anyone else. I love my wife. It wasn't my fault. I love her. I didn't mean to do it!

But you didn't do anything, a stranger's voice assured him—a strangely familiar voice. All you did was satisfy a little innocent male curiosity.

The man's voice had a pleasant, gravely timber that felt like cinnamon candy melting in Gavin's head. As the van went over another pothole, the fuzzy dice Katie had begged him to throw out rustled from the rearview mirror.

Nothin' wrong exercising your rights, the voice said. Nothin' wrong with bein' a man.

"Nothing wrong at all," Gavin agreed. The voice seemed to come from everywhere, from the porous vinyl seats to the cold hard plastic of the dash. From the fuzzy dice. From the musty air. It was the van speaking to him, Gavin realized—and all this time he'd been calling it a "she."

"Who the fuck is Tony?" he wondered, recalling the look of recognition and confusion from the dark-haired prostitute.

At this, the van remained silent.

The owner of the storage facility, an old man by the name of Grosvenor, hadn't mentioned a Tony, a Ton', an Anthony, or Antonio. The Ram had been gathering dust in a storage shed for six or seven years. When Grosvenor's brother Barrett died, the old man liquidated his assets, but the owner of that particular shed couldn't be found. "Old number, I guess," Grosvenor said. When Gavin asked if the owner would be upset, the old man answered, "Fuck 'im. I'm getting outta dodge, no pun intended. Gonna buy me one of them mobile homes. Get while the gettin's good."

Get while the gettin's good, the voice said. That's some excellent advice. There's a reason they call marriage an institution—it's a correctional institution. Marriage is a prison, and that brainy little wifey of yours is the warden.

"You're wrong," Gavin said. "She saved me."

Saved you? The van chuckled derisively. From what? Too much pussy?

Gavin flicked on the radio, trying to tune it out. He sang along with Tom Petty until the dial changed on its own.

Can't get rid of me that easy, compadre, the van said, speaking from the static between stations. We're takin the long way home, and you an' me are gonna pow-wow.

Gavin flicked off the radio. Relief washed over him in the silence that followed. Is this what it's like to lose your mind? he wondered.

Laughter as sharp as razor blades answered the unspoken query.

You really are pathetic, you know that? Sorry excuse for a human being, let alone a man.

Gavin tried to turn right at the next intersection, back toward home, and the wheel jerked out of his hands with a peel of tires. He tried to unbuckle, but the latch was stuck.

"Why don't you leave me alone?" he cried.

The man in the car beside them threw Gavin a queer look.

You an' me are gonna get somethin' straight. I'm runnin' the show now, got it? So just shut up, sit back, and let the smooth grooves of WTNY All Tony All the Time wash over you.

The van drove straight. Gavin did as he was told — Gonna hurt me more than it hurts you, he thought inexplicably

— but he didn't have to listen. So while Tony talked, driving him past ugly warehouses and rundown tenements, Gavin tried listing all the flower genera he could recall in his head: Astragalus, Bulbophylium, Begonia, Centaurea…

"…Gav?"

Katie stood at the top of the stairs, a towel around her midsection, the smaller one from the set perched atop her head. She called down the stairs again. "Gavin?"

No answer.

"Where is he?"

She'd popped in for a quick shower before bed, and had been in there a little longer than expected; having realized her legs were bristly, she'd taken the extra time to shave. She emerged, toweled and moisturized, hoping to find Gavin primed and ready on the duvet cover, but instead it seemed as though he wasn't in the house at all.

With her deadline quickly approaching, Katie played catchup, moonlighting in the flower shop while writing her novel by day — barely any time to breathe, let alone play. Tonight during dinner, eaten at the workshop counter, Gavin casually mentioned it had been two weeks since they'd spent any time together. Katie promised to rectify the injustice tonight, deadline be damned, but Gavin was nowhere to be found.

"That son of a bitch," she muttered, suddenly sure where to find him. Holding the towel to her breasts, she hurried downstairs. "Son of a bitch," she said again, bare feet stomping down the hall. She heard the engine rumbling even before she got to the kitchen door.

"Gavin!" Katie stepped out, moving toward the van while Mr. Big rattled its windows. She pounded on the back window before approaching the driver door.

Gavin sat in the driver's seat, staring off into the dark backyard. Several weeks back, he'd started going for long drives at night to God knows where while she worked on her novel. Secretly, Katie feared he was going through a midlife crisis -- that the van's nostalgia had regressed him. Secretly, she worried he was having an affair.

He turned at the sound of her knuckles on the window, fixed on a proper loving smile, and rolled it down. The twangy ballad spilled out into the carport, four overgrown boys longing to date the cool chick in school.

"Hi, honey," Gavin shouted over the music, oblivious. He looked her over, eyes lingering on the valley between her breasts where the towel pushed them up.

"Could you turn that off, please?"

Gavin gave the tape deck a queer look, as if he'd been unaware it was on. "Sure thing, hon'," he said, flicking off the music. "We were supposed to be doing something, weren't we?"

"You were supposed to be doing me. Instead, you're doing… whatever this is."

"Just letting off some steam. You know — unwinding."

"Well, I'm going to bed. Are you gonna come, or not?"

His grin was half snarl. "Oh, I'll come," he said, stepping out. He shut the door gently behind himself and turned, standing so close the hot breath from his nostrils warmed her forehead. "I'm sorry, babe," he said, smiling down at her. "I know you're stressed about your deadline. How 'bout I make you a drink? Give you a nice back rub?" He was already hard. It throbbed against her stomach as he drew her into his arms and kissed the crook of her neck. His tongue slid into the divot below her trachea, flicking up and down. Katie leaned in to him, getting wet. She wanted to be full of him — needed it.

The moment the door closed behind them, Gavin snatched off her towel. She yelped in surprise, rushing naked into the darkened hall, and he laughed as he chased her to the stairs. She laughed with him, couldn't help herself, bounding up two by two.

In the bedroom, Gavin whipped her around and pushed her down on the bed. Katie spread her legs, felt his fingers wedge into her, out and in, felt them pull out entirely and heard him suck them before the velvet head of his cock spread her wider. Delicious pain in a thousand nerve endings of her scalp made her cry out as he grabbed a handful of her hair, pushing deeper inside her. His hip bones smacked her ass, warm vibrations spreading up her spine.

His thrusts grew frantic. Suddenly he jerked her up from the bed, wheeling her around by her hair and hip to stand her against the wall, pressing her face and tits against its cool surface. She cried out, unsure if she meant it in pleasure or fear.

Gavin grasped her shoulder, mashing her further into the wall with each thrust until her tits throbbed and cheekbone ached. Then his fingers slipped around her throat—

"No," she breathed.

But his fingers closed around her trachea, dirty nails squeezing the thin veneer of flesh. Katie felt the airway close to a pinhole. Gasping now, she reached behind herself, throwing a blind fist at him, striking his thigh, his hip, feeling weak and very small. Gavin humped and humped until his body grew rigid, every muscle flexing but his fingers, which relaxed, a tender mercy. Before she had a chance to catch her breath, he fell against her with a mighty groan, pinning her to the wall, cock spasming as it spewed his hot seed inside her.

Gavin drew away from her then, staggering back. She heard
the springs creak as he flopped onto the bed, and stood there
panting, feeling the dull ache of at least one tear in her vagina,
maybe more, as his cold sperm trickled down the inside of
her thigh. Gavin had never been like that before. Never. Katie
couldn't begin to comprehend such a vast shift in behavior, so
she didn't try. She merely held herself and wept against the
wall until the pain and fear and confusion subsided, and all
she had left was anger.

When she finally turned, Gavin lay draped across the
bed, staring up at the ceiling, still hard after several minutes
untouched. "Never do that again," she told him. He turned to
her with a look of wide-eyed innocence. "Do you hear me?"
she said more forcefully.

Gavin nodded stupidly, looking like a hurt little boy.
This is going to hurt me more than it'll hurt you, Katie
thought. Isn't that what Deanie used to tell him?

"I'm going to wash off," she said, giving him a
measured look. "Sleep in the guest room, sleep on the couch,
you can sleep in that fucking van of yours, if you want. But
I don't want to see you in bed when I get out. You crossed a
line. I don't want to look at you again tonight."

Again he nodded, lower lip pooched like a petulant
child, impossible to tell if the words had sunk in. Katie held
his gaze for a moment, then strode out of the room, to hell
with the pain between her legs.

"I'm sorry!" he called after her, but she didn't return.

In the weeks since his first visit to Almond Street, Gavin
and Tony's "pow-wows," which mainly consisted of Tony
speaking and Gavin listening, became more frequent.
Picturing the man behind the voice, Gavin saw Tony as the
type of guy who sits at the bar swallowing two fingers of Jack

Daniels, dressed well but all in black, spouting off about all the shit straight white males are forced to endure at the hands of the demon Political Correctness — and despite Gavin's innate loathing of conservative pundits, it troubled him how much truth he began to see under all of Tony's bullshit. Gavin sang "Urgent" along with Foreigner on the way to Almond Street, beating his palms against the steering wheel, glad for Tony's conspicuous absence on this particular drive. The cassette collection old man Grosvenor discovered in the cabinet had sold him on the van. Gavin owned some albums on vinyl and many more on CD, but his first love had been Memorex. As a kid, he would stay up late with a flashlight waiting for his latest favorite to play on the radio; RECORD and PLAY and PAUSE already pressed, just sitting on the floor with his legs crossed and a finger hovering over PAUSE, waiting for the DJ to announce his song coming up in the next row of hits, or to hear those first few telltale notes. Gavin became so good at instant recognition he won a radio contest, although he hadn't been allowed to collect the five-hundred bucks because he'd been twelve.

"Those were the days, man," he told himself, wearing a goofy smile. He peered at his reflection in the rearview, brushing his dark hair out of his face. Crow's feet from his cold blue eyes betrayed his age, as did the lines on his forehead. Even the sides of his hair were starting to gray. Soon he'd be too old to fuck without taking a pill, and too ugly to find a decent piece of strange even if he did. Soon he'd be shitting and pissing in adult diapers, sucking all his meals through a straw.

Ain't that a bitch, Tony said. Best to live while the living's good.

Getting old was a bitch.

Katie could be a bitch too, Gavin thought. The way she'd

acted when he fucked her last night, after she practically begged him to fuck her, it was—

Uncalled-for, that's what it was, Tony told him. Hysterical. Just like a fuckin woman.

"Just like a woman," Gavin repeated, feeling Tony's influence like a thick finger probing in the steaming meat of his brain. "Maybe she was right about crossing the line, though. I mean, maybe I was a little too rough."

You just took what was yours, Tony assured him, the dead lights of the dash peering into Gavin's soul. She's your wife. You wanna break off a piece, that's your right as a man.

"My right as a man."

That's the undeniable truth.

"Undeniable," Gavin said, pulling up to the grimy curb at Almond Street. The woman named Indica clicked over on high cork-heeled sandals. A violet vinyl skirt hugged her thick thighs tonight, her lower stomach fold obliterating its waistline. Jade jewelry dangled from a raw hole in her navel. A flimsy piece of leopard-print fabric barely concealed her tits.

Gavin shut off the van.

"Back again, huh, sexy? You musta got your GPS set on speed-dial."

Having a smoke a few paces behind Indica, a young Asian in latex thigh-highs chuckled as she exhaled.

"Do you know a guy named Tony?" Gavin asked. The girl by the wall raised her penciled-in eyebrows and dragged eagerly on her smoke a few times, remaining quiet.

Don't go asking questions you don't want the answer to, Tony warned.

"That some kind of innuendo?" Indica said. "Like 'If You Seek Amy'?"

Gavin had no clue what she meant, and didn't care.

"Where's the dark-haired girl? The one with the lip piercing."
I'm telling you, man, you don't wanna go asking about me or
that girl.

"It's called a labret," the other woman said on a
breath of smoke.

Indica sucked her teeth and looked off. "You
mean Lola. She ain't workin tonight." She turned her thick
eyelashes toward Gavin. "But I can help you forget alllll
about that skinny-ass bitch."

"Thanks for the offer. I'm just looking for some
information. Maybe your friend knows something?" he asked,
indicating the smoker.

Indica threw a dismissive look over her shoulder.
"Got a taste for the Orient, huh? All right. I can tell when
I'm not wanted." Gavin relaxed when she stepped out of the
window. She sashayed toward another vehicle and another
john who'd pulled up behind the van, while the smoker held
up the wall, giving Gavin a sidelong glare.

"You know who Tony is, don't you?" he said.

"Everyone knows Tony," she said with a quick drag
and exhale. "That's why the other girls are avoiding your van
like it's got genital warts."

"Listen, would you mind...? I have money." He
took out his wallet. "I just want to know who he is. I need to
know."

You aren't gonna like what you hear, compadre.

"Put your wallet away." She came over, leaned her
elbows on the window. Squinting into the darkened van, she
saw the back filled with soil bags and hand tools and littered
with dark earth. "You sure you don't know Tony? You aren't
friends with him or anything?"

"I bought this van from an old guy at a storage
facility. I swear I don't know anyone named Tony."

The girl nodded, still wary. "What's with all the dirt?"

"I'm a florist," he said.

"I guess I shouldn't be afraid of a big bad flower man," she said, faux pouty, and opened the door. Sitting in the passenger seat, she flashed him a somewhat shy look, then held out her small right hand. "My name's Kitty."

Gavin shook it. "I'm sure you understand if I don't tell you mine."

Kitty smiled. She pushed Eject on the tape player and a cassette popped out. "Tom Petty and the Heartbreakers?" she said, turning it over. "What is that? Country music?"

Gavin started the van.

Well, hello, Kitty, Tony piped up a moment later. You know, you're prob'ly just gonna get horny again in half an hour.

Gavin ignored him.

"There's an alley where I take guys sometimes," Kitty said as they pulled away from the curb. "A few blocks over. It'll be more private there."

"I just want to talk," Gavin assured her.

Talk about the first thing that pops up, Tony said, and laughed uproariously.

"Sure. Talk. Fuck. Long as you've got cash, I'll walk on all fours and bark like a dog if you want."

"Now there's an idea." The words came out before Gavin could stop himself, Tony's thoughts from his mouth.

Atta boy! Guess you got a pair after all!

Gavin flashed Kitty an apologetic look. She merely smiled.

I love a woman who knows her place, Tony mused.

"Pull over in here," Kitty said a moment later, pointing to the dark, steaming mouth of an alley. Gavin pulled in cautiously, worried he might tear off the passenger side mirror in the narrow passage. Kitty rose to peer out her window. Her ass, a perfect heart caressed by black leather, was a distraction to driving. It was a distraction to rational thought; though rational thought had flown out the window the moment Gavin met Tony.

"You're good," she told him, and Gavin eased the van through.

Oh no, sister, Tony replied for him. I'm far from good.

"You know, you kinda look like Tony," Kitty said, scrutinizing Gavin's face in the dim light once he'd parked the van. "Cuter, though. Tony had a goatee."

Probably means a Van Dyke, Gavin thought. Not many guys have true goatees these days. He'd had a Van Dyke himself, in his younger days, but Katie had convinced him to shave it off a few months before the wedding. The clean-shaven look suited his face better, anyhow.

"You knew Tony well, did you?"

"We fucked a couple of times. Cheap asshole, though. Always trying to gyp me. Said I should be used to it, since 'my people' bargain all the time. I'm third-generation Canadian, I don't know what the fuck he was talking about." She flipped her sleek, straight hair with a hand. "He likes dark-haired girls. That chick you were asking about, with the labret? I haven't seen her around for a while."

"How long?"

"Like a month or so."

"And how long since you've seen Tony?"

"Six, maybe seven years." Shrugging, she said, "Tony's the type of guy when he doesn't come around, you count yourself lucky. Why you wanna know so much about him, anyways? He owe you money or something?"

"I'm just curious who was in the driver's seat before me," he said, patting the vinyl between his legs. Kitty took it for a cue and eased over onto his lap before he could stop her.

"You smell better than Tony did, too," she said. "I swear he must have bathed in Aqua Vulva." Straddling him, she leaned in to Gavin's ear. The heat of her breath prickled his spine as she nibbled on the lobe. "I'll call you Daddy," she said. She rose up on her knees and rubbed her small, hard tits over his dry lips. "I'll be your Mommy, if you want that too," she whispered, tugging on his belt buckle.

The idea repulsed him, all of it, but when he searched his heart for a reason not to let her keep going, he found it empty. Already crossed the line, he reasoned. Katie said so herself.

He helped her with his pants. His cock sprang up, and Kitty took him into her mouth. Her small, slender fingers matched the rhythm of her lips, mashing his balls against his bunched jeans. Kitty expertly reclined the seat without removing her lips from him and followed him down, taking him deep into her throat.

Gavin stretched out his limbs, ecstasy swallowing the whole world. But the feeling they were being watched nagged at him, and eventually he had to open his eyes. Tied up and gagged, the eyes of the dead girl in the passenger seat locked on his. She turned her gaze to the back where more bloodied, beaten women sat and kneeled, straight slash wounds festering on their skin, worms and beetles skittering and squirming in the moist earth. Each woman was stripped to her panties and tied up with nylon rope; each one as dead as Gavin's stepmother.

This was Tony's legacy: he'd raped and tortured and killed these young women, all six of them; black, white, Asian, and Aboriginal -- the girl with the labret. Their bodies were elsewhere — buried, left to the elements — but their tormented spirits haunted the van, bound to their killer in whatever passed for the afterlife of an abused and murdered hooker.

It was when he saw Madison Davis among them, the grieving widow, that everything fell into place.

Gavin stared into the bound girl's sorrowful eyes while the cold hands of the dead roamed his body, showing an eagerness no woman had ever displayed, not even Katie, and while Kitty sucked, a smile crept onto his lips. He grabbed the whore by the hair, thrusting her head down until she gagged, her eyes widening as he unburdened himself into her willing mouth.

His orgasm racking through him, Gavin felt free. He felt powerful. He felt like himself again, and he knew exactly what he had to do.

He didn't need Tony to tell him his next stop was home.

Earlier that night, Katie acknowledged Gavin's emergence from the workshop with a nod from behind her computer desk. Her book was speeding along at a good clip. Gavin ordered a pizza, giving her a wide berth since what she referred to as "the incident" the night before, and went upstairs to shower. He came back down smelling of fresh soap and the new cologne she'd bought him, and while the scent awakened her urges, she couldn't help but feel an undercurrent of disgust.

Katie ate her usual two slices in front of the screen with a desk lamp illuminating her corner of the open concept living room. Gavin polished off the rest watching the final season of The Sopranos, belching loudly when he was full.

"Could you turn it down a little?" she asked, not wanting to be a bother but unable to concentrate with all the macho bullshit onscreen. Instead, Gavin turned the TV off entirely. "I'm going for a drive," he said, getting up from the couch.

Katie watched him go. He'd never been as aggressive as he'd been last night, and she'd already decided to forgive him. She knew he didn't have the balls to try it again after what she'd said. They needed to put an end to the subtle hostility, to spend some time hashing it out — all night, if that was what it took — but her deadline loomed, and she returned to the incessant blink of the cursor. In her current state of mind, Katie found it difficult not to make her protagonist seem too put-upon.

That sort of behavior doesn't just happen, she thought, the words on the screen blurring as she chewed the ragged left temple of her glasses. He must have been thinking about it for a long time.

She thought of how gentle he'd been before, almost timid, and had to admit that until last night, she preferred the new Gavin's assertiveness -- at least in the bedroom. She could do without the mood swings, the late night drives, the blaring music from that awful van, and the all-around acting like a sullen, spoiled teenager.

I guess that would make me his mother, Katie thought dourly.

"That's not even the least bit funny," she told herself, and slipped her glasses back on, wondering what her editors would think if her straight-laced detective protagonist suddenly and brutally murdered her husband halfway through the book.

The words wouldn't come. The truth nagged at her. Did he rape me? Was it rape?

She'd said the word "no," that much was clear, but by then they were already engaged in the act. So maybe not rape in a technical sense, but certainly assault. She'd told him no, for fuck's sake, and still he'd choked her until he finished, using her like a fuck doll and leaving her to clean herself off.

It didn't sit well.

I can't sit well, she thought, shifting uncomfortably in her chair. I'm all cut up inside.

Thinking this brought a conversation with Gavin's stepmother to mind, in which Deanie revealed a long-kept secret, describing Gavin's adoption in a florist's metaphor.

"He's a cutting, dear," Deanie had said. "Snipped from his birth mother's garden, and transplanted into wonderful new soil. You have to be delicate with a cutting. They take patience, and nurturing. They're more fragile. They have to grow new roots, you see. They have to hold the soil." With this Deanie had leaned in, her breath smelling of the cinnamon candy she favored, which Katie had sneaked in to the hospital room. "But a hard wood cutting must be totally submerged. That's why Julian and I never told Gavin what I've told you today. And why he must never know, my dear…"

Naturally Katie had told Gavin soon after Deanie passed, and he hadn't seemed at all surprised. It had seemed to her that he'd already known, though he never seemed to show any interest in looking up his birth parents. He'd loved his stepparents dearly, but it was clear from what little he'd told her that they had been strict. When his mother was still living, he recalled phrases like "Spare the rod, spoil the child," and "This is going to hurt me more than it'll hurt you." After her death, it was easier to remember the good times, the loving times.

Why did I think of that just now? she wondered.

Katie eyed the photo of the two of them at Machu Picchu, snapped at the summit overlooking the ruins. Gavin's smile, partially obscured by that silly goatee he'd finally shaved off before the engagement photos, reminded her of better days, happier days. He told her she had saved him on that trip. She hadn't understood, and he'd never explained. She supposed she should have asked, but she'd assumed he had meant it metaphorically.

How could he hide so much anger?

She remembered thinking he seemed like a different person the night she'd sat on the cold floor of the workshop, the night his appetite became ravenous.

He was acting strange well before that, Katie reminded herself. Ever since he brought home that fucking van.

Katie flicked the word processor aside on a whim, and brought up the web browser. She typed in "vehicle registration lookup," and clicked the first link. She entered everything she knew about the van: make, model, year, license plates. When it asked for her credit card information, she provided it.

She drummed her fingers on the desk, awaiting the results.

What it revealed drew the breath out of her.

Before Gavin, the van was registered to a Tony Gleeson—but the address provided was 223 Dayton Street—this house, their house. Before that, Tony Gleeson had been living at the Leslies' bungalow with Gavin and Deanie and Julian, who had died when Gavin was twelve. The registry listed no prior owners.

"Who the hell is Tony?" she wondered. It didn't take long to realize Tony was a fake name; that her husband had been hiding a lot more than just the anger he'd shown in the bedroom the night before. That at one point in his life before her, he'd slept in a dirty van and from the look of that old, stained mattress had done a lot worse.

Headlights swept across the living room. A moment later, the van rumbled into the driveway. Katie closed the browser hastily and brought up her manuscript. Minutes passed while she chewed her glasses, waiting for Gavin to come in through the kitchen door.

She got up, tired of waiting.

Katie called out his name as she stepped out into the carport. The van idled there, thick exhaust eddying around it like mist the color of graphite. Someone sat in the passenger seat, and though she could tell it wasn't Gavin, in the dim evening light and the haze of exhaust she couldn't make out who it was — but from the small, slim figure, Katie thought it was a woman.

She crept toward the van. "Gav?" she said, becoming irritable.

Cold metal struck the back of her head. Blinding white pain shot across her vision. Katie cried out and fell forward, darkness overtaking her as she reached out blindly toward the van to catch herself before she hit the concrete floor.

The bitch woke with blood clotted in her hair.

His cuttings had whispered a warning in his ear, pawing at his chest, groping him, running their hands through his hair; the bitch wanted to take them away from him, and they wanted to be with him forever. There had been many flowers before but these were his only cuttings, snipped from the hard soil of prostitution and drug abuse and transplanted into Tony's Eternal Garden. They were his for all eternity, freed from the burden of lives filled with nothing but pain and misery. His birth mother had named him Tony and they were his cuttings; this was his van; this was his legacy.

A seventh flower had joined their Garden tonight: Kitty's cooling remains still graced the passenger seat, the wimp's sperm congealed in her esophagus. Tony had been obliged to strangle her himself because the wimp still had cold feet, and the bound girl — not one of his victims but his birth mother, the young prostitute Julian, and Deanie Leslie had adopted him from shortly before her untimely death — had howled in agony, but Tony had made the wimp silence the filthy cooze with the back of his hand.

Soon his Garden would welcome an eighth—but first, the bitch had to bend to his will. She had to tremble in fear of his power like a flower before the hurricane.

Gavin was kneeling before her when Katie's eyes snapped open. He looked insane, a wild man stripped down to nothing but a pair of argyle socks, fingernail scratches marking his chest and stomach. He was erect, the head of his cock crusted with dead sperm. In his left hand, he held a pair of gardening shears. A small, olive-skinned hand and wrist dangled from the passenger seat, ugly jewelry and painted nails, the first two torn at the quick. Katie saw this and struggled against the ropes binding her bare arms to her ribs, wondering what had happened to the man she loved, wondering where her clothes were, crying out with all of her breath as she tried to tongue away the gag from her mouth. Tony made Gavin's free hand pop in the cassette. A dark smile came over him as Mr. Big muted the bitch's cries. Great fucking tune, Gavin thought in Tony's voice, because he was Tony and Tony was him; he was turned on and tuned in -- WTNY, All Tony All the Time.

Katie watched Gavin grasp the large shears in both hands, his wild, incredibly vacant blue eyes burning holes in her. "This is going to hurt me more than it'll hurt you," he promised, chuckling softly, because that was what Deanie used to tell him when she gave him the belt. Katie shook her head wildly, screaming through the gag, praying for the neighbors to investigate the loud music. But they wouldn't. They'd had plenty of opportunity to complain in the months before and said nothing.

Gavin opened the shears. Had the music not been so loud, she would have heard a squeal of rust. She cringed away as he moved toward her on his knees. His dirty hands quivered. He hesitated, and for a moment, the burning hatred fell away and he fixed her with a look of pure sympathy.

The rusted blades located his target — and snipped.

The vile things plopped to the floor before the explosion reached Gavin's pain receptors. The shears fell from his hands and he reeled, staring down at the wet, oozing cavity he'd made at his groin. This was his legacy. His still-hard prick lay like a fat, wet slug in the loose soil; his testicles had oozed out of his scrotum, a pair of glistening pink orbs beside it. But Tony's cuttings were free — Gavin was free. The station had changed, and Tony Gleeson had left the airwaves for good.

Gavin looked up at Katie, and through her tears she saw him laugh, causing blood to spurt from the raw red and yellow meat where his genitals had been. "Tony's gone now," he said, before his eyes rolled back in his head, and he collapsed against the back of the driver's seat.

When the song ended, Katie's screams filled the silence.

CONDUCTIVE SALTS
DANIEL MARC CHANT

For Emma, the day had been marked by disappointment and frustration. She and Brett had been up since before sunrise, roaming the countryside with their metal detectors, and had found nothing but junk. With the day drawing to an end, she was in two minds about whether they should call it quits and head home. or keep going until the last dregs of daylight had faded.

The beach was their last hope. This desolate stretch of shore was the fourth location they'd tried that day and Emma had no expectations of it bringing more luck than the other three.

Brett walked slightly ahead, sweeping his detector from side to side as he took slow, steady steps along sand smoothed by the recently departed tide. Despite what experience should have taught him, he seemed forever convinced he was just a few steps away from an exciting discovery. Somewhere out there, a King's ransom awaited him and woe betide anyone who held him back from finding it.

A high pitched whine in her headphones told Emma

her metal detector was passing over something metallic. More in hope than expectation, she scraped at the ground with the side of her foot, pushing aside sand and creating a small hole that rapidly filled with water. She caught sight of something shiny, and bent down to see digging around it with her fingers.

"Anything?" Brett asked, pausing in his own efforts and placing his headphones around his neck.

Emma held up a crumpled sheet of tin foil, which had once perhaps held food for a picnicker or live bait for a fisherman. "What do you reckon? Should we get this in a bank vault before somebody kills us for it?"

"It's not been the most fruitful of days, has it? But that's metal detecting. You win some, you lose some."

"You're not usually this philosophical when we luck out."

"To be honest, treasure hunting is starting to lose its appeal. Maybe it's time to find another hobby."

Emma didn't like the sound of that. She and Brett had met at a metal detecting weekend and their love of searching for ancient artefacts was the glue that bound their relationship. In fact, it was one of the few things they had in common. And now Brett was proposing they give it up? Emma reckoned their relationship would fail within weeks if that happened.

"I don't want another hobby," she declared. "And nor does Bramble. He loves treasure hunting as much as we do."

"Talking of Bramble..." Brett looked over his shoulder. "Where is the little fellow?"

Bramble, their border collie, was every bit as much a part of the team as they were. Going treasure hunting without him was unthinkable.

Emma gazed down the long, narrow beach. She'd seen Bramble run ahead and supposed he must be hiding behind a rock or one of the wooden groynes that divided the

beach. "He's probably terrorising a stranded star fish."
Brett placed fingers in his mouth and whistled. "Here,
Bramble! Here, boy"

There was no response. Emma removed her
headphones. "Bramble! Where are you?"

"I swear that dog's going deaf." Brett scrambled to
the top of a dune to give himself a better view of the beach.

"There he is! I think he's found something.
Come on!"

Emma was both surprised and relieved at Brett's
excitement. Perhaps he hadn't lost the treasure hunting bug
after all.

Brett ran along the top of the dune, then came down
in an alarming series of leaps that could have landed him in
hospital if they'd gone wrong. With both hands clutching his
metal detector, it was a wonder he kept his balance.

Emma caught up with him at a large concrete block
housing a metal ring, which she figured must be for securing
boats or buoys. Bramble stood snarling at a hole beside the
block.

"What is it, boy?" Brett asked. "What have you got
for us?"

"He seems frightened," Emma observed. She was
beginning to get a bad feeling. "You don't suppose he's found
an old land mine?"

"My bet is he's picked a fight with a crab and lost."
Brett put his headphones over his ears and switched on his
detector. "There's definitely something there."

"It's bound to be junk. Let's leave it and go home."
Brett wasn't listening. He got down on his knees and scooped
out handfuls of sand. As he did so, Bramble backed away.

"Look," said Emma. "The dog's definitely afraid. We
should trust his instincts."

"Well, what do we have here?" Brett yanked an object out of the sand and held it aloft. "A statuette, I do believe."

Emma shuddered when she saw the thing in Brett's hand. It looked like brass and seemed to be a representation of some weird sea creature -- part snake, part squid, and part mollusc. There was no way, Emma thought, that natural evolution could have produced such a thing. It looked like the result of an insane laboratory experiment gone wrong. "Throw it away," she found herself whispering. "Please."

"Not on your life." Brett looked at her like she was mad. He rubbed his fingers over the statuette to clear away sand. "This is by far the most interesting thing we've found in a long time. I bet it's worth a bob or two."

Looking pleased with himself, Brett led the way back to the car. He seemed not to notice Bramble's reluctance to follow. Emma held back for fear that Bramble might run off. Reaching the car, Brett put his gear in the boot and reverently placed the statuette on the back seat.

"In you get," he said, taking Emma's metal detector from her. "It's my turn to drive."

As Emma climbed into the passenger seat, she noticed a smell that was a mixture of blood, iron, and sulphur. "That statue stinks," she complained, but her complaint fell on deaf ears.

"Come on, boy" Brett held open the back door. "Home time."

Bramble, who was usually keen to hop into the car, stood a short distance away and snarled.

"In you get. Now!"

"It's the statuette," Emma pointed out.

"I know what it is, thank you!"

"Okay. There's no need to shout."

With ill grace, Brett took the statuette and threw it in

the boot. "There! Now are you happy?"

They were halfway home before Brett spoke again. "I'm sorry I snapped. I don't know what came over me."

"You," Emma told him through clenched teeth, "were a real prick."

"Tell you what. Why don't I take you out for dinner tonight to make up for it? You name the restaurant and we'll go there. My treat."

As Emma dressed for dinner, it seemed to her that her relationship with Brett had reached a crossroads. Although they'd had their rows, Brett had never before snapped at her with such little provocation. For the first part of the journey home, he'd driven like a maniac, glaring at the road ahead and not so much using the gear stick as slapping it about. His uncharacteristic behaviour had frightened her to such an extent she'd almost demanded that he stop and let her out. It was only fear of how he might react that stayed her tongue. In the back, Bramble had made it known from his whimpering that he shared her unease.

And all over some stupid statuette, she thought as she slipped into the stylish black dress which she knew was Brett's favourite. Whoever made it must have been sick in the head.

Emma smoothed down the dress and then inspected herself in the wardrobe mirror. Looking good. Simple but elegant.

She finished dressing, grabbed her clutch bag and went downstairs to the living room where Brett stood with his back to her. His gaze was fixed on the statuette, which now, to her dismay, took a place of pride on the mantel above the fireplace.

Behind him, Bramble cowered against the wall, as far from the statuette as he could without leaving the room. His pathetic whimpering reminded Emma of the time he'd limped home with a thorn in his paw.

Emma's gut told her to demand that the monstrosity on the mantel be banished to the garden shed, but she decided on tact and caution. She would have a pleasant night out with her boyfriend and wait for the right moment to mention that she didn't want the statuette in the house. Why ruin a good evening by starting an argument?

"I'm ready," she said.

"What?" Brett was startled and momentarily disorientated. He must have been miles away. Without turning around, he inspected Emma in the fashionably distressed antique mirror hanging over the fireplace. "What do you mean you're ready? You think I'd want to be seen with you dressed like that?"

Stung, Emma was aware of tears in her eyes. "Like what?"

Brett span on his heels to face her. "Like a whore! That's what!"

For a moment, Emma was too angry to speak. She felt like she'd been physically slapped. When the shock wore off, she threw her clutch bag at Brett. "Don't you dare speak to me like that!"

The bag landed at Brett's feet. He kicked it away. "Are you going somewhere? Sneaking off behind my back to meet up with your fancy man?" He took a sudden step towards Emma, causing her to flinch. "Do you think I'm stupid? Do you think I don't know what's going on?"

"You keep away from me," Emma warned. "Or else." Laughing a nasty laugh, Brett raised his arm as if to strike. This was too much for Bramble. With a snarl, the dog put himself between the battling couple and barked warningly at Brett.

"Well, well, well," said Brett. "Now we see whose side the dog is on. The ungrateful mutt!"

Feeling protected, Emma decided to take control of the situation. "Me and Bramble are going upstairs to bed. You take one step into that bedroom and I'll call the police. When I come down in the morning, I want you and that statuette gone. Understood?"

"This is as much my house as yours. If anyone's leaving, it's you and that dog."

Emma slept fitfully that night. What little sleep she managed to snatch was plagued with dreams that faded swiftly from her memory. Sometimes she would wake up to find Bramble at the foot of the bed; other times he stood at the door, whimpering.

She could hear Brett moving about downstairs. From the heaviness of his footsteps and the other noises he made, he was clearly drunk.

This is not Brett, she told herself more than once. It's that damn statuette. It's somehow taken control of him. I'll get rid of it and he'll be his old self again.

Morning came and Emma awoke to find she had slept through her alarm. Bramble lay beside her.

"Late for work," she told the dog, sitting up and reaching for her dressing gown. "I'll phone in sick."

When she went downstairs, she was relieved to discover Brett had ignored her ultimatum to leave. He sat on the sofa, red eyed and clearly drunk. In one hand, he clutched a glass; in the other, an empty vodka bottle.

"I'm so sorry," he muttered pitifully. "So very sorry." Bramble jumped up next to Brett and gave his cheek a sympathetic lick. Lying down, he rested his head on his master's lap. It seemed all was forgiven.

Emma turned her attention to the statuette which still sat above the fireplace. Although it was without doubt the ugliest thing she'd seen in a long time, it no longer seemed as sinister as it had when she'd first set eyes on it. Now it looked like what it was; a lump of bronze that should be buried in the ground where it belonged.

She walked up to the fireplace to get a closer look at the statuette. As she did so, she noticed the sickly smell it gave off and realised she had been smelling it ever since she'd gotten up.

"Who do you think made it?" she asked. "It looks Babylonian to me."

"Not Babylonian." Brett's slurred speech was tinged with a hint of gruffness. "Tens of thousands of years older."

"That's impossible. You're talking about when men lived in caves."

"It has nothing to do with men! Look at it. Can't you see how alien it is? No man had a hand in making that statuette."

"Then who?"

"Somebody else. Somebody other."

Emma shivered and turned her back on the statuette. She couldn't stand to look at it any more. "I'll fix breakfast. You look like you need it."

Bramble leapt off the sofa and followed Emma into the kitchen. As always when breakfast was being prepared, he took up his station beside the fridge and watched patiently, knowing he would be fed at the same time as his owners. Emma busied herself making breakfast. She took bacon and eggs from the fridge and reached for a frying pan. Soon the pan was sizzling away on the stove, and the coffee maker was hissing and bubbling and filling the room with one of her favourite aromas. She turned on the radio and half-listened to the news.

Emma grabbed a spatula and flipped the eggs. With breakfast under way, she was able to pretend that everything was normal -- that she and Brett were getting along just fine.

"Can I help?" Without Emma noticing, Brett had crept into the kitchen. "Do you need a hand with anything?"

"You can cut the bread," Emma suggested.

"Sure. I'll do that." Brett took out a loaf from the bread bin and placed it on the table. "I really am sorry, you know. About everything."

"We'll talk about it over breakfast, I'm sure we can sort everything out."

Emma turned her attention back to the frying pan. Despite the heavy aroma of bacon and coffee, she could still smell the statuette, only now the smell seemed a whole lot worse. There was something about it that suggested rotten flesh and decaying corpses.

She felt sick.

"It's no good." She turned to face Brett. "I won't have that statuette in this house a moment longer."

Brett wiped a serrated bread knife on his sleeve. "Before there were men," he said, "there were the others. And before the others, there were the First Gods."

"That's enough, Brett! You're freaking me out and it isn't funny."

"Her name's Yrgasol."

"Who?"

"The statuette."

"You can't possibly know that."

"The gods demand their due. They thirst for blood." Brett looked directly at Emma as he dragged the knife across his throat. At first, blood gently bubbled out of the wound.

Then it erupted with such violence that some of it reached Emma and got in her eyes.

Through a red mist, she saw her boyfriend drop the knife and fall to the floor. There was a long, drawn-out scream and she wished it would stop -- which it did as soon as she realised it came from her.

Emma wiped her eyes and watched in numb disbelief as the pool of blood around Brett grew ever larger. She was vaguely aware of Bramble at her side, licking her hand.

"Yrgasol." She felt compelled to utter the name, and as she did, so she remembered her dreams from last night. She remembered a day millions of years ago when she had danced in a temple for the pleasure of Yrgasol. She remembered too the statue of the sea goddess. It was identical to the statuette in the living room, only a hundred times bigger.

"Yrgasol." Heedless of the blood she had to walk through, Emma took the knife from Brett's lifeless hand and went into the living room. She knelt before the statuette, just as she had done in a dozen previous incarnations. "The First Gods never died. They were just forgotten. And now they are remembered again, and they need blood."

Emma would have been pleased to sacrifice herself once more, but she knew the First Gods had other plans for her.

In the kitchen, the frying pan smouldered and the smoke alarm bleeped like a demented bird. As the kitchen filled with smoke, Bramble had no choice but to flee into the living room, where he pressed himself against the wall and cast a wary eye on his mistress.

Emma wiped blood from the knife on the sleeve of her dressing gown and called gently to Bramble. "Come here, boy," she said. "There's nothing to be afraid of. I won't hurt you. I promise."

SKIN
KAYLEIGH MARIE EDWARDS

It was a slow burn, but a hot one. Amy Cook winced as she pulled her hand back from her calf, which was already tender to the touch. She stared at the arachnid and shuddered as it sloped away. She wasn't the biggest fan of spiders and this particular one was behaving in an odd way; usually the little hell minions scuttled off, shying from the light that exposed them to bigger prey (which, in this instance, was most likely to be Amy's shoe). This spider, however, travelled with the nonchalance of one who had merely tipped his hat at her, rather than sinking its fangs into her flesh.

"Wait a minute, Ames." Martin insisted, putting himself between her and the beast before she could annihilate it.

"Nice to know whose side you're on," she mumbled, refocusing on her leg. It was a big spider, but even so, her wound was shocking. She could actually see the puncture wounds.

The bite was red and raw with a little blood oozing out. What concerned Amy, though, was the yellow ring forming around it. The patch of skin that fell between the bite and the yellow ring had already turned a shade a grey, as though the spider had drained the life right out of the immediate area. Bile started to rise in Amy's throat.

"Martin?"

"This is so weird." Martin replied, his attention completely devoted to the spider. He was on his hands and knees, following it as it strolled towards the nearest dark space -- under the bed. "You should see the markings on this thing's back. I thought it was one of those false widows, but this pattern is more like a star or something."

"If you let it run under my bed, I'm going to kill you!" Amy warned. Martin half-turned.

"No, not a star, a pentagram!" Martin turned back towards it, pointing. "I shall name you Satan!"

"Martin, for God's sake!"

Martin turned in time for Amy's shoe to collide with the side of his face. He shot her a look that denied pain but expressed annoyance, before picking up the weapon and squashing his girlfriend's attacker.

"Happy?" he demanded, planning on giving her a mouthful about shoe-related abuse. "Ames?"

Martin turned, ready to berate her. His girlfriend was unavailable for a telling off, however, because she was unconscious.

Amy had managed to live her fifteen years without spending a day in the hospital. A night hooked up to monitors and drips had been no fun, and though she would never admit it to Martin, a little scary. He was teasing her for fainting as it was.

She was glad to be home, but the doctors hadn't exactly been reassuring. She propped herself onto her elbows and shuffled up the bed, trying to find a comfortable sitting position. She still felt sick to her stomach, and a little light-headed.

Amy closed her eyes, heaved out a breath, and swung the duvet away from her leg. She opened her eyes, peering down at the wound, and immediately wished she hadn't. The yellow ring had turned a shade of gold with little blotches of green spreading through it. The pattern reminded her of marble -- if marble were an organic, rotting substance. The patch between the yellow ring and the bite had turned China-white and it throbbed with her pulse. The whole area was swollen and was beginning to give off a faint odour.
An allergic reaction to the spider's venom -- probably a false widow, they had said. She had even been scolded for not catching the beast for analysis.

'Inconclusive' was the word they used that had bothered her, and they had used it a lot. Two sets of blood tests were done, and both came back 'inconclusive.' The doctors blamed the new hematologist for the confusion, but for just a second, Amy had caught the look of perplexion on the doctor's faces. They took more blood and some urine, and sent her home to rest.

They didn't really think the hematologist had messed up, and neither did she. There was something wrong with that spider, and now there was something wrong with her too. She could feel it in her gut. Her stomach lurched suddenly.
She twisted out of bed, quite literally feeling it in her gut. She pressed her hand to her mouth, wincing as her feet hit the ground. Her whole damn leg was sensitive to the touch, right down to her foot. She'd have to suffer and run anyway or she would throw up on her brand new bedroom carpet.

Ten minutes later, Amy was back in bed with tears trickling from her eyes. She tried not to think of her mother

-- who had abandoned her years before -- but when she was unwell, she just couldn't help it. Her dad tried, but he didn't have the right touch. He was too abrupt, and as someone who never fell ill himself, lost patience quickly. Her mum had left them when Amy hit her teens, and she resented her for it.

Who was she supposed to go to with questions or problems? Puberty was stressful enough with a woman in the house, and a nightmare without.

A knock on her bedroom door suddenly snapped her back to the land of consciousness. She hadn't even realised she'd dozed off. The door creaked open, and Martin strode in, grinning.

"How's it going, puke breath?"

Amy gritted her teeth. Whenever Martin came over, her dad would suddenly 'misplace' any pictures of her looking pretty, especially the holiday pictures of her by the pool. Yet, he never failed to mention it if she had happened to vomit, burp, or break wind that day.

"I feel a bit better," Amy lied. Martin left the door ajar and approached the bed, jumping into a cross-legged position at the bottom. He opened his backpack, rummaging through the contents.

"Miss Prosser gave me your homework."

"Great," Amy smiled. She wasn't so fond of the homework, but she was fond of Martin in his shirt and tie. He always wore it a bit loose just to spite the school uniform rules. He'd been in detention many times, though as far as Amy's dad knew, Martin was a model student. He was even part of the band, Amy had beamed. That had lightened the mood a little; Amy's dad was also in the school orchestra back in his day, once a keen violinist. Martin wasn't in the orchestra, he played guitar in a band with his friends, but Amy accidentally on purpose forgot to correct her dad's assumption. He only just tolerated Martin as it was.

"Ames?"

"Hmm?" Amy opened her eyes, embarrassed that she had drifted off again.

"I said, when are you back in school?"

"Couple of days," she lied again. She was feeling worse by the second. Martin tutted and rolled his eyes.

"You're making quite a big fuss; it's just a spider bite! Can I see it?"

Amy clenched the duvet, yanking it up to her chin. Martin's eyes shifted to the edge of the blanket where her legs were, but before he could snatch away her cover, Amy's dad entered the room.

"We're out of milk," he declared, his eyes fixed on Martin. Amy's face dropped -- milk was the only thing she could stomach, which was odd, because normally when she felt sick, milk was the last thing she wanted. "Martin, would you mind popping to the shop? I don't want to leave Amy on her own right now."

"Can't you go? Martin can stay here with me," Amy rushed to ask, before Martin could refuse and show himself up as rude. Her dad's eyes shifted back and forth between them.

"I'm not leaving you two on your own."

"Thanks a lot," she mumbled, glaring at him. Martin continued to rummage through his bag, averting his eyes from both of them. Her dad sighed and mimicked her folded arm pose.

"What's the mood face for, Amy?"

"Nothing. Nice to know you trust me, that's all. You'll only be gone a minute, I don't know what you think we're gonna do."

She shot Martin a look as she spoke that warned him

not to smirk, but he couldn't help himself and lowered his head into his bag to hide it from her dad. She coughed, hoping her dad hadn't caught the glint in Martin's eye. He unfolded his arms and shifted his weight on his feet, before finally lowering his gaze.

"I suppose. Martin?"

Martin lifted his head, the colour draining from his face. He pretended he wasn't, but he was a bit afraid of Amy's dad. He shot Martin his 'any funny business and I'll kill you' smile.

"I'll be back in two minutes, maximum."

Martin nodded, returning his smile with a nervous, tight-lipped smile of his own. Amy's dad stared at them both for a moment, and then left, making sure he nudged the door all the way open before he descended the stairs.

As soon as they heard the front door close, Martin turned to Amy with a suggestive grin.

"We can't," Amy snapped, her fingers tightening on her duvet. Martin shrugged.

"You said you felt better just now. And it's been ages," Martin insisted, shuffling up the bed towards her. Amy smiled but Martin caught the blatant refusal in her eyes before she could argue her case further. He stood, yanking a book out of his bag, and tossed it onto her legs.

"Ow!" Amy reached down and pressed a hand to her leg, crying out as searing pain set her skin on fire. She yanked her hand back, composed herself, and then lifted the book off her injured limb.

"Read the first three chapters," Martin told her, pulling his backpack onto his shoulders and making for the door. His voice had turned from playful to cold, just like it always did when he didn't get his way. "You know, you're boring sometimes. We've already done it; I don't know what your problem is."

Amy felt the panic rise in her chest -- she was ill and her boyfriend was about to leave her alone, but that really wasn't the cause of the lump travelling up her throat. She had upset him... again.

Martin had approached her at lunch about five months before. At first, Amy thought it was a joke. He was a popular boy and he was in the year above her. He had his pick of the girls, and he had made his way through quite a few of them. Amy had always daydreamed about him, as had everyone else. She had always defended him against the trail of heartbroken girls he left in his wake, insisting that when he found the right girl, he'd stick around.

She couldn't believe her luck when he started sitting with her every day at dinnertime. She knew she was no model, and she'd never had a boyfriend before. She was the bookworm type, sometimes she had to wear glasses; she definitely wasn't like the girls Martin normally went for. The other girls thought she was weird because her idea of fun was a good read, and she really didn't have any friends. And yet, there he was, joining her at every given opportunity.

Once she had accepted that he really did like her, they had become inseparable. He told her she was pretty a lot, and she was beyond flattered. He was the first male in her life ever to pay her a compliment, and before she knew what was happening, she had got completely carried away. Her dad had resisted, but she persevered -- she and Martin were meant for each other, and nothing would stand in the way.

She had always promised herself, and her dad, that she would wait until she was in love before she gave her virginity to someone. Her dad had actually been pushing for her to wait until marriage, but Amy didn't think that was very modern. Plus her dad would never have to know. They had done it at Martin's house after school before his mum got home from work. It had hurt like hell, and it had happened within the first month of their relationship. Amy would have preferred to wait, but Martin had seemed upset. Didn't she love him?

Afterwards, Amy wasn't sure that she wanted to do it again, but since they already had, she didn't see a logical reason to refuse him. Plus, there were a million other girls just waiting for Martin to realise that she wasn't good enough for him -- all of whom were probably more than willing. So she had done it again. It didn't hurt as much as the first time, but it wasn't like the movies either. She hadn't felt good about herself for it, not one bit. She still didn't. She told Martin she wasn't ready to do it again for a while, but he didn't seem to understand.

"Martin, my dad said someone needs to stay…"

"He'll be back any minute anyway," Martin interrupted, nudging the door with his foot. Amy felt the stab of rejection in her chest, and the tense lump inched a little further up her throat. If she didn't get over whatever the hell her problem was soon, he was going to ditch her. Suddenly, she realised that the lump in her throat wasn't just the tears she was choking on. Martin left just seconds before she threw up over the side of her bed.

Sleep came whenever it pleased for the next twelve hours. She cried into her pillow, frustrated with herself for upsetting Martin, who hadn't called. One minute, she was so tired and angry about her inability to sleep that she grit her teeth hard enough to send pain into her gums, and the next, she was waking up from a feverish red haze.

Around four in the morning, she awoke from a

nightmare -- the details of which she could not recall. Yet, senses lingered; a white hot burn, like she was aflame, and a rancid smell. As her eyes adjusted to her dark bedroom, she realised those dream sensations were not only lingering, but intensifying. Her leg felt like it was bathed in acid.

She knocked her glasses off the nightstand as she fumbled for the lamp. She eventually found it after scattering plastic jewellery and her schoolbooks onto the floor, and pressed her hand to her eyes as light illuminated the room. It cast away some of the darkness, but none of the pain. She shuffled into a slouched position, trying to hold in her screams for fear of waking her dad up, and looked down at the shape of her leg. A dark, wet patch had spread all the way through the duvet. She closed her eyes, counted to three in her head, and tore the blanket away.

She couldn't hold in the scream this time. Her flesh, which was stuck fast to the fabric, tore away with the duvet as she threw it back. Blood seeped from her shredded leg in some places, and spurted from one area, where the most skin and tissue had come away. Instinctively she reached down and pressed both hands to it, cursing herself as her limb exploded with pain. She stared, wide eyed despite the light, at the raw wound. About a third of the flesh on her shin was now stuck to the blanket, torn completely away. As her heart quickened; she thought she could see her pulse dancing in the blood and puss that trickled out.

Her bedroom door opened violently enough to hit the wall, as her dad thumped the light switch on and raced towards her -- first angry, then almost as horrified as she was. He stopped in his tracks, his mouth hanging open. Amy looked at him, then followed his gaze back to her leg, which, under the main light, looked far worse. Not only had a huge chunk of her flesh peeled away, but her leg was now porcelain white from her toes to just above the knee. It didn't look human.

Amy realised her cheeks were wet, but couldn't make sense of the reason, though she could hear herself crying in machine-gun sobs. She looked at her dad, who was staring at her blood-covered hands.

"Amy..." his voice was soft, for the first time in her life. "Why would you do this to yourself?"

It had been a long and painful night for both of them. It had taken her a while to convince him not to take her to the hospital; she was terrified, and the last place she wanted to be was in an unfamiliar bed surrounded by sick people. She had thought for sure he was going to force her into the car, so she had resorted to the one line she knew he could never fight against -- mum wouldn't force me to do this.

Two hours later, she was back in bed on top of fresh sheets. Her dad had found some anti-septic lotion in the back of the bathroom cabinet, and had cleaned her leg and wrapped it in a bandage. The process had been agonising, and she couldn't watch. She focused on her dad's face instead, though his expression seemed to mimic her agony. As grateful as she was for his help, she was angry. He said he believed her, though she knew he didn't. He couldn't lie to save his life. He actually thought that she had pulled her own skin off.

She was alone, her only company the lamplight, but she retained her irritated, folded-arm posture. She couldn't believe that her dad thought she would mutilate her own body. He didn't know her at all. Not like her mum had. She looked at the ceiling, trying to suck the tears back into her glistening eyeballs. She would not cry another tear over her mum. She hadn't given a shit about her tears when she was leaving, so Amy doubted she was thinking about the state she was in now.

Martin dropped the math book onto the nightstand, avoiding eye contact with Amy. The episode the night before now felt so unbelievable that if it weren't for the raw pain of her bandaged leg, she might have believed she dreamt it.

She smiled at Martin, reaching for his hand. She managed to brush his fingers before he moved to the bottom of her bed, plopped down on the edge, and started scrolling through his phone. Her heart sunk and accelerated simultaneously.

"Dad said you can stay for dinner tonight, if you want?" she tried, hoping for even a hint of his interest. It was the first dinner invitation Martin had ever received from her dad. Come to think of it, it was the first time her dad was going to actually cook a dinner that didn't involve the microwave. He must be really worried about her, Amy figured. Martin didn't look up.

"I don't know why the teachers keep giving me your homework to bring over."

"Because you're my boyfriend?" Amy responded, scolding herself for allowing the statement to come out as a question. Her eyes danced over his face, his crumpled shirt, and his loose tie. The mere sight of him made her smile, despite the glaring truth that his feelings for her were rapidly vanishing. Her eyes lingered on his tie, and then his neck. There was a round, red, blotchy mark on his skin. It looked like a bruise on first glance, but she knew it wasn't. Tears stung her eyes. The house phone rang in the background, but she barely acknowledged the sound, it was like she was drowning in suspended time.

"Yeah, well, I'm not your slave. Get one of your friends to bring it next time," Martin sighed, finally making eye contact. His face flashed with cruelty as Amy's face crumpled. "Oh yeah, that's right. You don't really have any."

The pain in her leg suddenly felt like it was attacking her chest, her heart.

"Why are you being so mean?"

But she knew why. Martin's phone vibrated, and his eyes shifted back to it. He had intentionally made a dig, and it was nothing to him. He was talking to her like he talked to the nerds in his year that he and his friends thought were losers. Amy stared at him as he read his text, fighting to stop her lower lip from trembling as she watched the side of his mouth turn upward. She knew that look. It was a girl, probably the same one who had left the mark on his neck.

"Look, we both know this ain't working out, Ames. I think we should leave it."

Time stopped for her then. She was so angry with herself -- she knew this would happen. She should never have been stupid enough to believe he liked her in the first place -- to actually believe him. She should never have been stupid enough to let him... when she wasn't ready.

The anger left her as quickly as it arrived; then the devastation set in. She had known, realistically, that she was never good enough for him anyway, but, though he was being mean, she didn't want to believe he didn't want her.

"You said you loved me?" she whispered, cringing at how pathetic she sounded. Martin continued to stare at his phone, his thumb hovering over the keys as he responded to his text message.

"Yeah, well, that was before you strung me along. I thought you were different, Ames."

"I... different to what?"

"I just didn't think you were one of those girls who dangles it in a guy's face, then turns him down. Get a kick out of winding me up, don't you."

It wasn't even a question; he had made his mind up

about her.

"No... I..."

Amy pulled the duvet to her chin as though her blanket cocoon would stop her from shattering like frosted glass. Before she could humiliate herself further, footsteps pounded up the stairs. Her dad burst into the room, still clutching the cordless phone. His face was red, his eyes glassy. It reminded her of that red haze from her dreams. He strode across the room and gripped Martin by his collar, lifting him off her bed, and spun him towards the door.

"You little shit! I knew it!"

Martin's face twisted with terror as he was flung to the ground like a ragdoll. Amy's dad glared at him and pointed towards the door.

"Get out of my house! You ever come sniffing around my daughter again and I'll fucking kill you!"

Martin didn't need to be told twice; he bolted. Amy's dad turned towards her, the glaze in his eyes turning to tears.

"Why didn't you tell me?"

"Tell you what?" Amy brought her good leg up to her chest, feeling that she needed the defence.

"I knew it. I bloody knew it." He dropped his head into his hands and paced back and forth. "Jesus Christ, Amy, I thought I raised you better than this. Why didn't you come to me with this, instead of letting me hear it from some doctor at the hospital? This all makes sense now. I should have known when you started throwing up."

Amy's breath caught in her throat as the penny dropped.

"And don't try to tell me you didn't know you were pregnant, Amy, or I swear to God..."

The sobs exploded from within her, painful enough even to numb the pain in her leg. She howled into her hands as everything around her crumbled to ash. She hadn't known. She hadn't even missed a period. She had been stupid enough to sleep with Martin, and she had been stupid enough to listen to him when he insisted he didn't want to use protection. But even in that moment, she wasn't too stupid to realise that she was almost halfway into her pregnancy.

Convinced that she had mutilated her own leg due to the stress of her 'secret' pregnancy, Amy's dad went full babysitter on her. She was grounded -- probably for life, she reckoned -- and the next week was a nightmare. There was either something wrong with the pregnancy, or there was something wrong with her as well as the pregnancy. The real problem for Amy was her dad just wouldn't listen.

They had never been close; in fact, he had often been cruel, and even occasionally physical with her when she disobeyed or angered him. Even so, his disappointment sliced into her every time they were in the same room together. He simply couldn't look at her, and talking, other than to give her instructions, was out of the question. After the initial shock, and the tirade of abuse from him was over, he had gone mute. Days and nights passed by in an awkward, stilted fashion, and Amy felt truly alone. She would have preferred him to yell, but silence, as she knew her dad had worked out over the years, was really the best way to hurt her. She didn't feel, even in her current state, that her pain was worth his acknowledgement or attention -- and he knew it.

Her dad would probably never forgive her for 'shaming the family' and she wasn't allowed to talk to him. With an already broken heart, she had tried to explain that Martin was the only one, but her dad had already come to the conclusion that she had been off 'gallivanting,' and that once the secret was out, she'd be known as the town bike. He was keeping her home from school until he could figure out 'what to do' about the baby, and she was under strict orders not to tell anyone what was going on. Even if she were allowed to go to school, she was too ill to go anyway. The burn in her leg had spread to her hip, and her entire body had adopted the porcelain hue. Her dad assumed it was the pregnancy making her pale and wouldn't listen to her arguments -- he thought she was trying to detract from the real disaster.

Martin had been right with his snide comment about her lack of friends -- she hadn't received a call or a visitor, and didn't expect to. Being a bookworm didn't normally coincide with being popular in her school. Martin was the only thing she could think about besides her physical and emotional pain, and he wasn't exactly a comforting thought. She doubted he knew what the hell her dad had gone crazy on him for, and she was glad. Had he known about the baby, he probably would have ditched her earlier.

She was fifteen, motherless, and pregnant. She was in agony, she was sick, and she was terrified. She didn't even know what to be more scared of -- the sickness spreading from the leg wound, or what she considered to be the sickness inside her womb. The only thing she knew was that she was completely and utterly alone.

Fire...

Amy, in her sleep, crunched her teeth together, but a whimper still escaped. Her eyes fluttered open, the pupils so big her eyes looked almost entirely black.

Pain...

Sweat matted her hair to her face and her nightdress

to her body. She was soaking wet, and, for a moment, she was convinced that she had been set alight. A gurgle escaped her throat as she tried to call out for her dad. She tried to move, but she couldn't. She was wide-awake, but the red haze of her nightmares hovered in her vision instead of dissipating like normal.

She lifted an arm, reaching for her lamp, and screamed, but the sound caught in her throat. Memories of the night the flesh tore away from her leg returned as she realised why she couldn't move -- her entire body was stuck to the sheets, just like her leg had been. The sweat coating her body was unusually warm, and she croaked again as she recognised the velvet texture of the liquid not as sweat, but blood. She didn't need the light to know that the skin from her arm was no longer attached to her -- at least not for the most part. She tried to scream again, hoping to a god she didn't think she even believed in that her dad would just so happen to check on her at any moment. Hot tears streamed from her eyes, the salt stinging the layer underneath the skin, as the moisture trickled through her bloody cheeks. Every sensitive and inflamed inch of her skin was coming away from her body, exposing the nerves and the red raw layer underneath, and there was nothing she could do to stop it.

Shedding....

She lay there in the dark, becoming grateful that she wasn't able to turn on the lamp after all. She didn't want to see what was happening. She tried to remain motionless, but every now and then, the pain would barrel through her, pitching, and an involuntary spasm would wave through. Every time it happened, a piece of her came away, matted to the sheets.

Hers weren't the only sheets she had lost a part of herself in. In the quieter moments where searing torture dulled to mere agony, she cast her mind back to that first night with Martin and wished she could take it back. This was her punishment. Her dad was right -- she was a slut. Her mother was right -- she wasn't worth sticking around for. Despite her 'A' grades, her domestic capabilities, and her wonderful manners, she was no longer a good girl. She had ruined it, and she could never be what she was again. She was worthless now -- but deep down, she knew she always had been anyway. She had struggled with it for years.

By now, the whole school would know; Martin had a habit of spilling the dirty details once he was done with a conquest, and despite her better judgment, she had allowed herself to join those shameful ranks.

Make it stop...

Please, make it stop...

Time lost all meaning as she lay there, burning. Eventually, sunlight filtered through her curtains, and as the light grew, her pain seemed to lessen. Her radio came on automatically at eight, signaling her usual time to get up for school. She turned her head to look at it, and noticed that the movement didn't hurt so much. She closed her eyes, took a deep breath, and sat up. She screamed inside, but managed to keep her mouth shut, and then in one swift movement, swung her legs over the edge of her bed.

She rested a moment to compose herself as pain shuddered through her limbs and torso. After the wave had passed, she stood and, with stilted steps, made her way over to her full-length mirror. She looked at her reflection.

The metamorphosis was complete -- she had changed. She took in the new layer of skin, fancying that it was thicker and more durable than the last, though it was still raw, with small areas pumping out blood in little pools. Some of the old skin still clung on in places, but that would drop off. She tilted her head, examining the skull, noticing a clump of hair had fallen away along with the flesh.

She winced, taking a step back, and stared into her own eyes -- both black -- as numbness crept in. She would never be the same again. She smiled at her reflection as she realised that, and rested her hands on her hips. The pain was just a dull throb now, like background noise. Her thumbs connected with deep scratches, and, confused, she turned to examine her lower back in the mirror. An untidy, yet unmistakable, pentagram was etched into the soft, raw flesh. Blood trickled from the deepest points and ran down the backs of her legs.

She thought back to the day the spider bit her -- which now felt like it was years ago -- and recalled Martin's words as he examined the beast.

"You should see the markings on this thing's back. I thought it was one of those false widows, but this pattern is more like a star or something.... no, not a star, a pentagram!"

Her smile broadened; it had chosen her. She had transformed because she had been selected. Accepted. She continued to smile at her own reflection as her dad entered the room, completely unaware of his presence. She was also unaware of the warmth trickling out of her wounds, carried in her blood.

Amy's dad stood in the doorway, silent as usual, but for a different reason. He looked at his once beautiful daughter -- a picture of gore in her nightdress, bloody open scissors clutched in one skinned hand. A million thoughts raced through his mind, but it seemed that there were none at all. Reason and logic had deserted him. Rooted to the spot, he marveled that his mutilated daughter had even survived the attack on herself, let alone that she was able to stand.

Finally alerted to his presence by his shallow sobbing, she turned towards him. He collapsed to his knees in shame, guilt, and mourning. He didn't know who was looking at him, but he was sure that his daughter was dead.

"My little girl…"

Amy clenched her fists, feeling an obstruction in one of them. She looked down, noticing the scissors, and raised them to eye level. She didn't remember picking them up, yet she felt their impression in her palm and realised she had been clutching them for a long time. Strands of gnarled flesh clung to the points.

By the end of the day, she had helped her dad shed his skin too.

NEEDS MUST
A.S. CHAMBERS

It was a nice well; roomy, dank, and dark. There was just a glimmer of hurtful sunlight from the small aperture high above. This suited Odd Bod suited him fine. As he sat in the noxious gloop that constituted the well's floor, he scratched the infrequent tufts of hair on his scabrous scalp and decided that, overall, life had been very good to him. He had a safe place to live and there had been no hordes of angry villagers chasing him with pitchforks or other horticultural accoutrements.

The food, however, was becoming a problem.

Odd Bod tugged at a small bone that was lodged in the sticky floor and it parted company from the clinging substance with a wet pop. He blew at it and a piece of green slime dripped onto his knee. Absentmindedly rubbing at the slime with one hand, his other used the bone as an impromptu toothpick between his blackened incisors whilst he contemplated the issue of supplies.

There used to be plenty of food. It would come to the well, drop the wooden thing down to scoop up the wet stuff and, if he was hungry, Odd Bod would give the wooden thing a big tug, causing the food to come crashing down into his awaiting lap. True, it was a noisy experience when the food fell, and sometimes it needed convincing that it really was food, but on the whole, it worked to Odd Bod's satisfaction.

Recently though, the food had stopped dropping the wooden thing down. Odd Bod thought that this must be down to one of two reasons. It was either because the horrid wet stuff that the wooden thing used to scoop up had finally vanished or -- and this possibility troubled Odd Bod more -- that he had eaten all the food and there was none left.

Yes, that troubled Odd Bod a great deal. The thought of a world with no food was not a pleasant prospect at all, even if he did live in a very nice dark, dank well with very little sunlight.

He hoped that it was the lack of the wet stuff that had caused the food to go away; he truly did, because if the wet stuff came back, then the food would too. If, however, he had eaten all the food...

Odd Bod sadly shook his head. He had never been a fan of the wet stuff. It had always gotten everywhere and had made him feel as icky as the wet stuff itself. Odd Bod had fashioned himself small ledges between the crumbling bricks which had provided places for him to perch on when the wet stuff had risen up at certain times of the year. Then, over the last few years, the wet stuff had stopped rising. Instead, it had gotten lower and lower until all that was left was the gloop and the bits of broken bone that Odd Bod had discarded during his time in the well.

Odd Bod liked the gloop. It stuck nicely to his bony fingers and made his nose wrinkle when he sniffed it. Much more pleasant than the wet stuff.

However, if the wet stuff going away had caused his

food to disappear, then that was a bad thing -- whether Odd
Bod liked the wet stuff or not -- and something had to be done
about it. The melancholy creature looked up to the small hole
high above and sighed. There was only one way to find out
what had happened to his food. Had it gone away or had it all
been eaten? He had to find out or he would starve. It would
not be the easiest of jobs, but one that had to be undertaken,
nonetheless. His stomach rumbled and he whimpered
disconsolately, his shaggy whiskers quivering around his
mouth.

Odd Bod transferred the small bone from his hand to
between his freshly picked teeth and placed a bare foot onto
the lowest of the perches. He reached up with his hands -- his
cracked and broken nails searching out the tiniest of nooks
and crannies with which to heave himself up. A foot edged
up to another perch and his hands started to seek out more
holes where he could cling securely between the bricks. After
he had reached the same number of perches as he had fingers
on his left hand, he had to start work with the bone. Whilst
clinging on with one set of fingers, the others used the bone to
dig out handholds and footholds for him to utilise.

So it went on, time after time, transferring his weight
onto newly excavated holes whilst digging out more and more
spaces for his hands and feet. As he ascended the side of the
well, Odd Bod realised that the work was becoming harder
and harder. Down below, the wall had been soft and easier to
excavate. Up higher, it was tough and the bricks were much
more firmly cemented together, but Odd Bod knew there
could be no turning back. He peered down between his legs
at his comfortable home and whimpered plaintively. What
he would give to be settled down there once more with some
fresh food, happily enjoying the knobbly, gristly bits that
spurted goo all down his front as his teeth chomped into them.

Instead, his muscles ached and his throat was dry. Moreover, to make matters worse, he was starting to feel very warm.

Odd Bod looked up and saw the reason for the increased heat; the hole at the top of the well was getting much larger! He had thought it was starting to increase in width when he had reached about half way, but he had dismissed the notion as silliness. Now, however, here he was, much higher up and the round hole was definitely letting in more of the hated sunlight. Odd Bod blinked as the brightness hurt his eyes and he focussed yet again on the task at hand, digging furiously between two stubborn bricks. Even the bricks seemed to be suffering from the sunshine. Down below, they had been beautifully dark and shiny; up here, they were dry and much paler in colour. Odd Bod shuddered as he dreaded what the evil sunshine would do to him when he eventually emerged from the well.

He carried on climbing.

In time, his breathing became somewhat laboured as his throat felt parched. Odd Bod started to whimper as he began to fear that he was not going to make it to the top of the well. Despair started to wash over him.

What if he slipped and fell? Would he make the same noises that the food normally made when it jumped down to him?

What if he got to the top and discovered that he had eaten all the food? His stomach roared and he shook his head. No, he must not think such things. Food had to be out there. It had just gone away when the wet stuff had disappeared!

He glanced up and squeaked in both fear and excitement. Fear because the hole was now so wide that he could not see all the way around it. Excitement because he was only about an arm's length from the top. A broad grin of blackened teeth spread across his face and he clambered towards the rim of the well.

Odd Bod's stomach lurched as his foot slipped and
his arm swung free. Screaming loudly, he gripped with one
hand on the bone that was currently dug between two bricks.

Silly Odd Bod!

Silly Odd Bod!

He had let his excitement get the better of him and
had lost his concentration. With one firm tug on the bone,
he swung his loose arm up and grabbed at the tiniest of gaps
in the unforgiving brickwork. His nails prised themselves
in and he hissed in pain as the rough surface dug into his
grey flesh. Desperately, his feet scrambled at the sheer wall
below him, propelling his weight up towards the rim of the
well. He discarded the bone, ignoring the tool as it tumbled
down towards the dark, comforting gloop. Instead, he hauled
his hand up to the precipice above him. His fingers flailed
around, crumbling material on the rim until they found sound
purchase and the rest of his withered body scurried up the
last little distance. With one, firm lunge he heaved himself up
and over the edge of the well. He rolled head over heels and
landed with a thump on something that was most definitely
not gloop.

Odd Bod bent over onto all fours and peered closely
at the stuff. It covered the floor around the well. It felt strange
to his gloop-accustomed touch and consisted of a multitude of
little strands of near identical material that stood together in
the near vicinity.

He sniffed it. It wobbled as he did so.

Carefully, he picked some out and stuck it in his
mouth before chewing.

"Pah!" He spat the disgusting substance out and
wiped spittle from his face with the back of his dirt-encrusted
hand.

"Why are you eating grass?"

Odd Bod's head snapped up and his eyes located the source of the noise. It was food; a small morsel, but food nonetheless. He grinned.

The food giggled as it clasped its hands over its mouth. "You look funny," it laughed.

Odd Bod sat down on the horrid-tasting stuff and scratched his threadbare scalp. This food was strange. Food normally made noises like, "Oh, God! No! No!" or "Please no! I have children!" This one sounded different. In addition, it was not covered in delicious icky stuff.

He pointed with a chipped and broken fingernail. "Food?" his gravelly voice enquired.

"Sure," said the little red-haired girl. "I've got lots. Teddy and I are having a tea party on the blanket over there."

Odd Bod's eyes followed her small finger as it pointed over to a small furry thing sat on the thing called a blanket. "Food?" he asked again.

The little girl walked over to him and took his warty hand in hers. "Come on. We have plenty."

Odd Bod clambered to his feet and slowly lurched along behind her as she led him over to the blanket where the small, inanimate furry thing was propped up against a grey stone. In front of it were a number of round receptacles of different sizes, along with an object that had a handle on one side and a pointy bit on the other. The girl patted the blanket next to her and Odd Bod seated himself down, tucking his gangly legs beneath him. He frowned as his brain, used to years of peaceful solitude, tried to make sense of the situation.

As his grey cells bumped together in confusion, the little girl handed him one of the round things. "Here you go," she said. "Cake."

The very perplexed diner took the object in both his

hands and stared at it. It was flat and about the size of one of his hands. It was decorated around the edge with pink flowers. Not sure what to do, he shoved it in his mouth and started to chew.

"No!" exclaimed the girl, leaning over and dragging the thing out of his mouth. "Don't eat the plate. Eat the cake."

She proceeded to hold her own plate and apparently feasted on thin air.

Odd Bod did likewise. The air did not taste of anything. He frowned.

"It is only make-believe, you know," the girl whispered into his ear. "There isn't really any cake. Just don't tell Teddy. He'll get upset."

Odd Bod looked over at Teddy. The small, furry thing was making no apparent effort to eat the make-believe cake. Whatever cake was. Odd Bod sighed and glanced longingly over his shoulder to his well.

"Are you thirsty?"

"Thirsty?" Odd Bod asked.

The girl was now placing a different receptacle in front of him. This one was also decorated in flowers but was somewhat deeper in shape. "I'll pour some nice tea in the cups." She picked up the odd-looking thing with the handle and poured a clear liquid into the cups before offering one to her guest. "Here you go."

Odd Bod took the little cup awkwardly in his misshapen fingers and raised it to his mouth. His nose caught a whiff of its smell and wrinkled in disgust. He snapped his head back and grimaced.

"Now, don't be rude," the little redhead scowled. "Drink it all up."

Odd Bod looked across the rim of the cup to this strange piece of food that was not acting as it should, then peered down into the cup, unsure as to what he should do. Part of him wanted to reach over and gobble her up, but part of him felt he really ought to do as he was told. It was only polite.

He placed the cup to his lips.

The girl smiled and nodded for him to continue. "Down in one," she said.

Odd Bod did as he was instructed and gulped the liquid down.

He immediately regretted the decision.

Emily carefully tidied up the blanket and the tea set. She cautiously poured the remains of the so-called tea down the dry, foul-smelling well - the well in which her mummy had died. She had no idea what she had put in the teapot, but it seemed to have done the trick. It had been a concoction of all sorts of liquids from tins in the cellar, the labels of which had borne loud warning symbols.

It had worked a treat.

She had been terribly scared when the monster had climbed out of the well, but it had saved her the job of climbing down to do what had needed doing. Besides, Teddy had been there for moral support.

The thing that had eaten her mummy and so many other villagers lay dead at her feet.

She bundled Teddy and the tea set into the blanket, swung the improvised bag over her shoulder and skipped merrily home.

THE OCTAGONAL CABINET
IAN CALDWELL

I was surprised the invitation had found me, but I shouldn't have underestimated Lord Aries. He was an old University friend and it had been a privilege to know him. Over time, we had fallen into other circles, other lives. Lord Aries was one for travel and adventure, and I'm happy with a small world. But there it was, an invitation to Aries's country house; lunch followed by entertainment by the Host, ending with a buffet and dancing in the evening. How could I refuse? It was a chance to use my motorcar, and surely Harriet would love to be out of the city for a while.

      The day had started rather pleasantly, but grey clouds swept over head by the time we arrived. The staff took our bags at the door and directed us to the rear of the estate. There we found two silent men intent on clay pigeon shooting; with muffled ears, they didn't hear us approach. Harriet wasn't going to wait to be noticed, and stepped up to tap Aries once on his shoulder. He met her with a smile, and seemed even more pleased when I stepped forward to warmly shake his hand. It was only in taking my eyes off Aries that I recognised the man standing next to him. Sir Charles Darrow, the other member of our Old University triumvirate! A little larger for his years, but unmistakable.

I introduced Harriet to them both and was warmly congratulated on our engagement. We relocated to the veranda for a light lunch, and exchanged stories. Apparently, until the other guests arrived this evening, we three were his Lordship's only company. I apologised to Harriet, hoping she wouldn't get too bored with only old boys to listen to all afternoon. She shushed me and said she'd make interesting conversation of her own.

Darrow was slightly put out to learn Harriet was a journalist, but she gave her usual deft reply about women aspiring to be more than home makers, and in any case, she wrote under the pen name of 'H.R. Macmillan' and intended to keep to that habit even after we married. Putting down fusty Darrow won her to Aries's affections, and he wished her luck before standing to leave us, saying he needed a little time to prepare the afternoon's entertainment.

I took a seat closer to Sir Charles and quietly asked what had happened to make him settle his old feud with Aries. He told me nothing had changed except the passage of time, but his Lordship had made the gesture and he was going to take things at face value. Although Aries was unlikely to let his good intentions get in the way of testing a boundary, and while Darrow wished to rise above the old quarrels, he reminded me he had his limits.

It's sad one of my most treasured memories of University is also the structural fault that lies between Aries and Darrow. I had counted it a privilege to sit in between them as they talked, often at length and late into the night. Darrow taking the naturalistic and pragmatic view of the world, Aries forever hectoring away at his 'stale dogmas.'

The lively exchanges become ever more strident over time. until disagreements bled into personal disdain and finally publicly scorn against one another.

At that moment, Darrow was scorning me for leaving the civil service to buy a hotel -- facts he'd gleaned from Harriet. I told him after eight years of wasting my time, I was keen to do more with my life than grow old in a boring position so I could enjoy retiring from it. What's more, it was a quality lodging house and the city location meant I'd have the pick of who I had in. It would largely run itself, allowing me to finally catch up on my reading.

Darrow shook his head at it all; the woman going out to work while the man stayed behind to make house. I would apparently go quite mad stuck alone in that lodging house all day. I scowled at it all, but Harriet had to cover her mouth to hide a private giggle. Thankfully, Aries returned and gleefully announced he had a demonstration waiting for us upstairs -- one that would baffle and amaze us.

The Octagonal Cabinet stood much taller than a man, wide and heavy. Its dark wooden panelled surface was exquisitely detailed, revealing loving craftsmanship. At the top, tiny birds wheeled in the sky above the canopy of a vast forest; the tree roots stretched far down into the strata, snaking and twisting into other shapes, betraying the pleasant vista above.

These roots became devouring wolf heads, phallic shapes, and writhing naked forms. A door with an old ivory turn handle was the only obvious way in or out. It was set on a raised base, flush with its eight sides so that the door had almost a foot's clearance from the ground. His Lordship had gone further still, adding his own platform of a stunted table familiar to the kind Magicians use to assure the audience no trap door was involved in their cabinets of wonder.

A room in Lord Aries's manor house had been set aside just for this. The furniture was cleared away and even the carpet rolled back to reveal the floor boards below. The only other feature was a long rope hooked to the ceiling and coiling about the floor.

Aries did not explain the nature of the Cabinet to us straight away; instead he left it for us to examine freely while he regaled everyone with the tale of the thing's acquisition from Africa. Not a dull story at all, involving hidden dens where shadowy characters wielded great power. Harriet would stop him to ask questions, such as various conditions he'd laid down for the Cabinet's transportation back to England; and Darrow thought it all an embellished drama used to distract us and whet our excitement -- a typical magician's trick. Lord Aries playfully wondered how boring the conversations at Darrow's Royal Scientific Society must be if no one was allowed to embellish a good story.

"Well how much did you pay for it, if you didn't commission the thing yourself?" Darrow asked bluntly.

Aries took back the scene by simply replying: "My life."

After a dramatic pause, he told us the Octagonal Cabinet's previous owner had guarded it so privately it had been a game in itself just to see it at work. The owner had refused all offers for it, claiming the box to be worth more that material wealth. In the end it had boiled down to an insane wager -- a revolver with only one empty chamber and his Lordship's devilish luck. Sir Charles was torn between disbelief and condemnation, but settled on being dismissive. For whatever trick Lord Aries was about to perform it was just that -- a trap door, the secret compartment, the mirror at the certain angle; in the end you can only appear to defy natural laws, not break them.

Challenged by this, Lord Aries strode onto
the platform and opened the door. It creaked away to
reveal the fine scarlet velvet interior. Invited to inspect
it, I stepped up and went inside. The door was level with
the interior, which made me remember the base of the
thing. I tapped my foot and found the floor not all together
empty underneath. I wondered aloud about something in the
base. Aries seemed to agree -- a mechanism, maybe, he hadn't
yet checked.

I reached out to pull the door closed, but Lord
Aries reflexively clutched it back with a jolt and warned me
not to. This wasn't any vanishing box as I understood it, and
Aries could not guarantee my safety if I was inside. I stepped
out and stood back, waiting to be finally amazed.

Lord Aries pushed the door shut with a click, then took the
box with both arms. I saw it could turn and spin on its base,
which stood still. When it had turned enough so that the
door was now flush with another side of the octagonal base,
a deep clang resounded. His Lordship turned to smile at his
guests -- his moment of victory near. Opening the door,
he stepped away.

Harriet was the first to see what had happened and
let out a muted private oath.

Now the velvet floor was broken by a wide lidless
trap door. The three of us huddled up, unable to think
what to say as we took turns leaning in and looking down,
for, maddeningly, we could see a fine marble floor maybe
ten feet below the open hatch. We kept looking under
the raised cabinet and inside again, trying to reconcile the
two perspectives.

Darrow, ever the empiricist, knelt down on his knees
and dipped one hand through the hatch, while the other felt

along the underside of the platform. Yet the arm inside the box continued to sink inward, past the point where, had his hands been outside the box, one would have met the other.

There was no way to reconcile this. The Trap Door defied reality.

"Well now. Should we go down?" asked Lord Aries, grinning as he walked towards the box, the ceiling rope partly looped about one shoulder.

As he was the cause of all our woes, he volunteered to go first. A credit to her choice of profession, Harriet went next and I was last. Darrow played his own part, marching about the house, trying to find the room directly under the Octagonal Cabinet. Such a thing seemed unlikely, as the only way in or out of the secret room was the hatch we came in through.

The interior chamber was a long rectangle of carved marble, and at the other end was some kind of altar, raised on steps with a pillar at each corner. It was only as we got closer we saw what once must have been the golden jewelled knight in armour, laid out as if in repose. This was a tomb, apparently.

I credited Lord Aries on his trick. I did not know how he had forced the perspectives so that it appeared the under chamber was only accessible from within the cabinet. His Lordship assured me the puzzle was not even half done and, pressing us to cut short our exploration, had us climb back up top where Darrow was waiting.

We said nothing as Aries shut the door and began to turn the cabinet again, twisting it further away from the starting position. When it opened, we huddled once more, and only this time did we see it was a wholly different under room. We were at a dizzying height over a vast chamber; its walls and floor were finely painted but faded with time.

Darrow muttered something of the Library of Alexandria, and Harriet dropped a penny into the hatch.

I couldn't fathom any of it. How could the under chamber change so drastically and so quickly without a ludicrous amount of stage hands and mechanics. Ridiculous. Lord Aries revealed that what was accessible through the trap door changed depending upon which side the door was aligned to.

I should point out some of the chambers were no longer accessible; two were nothing but rubble piled to the trap door. One was an underground cave system that was completely flooded and in darkness. The other four all led to strange but stunning underground chambers that were part of the box's magical world.

In addition to the Tomb and the Library vaults was the Great Hall; a room of grey stone, carved and high vaulted. A giant fireplace dominated the space made for an owner with the dimensions of a giant. Whatever the original intention of the room, it had been repurposed into an armoury, with ancient weapons of sword, shield, pike, and axe piled into the brittle wooden alcove shelving. When lamps were sent down for better light, we noticed dark lines chalked in black upon the floor; these linked in a zig-zag to a single common point before the wall directly opposite to the great fire place. We found four holes arranged in a square upon the ground there and speculated about a removed altar. Or worse, perhaps -- a giant's throne.

The last chamber was beautiful. The ceiling was low enough to the ground that I was able to leap down and jump back onto the hatch without the rope.

This chamber was stained a deep cerulean by an endless film of water which gently ran down walls. It channelled along grooves in the ground to a central point, where it guttered into a curved font guarded on either side by two giant cats, sitting like sphinx, facing one another. Of all the chambers, the font room unnerved us the least.

Back in Aries's house, we sat upon the floor and just talked to each other, trying to understand what this object was. Lord Aries told us what he knew of the lost rooms. Of the two in rubble, one was known as the 'mosaic room,' and if you dug about in the rocks fragments, coloured tile could be found; the other was known as the 'market place,' and he knew not much beyond that. Although the flooded cave was lost to darkness now, but had once been an underground waterfall bright with luminescence.

We listened to Lord Aries without interruption. Without a doubt, he possessed something unique and seemingly magical. He confessed his eagerness to know Darrow's thoughts on all this, but the man seemed quiet and clearly distracted; at best, he grudgingly admitted he had no answers at the moment. Lord Aries was disappointed at so poor a concession and ushered us out the cabinet room so he could lock it up. His party guests were gathering and he didn't want any of them to stumble into there. Also we were not to speak of the box to anyone else -- not for the moment anyway. The gas lights were lit as the evening encroached upon us. Aries was now off playing host, and Darrow was silently helping himself to food and drink. Harriet kept asking me more questions about Aries but I couldn't stop thinking of the magic box. I just wanted to return to that room and check that it had all been real.

Harriet and I danced briefly and ate a little fruit just to keep ourselves going, but neither of us had much appetite. When we saw Darrow sitting alone in the corner, looking dazed, we both went over, knowing exactly what he must have been going through.

Darrow still spoke in terms of: 'If it is true,' as if the afternoon with the box had been just a story for him to ponder on. He wondered if the mechanism in the cabinet's base functioned like the junction of a telegraph services, connecting the interior of the box to other places about the world. If those underground room were actually out there, what would happen if we dug our way up and out to the surface? And if such a mechanism could be studied and replicated, one might be able to go from Tooting Bec to Timbuktu as easily as walking from one room to another. Harriet kept thinking of things she wished she'd done when she had the chance, like leaving an object in one chamber and the returning to it later; and if that worked, try again -- this time with a volunteer staying behind. Soon we were all adding to this list of activities. Together, we resolved to do the obvious thing.

The people surrounding Lord Aries were just so much furniture as we worked our way past them for his attention. Guessing our motives, he apologised to everyone else and took us outside into the cool, quiet air. Harriet started charmingly to lay out our case, but Aries soon brought it to a halt. Using the box at night was out of the question; he might entertain something tomorrow, but for the moment, it was impossible. Darrow demanded to know why and his tone was suspicious.

It was then we learned the darker nature of the box, for at night the chambers accessed were of another quality than the ones found in daylight. I just absorbed his words and felt giddy, but Darrow scoffed and labelling it a weak excuse. Harriet asked for a quick look in on the night chambers -- surely that would settle it. Aries asked what I thought, and after baffled mumbling, I said it was obviously up to him, even if it was just all a trick on his part. He thought for a moment then. to everyone's surprised. relented.

"I will show you one. The tamest of them," Lord Aries informed us as we stood nervously before the Octagonal Cabinet again. The box was carefully turned to an exact position; clearly his Lordship had some foreknowledge of what location yielded what.

When the door opened we were assaulted by a tinnitus-like pitch, a moribund howl; the mood in the room sank into quick depression.

The Light from below was pale and grey, and looking down, I saw only a narrow path standing out of a dark oily sea. His Lordship pulled the rope close and asked which of us was game enough to go down -- expecting no takers. I shook my head; it was too much. Harriet sighed and began to put on her gloves, but then Sir Darrow offered to go in her place, which seemed to please Aries. Charles was nervous, but I could not deny his bravery.

Once lowered, he spoke of seeing a circular chamber of dark rock -- a lake all about it, with only his catwalk to stand on. And he described seeing human figures carved into the walls -- all of them screaming and reaching out toward him. He wandered out of view, inching along the path, occasionally muttering a response to a question from Harriet. Then he yelped and darted back underneath us and screamed to be pulled up immediately.

The poor man wasn't content just to get out. He staggered out into the hallway to lean on a wall, gasping, pale, and trembling. Aries ordered us to take him down to his private study for a stiff drink while he locked up again.

Darrow was soon calmer, but obviously shaken. He stood at the fire place, half resting on the mantel with an empty glass in hand. He told us of putting one hand into the black water and feeling something, not with touch, more a sensation like a mass moving down in the depths.

Lord Aries refilled Sir Charles's glass and reminded us that was just the tamest of rooms, and that others had deeper horrors. He said he had names and warnings for all of them. The Tome Chamber, the Forest of Cages, the Penitents' Slough, The Three Iron Judgements, the Sinner's Catacombs, the Mausoleum of the Beasts, and the Tapestries of Flesh. He let his words linger slowly on this last. Clearly Darrow's terror was an important private victory.

With a quivering voice, Darrow offered all the resources of the Royal Society to uncover the truth of the box's nature, whatever that might be. Aries just snorted at the idea and accused him of wanting to steal the thing back to London for himself. So long as it was on his property, those chambers and their secrets were on his land. The point was argued back and forth for a moment until Darrow let out a quick sharp laugh that made me jump. He turned to Aries and openly accused him of orchestrating everything.

Hadn't Lord Aries been in control of the situation the entire time? And the master stroke, baiting us to ask for more and giving us a grand finale? Of course the box couldn't be moved; the trick wouldn't work in London, would it?

Lord Aries lost patience with him and angrily called him a few choice names before eagerly inviting him to wait out the night in the box if he truly believed anything he'd just accused Lord Aries of. Taunted, Darrow threw his drink into Aries's face; his Lordship blinked in pain but was on him. Darrow resisted and soon they were grappling like school boys. They were both red faced and grunting, Darrow being pushed hard onto the mantel, staggering a pace or two before being hauled right back as if Aries was intent of shoving him into the fire.

I was a statue before this scene. Harriet just seemed to stare at it all with fascination. It was only when Darrow kicked Aries in the knee, causing him to drop to a crouch, that I realised I must step in to hold Charles back from pressing his luck. I paid for that; I was on the ground now with a seething pain in one shoulder. Lord Aries stood over me with a poker in one hand.

Harriet came down to me as I twisted about, trying to manage the agony. Feeling a giddy sickness, I fought the urge to throw up. Darrow staggered out of my view, letting out a sob. To his credit, Aries offered a full and total apology for his poor aim and promised me he would never have wished me any harm. He inspected his handiwork, something likely fractured -- perhaps my collarbone. He said he'd get his doctor in the morning and would pay my bills in full until I recovered.

I do not fully recall the next series of events, except being led out with the support of my two friends; the faces of the other guests all on me as I wept my way past them all. On my bed, I was painfully stripped of my jacket, shirt and shoes. Aries made up a kind of sling for me and retrieved a measure of laudanum.

I must have slept, or at least drifted in and out. I remember Harriet being there, trying to assure me. Everything was so quiet; apparently Aries had angrily ordered everyone to go home and turned in. Darrow had crashed also.

I remember pleading more than once for Harriet to stay with me; a childish fear of being left alone in pain overwhelming me. The last I heard from her was a gentle arguing to hush.

I must have stared at that ceiling for some minutes before I realised I was awake and feeling very cold. My good arm reached over to where she had been sitting in a chair next to my bed. Nothing. Very slowly I sat up, turned and placed

my numb feet down unto the ground. A grey fog was all I
saw when I looked down, and it took a few moments before I
realised it was real. A layer of fine mist obscuring the carpet,
leaving it wet with dew.

I'm not sure what propelled me, I wanted Harriet, yet
my steps took me dreamily back towards the cabinet room.
I registered the room's door was unlocked and staggered
quick to the threshold to stare in. The source of the miasma
was, of course, the cabinet, turned into a chamber, its door
ajar. A sickly yellow light pulsed and faded within. I mouthed
Harriet's name over and over, my mind a numbing blank as I
tottered into the room and towards the black column of
the box.

I almost tripped over the body of Darrow, obscured by
the fog and laying on his side. His eyes were open and mouth
agape in silent, fatal horror. The next I knew, I was gasping
and banging on Aries's door. Stirred, he soon realised what
had happened before I could burble it all out. A quick check
of his desk, he snapped something about a missing key and
stormed off down the cabinet room, hissing Harriet's name.

He slammed the cabinet shut and turned the box to
the safe setting before opening it again. Long animal-like
claw marks were on the door's velvet interior. Aries dismissed
the idea of a monster and insisted Harriet must have scored
them. He speculated Harriet had enlisted Sir Charles to aid
her in a descent that had gone awry. Whatever had happened,
Darrow had fallen away with a fatal heart attack or a stroke of
some sort, pulling the rope back up as went.

But what of the claw marks? If the door was open,
surely she would have stepped out if she'd gotten this far? His
Lordship went pale. No, she'd been sealed in by Darrow, who
had turned the cabinet to some other chamber. Maybe she'd
had that idea, and that next under room had proved chillingly

fatal for him.

"But she's at the threshold of one of the chambers!" I pointed out. How else would she claw at the door? Aries was trembling. Nevertheless, he turned to me and nodded. And so we began the terrifying challenge. A new game of five bullet Russian roulette was about to be played.

Aries guessed Harriet's chamber was the one just before the mist room, and turned the box to that alignment. His shaking arm reached out and slowly touched the ivory handle. His fingers tightened as he gently he turned it until, with a click, the door silently opened.

His Lordship leaned gently in and gazed inward into what was below. After a moment, he turned to me and said he could see her, but she was prone and the other side of the lower room. He tied the rope about his waist and went down while I stood stationed above, steadying the lifeline and looking on.

Vile earth banked the floor of the chamber and sloped into a wide circular pit. If you looked long enough, you could see the silt move, sliding ever so slowly and unfalteringly into the abyss. Harriet was folded over on herself like a broken puppet on the far side of the pit. With careful footing, Aries slowly navigated his way around and spoke of wailing voices, but I told him I could hear nothing.

He turned to look back up at me, perhaps to urge me to be quiet, but he froze, looking back at me -- his eyes filled with horror. When I saw the dancing light about his eyes, I realised he was not looking at me but all about me, toward the ceiling of this horrid place. I felt a creep go down my spine as I started to lean in. All this time Aries mouthed:

"Don't. Don't."

I saw them now. Black and huddled, shifting, hugging

the roof of this vault; an indistinct sea of limbs and bodies, small hideous faces, all glaring with yellow-eyed menace down onto Aries.

I gave a yelp as I felt a tug at my back and twisted to see a maid crouching down next to me with a lantern. It took me vital seconds to process it all. Had she stumbled in here to investigate the mist and found the body? She was stammering loudly. I haven't a clue what she was saying. I just had to shut up her up. They mustn't know -- they mustn't know.

It's all a little disjointed from here on. I remember pressing her up to a wall and covering her mouth with my good hand, and keeping it there until she finally crumbled downward -- a faint or something, I expect; her face red and blotchy.

Then I saw it. That dark, ghoulish figure rising, pressing itself up by its palms on either side of the hatch, and already clear to its waist. Its jaundiced eyes widened as they fixed upon me. The scream I heard was my own, but with the bravery of a madman, I took three paces toward the creature and slammed the cabinet door tight shut. Next a hard kick to the box's side, I turned it, creaking out of position. I staggered backwards, feeling my heart pulse throughout my body.

I remember throwing the maid's lantern down onto the rolled up carpet and watching it bloom as the fire took. I staggered out of the silent house as flickers of orange grew behind me, and I kept on walking whatever path was in front of me until the blue of morning was overhead and only a distant column of ugly brown smoke was behind me.

I soon organised a new version of events. The shoulder wound was from a foolish tumble. I'd been woken in the night by someone shouting fire, and still dazed on laudanum, wandered away, not thinking of Harriet. I just kept telling everyone that story over and over, adding no detail for fear of being caught out. If I was pressed for more, I would deflect it by acting enraged with myself for abandoning her there, blaming myself for the most ludicrous of things but never the truth. I just kept telling them -- telling everyone I just wanted to be alone.

In the end, I was. But I'm sure the ghosts of all of them linger about me. I see flashes of them from time to time in the guests at my lodging house -- even that unfortunate maid. The fear used to twist inside me; made me feel sick for needing these strangers to keep coming ... but you know, I've realised something obvious. I finally realised my lodging house has seven guest rooms; the same as that Octagonal Cabinet. It brought a calm to me I hadn't felt in years, for the nature of rooms changes at night. Obvious what needs to happen next isn't?

I will wait until they're all asleep and visit each chamber in turn.

HAPPY ANNIVERSARY
PAUL TOWNSEND

It always happens. We get the time together to do something nice or go somewhere different, and what happens? We have an argument -- usually over something so stupid. I don't think me and my wife are supposed to live in non-pressured environments. Well, not with each other. I don't think we know how to live like normal people.

Chrissy's a paramedic -- damn good one too. Helped a shitload of people stay alive long enough for the doctors to save 'em. Me, I'm in the fire department. We go from one extreme to the other. It's either helping little old ladies' cats outta trees or pulling a dozen people out of an inferno.

Tonight was our wedding anniversary. Only our second but, hell, still something to celebrate; least I thought so. I'd got a restaurant booked -- a nice fancy one for once. I'd saved up my overtime money and figured we deserved something special.

I'd left a note for Chrissy, telling her to get dressed up to the nines, and that I was going to be home a little late. I didn't get any texts -- no phone calls -- so I thought we

were all good. The reason I was going to be late was because
I'd been out and hired a tuxedo, and been to the barber's.
Basically, I'd gone to town on this. And her face when I
walked in? Ha! She just kept staring and staring.

Mind you, she wasn't the only one. I was staring at
her too. She had really gone for it when I told her to dress to
the nines. When I'd walked in the door, she came out of the
lounge in her little black dress. I tell you that dress clung to
all the right curves in all the right ways. She'd done some
gorgeous twisting thing with her hair so that it curled around
her head. Have you noticed, brunettes can get away with
doing things like that and it just seems to work?

And she has this fantastic perfume; it's kind of light,
but when you get close, you get this real hit of orange -- not
like some of those ones that make a woman smell like she's
been marinating in it, you know?

When I finally got her to speak again, she kept saying
how I didn't look like me, how well I scrubbed up... and she
also kept asking me how much the tux had cost, which took
the edge off my good mood, you know? I'd gone to the effort
of making things good for our anniversary and all she wants
to talks about is the money. I tried to tell her not to worry
about it, that I had it covered, but the more I tried to calm her
down, the more she wanted to know. She even threatened not
to come out.

It was about then that the car arrived. See, when I
told the restaurant it was our anniversary; they said they could
do me a deal on a chauffeur and car to pick us up and take
us home.

So he knocked on the door. Chrissy opened it before
I could get to it. She saw him there -- uniformed, limo parked
on the sidewalk -- and she hit the roof. Really laying it on
about bills to pay, work that needed doing that was more

important than this waste of money, so on and so forth. I tried explaining to her that it was coming from my overtime, not the joint account, but she was too far gone to listen.

I used a few choice words to remind her that this was my anniversary as well as hers, and that I had saved my money so we could have a real celebration for once. It didn't calm her down, but she got in the car.

You could have cut the atmosphere with a knife on the drive over. Poor limo driver; guess it wasn't really what he'd signed up for tonight. At least he just stuck to the driving and didn't try to 'lighten the mood.'

I could see Chrissy's eyes giving the place the once over when we pulled up; all she could see were dollar signs. So much for the great celebration. I had hoped that once she'd had a drink or two she'd loosen up, but she took one look at the prices and asked for soda. I ordered a fancy wine. I'd be damned if her penny pinching was going to stop me spending my money.

The waiter showed us to our table. It's that one over there, with the beautiful view of the city and the balcony. You can really see it all laid out for you, glittering like so many gemstones against the night. We ordered, the waiter left. Then the silence came down on us -- long, awkward silence. I tried to make conversation, tried to engage her with the view -- anything to try to bring her out of her shell -- but she didn't want to, and she's nothing if not stubborn; helpful when trying to save lives, not so useful when trying to reach a compromise.

She excused herself to go to the bathroom. Ten minutes later, the matrie d' came over and discretely explained that Chrissy had decided to go home and that the chauffeur was taking her there now.

I poured myself another glass of wine, and gave a

toast to myself and my fantastic marriage. I could feel the
eyes of everyone else on me at some point; that second bowl
of soup mocking me as I was sitting there alone. God only
knows what they thought. I didn't care; I'd paid for it with
money I'd earned doing a decent day's work.

"Fuck 'em," I thought.

The waiter came over, asked if everything was okay.
I told him with the food, amazing; with my marriage, less
so. He asked if I wanted to wait for "the lady," he called her.
Ha! "The lady" -- the little madam, more like. The bitch that
ruined our anniversary. I hope she's eating damn McDonald's
alone at home.

I told him not to bother waiting, and asked him for
another bottle of wine. He gave me one of those refined half
bow, half nod things and went away.

Pouring myself the rest of the bottle, I stared out of
those windows. The night was getting dark and I couldn't help
wondering if there was a fire out there somewhere I could
have been at, rather than being here. I didn't realise until
I saw my reflection in the window that I was playing with
my wedding ring, rolling it back and forth, as though I were
getting ready to pull it off my finger.

Catching the waiter's eye, I asked him if it would
be okay to go and grab a drink here at the bar. He said that
it wasn't really the done thing, but could see that I'd had a
rough night, and said that he couldn't see any harm in it. He
told me he'd come and get me when my main course was
ready. And that's why I'm sat here drinking whiskey and
talking to you on my wedding anniversary.

Oh, gotta go. My man's giving me the nod. Have
yourself a good evening. You gotta... you listen well, you
know that? Thanks. I- I mean that. Thanks for listening.

I walk back to my table slowly. I can feel the alcohol starting to get to me. The edges of my world were becoming a little hazy, and I had the feeling that my feet might do something stupid like trip me up if I wasn't careful. I rest my fingertips against the white linen tablecloth and take a deep breath to fight down off the blurry vision. I give the waiter a nod as I gingerly sink back down into the seat.

I turn my attention back to him and mumble, "Thanks, for everything tonight. You're solid, man."

He nods in gracious acceptance of my compliment before asking, "Is there anything else, sir?"

God, I don't belong here. I'm making an idiot of myself. It strikes me so hard that I really don't know how to live a normal life, like a normal person doing normal person things like going to a restaurant with my wife on our anniversary.

Glancing back at the plate of glazed spiced meat, vegetables, and spicy potatoes, I shake my head.

"Nah, it's all good."

He walks away and drifts off to another table. My eyes turn down to the thick slices of meat and my stomach growls hungrily. I ease my fork into it, gauging the resistance -- firm but yielding. Drawing the knife across the thick strip, I watch as it slices easily.

Placing a folded piece in my mouth, I could taste all the spices blossoming on my taste buds. There was so many flavours in the mix, I was having trouble identifying all of them. Sinking my teeth into the chicken, I think that was what the menu said -- the juices flow out -- and I can't help enjoying having spent so much on this meal. Setting down my knife and fork, I chew the meat, slowly savouring each new taste. There was cinnamon, some sugar maybe, definitely onion, garlic, chillies, peppers... possibly a bit of orange, maybe some other fruits. Just a whole lot of wonderful tastes that made me so glad I'd come here.

"It's such a shame that Chrissy didn't try this; she'd love it," I thought, then pushed all thoughts of her out of my mind. She didn't want it, so tough.

I continued eating the sumptuously prepared meal, savouring each bite as though it was my first, and at the end, I sat comfortably full and my anger dissipated.

The waiter arrived at my table as I eased the plate away.

"You enjoyed your meal, sir?"

"I certainly did, thank you."

"Do you want anything else? A dessert, maybe, or perhaps a coffee?"

I mused over the choice for a moment then smiled, "Yeah, a coffee would finish things nicely."

He seemed to drift away from my table once I'd made my choice, I watched him passing two or three other couples, bending to attend to them as he went. I had little time to wait or admire my surroundings before he was back with my coffee. Thanking him, I dropped a couple of sugar lumps in and stirred the tar-black coffee. The rich, slightly bitter, aroma curled up and lovingly caressed my nose.

I spend another ten minutes enjoying the coffee before laying down a twenty dollar tip for the waiter. He deserves it for everything that had happened tonight.

Taking a deep breath, I stood, my stomach full and my head a little clearer having soaked up some of the alcohol. I made my way to the matrie d' as he stood by the entrance and showed him my booking reference.

"Ahhh yes," he held up one finger, his eyes roaming for a cashier. With a single brief motion, he summoned one to us and smoothly withdrew from the proceedings. The young man surveyed my booking reference. He withdrew a tablet from the inside of his jacket pocket and tapped in the reference.

"I can see the meal has already been deducted from your card. So it is just the cost of the drinks to pay for, sir."

We did the familiar dance of the portable card swipe. He tore off my receipt and handed it to me with the card. The matrie d' reappeared beside me as the cashier departed.

"I've called your chauffeur to take you home, sir."

"Thank you. It's a wonderful restaurant you have here," I complimented.

"Thank you sir, we try our best. Ahhh, here is your car," he indicated with one white-gloved hand at the limo through the glass door.

"Night." I reached out to shake his hand.

"Good night, sir." He nodded politely, leaving my hand hanging. I withdrew it sheepishly before heading out the door before I made more of a fool of myself.

The limo driver had gotten out and had the back door open before I was out from under the restaurant's awning.

"Thanks," I slid onto the back seat, and waited for him to get back in the front and ease us into traffic.

"Good meal, sir?" he asked catching my eye in the mirror.

"Yeah," I sighed contentedly, "the meal was something else. My wife," I looked out of the window at the city lights as we glided through the busy inner city streets, "she's a different kind of something else. Say, how was she when you took her home?"

"Honestly?" he glanced in the mirror again.

"Yeah, honestly."

"She was mad as hell, sir."

"Shit!" I rubbed my face with one hand as I thought

of the fight that was going to be waiting for me when I got in.

"This is gonna be a fight and a half." I muttered shaking my head. "Happy anniversary, jackass."

"Sir?"

I woke with a start.

"We've arrived, sir... at your house," he added when I stared at him blankly.

I rubbed my eyes with the heel of my hands and I glanced out of the limo's window. The place was in darkness.

"Hopefully she's gone to bed." I turned my attention to the driver. "Thanks for the ride, and... I'm sorry you had to get caught up in all our shit tonight."

He shrugged. "Unfortunately, it's one of those things that happen. Enjoy the rest of your evening, sir."

I climbed out of the limo and walked up the front grass towards the front door, hands thrust into the pockets of my tuxedo pants, my head down, as he rolled off down the street. The long white limo turned around a corner and was gone, out of my life as though it had never happened.

"Time to face the music, I guess." I took out my keys and tried to unlock the door as quietly as possible.

There were two possibilities for why the house was in darkness. First, Chrissy had gone to bed, I was going to have to sleep on the couch, and we were going to have the mother of all shouting matches in the morning. Second, she'd been sitting in the dark since the chauffeur had dropped her off, waiting for me to come home, winding herself up hour after hour, and we were going to have the shouting match tonight. I hoped to God, it was the former. Something from my meal, probably the richness of it, was starting to repeat on me and, as I leant against the door jamb, a sharp pain gripped my stomach. I sucked down several long breaths, trying to get rid of the sudden pain. I spat a mouthful of acidic tasting saliva onto the grass.

"Ohhh, this isn't going to end well."

I stared at the door, trying to guess what my wife had chosen to do, and I knew I couldn't face the fight tonight.

I rested my head against the door taking more deep breaths.

"God, please let my pager go off. Please let someone set fire to something so I don't have to face this now."

I gave it to a count of thirty before I gave up, realising that God wasn't going to help me out of this one. I turned the door handle and pushed it open gently.

"Asshole," I muttered softly as I stepped inside.

Treading lightly across the carpet, I stopped when I felt something crack under my foot. It was a delicate sound, like glass. I retraced my steps to the door and cautiously flicked on the lights, unsure what to expect.

The scene of destruction struck me like a prize fighter's fists. Everything had been ransacked; books swept off shelves, drawers wrenched out, emptied and discarded. Picture frames, jars, and vases lay in fragments. Someone had dragged the television halfway across the room before abandoning it.

Even as I tried to take in what was in front of me, some tiny rational part of me was still working and I could feel words pushing their way out of my mouth before I even realised what they were.

"CHRIS?" The word erupted from me. To hell with burglary and property damage; I needed to know that my wife was okay. "CHRISSY?"

My feet carried me across the debris even as I

hollered her name. I felt pieces of glass and pottery break under my feet as I went. I leapt up the stairs two at a time, flinging open every door, screaming my wife's name as I tore through the house. Each room is in the same state, ransacked and destroyed and yet, somehow, I know this isn't Chrissy's doing. Something had happened to my wife but I don't know what, or even where to begin.

My stomach lurched as the impact of everything caught up with me. I barely made it to the bathroom where I collapsed in front the porcelain throne, my shaking hands clutching the rim as the acidic bile rose up my throat. My eyes streaming from the taste as it reached the back of my mouth, my stomach clenching as it tried to expel its contents. A watery steam of yellow fluid spattered the bowl; again and again I retched, bringing up pieces of that fantastic meal. Why hadn't I come home when she'd left? I could have been with here whenever... this had happened. I'd at least know where she was. My stomached tightened again and the acrid taste filled my mouth once more as I retched into the bowl. While I held onto the toilet and shivered, my throat continued gagging to purge the bile; the scent of orange zest fought to overcome the sickening stench of vomit. It took me a couple of seconds to recognise it as the tears continued to streak from my eyes.

I tried to lift my head and look around for Chrissy. I knew she must be close if I could smell her perfume. Rising to shaky feet, I put one hand against the wall for support and shuffled out of the bathroom into the hallway.

I looked around through watery eyes, trying to find my wife.

"Chris?" I managed though the lingering taste of the vomit in my mouth. I waited, listening to the darkness but there was no reply.

Making my way towards the bedroom, I realised that I couldn't smell her perfume any more. I turned around dumbly, shuffled back to the bathroom, and once more, a hint of orange perfume tickled my nostrils.

I went back into the bathroom to flush the toilet and wipe the vomit from my mouth when the scent of Chrissy's perfume hit me again - tangy, vibrant orange.

Struggling to understand where it was coming from, I reached forward to push the flush and froze, eyes down focused on the contents of the bowl. The undigested pieces of that fantastic meal that floated amid the bile and vomit -- the pieces of my Chrissy those bastards had fed me.

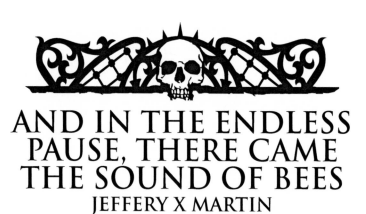

AND IN THE ENDLESS PAUSE, THERE CAME THE SOUND OF BEES
JEFFERY X MARTIN

Bobby loved Shonda, and he reckoned she loved him, and there wasn't a damned thing he could do about it. He was only the Caretaker for the Colony while Shonda was a Princess. One day, she would be Queen of the whole place. She was also about six years younger than he was. It was awkward all the way around, but she couldn't stay away from him, and he didn't want her to.

The Colony was much like a kingdom, although they had never known a king. Being a small community, they endeavored to be as self-sufficient as possible. They derived what little electricity they needed from wind-powered turbines. The land was fair, and the community garden flourished in season. There was game in the woods that bordered the property -- rabbits and some deer -- so they hunted their own food. In the center of the Colony was a large fire pit, where the citizens would gather to talk and cook and come together as a community. This was not some kind of half-baked attempt by faddish city-dwellers to get back to nature. Outsiders were rarely welcomed. It was simply how things had always been.

The largest house in the Colony was the Queen's Palace, a luxurious doublewide mobile home set on a permanent foundation. It was the only home in the Colony to have a wooden deck which wrapped around the entire structure. The other trailers were pop-ups or singlewides, with only three or four concrete steps leading up to the door. On the rare occasions that the Queen would address the Colony, she would stand on the deck while the citizens of the Colony gathered around to hear the Royal Edicts. She never appeared in public besides those times, and there was always a guard stationed at both the front and back doors. Without invitation, no one could get into the Palace.

But that never stopped Princess Shonda from getting out.

Bobby was strong, with yellow hair, and a constant countenance of kind-eyed concern. Every morning, Bobby would make his rounds through The Colony, checking on the welfare of everyone who lived there and making sure they understood their work assignments for the day. He patrolled the Colony at night also. Bobby slept lightly, and at the slightest odd noise, he was out of bed and investigating the source, fully armed and duty-sworn to protect the Colony and the people who lived there.

Even from an early age, Princess Shonda had been fascinated with Bobby; intrigued by the aura of calm power he exuded, and amazed at how he could take a broken thing and make it work again. She would watch him through the blinds of her bedroom window for hours. As a Princess, Shonda could have anything she wanted and was pampered, as per her station. What the Princess wanted more than anything, though, was to go outside and walk with Bobby, talk to him, and learn the things he knew.

"How much longer you figure there, Bobby?" Leo asked. Leo was one of the finest hunters in the Colony. Bobby was sweating in the late afternoon sun, attempting to repair the compressor on Leo's ancient air conditioner.

"I don't know, Leo," Bobby said. "Maybe forty, maybe forty-five minutes?"

Leo nodded. "I appreciate it," he said. Then he made an odd sound, as if he were about to say something but had suddenly swallowed a bug. Bobby looked up from his work, and was surprised to see Leo kneeling down on one knee.

"It's just a compressor, Leo," Bobby said. "No need to get all fancy."

Leo shook his head violently and pointed. Bobby turned. There next to him was Princess Shonda, resplendent in a torn black heavy metal t-shirt, yellow leggings, and furry boots. Bobby immediately dropped to the ground as Leo had and bowed his head.

The Princess stared at the two for a moment, loudly snapping her chewing gum. "What are you doing?" the Princess asked.

"I am fixing an air conditioner, Your Highness," Bobby said, not daring to face her.

"That's cool," she said. "Arise, y'all."

Bobby and Leo stood up.

"Show me," the Princess said.

"Show you what, Your Highness?" Bobby asked.

"Show me what you're doing to this thing," she said, pointing at the air conditioner. Bobby and Leo looked at each other for a second. This was not what they had expected their first brush with royalty to be like.

"Well, Leo's air conditioner stopped working and I'm pretty sure it's the compressor that's gone out, so I'm removing it with a wrench to see if that's the problem."

"Huh," Princess Shonda said, and blew a bubble with her gum. "Can I watch?"

"Sorry?"

The Princess shrugged. "Can I watch? I want to know what you're doing."

"Sure," Bobby said. "It's not real exciting."

"Neither is sitting in my room all day," Shonda said. Bobby smiled. "Well, if it's like that, do me a favor and hold this." Bobby handed her his wrench. She grinned and took it, holding it like a magical sword.

"My name's Shonda," she said.

"I know," Bobby said. "I'm Bobby."

"I know."

Princess Shonda watched intently as Bobby examined the compressor. The attention, especially from the future matriarch of the Colony, made Bobby nervous, and sweat rolled down his back. That was all it took.

This went on for months. The rest of the Colonists soon got used to seeing Princess Shonda out and about, walking the grounds with Bobby, helping him do whatever he had to do. If a truck needed fixing, the Princess would be there with him, crawling under the vehicle, holding a flashlight or handing Bobby different sized sockets. If anyone thought something was amiss or improper, they never said a word about it. For all they knew, Princess Shonda was acting as an emissary of the Queen, keeping an eye on the Colony and reporting her findings to Her Majesty or, even worse, the Palace guards. Best to just let it go.

"I'm worried," Princess Shonda said one evening, while helping Bobby work on the tractor. The sun was setting and, as usual, the Princess was holding a flashlight.

"Me too," Bobby said. "I think I'm going to have to replace this fuel line."

That earned Bobby a punch to the arm. "I'm being serious, Bobby."

"What do you have to be worried about, Princess?"

"That," she said. "That exactly."

Bobby put down his flat-head screwdriver. "Alright, Princess. You have my full attention. What's up?"

Princess Shonda sighed. "I'm not going to be Princess for much longer. I'm going to be the Queen soon."

"You don't know that."

"I do know that. I feel it, Bobby. I can sense it. Everything is tense and weird at home. And I can feel my body changing, too. It hurts. It feels like it's gearing up for something."

Bobby cleared his throat. "I'm probably not the right person to talk about this to, Princess."

Shonda made a petulant fist and hit the ground. "Who am I supposed to talk to about this, Bobby? Should I go talk to Leo? My mother, the stupid Queen? Nobody understands me the way you do, Bobby."

"You're at that age, Shonda," Bobby said, choosing his words with care. "Nothing's going to stay the same. There are things that have to happen. It can't be stopped. It's just the way it is."

"I know all that gross facts of life stuff," Princess Shonda said. "The guards told me about it. I ain't ready for that yet. Hell, I just barely started being a kid. I don't want to be an adult, especially one with responsibilities."

"Being responsible isn't so bad," Bobby said. "Everybody needs to work together. That's what makes the place run."

"Don't you ever want to get away, Bobby? Think about it. We could go anywhere."

"Leave the Colony?" Bobby laughed. "Nah. Ain't

nothin' out there I want. This is my home. Yours too."

"I would go anywhere with you, Bobby," she said.

"The only place you need to go is back to the Palace, Princess," Bobby said. "It's getting late."

Bobby rolled out from under the tractor first. He stood up and held out his hand. Shonda grabbed it and Bobby pulled her to her feet. Her hands were greasy and sweat streaked her face. The sunset was at peak color, and the sky burned a violent purple. The air was starting to take on the coolness of evening. Behind them, they could hear people gathering around the fire pit, laughing and telling stories of the day while dinner began sizzling over the flames.

"I wish everything could stay like this forever," Princess Shonda said. Bobby stared at the burning sky and nodded his assent.

Two weeks later, Princess Shonda awoke from a sound sleep with her stomach in knots and her white sheets soaked with blood.

The next day, one of the servants heard the sound of breaking glass. Upon investigation, he discovered the Queen in her bed, eyes rolled back in her head. The salty scent of urine filled the air. The queen had been watching a syndicated afternoon talk show and drinking her customary sweet tea. When her heart stopped, the glass slipped from her hand and shattered on the floor. The weeping servant rushed to the Palace guards to tell them the news.

The Queen was dead.

Long live the Queen.

As Caretaker, it fell to Bobby to burn the Queen's body. He spent a day cutting wood for the pyre, his sweat a substitute for tears. The Colony was in mourning for their fallen

leader, and Bobby could feel the weight of their grief on his
shoulders. It was as if the entire camp had a different smell
about it -- the aroma of despair, and the scent of pain. Bobby
absorbed it all, distilled it, and used it as energy for his task.
He would not allow himself to stop until he was finished.
At dusk, the people filed out of their homes and approached
the wooden structure. Some of them tossed flowers onto the
wood. Others helped Bobby finish stuffing hay into the open
spaces between the logs, fuel for the fire to come. When
the pyre had been decorated, the French doors of the Palace
swung open wide. Four Palace guards exited, carrying the
body of the Queen on a piece of black plywood. The Queen
had been bedridden for most of her life, only venturing to the
bathroom and the kitchen. Exercise had not been a priority.
The men struggled under her dead weight and with their grief,
which they had a difficult time hiding. It took a couple of tries
for them to heave the body of the Queen atop her final resting
place. When that was accomplished, the men joined the
Colonists, who had formed a circle around the pyre.

　　　　Through the open doors of the Palace stepped the new
Queen, the former Princess Shonda. She cleared her throat,
and everyone turned to stare. Bobby sucked in his breath. She
looked so different, even from just two weeks before. The girl
was gone and in her place, a beautiful woman had emerged.
He had never seen her dressed up before, and although her
black mourning dress was simple, it represented a striking
difference from the friend he had known. Her face seemed
fuller, among other things. She stood straighter. Shonda
had always been taller than everyone else in the Colony,
including her late mother, but now she seemed like a giantess.
She didn't avoid anyone's gaze, but met the eyes of all her
subjects in turn. She exuded command, confidence. A week
ago, she had been a little lady in waiting -- a Princess and

nothing more. Now, she gazed upon her Queendom as if it had always been hers.

"It is never easy to lose a Queen," she said, in a loud, commanding voice. "We all loved my mother. She inspired respect and adoration. The impulse to weep and remember is normal. This is the time for that. Take tonight to mourn. Get your crying done. Tell your stories. Remember your former Queen. Tomorrow, we go about things as normal. The Colony will survive under me, as it did under my mother, with your dedication and hard work."

She looked at Bobby and gave him a decisive nod. Bobby nodded back, and stepped towards the funeral pyre. He produced a candle lighter from his pocket, ignited it, and held the flame against the dry straw. He repeated this action three more times, in different spots, until the entire structure was fully ablaze. The firelight reflected off the aluminum of the trailers, turning the whole camp red.

The Queen came down from the porch and stepped into the circle next to Bobby, tearless, watching the body of her mother burn, the smoke drifting upward, bearing her soul to the afterlife, the whole area filling with the strange sweet smell of flesh and honey. She grabbed Bobby's hand and he blushed, his face unbearably hot from the fire, both within and without.

The fire began to die down and the colonists began to meander away, back to their homes. The guards began walking towards Shonda, the new Queen, motioning that it was time to leave. She held up a finger and they stopped in their tracks.

"How are you doing?" Bobby asked.

"It's so weird, Bobby," the Queen said. "Everything's different now. But I'm okay. A little scared, I guess. But okay."

"Good," Bobby said. "I worry about you."

The newly crowned Queen Shonda squeezed his hand. "I'm going to need you, Bobby," she whispered. "Now more than ever."

Bobby nodded and stood resolute, watching the fire die. Reluctantly, the Queen let go of his hand and joined the guards, who walked her back to the Palace. Bobby caught one last glimpse of her before the doors closed; her tear-streaked face stared back at the Colony, and then briefly back towards him, as if she had just remembered something she wanted to tell him. But then she was inside and there were only the guards, the fire, and the invisible line between royalty and colonist.

Bobby didn't see Queen Shonda again for three years.

The separation was difficult. Bobby had grown accustomed to her presence. There were times he found himself confused in the middle of a repair, having no one to help him. He kept to himself more, staying quiet even during dinner around the fire pit. It wasn't that he didn't like his fellow colonists; he just didn't have anything to say to them.

On his morning rounds, he found himself spending an inordinate amount of time staring at the Palace, looking for some motion behind the constantly drawn blinds. He wondered if she was secretly watching him or if she had forgotten about him completely, his memory a victim of politics and position.

He forsook his bed for the living room couch, and Bobby found himself staying up late at night, listening to talk radio, hoping for a knock on the door. He would awake, startled and angry, wondering if he had missed a secret visit from the Queen. In the morning light, nothing indicated that he had. His whole life began to feel like trying to remember a fleeting dream, so he could prove to himself that it hadn't been a dream at all, but reality.

The banging on his front door came early in the morning. It was still dark outside and Bobby, who had been thinly asleep in a mead-induced haze, was instantly angry. It was probably Leo. That guy was a supreme pain in the ass. Nothing worked for him. His air conditioner was always on the fritz. Light switches stopped working for no reason. It was probably a plumbing problem this time.

Bobby rolled off the couch, his boxer shorts crammed halfway up his ass, his hair sticking out in bizarre anime angles. The knocking came again, the force of it rattling the windows in the door. "I'm coming!" Bobby yelled. "Keep your pants on." Bobby unlocked the door and threw it open.

It was not Leo.

The palace guard on Bobby's doorstep wrinkled his nose in effete disgust. Bobby stared at him, stunned and slack-jawed. Embarrassment overcame Bobby, and his cheeks burned red.

"Your Queen wishes to see you," the guard said, disdain evident in his voice.

"Really? Can I get dressed first?" Bobby asked

"I would suggest it," the guard replied. "I shall wait here. I have been asked to escort you to the Palace myself."

"You can come in, if you want," Bobby said, gesturing towards his living room.

"I'm fine," the guard said. He turned his back to Bobby and closed the door.

Running on panic and instinct, Bobby took a quick shower, shaved haphazardly, and put on the clothes that smelled the cleanest. He checked his look in the mirror. He was still a wreck, but he looked a damn sight better than he did before.

He opened the door. The guard was still there, waiting for him. "Let's go," Bobby said.

The guard nodded and they walked towards the Palace, Bobby trailing only a few inches behind the guard, his excitement tempered by his trepidation.

They climbed the wooden steps (the second step had a nail that wasn't quite flush; Bobby made a mental note to fix that later) to the Palace deck. The guard brought a set of keys out of his pocket with which he unlocked the front door. He held it open wide for Bobby, offering neither direction nor instructions. Bobby simply stepped in, and the guard shut and locked the door behind him.

It was dark in the Palace. Bobby assumed he was in the living room; maybe royalty had a different name for it. The Arena of the Grand Sectional Couch. There was a small light on in the kitchen (the Royal Food Preparation Area). The counters were totally empty. Not even a salt shaker was visible.

"Back here, Bobby!" she was calling to him. "Through the kitchen."

"It's dark," he said.

"Well, turn on the light, silly."

Bobby walked through the kitchen, down a narrow hallway, past the water heater and utility closet. He could hear music playing, some drop-D metal song. Some things hadn't changed; Queen Shonda always had lousy taste in music. He followed the sound of double kick drums and growling to a cracked open door. It was her bedroom -- the Regal Suite of Nocturnal Activities.

He knocked, and the door swung open with the impact.

"Oh, my," Bobby whispered.

Candles, twenty, maybe thirty of them, dotted the room. Incense was burning in a holder -- honeysuckle, if Bobby reckoned correctly. Pink draperies hung from a central hook over the bed, cascading down like a child's mosquito netting. Mirrors of different shapes and lengths hung on the walls. All the candles made the room hot, and Bobby was dripping sweat in no time.

The draperies rippled, and a hand emerged from behind them, grabbing the fabric and pulling it aside. Sitting on the edge of the bed was Her Majesty, Queen Shonda. She had grown up. The Queen was almost wearing a sheer yellow nightgown that buttoned up the front; she had neglected the buttoning part.

"Hello, Bobby," she said.

"Hello, Your Highness," Bobby said, and he felt compelled to bow.

She laughed. "Stop it," Queen Shonda said. "That's silly."

Bobby put his hands in his pockets. "So! This is nice. I always wondered what it looked like in the Palace."

"They wouldn't let me redecorate how I wanted to," she sniffed. "I guess my ideas weren't regal enough. The guards came in and took down all my posters and put all this shit up."

"I like it," Bobby said. "It's colorful."

"It's okay. I'm not a child anymore, Bobby," she said, stating the obvious. "Everything changed, Bobby. It changed so fast." She patted the bed. "Come here. I'll show you." Bobby raised an eyebrow. "What's going on here, Shonda?"

"I think you're supposed to call me Your Highness now." Queen Shonda patted the bed again. "Come. Sit next to me."

And then he understood. Bobby hesitated briefly, as fear and desire waged a battle in his brain. That small war ended quickly, and Bobby took his place on the right side of his Queen. He had never felt satin sheets before. They were like trying to sit on water, and he was afraid he might slide off the bed. He felt the Queen's fingers on the back of his neck, caressing and stroking gently. It was like she was scratching an itch he didn't know he had.

"I am extremely uncomfortable right now," he whispered. A bead of sweat dripped from the tip of his nose.

"I understand," she said. "You've never done this before."

"Have you?" Bobby asked.

"No," she replied. "I wanted you to be the first. That was always the plan. Didn't you know?"

Bobby shook his head.

"Well, it's true. All those times we sat in your place, late at night, just talking about whatever, you never thought..."

"No. Not one time."

"You're a liar," Queen Shonda said, smiling.

"I can't lie to you," Bobby said. "You were the Princess and I was honor-bound to serve you."

Shonda lay back on the bed, her head on a stack of pillows. It was then that Bobby noticed her evening gown was crotchless. He tried not to stare, but failed.

"Now I am your Queen. You are no less honor-bound."

Bobby had never seen a naked woman before, except on television. It was nothing like he expected. There were so many different smells; fading deodorant, expectant sweat, something else dark and primitive he couldn't define. It was like being drunk, but better -- more focused.

"This is what you were made for, Bobby," Queen

Shonda said. "I am the entire reason you were born. Do you know this?"

He nodded.

"Then come to me," she said, and Bobby obeyed at last.

He awkwardly took off his clothes, keeping his eyes on his Queen, who was languorously stroking herself between the legs. He was amazed as he watched her nipples grow hard.

"I don't…"

"I know," she said, her voice soft and reassuring. "It's okay. It's going to be all right. This is your destiny, Bobby." She spread her legs wide and waited.

Bobby was still mostly soft when he entered her, but once his nerve endings registered the warmth and tightness, his penis swelled to its maximum length. Whatever modicum of control he had managed to retain slipped away. An urgent adrenaline rage shot through his bloodstream. He gripped the Queen tightly, stabbing his fingernails into her sides. She yelped in pain, then laughed deep in her chest. In return, she grabbed his hair, clumps of it coming loose by the bloody root in her hands. Her back arched until Bobby was sure they were no longer on the bed, but floating above it. The pressure in his groin was unbearable, but he wanted this new sensation to go on forever. His eyes bulged with the effort of keeping it in, but his lack of experience made it a battle he could not win. She shifted her hips slightly, drew in her breath and he felt his testicles slip into her vagina. This was unexpected, and the wet shock of it pushed him closer to the edge. The Queen tightened and twisted simultaneously. Agonizing pain shot through his lower half, making his toes straighten and crack. Bobby orgasmed then, more out of reflex than desire, and his scream was ear-piercing.

The entire act took less than five seconds.

Bobby wondered if it was like that every time. Even if it were, he thought he would still like to do it again. People on television said the first time was always weird. He stared into Queen Shonda's eyes, tears and sweat falling on her neck. He saw with some surprise that she was also crying, and gave her a questioning look.

"Did it hurt you too?"

"I'm sorry, Bobby," she said. "I'm so sorry."
He was wet down there, more than he reckoned he should have been, even with the commingling of fluids. He reached his hand down to feel and drew his fingers back. They dripped with blood and semen. But there was something else.

"See, everything's different now, Bobby," Shonda continued. "It all changes when you become the Queen, but I didn't know; I swear I didn't know to what extent! It's not just a change in power or position."

Bobby reached down again to his crotch and a horrible realization began to sink in. He felt dizzy, light-headed. He fell backwards off the bed, too in shock to scream.

"I have to keep it, Bobby. I have to keep it to make sure. Don't you understand? Please, tell me you understand!" She was crying harder and her words trailed off into a spasm of weeping.

The blood was puddling around Bobby's naked bottom from the rough hole in his body. Other organs were feeling the pull of gravity, and starting their downward slide to freedom. He looked at his Queen for comfort, but all he could see was the jagged stump of his cock sticking out of her royal vagina, still weakly spasming, shooting seed from his detached and deflating scrotum, which hung in front of her ass crack like a door knocker.

"It's for the Colony, Bobby," Queen Shonda said. "That's how it's always been."

"At your service," he whispered, and his eyes closed.

After a while, the men from the Nursery came. They were thin-lipped and grim, rarely speaking to each other or the Queen. They carried buckets and industrial-strength cleansers and an old wet-vac they had salvaged from someplace. They sopped up blood, scooped up shit and piss, and shoved things back into the appropriate cavity. When everything was clean, one of the Nursery workers suggested that the Queen burn some more incense. She did and for a few days afterwards, the Royal Bedroom smelled of sandalwood and meat.

A boy named Stephen grew into Bobby's position within the Colony. No one asked any questions; it was a gradual, seamless progression from one Caretaker to the next. If Bobby was missed at all, it was in silence.

Nine months later, Queen Shonda gave birth to a healthy male child. Before she handed him off to the men who oversaw the Nursery for raising, she gave specific instructions to name the child Robert. They nodded and carried the child away. She would spawn many more children before her time in the Palace was over, and Queen Shonda never gave Bobby's baby another thought.

EPILOGUE

Antonio removed the dagger from the miser's heart.

"So, old man, someone has robbed me of the chance to kill you. Never mind. It is not your life I seek. It is your Book."

So saying, Antonio began a methodical search of the house. With midnight approaching, there remained but one room left to be searched, and its door was locked.

Peering through the keyhole, Antonio tasted disappointment at the sight of bare walls. Where was the old man's fabled library? Perhaps, after all, there was no Book.

"No!" Antonio whispered fiercely. "The Book had to be in the locked room. It has to be!"

The door swung open and permitted Antonio to enter. It closed behind him, but he scarcely noticed. His attention was fixed on the corpse lying in the middle of the room. Its face was distorted in terror and would have sent most men running. But not Antonio, for the dead man clutched a book to his chest.

"Mine at last!" Antonio prised the ancient volume

from dead fingers. He opened the book and his joy turned to despair. The pages were blank! "No! It cannot be! This is the Book! I know it is. But where are the words?"

As he spoke, the page in front of him turned to gold. Black spots formed on the gold and grew like ink blots, joining together to form three words which, though they had no meaning to him, Antonio felt compelled to read out loud.

"Pasher tagoth imra!" The house sighed and Antonio repeated the words. "Pasher tagoth imra!"

This time, something whispered back.

THANK YOU

Serial killers. Giant spiders. Haunted houses. A zombie
apocalypse. Murderous clowns.

Chances are, at least one of these things sent a shiver down
your spine or made your pulse quicken; we all have a unique
list of fears, phobias, and things that make us clutch the
covers at night. But what scares one person half to death may
be a yawn-fest for the next. It turns out that "scary" is quite
subjective.

Psychologists believe that we seek out horror books and films
in an attempt to exercise the amygdala - the fear centre in
our brains. For thousands and thousands of years, humans
encountered frightening situations each and every day,
sending a rush of adrenaline and other hormones surging
through our brains. Our bodies are well-prepared to run away
from a lion, wrestle with a crocodile, or head out into battle --
and to relish the "high" that comes from a narrow escape.

In modern times, most people live in cities or towns far
from carnivorous prey or daily war, yet our evolutionary
instincts still survive. Reading a horror novel is a way for
us to encounter sheer terror and get our heart pumping,
all within a controlled, safe environment.

General horror tropes such a vampires, werewolves, killers, poltergeists, and ghosts all work to evoke the existing fear responses that we have ingrained in our psyches. An author works to build suspense and uses vivid imagery to help us imagine ourselves running down a rickety staircase away from a monster, and this transports us back thousands of years to a time when our ancestors ran through the wilderness away from a bear.

Just as different people seek out different thrills in sport, travel, and entertainment, different people also are aroused by different fear stimuli. It's the same basic reason that humankind suffers from such a diverse and strange list of phobias (omphalophobia -- the fear of belly buttons -- actually exists). Part of this is evolutionary, and most likely hardwired into our brains from a combination of genetics and chance.

However, many of our fears are a result of our own past experiences. A fear of clowns may result from a particularly scary birthday party, at which a clown made you cry. A fear of rabid dogs may stem from being bitten as a little one. You can probably think of a fear that you struggle with, which can be connected to a traumatic experience.

We all have our own histories and different genetic profiles, and so it is completely natural that we find different horror genres appealing (and by appealing, I mean terrifying). What scares you and gets your imagination running wild may completely bore the next person -- and that is part of what makes the horror genre so fantastic and appealing. You can always find a niche subject that seems designed to frighten only you, and bask in the afterglow of adrenaline coursing through your veins.

Whatever horror genre is particularly terrifying to you, I'm certain you found something to quicken your heart and send a shiver down your spine in The Black Room Manuscripts.

And you helped a wonderful cause.

So thank you.

Daniel Marc Chant, March 10th 2015.

HORROR AS A UNITING FORCE

AFTERWORD BY JENNIFER HANDORF
(PRODUCER OF 'THE BORDERLANDS')

Horror has long been the whipping boy of the arts. Is your teen lashing out? Check his shelf for Clive Barker. Society in the gutter? Probably all of those Horror films showing down the local cinema. But if the cultural fear mongers would only give us a chance, they'd realise Horror fans nearly always wear their dark hearts on their sleeves. We like to explore and express the gory and the gross right out in the open, because it isn't something we want to let fester inside us. Instead of ignoring our nightmares or pretending they don't exist, we prefer to confront our demons in the bright light of media. And why wouldn't we? The arts are the safest place to explore these notions. Where else could you be teetering on the brink of madness, only to pull yourself back by closing your eyes and repeating, "It's only a movie... It's only a movie." Horror is like a rollercoaster for the emotionally brave. If you're willing to take yourself to the edge of fear, to experience the adrenaline of near death, only to be flung back into complete and utter safety... well, there's nothing better.

I can't remember when I first became addicted to the thrill
ride of Horror, but it seems like it's always been with me. I
remember my brother reading me "Scary Stories to Tell in the
Dark" as thunder storms cracked around us. I was too young
to read them myself, but that didn't mean I didn't crave the
excitement and the fear. I'd pull the duvet tighter and tighter
as I felt my insides twisting with the growing tension. And
then it would come -- a gasp, a jump, or, if my brother had
told the story particularly well, a full blown scream. But that
fear was always followed by a fit of giggles -- the absolute
delight of having defied death, though be it a fictional one.

I don't think it so strange that the two should be closely linked
-- laughter and screaming. When you think about it, they're
really two sides of the same coin. Mounting tension creates
an emotional pressure inside us that builds and builds until it
explodes into one or the other. But, and I may be biased here,
I do think that a scream is the more noble of the two. It's more
honest for one -- I've never heard someone fake a scream in
the cinema. But it's also more enduring. Explain a joke, and
it ceases to be funny. Explain why something frightened you,
and suddenly you've passed that fear to someone else.

In that way, you see how Horror -- rather than tearing a
community apart -- can actually be a uniting force. It's primal
-- universal even -- as is evidenced by the millions of Horror
fans in thousands of communities around the Horror world.
Phobias seem to cross borders of culture and language. But
it isn't just the common fears that bring Horror fans together.
It's the real joy of exposing ourselves to those fears alongside
each other. Perhaps it's because there is safety in numbers.
But I think it's more to do with the honesty of the experience.
When we allow ourselves to be afraid, we're really allowing

ourselves to be vulnerable. Which is pretty frightening in and
of itself.

Perhaps that's why Horror is so often picked on. The censors
and the Stepford Wives aren't afraid of what they'll be
exposed to, but, rather, they're more frightened of what will
be revealed of themselves. As much as you can close a book
or switch off the TV, what that experience has shown you
about yourself can follow you forever. For those audiences
who have not spent time exercising their own demons through
the arts, that must be a terrifying notion. Can you even
imagine the fear of what may lie in the depths of your own
unexplored psyche?

This is what I think of whenever someone casts a worried
look. I need it. I need it because it's fun. I need it because it's
what I do with my friends. But, more than anything, I need it
to illuminate my own demons before they have a chance to
creep up on me in the darkness of my mind.

CONTRIBUTORS

Jim McLeod has been a fan of Horror ever since that fateful Friday night when he snuck down the stairs to watch Hammer's "Dracula" on late night television. He set up Ginger Nuts of Horror six years ago, and in that time, it has become the largest independent horror review and interview website in Europe. One of the many highlights of his time on the website was when he interviewed Joe Hill in front of a packed-out audience at The Pleasance in Edinburgh for the release of Joe's novel, "NOS4R2."

Danny King is an award-winning British novelist and screenwriter. Born in Slough, United Kingdom in 1969, he has worked as a hod carrier, a supermarket shelf stacker, a painter & decorator, a postman, and a magazine editor, and today uses these rich experiences to dodge all of the aforementioned. He has written fourteen books to date -- eight of which were originally published by Serpent's Tail, two by Byker Books -- as well as screenplays for both the big and small screens. His first book, "The Burglar Diaries," won the 2002 Amazon.co.uk Writers' Bursary Award and was the basis of his BBC sitcom, Thieves Like Us (2007). And his first feature film, Wild Bill, won both the 2012 Writers' Guild of Great Britain Award and a BAFTA nomination for Outstanding Debut. He lives in Chichester, West Sussex with wife, Jeannie, and two children, and divides his time between writing and wondering what to write about. For further details, go to www.dannykingbooks.com.

Detecting the tiniest crack in the containment pod, **Duncan P Bradshaw** managed to break free of the mind control routine after morphing into liquid form. He oozed through the fracture and to freedom. Living under an assumed name, he walks the streets amongst you. He eats where you eat. Drinks where you drink. Flytips in the same layby as you. In a life reserved for another, he now writes down the horrifying dreams that plague his waking moments -- the things which reside just beyond sight. In the darkness, they shriek his name... Dddduuuunnnccccaaaaannnnn, they call. He answers not, for to do so would awaken his Nemesis, "Nacnud," and spark all-out war. Duncan's debut novel, a zom-com, "Class Three," was released in November 2014. The first book in the follow-up trilogy, "Class Four: Those Who Survive," ambles into existence in July 2015. For more information, check out www.duncanpbradshaw.co.uk

Vincent Hunt is a graphic designer, illustrator, and creator of the acclaimed self-published comic book series, "The Red Mask From Mars." Being a huge horror fan, he jumped at the chance to contribute to The Black Room Manuscripts, and also designed the cover artwork. Visit jesterdiablo.blogspot. com or follow him on Twitter (@jesterdiablo) to see more of his work. "Hide and Shriek" is his first published prose work, but he has threatened that it won't be his last.

Adam Millard is the author of twenty novels, ten novellas, and more than a hundred short stories, which can be found in various collections and anthologies. Probably best known for his post-apocalyptic fiction, Adam also writes Fantasy/Horror for children. He created the character Peter Crombie, Teenage Zombie, just so he had something decent to read to his son at bedtime. Adam also writes Bizarro fiction for several publishers, who enjoy his tales of flesh-eating clown-beetles and rabies-infected derrieres so much that they keep printing them. His "Dead" series has recently been the filling in a Stephen King/Bram Stoker sandwich on Amazon's bestsellers chart. When he's not writing about the nightmarish creatures battling for supremacy in his head, Adam writes for This Is Horror, whose columnists include Simon Bestwick and Simon Marshall-Jones. For further details, go to www.adammillard.co.uk/.

J R Park writes Horror fiction, drawing from the crazy worlds of exploitation cinema and pulp literature for his inspiration. His family are both equally proud and disturbed by his literary output, dragged from a mind they helped to cultivate. He resides on the outskirts of Bristol in the UK and hopes one day they'll let him in. For more information, check out www.jrpark.co.uk

Madeleine Swann's collection of short stories, "The Filing Cabinet of Doom," was published by Burning Bulb. She has stories in anthologies including "The Strange Edge," "Bizarro Central," "American Nightmare," and "Weird Year." She has also written for magazines such as Bizarre and The Dark Side. You can find it all on madeleineswann.com.

Craig Anderson-Jones was born, and still resides, in Southampton, Hampshire UK with his wife and two children, Elijah and Oki. A fan of science fiction, specifically the Alien franchise, and the works of A C Grayling. His main passion however is for fitness, and he spends countless hours in the gym at ridiculous times in the morning. Or playing golf. But he still hasn't transitioned into Justin Bieber yet despite countless attempts.

Leo Stableford lives in South Wales with his wife and cat, and is quite content. By day he runs a media business, recording audio and video for private clients and community projects. By night he writes thoroughly modern fairy stories, and invites people to play a variety of diverting story games. For further details, go to www.leostableford.com.

Martin Jones was introduced to Horror at an early age by two people in his life; his Mum and his Granddad. One by accident, the other by design. Mum would leave him in the kids section and go off to choose her books for the week (he could be trusted in those days), and she was a big Horror fan whose books unwittingly found their way into his grubby mitts. His Granddad would tell him about Horror films -- Hammer and Universal in particular -- and would explain the plots in great detail. Over the years he could not begin to tell you how many genre books he's read or how many films he's have watched. It's a lot. He had never considered making a film or writing a book -- instead considered himself a spectator, and happily so. In 2013 he met a fellow fanatic who wasn't satisfied with him being a spectator, and this crazy bastard actually believed he had his own story to tell; this forced Martin to put pen to paper and start his writing journey. Hopefully he doesn't get lost on the way. Follow him on Twitter: @Jonesanory.

Thomas S Flowers was born in Walter Reed Medical Center, Maryland to a military family. He grew up in RAF Chicksands, England and then later Fort Meade, and finally Roanoke, Virginia. Thomas graduated high school in 2000 and on September 11, 2001, joined the U.S. Army. From 2001-2008, Thomas served in the military police corps, with one tour in South Korea and three tours serving in Operation Enduring Freedom and Operation Iraqi Freedom and, following his third and final tour to Iraq, decided it was time to rejoin the civilian ranks. Thomas was discharged honorably in February 2008 and moved to Houston, Texas where he found employment and attended night school. In 2014, Thomas graduated with a Bachelor in Arts in History from University of Houston-Clear Lake. He is the author of two published short stories: "Hobo: a Horror Short Story," and "Are You Hungry, Dear?" Both are available on Amazon Kindle. And most recently, Thomas has released his first published full length book, "Reinheit," also available on Amazon Kindle. You can follow Thomas on Twitter: @machinemeannow

Kit Power lives in Milton Keynes, England, and insists he's fine with that. His short fiction has appeared in various venues, including Splatterpunk Magazine, "The Widowmakers" anthology, and themed collections from Burnt Offering Books and Black Beacon Books. He also has two loosely linked novellas available ("Lifeline" and "The Loving Husband and The Faithful Wife"), and his much-delayed debut novel "GodBomb!" is expected to finally drop in early spring of 2015. He once visited Doc Holliday's grave in Colorado, which is the closest he's ever come to a real cowboy. You can follow Kit on Twitter: @KitGonzo

David Karl Ryan was born in Leicestershire, and grew up in the village of Sileby. His exact age is unknown, but he is believed to have been born around the year 1972. His love for writing came late, but after being recognised for his short story, "The Demon And Me," he decided to put all of his efforts into writing and self-publishing his serial killer novel, "Family Perfect." He lives with his wife and two children in Western Australia. Follow him on Twitter: @dkryanhorror.

Dave James is a massive geek. In both outlook and personal proportion. He's been flapping fingers at keyboards since he was far smaller though, and has spent the last decade writing about games and technology for various outlets across the globe. That hasn't stopped him from stretching his creative muscles every now and then though... His literary heroes include Iain Banks, Charles Bukowski, and Hunter Thompson, but he's certainly not deluded enough to think he'll ever get close to their craft. Follow him on Twitter: @Not_the_GK

Since a very young age, **Duncan Ralston** has wanted to disturb you. In the 2nd grade, when he came to class dressed as the devil for Halloween, the teacher rolled his eyes and said, "How appropriate!" By Grade 7, he had given up trick-or-treating -- not to hand out candy but to scare the bejeezus out of kids and adults alike. His ghastly terrors on pulleys and hooks brought parents and children from neighboring towns to see the haunted house. As a "grown-up," Duncan lives with his girlfriend and their dog in Toronto, where he works behind the scenes in television. He writes Horror about the things that frighten, disgust, and delight him. In addition to his dark and twisted short stories found in Gristle & Bone, his debut novel, "Salvage," will haunt various booksellers in September 2015. Follow him on Twitter: @userbits

Daniel Marc Chant is an up-and-coming author of Horror and strange fiction. His passion for H. P. Lovecraft genre and the films of John Carpenter inspired him to produce intense, gripping stories with a sinister edge. Currently based in Bath -- a picturesque town in Somerset, UK -- Daniel launched his début, "Burning House," to rave reviews, and swiftly followed with the Lovecraft-inspired "Maldición," the story of a lone survivor of a desert island plane crash fighting for his life with an ancient predator. Daniel continues to hone his craft with a number of dark titles waiting to hit shelves, including "Mr. Robespierre" and "Devil Kickers." Follow him on Twitter: @danielmarcchant.

Kayleigh Marie Edwards is a freelance writer and entertainer based in South Wales. She writes Horror and Comedy, and on wild occasions when she feels like getting down with her bad self, she even meshes the two. Her greatest loves are zombies and Stephen King stories, and she's really partial to cheese. Cheddar, Edam, camembert... Well, she's a major fan of the whole cheese scene, but apparently that's irrelevant. Her most recent works include two Comedy/Horror theatre productions, and several short stories. She rambles at www.kayofthedead@wordpress.com, and contributes at www.gingernutsofhorror.com.

Ian Caldwell currently lives in Australia where he tolerates the garish sun and the abundance of happy, healthy people. He emigrated from the UK in 2005, leaving behind his job editing audio books for BBC. He enjoys creating stories, RPG's games, and other distractions. For the last two years, he's helped produce a Podcast called "Revenge of the 80's Kids," which retrospectively covers the Horror, Sci Fi, Fantasy, and Actions films, as well as TV and other media of the last forty years. You can find him at https://www.facebook.com/RevengeOfThe80sKids

By day, **A S Chambers** is a mild-mannered genealogist, armed only with a tweed jacket and a finely sharpened HB pencil. By night, he is the top-hatted creator of Lancaster's long-suffering Sam Spallucci - investigator of the paranormal and all things weird. He has a rather nice website at www.aschambers.co.uk and actively encourages people to look him up on Facebook, Twitter, and Pinterest, where he spends far too much time posting snippets about things that lurk in the shadows.

Paul Townsend has been writing for the past 10 years or so, and has tried his hand at poetry, short stories, flash fiction and, more recently, script work for stage, short indie movies, and radio. His two main genres of interest are Science Fiction and Horror; growing up in the 80s with an over-abundance of both good and schlock in books and movies has heavily influenced his writing.

Jeffery X Martin lives with his family somewhere in the Great American South. He is the author of "Black Friday: An Elders Keep Collection" and "Short Stories about You." Martin is a highly sought-after podcast guest. He is also the creator of "Kiss the Goat," a top-rated podcast he hosts with his wife, which covers the sub-genre of Devil movies from the past fifty years. He writes pop culture articles for the Toronto-based website, Popshifter. He is a partner in Grave Folk Productions, and has several film scripts in pre-production. In his spare time, he enjoys watching professional wrestling, Eighties Goth music, and a nice giallo. Follow him on Twitter: @JefferyXMartin.

The career of **Jennifer Handorf** began at Columbia University, where she was presented by the Academy of Motion Picture Arts and Sciences with the prestigious Student Academy Award for her producing work on a short entitled "POPFOUL." Jen has produced dozens of shorts and five features which have been programmed at over 100 festivals worldwide -- including the Sundance Film Festival -- with many of her films taking top prizes. After receiving her Master's Degree from USC's Peter Stark Program, and working for Sanford Panitch at Fox International Productions in Los Angeles, Jen returned to London. Here she produced several films, including BAFTA-recognised "FORNA," and Ben Wheatley's short film "PRECINCT 13." She has also produced for television, collaborating with the National Literacy Trust and Sky Arts to bring performances of classical authors by Stephen Fry, Eddie Marsan, Simon Callow, Karen Gillan, and others to screen. Her first feature, "THE DEVIL'S BUSINESS," was described by critics as Pinter-esque and praised for its art house qualities as much as for its scares, with The Observer calling it "genuinely literate and scary." Her most recent production, "THE BORDERLANDS," was released by Metrodome Distribution in the UK and has been met with critical and commercial success. Mark Kermode praised it in the Guardian as "properly alarming scary fair" and Peter Bradshaw called it "A very punchy, funny, scary movie... fantastically unnerving." Jen has recently wrapped production on "NATIVE," a Science Fiction thriller starring Rupert Graves and Ellie Kendrick. Jen hopes to continue bringing high-concept story-driven genre films to the British screen with her upcoming projects, "CHAMBER," co-produced with Optimum founder Paul Higgins, filming later this year, and "BELLY OF THE BULLDOG," starring Rupert Evans. Jen is also the Head of Production for the Metrodome and is currently supervising development and production on their slate of films.

Editor of The Black Room Manuscripts **Cheyenne DeBorde** is a Wordsmith who's been balancing for years between convincing others it's a "real job" and accepting that it might

not be. She is the co-founder of Ember Ink Wordsmithing
(https://emberinkwordsmithing.wordpress.com), which allows
her to live out not only one dream job, but many in the duel
form of editor and writer. Starting to write at a young age
and starting to edit as soon as she mastered grammar, she
was doomed from the beginning. Cheyenne has ghost written
enough novels to call herself an authoress (but don't tell
anyone), and has her name proudly brandished in books
she's helped polish and reach the finish line. She spends her
days in the southern Arizona sun, over-thinking the universe
and making trouble for her characters, while helping others
make more trouble for theirs.

Composer of The Black Room Manuscripts theme,
Ben Steed -- AKA Windfallen -- is a British videogame and
media composer, as well chiptune artist and manager for the
netlabel PegasiaMusic. Most recently, his work has featured
in Retro Ronin's virtual reality MMO Voxelnauts. More
information and music can be found at windfallen.net, and
you can listen to the official The Black Room Manuscripts
theme here: https://goo.gl/h1xTAA

ACKNOWLEDGEMENTS

Thanks to Danny King, Adam Millard,
Paul Townsend, Madeleine Swann,
A S Chambers, Duncan Ralston, Jeffery X Martin,
Thomas S Flowers, Kayleigh Edwards,
Craig Anderson-Jones, Martin Jones,
D K Ryan, Ian Caldwell, David James,
Leo Stableford, Kit Power, Jim McLeod,
Jennifer Handorf, Duncan P Bradshaw, J R Park,
Vincent Hunt, and Cheyenne DeBorde for
their generosity and talent.

This anthology wouldn't exist without your work,
kindness, and help. I can't thank you all enough.

This book is dedicated to the animals of
Blue Cross UK -- to all the unwanted cats,
dogs, small pets, and horses that they
look after with nothing but the
kindheartedness of the public.

ABOUT BLUE CROSS UK

Sick, injured, and homeless pets have relied
on them since 1897. Thousands of abandoned or
unwanted, ill or injured pets turn to Blue Cross UK
for help every year. Their doors are always open to
them, and with your support, they always will be.

Each year, thousands of cats, dogs, small pets,
and horses turn to their animal hospitals,
clinics, and rehoming services for treatment and
to find them the happy homes they deserve.

For more information and to donate please visit
www.bluecross.org.uk

SINISTERHORRORCOMPANY.COM